TK

MY
OXFORD
YEAR

MY
OXFORD
YEAR

MY
OXFORD
YEAR

A NOVEL

JULIA WHELAN

WILLIAM MORROW

An Imprint of HarperCollins*Publishers*

MY OXFORD YEAR. Copyright © 2018 by Temple Hill Publishing. All rights reserved. Printed in the United States of America. No part of this book may be used or reproduced in any manner whatsoever without written permission except in the case of brief quotations embodied in critical articles and reviews. For information, address HarperCollins Publishers, 195 Broadway, New York, NY 10007.

HarperCollins books may be purchased for educational, business, or sales promotional use. For information, please email the Special Markets Department at SPsales@harpercollins.com.

FIRST EDITION

Designed by Diahann Sturge

Library of Congress Cataloging-in-Publication Data has been applied for.

ISBN 978–0–062740649

18 19 20 21 22   LSC   10 9 8 7 6 5 4 3 2 1

To those we have lost.
Particularly fathers.
Particularly mine.

I envy you going to Oxford: it is the most flower-like time of one's life. One sees the shadow of things in silver mirrors. Later on, one sees the Gorgon's head, and one suffers, because it does not turn one to stone.

Oscar Wilde, letter to Louis Wilkinson,
December 28, 1898

MY
OXFORD
YEAR

CHAPTER 1

While the chaffinch sings on the orchard bough
In England—now!
Robert Browning, "Home-Thoughts, from Abroad," 1845

Next!"

The customs agent beckons the person in front of me and I approach the big red line, absently toeing the curling tape, resting my hand on the gleaming pipe railing. No adjustable ropes at Heathrow, apparently; these lines must always be long if they require permanent demarcation.

My phone rings. I glance down. I don't know the number.

"Hello?" I answer.

"Is this Eleanor Durran?"

"Yes?"

"This is Gavin Brookdale."

My first thought is that this is a prank call. Gavin Brookdale just stepped down as White House chief of staff. He's run every major political campaign of the last twenty years. He's a legend. He's my idol. He's calling me?

"Hello?"

"Sorry, I—I'm here," I stammer. "I'm just—"

"Have you heard of Janet Wilkes?"

Have I heard of—Janet Wilkes is the junior senator from Florida and a dark-horse candidate for president. She's forty-five, lost her husband twelve years ago in Afghanistan, raised three kids on a teacher's salary while somehow putting herself through law school, and then ran the most impressive grassroots senatorial campaign I've ever seen. She also has the hottest human-rights-attorney boyfriend I've ever seen, but that's beside the point. She's a Gold Star Wife who's a progressive firebrand on social issues. We've never seen anyone like her on the national stage before. The first debate isn't for another two weeks, on October 13, but voters seem to love her: she's polling third in a field of twelve. Candidate Number Two is not long for the race; a Case of the Jilted Mistress(es). Number One, however, happens to be the current vice president, George Hillerson, whom Gavin Brookdale (if the Washington gossip mill is accurate) loathes. Still, even the notoriously mercurial Brookdale wouldn't back a losing horse like Wilkes just to spite the presumptive nominee. If nothing else, Gavin Brookdale likes to win. "Of course I've heard of her."

"She read your piece in *The Atlantic*. We both did. 'The Art of Education and the Death of the Thinking American Electorate.' We were impressed."

"Thank you," I say, gushing. "It was something I felt was missing from the discourse—"

"What you wrote was philosophy. It wasn't policy."

This brings me up short. "I understand why you'd think that, but I—"

"Don't worry, I know you have the policy chops. I know you won Ohio for Janey Bennett. The 138th for Carl Moseley. You're a talented young lady, Eleanor."

"Mr. Brookdale—"

"Call me Gavin."

"Then call me Ella. No one calls me Eleanor."

"All right, Ella, would you like to be the education consultant for Wilkes's campaign?"

Silence.

"Hello?"

"Yes!" I bleat. "Yes, of course! She's incredible—"

"Great. Come down to my office today and we'll read you in."

All the breath leaves my body. I can't seem to get it back. "So . . . here's the thing. I—I'm in England."

"Fine, when you get back."

". . . I get back in June."

Silence.

"Are you consulting over there?"

"No, I have a . . . I got a Rhodes and I'm doing a—"

Gavin chortles. "I was a Rhodie."

"I know, sir."

"Gavin."

"Gavin."

"What are you studying?"

"English language and literature 1830 to 1914."

Beat. "Why?"

"Because I want to?" Why does it come out as a question?

"You don't need it. *Getting* the Rhodes is what matters. Doing it is meaningless, especially in literature from 1830 to 19-what-ever. The only reason you wanted it was to help you get that life-changing political job, right? Well, I'm giving that to you. So come home and let's get down to business."

"Next!"

A customs agent—stone-faced, turbaned, impressive beard—waves me forward. I take one step over the line, but hold a finger up to him. He's not even looking at me. "Gavin, can I call—"

"She's going to be the nominee, Ella. It's going to be the fight of my life and I need all hands—including yours—on deck, but we're going to do it."

He's delusional. But, my God, what if he's right? A shiver of excitement snakes through me. "Gavin—"

"Listen, I've always backed the winning candidate, but I have never backed someone who I personally, deeply, wanted to win."

"Miss?" Now the customs agent looks at me.

Gavin chuckles at my silence. "I don't want to have to convince you, if you don't feel—"

"I can work from here." Before he can argue, I continue: "I will make myself available at all hours. I will make Wilkes my priority." Behind me, a bloated, red-faced businessman reeking of gin moves to squeeze around me. I head him off, grabbing the railing, saying into the phone, "I had two jobs in college while volunteering in field offices and coordinating multiple city council runs. I worked two winning congressional campaigns last year while helping to shape the education budget for Ohio. I can certainly consult for you while reading books and writing about them occasionally."

"Miss!" the customs agent barks. "Hang up the phone or step aside." I hold my finger up higher (as if visibility is the problem) and widen my stance over the line.

"What's your date certain for coming home?" Gavin asks.

"June eleventh. I already have a ticket. Seat 32A."

"Miss!" The customs agent and the man bark at me.

I look down at the red line between my sprawled feet. "Gavin, I'm straddling the North Atlantic right now. I literally have one foot in England and one in America and if I don't hang up they'll—"

"I'll call you back."

He disconnects.

What does that mean? What do I do? Numbly, I hurry to the immigration window, coming face-to-face with the dour agent. I adopt my best beauty-pageant smile and speak in the chagrined, gee-whiz tone I know he expects. "I am so sorry, sir, my sincerest apologies. My mom's—"

"Passport." He's back to not looking at me. I'm getting the passive-aggressive treatment now. I hand over my brand-new passport with the crisp, unstamped pages. "Purpose of visit?"

"Study."

"For how long will you be in the country?"

I pause. I glance down at the dark, unhelpful screen of my phone. "I . . . I don't know."

Now he looks up at me.

"A year," I say. Screw it. "An academic year."

"Where?"

"Oxford." Saying the word out loud cuts through everything else. My smile becomes genuine. He asks me more questions, and I suppose I answer, but all I can think is:

I'm here. This is actually happening. Everything has come together according to plan.

He stamps my passport, hands it back, lifts his hand to the line.

"Next!"

WHEN I WAS thirteen I read an article in *Seventeen* magazine called "My Once-in-a-Lifetime Experience," and it was a personal account of an American girl's year abroad at Oxford. The classes, the students, the parks, the pubs, even the chip shop ("pictured, bottom left") seemed like another world. Like slipping through a wormhole into a universe where things were ordered and people were dignified and the buildings were older than my entire country. I suppose thirteen is an important age in every girl's life, but for me, growing up in the middle of nowhere, with a family that had fallen apart? I needed something to hold on to. I needed inspiration. I needed hope. The girl who wrote the article had been transformed. Oxford had unlocked her life and I was convinced that it would be the key to mine.

So I made a plan: get to Oxford.

After going through more customs checkpoints, I follow signs for the Central Bus Terminal and find an automatic ticket kiosk. The "£" sign before the amount looks so much better, more civilized, more historical than the American dollar sign, which always seems overly suggestive to me. Like it should be flashing in sequential neon lights above a strip club. $-$-$. GIRLS! GIRLS! GIRLS!

The kiosk's screen asks me if I want a discounted return ticket (I assume that means round trip), and I pause. My flight back to Washington is on June 11, barely sixteen hours after the official end of Trinity term. I have no plans to return to the States before then, instead staying here over the two long vacations (in December and March) and traveling. In fact, I already have my December itinerary all planned. I purchase the return ticket, then cross to a bench to wait for the next bus.

My phone dings and I look down. An e-mail from the Rhodes Foundation reminding me about the orientation tomorrow morning.

For whatever reason, out of all the academic scholarships in the world, most people seem to have heard of the Rhodes. It's not the only prestigious scholarship to be had, but it's the one that I wanted. Every year, America sends thirty-two of its most overachieving, über-competitive, social-climbing, do-gooder nerds to Oxford. It's mostly associated with geniuses, power players, global leaders. Let me demystify this: to get a Rhodes, you have to be slightly unhinged. You have to have a stellar GPA, excel in multiple courses of study, be socially entrepreneurial, charity-minded, and athletically proficient (though the last time I did anything remotely athletic I knocked out Jimmy Brighton's front tooth with a foul ball, so take that criterion with a grain of salt). I could have gone after other scholarships. There's the Marshall, the Fulbright, the Watson, but the Rhodies are my people. They're the planners.

The other finalist selected from my district (a math/econ/classics triple major and Olympic archer who had discovered that applying game theory to negotiations with known terrorists makes the intel 147 percent more reliable), told me, "I've been working toward getting a Rhodes since freshman year." To which I replied, "Me too." He clarified, "Of high school." To which I replied, "Me too."

While, yes, the Rhodes is a golden ticket to Oxford, it's also a built-in network and the means to my political future. It ensures that people who would have otherwise discounted me—this unconnected girl from the soybean fields of Ohio—will take a second, serious look. People like Gavin Brookdale.

Going after things the way I do, being who I am, has alienated my entire hometown and most of my extended family. My mom hadn't gone to college and my dad had dropped out after two years because he'd thought it was more important to change the world than learn about it, and there I was, this achievement machine making everyone around it vaguely uncomfortable. *She thinks she's better than everyone else.*

Honestly, I don't. But I do think I'm better than what everyone, besides my dad, told me I was.

I WAKE UP in a moment of panic when the bus I'd boarded back at Heathrow jerks to a stop, sending the book on my lap to the floor. Hastily retrieving it, I force my sleepy eyes to take in the view from the floor-to-ceiling window in front of me. I chose the seat on the upper level at the very front, wanting to devour every bit of English countryside on the way to Oxford. Then I slept through it.

Pushing through the fog in my head, I peer outside. A dingy bus stop in front of a generic cell-phone store. I look for a street sign, trying to get my bearings. My info packet from the college said to get off at the Queens Lane stop on High Street. This can't be it. I glance behind me and no one on the bus is moving to get off, so I settle back into my seat.

The bus starts up again, and I breathe deeply, trying to wake up. I jam the book into my backpack. I'd wanted to finish it before my first class tomorrow, but I can't focus. I was too excited to eat or sleep on the plane. My empty stomach and all-nighter are catching up to me. The time difference is catching up to me. The last twelve years spent striving for this moment is catching up to me.

Inside my jacket pocket, my phone vibrates. I pull it out and see the same number from earlier. I take a deep breath and pre-emptively answer, "Gavin, listen, I was thinking, let's do a trial period of, say, a month, and if you feel that I need to be there—"

"Not necessary."

My throat tightens. "Please, just give me thirty days to prove that—"

"It's fine. I made it work. Just remember who comes first."

Elation breaks through the fog. My fist clenches in victory and my smile reaches all the way to my temples. "Absolutely," I say in my most professional voice. "Thank you so much for this opportunity. You won't be disappointed."

"I know that. That's why I hired you. What's your fee? FYI: there's no money."

There's never any money. I tell him my fee anyway and we settle on something that I can live with. The Rhodes is paying my tuition and lodging and I get a small stipend for living expenses on top of that. I decide right then that what Gavin's going to pay me will go directly into my travel budget.

"Now go," he says, "have fun. You've clearly earned it. There's a pub you should visit in the center of town. The Turf. See where one of your fellow Rhodes scholars—a young William Jefferson Clinton—'didn't' inhale."

"Ha, got it. Will do."

"Just take your phone with you. Your phone is an appendage, not an accessory. Okay?"

I nod even though he can't see me. "Okay. It's a plan." Just as I say this, the bus rounds a bend and there she is:

Oxford.

Beyond a picturesque bridge, the narrow two-lane road continues into a bustling main street, lined on each side by buildings in a hodgepodge of architectural styles, no room to breathe between them. Like the crowd at the finish line of a marathon, these buildings cheer me on, welcoming me to their city. Some are topped with sloped, slate roofs, others with battlements. Some of the larger buildings have huge wooden gates that look as if they were carved in place, a fusion of timeless wood and stone that steals my breath. Maybe those doors lead to some of the thirty-eight individual Oxford colleges? Imagining it, dreaming of it all these years, doesn't do it justice.

I look skyward. Punctuating the horizon are the tips of other ancient buildings, high points of stone bordering the city like beacons.

"The City of Dreaming Spires," I murmur to myself.

"Indeed it is," Gavin says in my ear. I'd forgotten he was still on the line.

That's what they call Oxford. A title well deserved. Because that means, before it was my dream or *Seventeen* magazine girl's dream, it was someone else's dream as well.

CHAPTER 2

Light, that never makes you wink;
Memory, that gives no pain;
Love, when, so, you're loved again.
What's the best thing in the world?
—Something out of it, I think.
Elizabeth Barrett Browning, "The Best Thing in the World," 1862

I wish I could say that Oxford smells like parchment and cinnamon or something poetic, but right now it just smells like city: bus diesel, damp pavement, and the aroma of French roast wafting from the coffee shop across the street.

The sidewalks are narrow on High Street, edged by tall stone walls on one side and low, worn curbs on the other. The narrowness heightens their crowdedness. Students rushing, tourists lingering, the former annoyed by the latter. Those who speak English are almost as incomprehensible to me as those who don't. My ear hasn't yet adjusted to the accent and passing dialogue is entirely lost on me.

It's just another day in Oxford, but to me it's magical.

As the bus pulls away I gather my luggage and try to sidestep a large family bowed over a map, their voices agitated and overlapping. After a moment, the father's head pops up and he lifts the map into the air, out of reach, his patience snapping. "Aw-right, awright, step off it now, wouldya? We're goin' this way!"

Before I can steer clear of the family, a flock of bicycles, a veri-table swarm, goes flying past, grazing my luggage and whipping my hair in its wake. Their riders wear some kind of sporting attire (rugby, maybe?), smelling of boy-sweat and new-mown grass as they go by, hooting and hollering. Boys are boys in any country, apparently. The last rider snatches the map right out of the father's hand, lifting it victoriously, crying out, *"Et in Arcadia, ego!"*

Oxford: where even the jocks speak Latin.

THERE'S NOTHING I have to do for the Rhodes, per se. It's not a degree or title in its own right. What I do—or don't do—at Oxford is between my academic department and me. Also, be-tween my college and me.

The college I'll be affiliated with is Magdalen, which, for rea-sons unknown to me, is pronounced "maudlin." Founded in 1458, it boasts a great hall, a deer park, an iconic bell tower, medieval cloisters, and approximately six hundred students. I did not request Magdalen because of some heavily considered academic reason; I requested Magdalen because it was Oscar Wilde's college.

I approach the gate, carefully navigating the people streaming in and out, and lug my baggage into a portico. In front of me, straight out an open Gothic-style door, I glimpse a cobblestone courtyard with a charming three-story sand-colored dormered building in the distance. On the portico's flagstones, sandwich boards announce the times of day the college is open to visitors and advertise a tour of the fifteenth-century kitchens. To my left are glass-enclosed bulletin boards with notices and reminders posted haphazardly: "Have you paid your battels?" "Get all your uni gear! New Student Discount at Summer Eights on Broad, show your Bod card." "Fancy a nip before Hilary's first OKB bop? 8, Friday noughth week, JCR." Seeing the words in writing, I realize the accent isn't the only obstacle. To my right, wood paneling and two arched glass windows cordon off a sort of office, like an Old West bank just asking to be held up.

I round the corner and spy, behind the glass, an older man in a red, pilled sweater, white collared shirt, and tie. He stands over an archaic copier the size of an SUV, his shoulders hunched in consternation, long neck and mostly bald head giving him the appearance of a Galápagos tortoise. He mutters something and kicks the bottom of the machine. It whirs like a propjet engine and slowly spits out sheets of green paper.

"Hi!" I chirp.

"Help you?" he asks, not looking up, paging methodically through another stack of papers, occasionally licking his finger.

"I'm . . ." I hesitate. "Checking in? I guess?"

"Student?" he asks.

"Yeah. Yes."

"Fresher?"

I have no idea what he just said. "What?"

"Fresher?"

I don't answer. I'm afraid to answer.

Finally he looks up, exasperated, and I realize he's been counting the papers and, more, that I've interrupted him. "First year. Are you a first year?"

"I'm a graduate student. But I'm flattered, sir."

He sighs. "American. Name?" He goes back to counting.

"Eleanor Durran. But, please, call me Ella."

He does no such thing. He moves to a long wooden desk and hands me a piece of paper and a pen. I glance at it. It's a contract that says I can't burn down my room. I sign. He slides an envelope the size of a playing card across the counter to me, my initials written on the front. He walks around the long desk and comes out a side door, moving to a wall of small cubbyholes, similar to the kind in a kindergarten classroom. As he speaks, he bends one green paper into each hole.

"This is your pidge. Check it daily for post. You're room thirteen, staircase four. That's Swithuns staircase four, mind you. We don't make a habit of housing graduate students inside walls, but there's a shortage in graduate housing this year. Besides, I've found Americans rather enjoy being 'behind the gates.' Something to do with that boy wizard?"

"Harry Pott—"

"Meals are at your discretion. We have Formal Hall on Sunday, Wednesday, and Friday. Gowns must be worn. Nip into a shop on Turl for one. Boiler won't come on till October fifteenth, no heat till then, so don't ask for it. You'll find two keys in the envelope; the electronic card will get you in the gates and any of the public rooms after hours, the other is a proper key for your room. It is irreplaceable. Don't lose it."

I understand maybe half of what he's said. "Thanks. What's your name?" I ask.

His turtle neck recedes. "Hugh," he grunts, turning back to the pidges.

"I'm Ella."

"We've established that, Miss Durran."

"Well," I say, grabbing the handle of my suitcase, "I think this is the beginning of a beautiful friendship, Hugh."

"Of all the gin joints, Miss Durran," he mutters. But I can see the hint of a smile. I mean, it's reluctant and has a rusty, unused quality about it, like an old bicycle pump, but it's there. "You'll be finding staircase four just outside the lodge—" I open my mouth to speak, but he forges on, "This is the lodge, and you will exit through that door there, cross St. John's quad, turn left at Swithuns, and then you will pass, on your left, staircase one, and then you will pass, also on your left, staircase two, and if you persevere you shall invariably come to staircase four." I try again, opening my mouth to speak, but he deftly continues: "At which point, your room will be on the left of the uppermost landing, at the very top."

The words "the very top" give me pause. I'm once again reminded that I haven't eaten since I left the States.

"Hugh, would you mind if I left my bags here and got some food first?"

"As you will, Miss Durran."

"I'll be quick," I assure him, but Hugh's turned back to his copier. "Any recommendations?"

"Plenty of options on the High."

The High. So much cooler than High Street.

I wheel my bag next to the copier, take my book out of my backpack, turn to go, and stop abruptly. A boy pokes his head around the entrance to the lodge and tentatively steps forward. He moves like a mouse. He's pudgy around the middle and his hair is styled in two pointed fans on the top of his head, resembling ears. He looks like Gus Gus from *Cinderella*.

I'm so tired.

"Yes," Hugh snaps at the boy, instantly impatient.

He looks as if he wants to flee, but says, "Yes, erm, sorry, sir, I'm going to, erm, uh, Sebastian Melmoth's room?"

"Not again," Hugh mutters. "Posh prat." I can't help but smile. Someone actually said "posh prat" in real life, in real time, right in front of me. Hugh then barks at the boy, "Don't just stand there, come in, come in." Gus Gus scurries past us. As Hugh shakes his head, I walk back out to the High.

Taking an arbitrary right, I journey back the way I came, glancing at my watch. As if on cue, a clock tower somewhere begins belting out five resounding chimes. Goose bumps crawl up my arms. If I weren't exhausted I'd probably start crying.

I glance across the street and stop.

I can't believe what I'm seeing. The sign still looks exactly like it did in the magazine.

The Happy Cod Chip Shop.

I look left and move to cross the street, dropping one foot off the curb when the sudden bleat of a horn makes me leap back onto the sidewalk. I clutch my book to my chest, keeping my heart from falling out. A classic silver convertible, like something out of a Bond movie, flies past, nearly running me over. I catch a glimpse of the careless driver, whose longish brown hair swirls in the wind as he zooms off. In the passenger seat, an equally windswept blond woman turns around to stare at me, her mouth wide open in a shocked, but unabashed, laugh.

"Not funny!" I want to shout after them, but they're already well past me. As my heart begins beating normally again, I take a deep breath and step off the curb once more. This time, making sure to look right.

A tiny bell jingles as I enter the Happy Cod. The proprietor, a stocky, red-nosed man with a white towel slung over his shoulder, glances up cheerfully. "Hallo!"

The small, charming room has a row of wooden booths on one side and a bar with stools on the other. The man stands at the back, behind a small service counter. There's a stool there as well. He pats the counter in welcome. "What can I get you?"

"Fish and chips!"

"Comin' right up." He turns to his fryer as I settle in, running my hands along the old, worn wood and moving around on the squishy black vinyl seat. Everything feels just as I imagined it would. Smells just as I imagined it would. Even the proprietor is exactly as I imagined.

"I'm Ella, by the way."

He spins back, ceremoniously wipes his hand on his towel, and offers it to me. "Simon." I take his hand, meeting his firm shake with one of my own. He grins. "Where you from, Ella?"

"Ohio, originally." Simon nods vaguely and leans his elbows on the counter, looking down at the book I've put there.

It's a meager hardcover, bound in that linen material that only academic books are covered in. It cost me eighty dollars on eBay; the price of these books is inversely proportional to the size of their audience. He reads the title aloud, picking over each word as if he's selecting ripe tomatoes: "*The Victorian Conundrum: How Contemporary Poetry Shaped Gender Politics and Sexuality 1837 to 1898,* by Roberta Styan." He glances up at me dubiously.

"It's a real page-turner," I say, and he guffaws. "No, I'm doing a master's." I tap the author's name on the cover. "Mostly with Professor Styan. Do you know her?" Simon shakes his head and a beeping noise comes from the fryer. He moves to it. "She's, like, a deity in the lit crit world. Her specialty is Tennyson, which isn't exactly my area. Not at all, actually. I work in politics. American politics. But this whole year for me is about pushing boundaries, and exploring new things, and basically just, like, leveling up. As a person?" Why am I rambling? Why do I feel like a fog is rolling into my head? Oh. Jet lag.

Simon wraps my whole meal in a cone of brown butcher paper surrounded by newspaper and offers it to me like a bouquet of roses. "Tradition," he boasts. "Some other chippies use them plastic takeaway containers. Flattens me." He hands me a paper plate, saying, "For sauce," and gestures to a counter full of condiments at the front of the restaurant. "That's me own twist on tradition. Used to be you'd come in here and get curry or peas or tartar and that was that. Give 'em a go. Promise you won't be disappointed." He winks at me.

Before I can reply, the bell jingles, and Simon turns his attention to the door. "JD!" he exclaims with a bright smile, opening the hinged counter and moving toward the entry.

"Simon, my good man," a male voice replies.

I focus on the culinary perfection in front of me. God, the smell. I take a bite. Heaven. I have to restrain myself from moaning.

I hear the man say, "Two fish and chip and two fizzies. Cheers, mate." His voice is so melodious, so low and soothing, it should be accompanied by choral music.

Then a female voice says, "No chips for me. And make mine diet."

Peripherally, I sense them settle in at a booth near the door as Simon comes back around. I take another mouthful of the perfectly prepared fish and this time am not so successful at stifling my moan. Simon, tending to the fryer, throws me a grin over his shoulder.

I hear the woman behind me murmur, "I thought you were taking me to the best place in Oxford."

"And so I have," the man says.

Pulling another chip out of the cone, I'm absorbed in trying to read bits and pieces of the newspaper's stories and advertisements, but the fog keeps rolling in. A few minutes later, Simon pops the countertop once more and lumbers over to the couple, delivering their meals. "Cheers," the man says, then, as Simon comes back through the counter, "Behold the potato! Divine tuber. Staple of the gods. How we adore thee!"

"They give you a fat arse," the woman replies.

"No, no," the man argues, "The oil does. The oil! Yet the potato takes the blame. It's a bloody outrage, I tell you." He laughs. She doesn't.

Simon catches my eye and rolls his. I roll mine back and we smile, comrades-in-arms. He nods toward the condiment station, whispering, "Really, give 'em a go."

"Oh, right! I forgot." I pick up my plate and walk to the counter to survey the many options.

I hear the man continue, "Now, the Irish! They knew the value of the potato. Did you know that when the Irish were deprived of the potato for just a few years, a million people died?"

There's a pause. "Why didn't they just eat something else?"

My hand punches the tarter sauce pump and the thick paste overshoots my plate, splattering onto the counter.

"What, like cake?" the man asks dryly.

"Sure," she answers, immune to sarcasm.

I pick up a bottle labeled *Brown Sauce* (not exactly descriptive) and pour that onto my plate, too. Then I take a squeeze of mustard, a dollop of mayonnaise, something that looks like chutney but I'm not sure. I feel obligated to take a little of everything, not wanting to disappoint Simon. The plate looks like a painter's palette.

I hear Golden Voice get out of the booth. "Why didn't they just eat something else? Excellent question! Let them eat cake! But, see, they'd run out. Not a slice of cake in the entire country. Bloody awful. What was the Empire coming to, eh?" Dry British wit on full display. Always entertaining and yet somehow thoroughly obnoxious. "Now," he continues, "there's a home-cooked meal in it for you—"

She cuts him off, using a low, come-hither voice. "I'd rather those earrings we saw earlier."

"You'll have to do a bit more than trivia for diamonds, love," he says offhandedly. The jerk. "A home-cooked meal if you can tell me the year the Potato Famine occurred. You have ten seconds. Ten. Nine. Eight—"

I realize I'm just standing there in my encroaching fog, listening to this ridiculous conversation, letting my fish and chips get cold. Snapping out of it, I turn around to head back to my seat and crash spectacularly into Golden Voice. Two planets colliding. The entire plate of condiments flips backward into my chest and I teeter, about to go down. A knightly hand reaches out and clutches my forearm, steadying me. My other hand grabs his shoulder.

Maybe he's not a jerk, after all.

Righting myself, I catch sight of the woman he's been talking with. Long blond hair. Windswept. Mouth open wide in a shocked laugh.

My gaze whips back to him, just as his head pops up, brown hair mussed.

Our eyes lock.

The fog lifts and I blurt, "You!"

CHAPTER 3

He sits in a beautiful parlor,
With hundreds of books on the wall;
He drinks a great deal of Marsala,
But never gets tipsy at all.
Edward Lear, "How Pleasant to Know Mr. Lear!," 1871

M e?" he inquires, a deer-in-headlights look in his eyes.

"You!" I repeat.

We're still facing each other. He's still grasping my forearm, I'm still clutching his shoulder. We're right up against each other, face to face, eye to eye, plate to breasts.

His stare activates. He comes to life. "Right, okay, here's what we do. Simon?" he calls, but Simon's already tossing the towel from his shoulder and You deftly snatches it out of the air. "Lean forward," he encourages. I bend at the waist and he peels the plate away. I watch the myriad sauces plop from my chest to the linoleum floor, a poor man's Jackson Pollock.

The blonde laughs.

I stand upright as the man sets the plate on the counter, then moves toward me with the towel, heading for my chest.

My hand shoots out. "Don't. I got it." With my bare hands,

I rub at my shirt like a finger-painting toddler, making it ten times worse. The clamminess is starting to seep through the fabric onto my skin. I feel him staring at me. "What?" I ask, all contained calm.

"Do we know each other?"

"You almost hit me with your car!"

"Was that you?"

I grind my jaw, keeping my mouth shut.

"May I . . . assist?" the man lilts with a tone that only ever means one thing.

I freeze.

He can't be.

I look up at him.

He is.

He's flirting with me. Holding the towel poised and ready, all dashing smile and twinkling eyes.

My head explodes. "Are you kidding me?"

"I would never dare kid about such matters," he charms.

"You're flirting? You should be apologizing!"

"For flirting?"

"For nearly running me over!"

"You're suggesting I apologize for something I didn't intentionally do? I'd rather apologize for the flirting." He's smiling.

"Y-you . . . you posh prat!"

"Ooh. Posh prat. Nice choice of alliterative spondee." He's still smiling. "So you're American. Right, here's the one thing I know about Americans: they tend to get themselves run over in this country by stepping directly into oncoming traffic."

"So it's my fault?!" I shout.

"Another thing I know about Americans: they tend to shout. Here." He reaches into his pocket, pulling out a brightly colored wad of money. He peels off a bill. He holds it out to me.

"What is that?" I seethe. Quietly.

"Specifically? It's a fifty-pound note."

"I don't want your money! I want . . . I want—" What do I want? The fog is thickening again.

"Oh, don't look so outraged. Take it. You said it yourself. I'm the posh prat." He holds the money out again. "The unemotional cad who—absent any genuine remorse or feeling—can but only buy the regard of others."

I jerk my head to the blonde. "So I see."

This strikes him. His face changes. The open, breezy, devil-may-care smile drops away and a curtain closes behind his eyes. The show is over. He actually looks hurt. Good. "Keep your money," I say, capitalizing on this moment of clarity, of the tables having turned, seizing a parting shot. "Buy the historian some carbs."

Walking back to the counter, I pick up my book and coat, digging in the pocket for some cash. I plop down twenty pounds, grab what remains of my fish bouquet, catch Simon's smiling eyes, and head for the door. "See you later, Simon!"

"Looking forward to it, Ella from Ohio!" He chuckles.

"Bonne chance," the man calls dryly, clearly having rallied. Then, adopting an even plummier, more clichéd British accent, adds, "Keep calm and look right!"

Ignoring him, I open the door. The bell jingles and I pause at the threshold. I can't resist. I turn back to him. "The Potato Famine was in 1845. Asshole."

So that went well.

Foggy, filthy, and suddenly exhausted, I hoof back to Magdalen, shoving fried fish into my mouth as I go. It's not my imagination that people give me a wide berth.

Now that I'm out in the fresh air, the beginning twinges of

embarrassment set in. Yes, I'm jet-lagged, out of my comfort zone, but still . . .

I hate guys like that. I went to college with guys like that. I interned on the Hill with guys like that. Guys who think they can buy respect with Daddy's money, and then seal the deal with a wink and a smile. Guys who play a game, who set their trap as if it's the most ingenious feat of engineering ever devised and expect you to fall all over yourself congratulating their effort.

Look. I'm not drop-dead gorgeous or anything, but with the right lighting, the right hair and makeup effort on my part, I've been known to turn a few heads. I have this wild Irish hair that goes everywhere, a wide Julia Roberts mouth, and big, round eyes that make me look more innocent than I actually am. The approachable, girl-next-door type. The type who might be flattered, for instance, by your flirting after you've nearly run her over and then destroyed her shirt.

Unfortunately for guys like that, looks can be deceiving.

I stumble through the Magdalen gates and into the lodge. No Hugh. I continue on through the other door and into the courtyard. The sun dips in the sky and the sandstone buildings are hued pink. I wobble across the cobblestones and try to follow Hugh's directions in my clouded head.

A large L-shaped building appears, embracing a giant lawn so finely coiffed it would shame a golf course. Every thirty feet or so, little staircases, bordered by mullioned windows, ascend into the depth and darkness of the building. I find number four and start my climb with the single-minded determination of the proverbial horse returning to the barn.

The first few stairs are granite, but they soon become old slabs of stone, each step worn into a bowed smile from centuries of shoes. The stairway continues to spiral and soon narrows into planks of rickety wood. It's so steep that I find myself climbing the steps as if they were a ladder, ending up on hands and knees on a small five-by-five landing, a door on each side of me.

I'm about to stand and dig in my pocket for the key Hugh gave me when it occurs to me that my bags are still downstairs in the lodge. I tip over onto my side with a loud groan. I could sleep right here. I just might.

The door on the right opens and Gus Gus quickly emerges, stepping over me casually as if I'd been there as long as the staircase, and disappears down the stairs. A voice from the open door calls after him, "Your beauty will fade, as will my interest. Be gone with you!"

A figure appears in the doorway and recoils at the sight of me. It's wearing a red dressing gown and holding a tumbler of amber liquid. Its free hand finds the gap in the robe and clutches it closed, like an aging Tennessee Williams heroine.

"Hello!" I croak.

"Hel-lo," it replies haltingly, a small, willowy male with wavy, chin-length, chestnut hair. He peers at me then murmurs, almost to himself, "Is it lost?"

Hey. When I use a dehumanizing pronoun, I only think it. I don't say it right to the pronoun's face. I stumble to my feet. "I live here." I gesture to the door behind me. "I'm Ella." He looks me over, nose crinkling at either my appearance or smell, I can't tell which. Both are on par with a county-fair trash can at the moment. I soldier on, remembering who Gus Gus told Hugh he was looking for, back in the lodge. "And you're Sebastian Melmoth, right?"

Now he gives me the side-eye, suspicious. "That's right. It's a family name. But how—"

"Oh yeah?"

"Yeah," he drawls, mocking my accent. "Goes back centuries.

But how did you—"

"I didn't know that was possible."

"What?"

"To be descended from someone who didn't actually exist." He side-eyes me from the other direction. "Correct me if I'm wrong, it's been a while since I read his stuff, and I'm tired, jet-lagged, and, you know, American, but Sebastian Melmoth was Oscar Wilde's pseudonym. Right?"

Admittedly, I'm getting a certain perverse pleasure from this.

Called out, the guy just glares at me, then heaves a conde-scending sigh, turns on his heel, and goes back into his room, slamming the door for good measure.

I take a stabilizing breath, retrieve the ancient-looking key from my pocket, and assess the antique keyhole lock. I slide the key into it and turn. It sounds like I'm unlocking a vault. I push open the tired hinged door and enter the room. My room.

The sun has almost set, so the room is dim. So dim that I fail to see my luggage in the middle of the floor and trip over it. Still, Hugh is my hero right now. I fumble for a light switch and find it to the right of the door.

The room is quaint, with an A-frame ceiling and exposed wooden beams. Between the beams, the ceiling is painted white and the walls are Victorian-era plaster, even peeling romanti-cally in places. Pushed up against the far wall is a single twin bed centered to the apex of the roofline. There's a functional dresser on one wall and a low built-in bookcase beside it. To the left there's a little bathroom with an RV-sized shower and Bar-bie doll sink, and to the right is a single, double-paned dormer window. I go to it.

The light is fading, but I glimpse the outline of a spectacular view. I can see Magdalen Tower from here, and slate-shingled rooftops in between and beyond. The top of one of the oak trees in the quad below fills in the bottom border of the window.

I could get used to this.

I quickly shower off, reluctantly throw away my shirt, change into some sweats, connect to the college WiFi, and check my e-mail.

Four sequential messages from my mother greet me.

Just checking in. Let me know when you land.

Let me know when you get settled.

Are you settled? Is something wrong? Something's wrong, isn't it?

Ella please respond. I would call the college but I don't know how to call international and the Skype thing you set up for me says I need money to call. I thought the point of it was that it's free??? Anyway, just let me know you're safe because in my bones I think something might be wrong.

I heave a sigh. Now is not the time for her to go all Chicken Little on me. I type:

Tell your bones to relax. I'm fine. Just exhausted. Will write more tomorrow.

I hesitate, as I always do at writing "*I love you*," so I just write, *XO, E.*

I glance at a few more e-mails in my in-box, but everything is becoming one big blur. I look at the clock on my computer: 6:30. A totally reasonable bedtime.

For the most part I sleep soundly, but every time the clock tower chimes, my dreams change like slides in a projector. At the seven o'clock chime, the door to my room opens.

It takes me a moment to realize I'm no longer dreaming.

CHAPTER 4

Awake! For Morning in the Bowl of Night
Has flung the Stone that puts the Stars to Flight . . .
Edward Fitzgerald translation, *Rubaiyat of Omar Khayyam*, 1859

bolt upright. A squat, white-haired woman wearing a functional gray apron walks into my room, humming.

I scream.

She screams.

We look at each other.

"Oooh!" she exclaims, grabbing her chest. "You put the heart crossways in me, love!" She shuffles farther into my room. "Go back t' sleep, don't mind old E."

My eyes begin to clear and I notice she's carrying a bucket. She waddles into the bathroom.

I get out of bed and stagger after her. She's bent over the toilet, scrubbing and humming away. "Oh, y-you don't have to do that," I stammer.

"Bless you." She keeps right on doing it.

I hold out my hand. "I'm Ella."

She doesn't take her eyes off the task at hand. "Eugenia, love."

I drop my hand. "So, you're a maid? We get a maid?" I cringe.

"I mean, a housekeeper? Or room attendant, or—"

She stands upright and looks at me sternly, a schoolmarm in a past life. "I'm yer scout, dearie." Then she moves to the shower, wiping it down with a rag. "Did that muddleheaded porter of a Hugh not tell ya you'd be havin' a scout?"

"How often do you come?" I ask.

"Why every day, o' course!" She turns to the sink, polishes the knobs. "'Cept for Saturdays. And Sundays. And bank holidays, fer certain. Seven sharp, on the chime." She grins at me. "But don't worry, love. Quiet as a church mouse, in and out in two minutes without anyone knowin' the wiser. Just ask yer neighbor. Been cleanin' his rooms for four years now and I only ever seen him with his eyes open but once, and that was comin' home after a night out." She laughs to herself. "He's a jolly one, he is." She changes the trash bag with a magician-like flourish of the wrist.

This whole arrangement is very *Upstairs, Downstairs*. And she's no spring chicken. My midwestern side is uncomfortable having a septuagenarian in service to me, no matter how much pride she seems to take in her job. "Eugenia, you really don't have to come every day."

She's already at the door, bucket in hand. She smiles, grabs the doorknob, and says, "Right then, see you tomorrow, love." And she's gone.

AFTER CUTTING THROUGH some texts and e-mails (three from Gavin), I shower, twist my hair into a messy topknot, slap on some mascara and lip gloss, and slip into one of my more responsible-looking blazers. I'm out the door by nine with an unearned sense of victory. I thank Hugh for his very *Remains of the Day* baggage-delivery service last night and get a distracted grunt in reply.

With an hour to spare before the Rhodes orientation, I grab a bottled Frappucino and some cookie-like thing called a flap-jack from some bodega-like thing called a newsagent's and start wandering.

The High is quiet this early, the shops' gates still down, the restaurants dark. But a simple right turn, just before a medi-eval church, puts me in a cobblestone alleyway that opens up to a city alive. I'm in Radcliffe Square, and I stop to take it all in. The iconic, cylindrical Radcliffe Camera stands before me, with its neoclassical architecture and golden walls. It's as if I've stumbled onto an anthill. Students and tourists go in and out of gates on the square's periphery, disappearing into the basement of a church, emerging with coffee and pastry bags. Interesting. I regret my bottle of newsagent's coffee.

I'm just turning around like the second hand of a clock, tak-ing it all in. The architecture, the landscaping, the way people are dressed, the way they sound. The constant *tring-tring* of bicycle bells. I move through the square, past the Bodleian Library, and around the Sheldonian Theatre, its surrounding pillars topped with thirteen stone busts of nameless men. Across the street, tourist shops hawk Oxford gear next to a couple of charming-looking pubs and a few gated colleges. The stores are painted in cheery blues and reds, yellows and whites. A couple of Union Jacks fly out over the sidewalk, where a smattering of café tables and chairs waits for patrons in the dewy early-morning chill.

It's a more cosmopolitan environment than I expected. It feels old, yes, but it's thriving. History with a pulse. Warm-blooded ruins. I hear Mandarin, Italian, French, Arabic, and an assort-ment of English accents. There's a startling number of Ameri-cans. It's as if this city belongs to everyone. If you're here, you belong here. It's like a timeless, ramshackle, international space station.

At the end of Broad Street, in front of Balliol College, there's an innocuous-looking cobblestone cross embedded in the street. A memorial, it turns out, for the three Oxford Martyrs, Protestant bishops who were burned at the stake by Queen Mary in the 1550s. I realize, with a start, that one of these men was Thomas Cranmer, the man responsible for annulling the marriage of Mary's parents, Henry VIII and Catherine of Aragon.

My brain tries to reboot. I'm standing on the spot where Thomas Cranmer died. It's not blocked off, no one's charging admission. It's barely even marked. It's just part of the Oxford landscape. And not thirty feet away, I can buy Oxford University sweatpants and Tardis cookie tins.

A chill goes up my spine. This moment of cognitive dissonance is just the beginning. Toto, we're not in Ohio anymore.

Gauging distance in this town is impossible. Maybe it's the uneven, cobblestoned terrain. Maybe it's the pods of tourists taking up every inch of sidewalk. Maybe it's the meandering streets and alleys. I love every cobblestone, pod, and meander, but I misjudge how long it will take to get to the Rhodes House and I end up finding it with less than a minute to spare.

I race up the steps. Just as I grab the door handle, my phone rings. *Shit.* Even though it's only five A.M. in Washington, apparently we're open for business.

"Gavin, hi!" I answer.

A chuckle greets me from the other end of the phone. "Sorry to disappoint, but this isn't Gavin."

I freeze, still holding the door handle. "Senator Wilkes," I manage. "W-what a nice surprise."

"Ella Durran. I'm a fan."

I can't believe this is happening; I'm here, I'm there, I'm— starting to hyperventilate. *Chill.* "I'm a huge fan of yours," I gush. "I'm so excited to—"

"Excuse me?"

I spin around. I'm blocking the entrance. "Sorry," I whisper to the woman trying to get around me. I glance inside the building as she opens the door. The place is packed. I'm two minutes late. They're starting.

There's no way I'm hanging up on the next possible president of the United States, who says breezily, "Well, let's get to it. Education is going to be the cornerstone of my campaign and you are a key part of the strategy. I loved what you wrote. I had three boys in the Florida public school system while trying to put myself through grad school in my thirties. Trust me, I get it."

Through the door, I hear the squeal of a microphone coming to life and then an amplified British voice saying, "Everyone, please take your seats . . ."

"Senator—"

"Call me Janet."

"Thank you, I just want to say . . ." Breathe. Speak. "Anything you need, anything at all, I'm here for you and Gavin. It's an honor to be working for you."

"Working *with* me, Ella. This is a partnership. We're going to do great things together. That said, we'll try to bother you as little as possible. We want you to enjoy your time at Oxford. Right, Gavin?"

"Absolutely," I hear him say in the background in a tone of voice I haven't heard from him before. It's patient and ingratiating. Just as he's my boss, she's his.

The door to the Rhodes House opens from the inside, and a man steps out, bending his head and bringing his cell phone to his ear. He answers it lowly. "This is Connor."

We glance at each other with mirrored looks of chagrin. He has a really nice face: chiseled jaw, sloped nose, bright brown eyes, and Stephanopoulos hair. This is what I used to imagine a

Rhodes scholar looked like. The prep school quarterback from a J. D. Salinger novel.

"Well, Ella, I won't take up any more of your time. I just wanted to say welcome aboard."

"Thank you. I won't let you down."

"Never crossed my mind. Wait, Gavin wants to say something. I'll hand you over."

Do I tell him I'm missing orientation? Do I tell him I'll call him back? Do I have a choice? Gavin's voice comes on the line. "You have a minute? I can get Priya Banergee right now for a conference call. You in?"

Priya Banergee is a pollster. I should hear what she has to say. I look wistfully at the Rhodes House door even as I say, "Of course." They patch Priya in as I plop down on the top step. My partner in cell-phone purgatory takes up residence on the other side of the stair. We give each other a resigned grin. As he speaks into his phone, I find myself assessing him.

Jesus. That is one attractive Rhodie.

TWENTY-FIVE MINUTES LATER, after listening to an endless stream of data and contributing almost nothing to the conversation, we wrap up. I disconnect and take a breath, then glance over at the guy, who's also just hanging up.

Smiling, he says, "Can we just agree that anything either of us might have overheard doesn't leave this stoop?"

I snort. "Deal. But can I ask who you work for? Lobbyist?"

He nods. "Health care."

"Which group?"

"PMR?" Public Medical Relations. The biggest health care lobbying group in D.C., and he says it as if questioning whether I've heard of it. Like when you ask someone where they went to college and they say, "Harvard?"

"You're inside the Beltway as well?" he asks. I nod. He leans over, bracing a palm on the cool marble step and extending his other hand to me. "Connor Harrison-Smith."

"Ella Durran."

God, he has a killer smile. Wouldn't that be just my luck; I come all the way to England and fall for a guy who probably lives a block from me in D.C. He gestures toward the door. "You wanna?" I nod and we both stand, collecting our things. "So, not that I overheard anything, obviously, but this is a new job for you?"

"Yeah. You?"

"No. I quit. I'm just helping out until the new guy's up to speed."

I make a show of contemplating this. "Interesting. So you're just gonna, like, study for the year?"

"I'm just gonna, like, drink a lot of really good beer, is what I'm gonna do." We both chuckle. "I'm doing a master's in global health. You?"

"Literature."

"Really?"

Everyone always sounds surprised when I say this. "Yup; 1830 to 1914."

We move toward the door. "Huh." A wrinkle appears on his brow as he puzzles this out. He's adorable. "Where'd you do your undergrad?"

"Georgetown. You?"

"Harvard?"

I smile.

He opens the door and holds it for me. A gentleman.

After getting an abbreviated orientation from a harried administrator (go here, do this, see this person for this thing, don't do this, sign this), I glance at my watch, and I only have ten minutes to get to my first class at the English faculty building. I seem to be the only person rushing out. I think I'm definitely the only one doing a master's in English. Whenever I say what I'm studying, people tilt their heads at me. What is this literature of which you speak?

I head outside only to be slowed by Connor's voice calling, "Ella, wait." I turn back, see him standing on our stairs. "Why don't I give you my number? In case you wanna drink some beer."

I smile at him and take out my phone. "It's a plan."

THE ENGLISH FACULTY building is a blocky, midcentury cement blight. Not exactly what I had expected. One of the linear, unimaginative departments should have this building. Something like chemistry or mathematics or, well, global health.

I arrive at the designated lecture room ten minutes after the class's start time, once again a day late and a pound short in this city. Collecting myself, I softly open the door, fully expecting to interrupt the class.

I don't.

A group of about ten people is scattered around a horseshoe table, some murmuring to each other, others reading, others looking at their phones. No one is at the lectern.

I cross to a cluster of empty seats. As I pass behind one of them, a girl mutters, "Sorry! This doesn't need to be here," and quickly lifts her bag off the seat directly in front of me. I keep moving toward another empty chair, opening my mouth to tell her it's okay, but she keeps talking. "So sorry. My apologies, really. Selfish."

In America, there'd be a good chance her apologies were sarcastic. From the corner of my eye, I take her in. She's dressed conservatively (boat-neck tweed sheath dress under a canary-yellow cardigan, ballet flats), and her hair is styled in an intricate sixties beehive. Only, it's pink. She appears innocent of any sarcasm.

I consider introducing myself to her, but she looks as if interaction with a stranger might push her over the edge. I guess this must be the famous British reserve.

Just then the door bangs open, causing everyone to jump, and a guy, outfitted like Robert Redford in *The Sting*, strides in. "I have arrived," he announces. "We can begin." So much for British reserve. With a start, I realize that I know him.

"Sebastian Melmoth!" I say.

He stops and peers at me. The girl's pink head swivels from him to me, eyes bulging, before whipping back to him. "Charlie! You swore you'd stop doing that!"

He drops his head theatrically to his chest and sulks toward us.

The girl turns back to me, doe-brown eyes sympathetic. "How did you meet this git, then?"

"We share a staircase," I answer as he drops into the chair on the other side of her.

She spins back to him, smacking him on the arm. "And you didn't recognize her?"

"In my defense," he begins, "she was disguised as a vagrant. The old crone in a Breton lai who is actually a beautiful sorceress. Clever bitch gets me every time." He looks past the girl, to me. "So, having failed the moral aptitude test, what shall it be, eh? Seven years as a toad? Eternity as a Tory? Or shall we dispense with further discord?" He extends his hand. "Charles Butler, *veritas et virtus*."

I can't help but smile. "Ella Durran."

He drops my hand and settles back in his chair. "Come to mine tonight." It's not an apology, but it's clearly a peace offering. "We'll have a dram."

"Will do. Thank you."

He nudges the girl. "Join us."

"All right."

"Bring your Scotch."

The girl rolls her eyes, but just then, Professor Roberta Styan walks in. Everything stops. She typifies the absentminded professor, stumbling up to the lectern, arms overflowing with paraphernalia. Briefcase, papers, umbrella, jacket, muttering as she walks, "Hello, hello, sorry, apologies for the delay."

At the podium, she doesn't set anything down, just stands behind it looking out at us. Then she says, "Right, so: tragic news, I'm afraid. I've just been named head of graduate studies. Which means I'm far too important to be teaching you lot." Before we can respond, she continues, "Please, shed no tears! Rend not your garments! My replacement is more than able. In fact, he's my most brilliant JRF. After two minutes with him—not to mention his skinny jeans—you'll forget I ever existed." She takes a breath, then smiles. Off our lack of reaction, she quips, "You were meant to scoff at that. Ah well. Without further ado, meet Jamie Davenport. Jamie?" She gestures toward the door.

Wait. Hold on. The person I came to Oxford to study with is leaving? But I've read all of her books, all of her papers. I watched all three of her YouTube videos. (It's not her fault. Victorian sexuality and linguistics is a niche market.) This isn't happening. She was my Oxford destiny, my Gandalf, my Mr. Miyagi, my whatever-Robin-Williams's-Character's-Name-Was-in-*Dead-Poets'-Society*. What does she mean she's not teaching?

Styan hobbles away from the podium, and the TA gives her a squeeze on the shoulder before taking the lectern. "Sorry to disappoint, my skinny jeans are at the cleaners." He smiles charmingly at the group and everyone responds with an appreciative chuckle.

Except for me. I can't respond. I'm too busy having my world reordered.

The new professor is the posh prat.

CHAPTER 5

Out flew the web and floated wide;
The mirror cracked from side to side;
"The curse is come upon me," cried
The Lady of Shalott.
Alfred, Lord Tennyson, "The Lady of Shalott," 1831–1832

Jamie Davenport takes his time spreading his notes out on the podium. Then he looks up at the class and smiles impishly. "Please, be gentle."

What would happen if I left? This is only one of my courses and it only meets once a week. Maybe I can join another group. Maybe I can track down Styan and convince her to work with me privately. I refuse to allow this teaching assistant to be my only option. This cannot be my "Once-in-a-Lifetime Experience." That's supposed to be a good thing.

"Five years ago," he begins, "I sat right where you are now. Styan walked in and I thought, 'So this is who'll bore me to tears for the next two months?' I mean, I love poetry—why else would I be here, eh?—but bloody Victorian? Could anything be worse? Ghastly old men in top hats, big bellies, muttonchops out to here, banging on about the glory of foreign wars and the sanctity of the marriage bed? Frankly, I wanted to slit my own throat."

Peripherally, I see the other students smile. I don't.

"Never in my wildest dreams," he continues, looking out into the room, "did I expect to find in the work of the Victorians such despair. Lust. Terror." He makes eye contact with a different person at each word, a politician "connecting" with his audience. "Wisdom. Love."

And bam. His eyes lock with mine and there's a whisper of hesitation in his voice, like the momentary skip of an old record. No one else notices. But I do. And he does. He quickly looks back out to the group. "Do you believe me?" he asks.

Not on your life, I think.

He claps his hands. "Any questions, then? Before we start?"

I raise my hand.

"We don't raise hands here. Forty lashes and no grog for you." He smiles at me. The gall.

"Do you have a syllabus we can look at?" I ask, sure he doesn't.

"A syllabus?"

There's a titter somewhere in the class. He cocks his head at me. "Yes," I continue. "A document in which you outline the weekly reading, due dates, grading standards, expectations?"

"Ah, good question," he says easily. "You don't need to prepare any of the material ahead of time, and I don't foresee any papers, but if we do have one it'll be set at your convenience, and lastly, I'm not responsible for marking. So . . ."

By the snickers from some of the other students I glean that this is common knowledge. I look down at the table, realizing that I might be on the verge of embarrassing myself. "Okay. No syllabus is an Oxfordian thing that I'll just have to get used to."

A voice pipes up across from me. "Oxonian, actually."

I glance over. A girl who looks like an English rose cameo

you'd find on an antique pin scribbles something in her note-book, not looking at me.

"Tomato, to-mah-to," I reply, with forced geniality.

"It's not a matter of pronunciation, of dialectology," she coun-ters in a low, luxuriant voice. She keeps writing. "It's not a lin-guistic schism from the colonies, it's quite simply and literally a different word."

My face heats. "Oh yeah?"

She deigns to look up. "'Oxfordian' refers the theory pur-porting that the seventeenth Earl of Oxford authored the works of Shakespeare. A theory that has fallen predominantly out of favor amongst most legitimate academics."

The way she says "legitimate academics" feels like a slap. "Okay, cool," I say. "Thanks for the tip."

She smiles tightly and looks back down at her notebook. I bury my face in mine as well. If I could disappear right now I would.

"All right, then, Oxonians," Jamie Davenport says buoyantly, "Onward!"

EVERYONE IN THE class is obviously smart. The pink-haired girl next to me hasn't said anything, but has at least ten pages of notes. Charlie, who never even pulled out a notebook, rattles off crisp and cogent comments with about as much effort as a yawn. And the English rose drops her observations quietly yet delib-erately, with perfectly chosen words and no extraneous "uhs" or "likes" or "you knows." How is that possible?

I haven't said anything.

I wasn't an English major in undergrad. I was, perhaps unsur-prisingly, poli sci and history. I took English classes for fun, and am well read, but I didn't live, breathe, and eat it the way these people did. They are here, doing a master of studies in English at Oxford University, because they earned it.

I basically won a contest.

No disrespect to the Rhodes, but it's true. I got the scholarship because of the overall applicant I was, not because the committee knew I would excel in the study of English literature and language, 1830–1914. How could they know I'd be good at this? They were all hedge-fund execs and mathematics professors and social entrepreneurs.

What am I doing here?

A thought runs screaming through my mind like an escapee from an insane asylum: if I had actually applied to Oxford, I probably wouldn't be here.

Somehow this fact never occurred to me until just now while someone says, "Yes, but as Stanley Fish would have us believe," and another person says, "Harold Bloom would disagree with you there," and another replies, "Well, Bloom," as if that's retort enough, and then there are just words: "Derrida" and "Said" and "New Historicism" and "Queer Theory" and everything is "Post" (Post-Modernism, Post-Feminism, Post-Christian), until I honestly don't know what we're talking about anymore.

I realize that as much as I'd like to get out of this class and ask Styan about other options, I have no right to. The political operative from Ohio thinks the posh prat of a TA is beneath her? Because the truth is, all my anger, embarrassment, and hurt pride aside, I have to admit he's giving a damn fine lecture. He hasn't looked at his notes once. He's fielded questions with ease, moderated discussion with finesse, and managed with tact to tell certain people, "That's an interesting point, but have you evidence?" when he obviously means, "That's stupid, shut up."

Jamie Davenport comes around to the front of the podium, nodding along to whatever English Rose is saying. "Right, Cecelia, exactly. There's a theory that Shakespeare's plays taught us how to be human, how to understand ourselves. I believe that poetry teaches us how to feel." He looks out to the rest of the group, and says:

> *"My candle burns at both ends;*
> *It will not last the night;*
> *But ah, my foes, and oh, my friends—*
> *It gives a lovely light."*

Then he smiles cheekily at us. "Author?"

The class is silent. No one knows. I'm so surprised no one knows that it takes me a moment to realize that I do. I know this! My hand pops into the air like a marionette.

He smiles, and with that mellifluous voice says, "Remember? No raising of hands."

I immediately drop it. The class chuckles. I join them. *See, I'm a good sport,* and then go in for the kill. "Edna St. Vincent Millay, 1912."

He inclines his head in surprised approval. "Well done. Dates are most definitely a strong point. Ella from Ohio."

Potato Famine, 1845. Against my will, my cheeks flush. Charlie and Pink Hair's heads (and every girl's in the room, actually) whip toward me. I don't look at anyone.

"So," Davenport continues, heading back behind the lectern and looking at his notes, "I know this is your A course and all we're meant to do is reconnoiter the selected reading each week, but where's the fun in that, eh? The English faculty cocked up and gave me teaching responsibilities, so by God I'm going to teach! When I was doing my master of studies here, I often felt a bit adrift, so here's what I propose: I'll only do this once, don't worry, but I'd like to have everyone dash off a quick paper for me, and we'll have a chat about it." He looks, again, at me, "I forgot to mention I have the right to change my mind at any given moment. Apologies." To the rest of the class, he says, "The paper will serve to educate me, your humble Strand Convener, about your perspectives and predilections and help me guide you to the appropriate adviser for your dissertation in Trinity Term. I know, seems far off, eh? 'Miles to go before I sleep . . .'" He looks to me and extends his hand, begging an answer to his unspoken question.

"Robert Frost, 1922," I say. Without raising my hand. Nailed it.

"A little-known American Poet." He grins at me again. "Dates. Definitely a strong point."

English Rose lifts her head. "Didn't he write those quaint little children's songs?"

I take a fortifying breath while Jamie Davenport says, "I don't actually know," then looks out at everyone else. "I'd like you to pick a poem, and give me a page on it. Don't explicate rhyme scheme, meter, et cetera—this isn't sixth form. Speak of it as you would a friend. Describe its charms and quirks, its faults, how it achieves its intended effects. Does it flirt, offend, mislead? How does it make you feel?"

Besides the fact that he might as well be talking about himself right now, this assignment actually excites me. This I can do. I will write the ever-loving shit out of this. I will redeem myself. I glance around the room. Everyone else looks very British about it, like this is where fun comes to die.

"Send them to me via e-mail and we'll schedule a tute. Have a great week, everyone."

He begins collecting his papers. The Jamie Davenport Show is over. As I slip toward the door, I feel Charlie next to me, questions seeping out of him.

"Ella?"

I stop and look back at the lectern.

He's not looking at me; he's still fiddling with his papers. "A word, please?"

Charlie gives me a slight push forward and then he and Pink Hair slip reluctantly out the door. I gather myself and step in front of the podium. Davenport looks up and nails me with his eyes and suddenly I'm a boat caught in a current. What is it about those eyes?

"Yes?" I ask.

"Was it ruined?" he mumurs. "Your blouse?"

"Among other things."

His face is open, receptive. The smugness from last night is gone, the performance of the last hour is gone. He is startlingly focused. We continue to look at each other. "Apologies," he finally says. "For every bit of it. I won't make excuses, but I will explain. I'd had a spot of bad news earlier and I'd had a drink and I was entirely too slow to recognize the affront I'd caused."

My reply is quicker than my thoughts. "It's not necessary—"

"Please, I understand if this apology comes as too little too late, and I have no expectation of forgiveness, nor do I, arguably, deserve it, but do know that I acted without malice and my idiocy was nothing more than that. Sheer idiocy. You simply got tangled up in it. It was, invariably, an act of treason against my own better judgment, and . . . well," he concludes. "There it is."

I've got nothing. I was sure I'd have the perfect, cutting retort, but that was a Mr. Darcy–caliber speech. Not to mention his voice makes me feel as if I'm lying in a hammock. He's waiting for my response. I'm having trouble talking.

Finally, the words "apology accepted" drop out of my mouth. I can't stop staring at him. He has a classically proportioned face. Strong forehead, protractor jawline, straight nose, full lips.

The kind of face that on anyone with less personality might seem benignly handsome. I like guys with something distinctive, a crooked nose or a scar across an eyebrow, something that hints at a story. Jamie Davenport's face is a blank page. Except for those eyes, that is.

Still staring. It's starting to feel like a contest.

I break the spell and nod once, turning to go, but then I hear, "You could have waited."

I spin around. "For what?"

"Blurting out '1845' like that. She had seven seconds left," he deadpans.

I can't help the smile that pulls at my lips. "I don't think either of us believes time was the issue."

He grins, a knowing, appreciative grin. My stomach inexplicably flops and I realize I've barely eaten today. That must be it. "Anything else, Professor?"

"No, that will be all," he murmurs. "Ella from Ohio."

"Okay, then . . . posh prat." I turn and walk to the door. Glancing back (the kind of glance you can always disavow if necessary), I see he's shuffling papers again and biting his bottom lip, as if to keep from smiling. Someone brushes past me into the classroom. English Rose. She approaches the podium and I find myself pausing in the doorway to adjust the strap on my bag.

I hear her say, "Congratulations, Professor."

"Shh," he replies. "The real professors will hear you."

"You're quite wonderful, Jamie. I was well impressed."

"Cheers, Ce."

"If my being here is too distracting, surely I can switch out—"

"Come now, don't be daft, Ce. I love looking out at a sea of dubious faces and finding yours."

My bag slips from my hand and thuds to the floor. They both turn at the disturbance. "Sorry," I mutter, grab my bag, and escape.

CHAPTER 6

I took my scrip of manna sweet,
My cruse of water did I bless;
I took the white dove by the feet,
And flew into the wilderness.
Richard Watson Dixon, "Dream," 1861

Outside I am greeted by the sight of my two classmates huddled in a pocket of sunshine, arguing quietly. She shakes her pink head while he throws his back and groans.

"Hey," I say, stepping forward.

They break apart and give me two big, fake smiles. "Hello!" she squeaks. "I'm Margaret Timms. Sorry, Maggie, actually. You made quite the impression in there. With those dates. And whatnot." She has the most adorable baby voice, a little husky, but high and bright.

I stick out my hand. She looks surprised, but takes it. "Thank you. Ella Durran." I worry I'm crushing her thin little bird fingers, but she keeps smiling.

The three of us stand at the precipice of an awkward silence until Charlie, putting on sunglasses, says, "Maggie was actually wondering . . ."

I turn to Maggie. She looks as if she's being held at gunpoint. "No, I—sorry, I was just—" she stammers. I quirk my head. After one more excruciating moment, she bursts. "I was just wondering if you know that 'Oxfordian' also happens to be the geologic designation for the early stage of the late Jurassic period?"

Charlie and I stare at her with Tweedledee/Tweedledum looks of confusion.

"It's science," she adds, wringing her hands together. Then, looking at her feet, "Sorry."

Charlie slowly shakes his head. "I should have never let you shag that geologist." He turns to me. "Maggie was attempting to ask you to join us for tea this afternoon."

"Charlie," Maggie groans, "I was getting there."

"Had we waited for you to get there we would have missed tea altogether."

I can't help but ask Charlie, "Is this invite from just her?"

He stiffens slightly, cocks his head back, and assesses me. "I would not wish to be mistaken for having any carnal intentions."

Seriously? I try not to laugh. "I wouldn't have."

"And why is that?"

"Because you're gay?"

He side-eyes me. "You don't think I'm just eccentric and terribly British?"

"Definitely. And gay."

Maggie gives me a grateful look and then, vindicated, pushes Charlie. "See?" She turns to a cool, vintage bike (that is, yup, pink) and unlocks it from the rack. "We call him the closet door."

Confused, I glance between the two of them. Charlie sighs. "They go through me to come out." A laugh erupts from me, but Charlie is unfazed. "So. Tea?"

Smiling, I nod. "I'd love to. Thanks."

"Huzzah. The Old Parsonage in a half hour. Maggie has to . . . collect something."

She gives me the same repentant smile as before. "Sorry."

She climbs on her bike, demurely smoothing her dress over her legs, and is about to push off when I say, "A bike. Now, that's something I could use. I hate being late to everything."

She smiles. "It's essential. Everyone has one."

"Some travel under the power of our own dignity instead," Charlie mutters.

Maggie ignores him. "Actually, a friend happens to be selling one for a pittance at the mo. I'm off there now. Fancy joining me?" She pats her handlebars.

"Great!" Having said that, I approach Maggie's handlebars cautiously. I've never done this. How do I do this? I straddle the front tire and inelegantly struggle into position while Maggie—showing a surprising amount of upper body strength—holds the bike still.

I hear Charlie murmur, "You are not to speak of anything without me," and Maggie mutters back, "Oh, shut it." Then, cheerily, to me, "Settled?"

"I think so!" I reply, all feigned confidence. Charlie gives us a reluctant push and we're off.

WE RIDE THROUGH the city for about five minutes, over lots and lots of cobblestones, until we reach a large park. Across the street from it, Maggie pulls up to a curb and I hop off, letting the blood flow back to my cobblestoned ass. Maggie locks her bike to a lamppost and bounds up yet another ridiculously steep staircase. They should really just call staircases ladders in this country and be done with it. I join her as she presses a key on a call box, eliciting the sound of static, which then crescendos into a loud screech before cutting out entirely. She glances at me. "Sorry."

A voice calls out from behind the door, "Coming, coming!" When it finally opens, a gangly boy stands on one leg like a stork, holding his other shin and grimacing. "Bugger and blast, banged my shin on the brolly stand," he informs us by way of introduction. His golden-brown face is framed by black caterpillar eyebrows at the top and a wispy, scraggly, little-beard-that-could at the bottom. Shaggy midnight-hued hair spouts from his head in every direction.

"Hello, Tom!" Maggie chirps.

Hello, Mags," he exhales, dropping his shin. Then he sees me. "Oh! New person!"

"This is Ella," Maggie informs him. "She's American."

"Ah! Well, then!" Beaming, Tom raises a fist to me, inviting a bump. As if it's the way one greets Americans? Gamely, I raise my fist and meet his. He pulls his back and jazz-hands it, making an exploding noise. Then he giggles. "Always wanted to do that."

Maggie smiles brilliantly at him. "You're looking good," she effuses. "I like your new haircut—"

Tom turns back into the vestibule and exclaims, "Come in! Come in! Just mind the—" I'm sure he would have said "rug" had he not, at that moment, tripped over it.

Maggie and I enter a small hall filled with boxes and an overflowing umbrella stand. He forges ahead, leading us through an open door.

Into a closet. We're standing in a big closet with a small bed. The "room" is completely occupied, floor to ceiling, with books. "Make yourselves comfy," Tom says. Options limited, Maggie and I perch on opposing arms of a chair. I glance at the end table next to me. Peeking out from under a book, a framed picture shows a young, beaming Tom in Mickey Mouse ears standing between a tall man with Tom's jovial, wide-eyed face, wearing a Sikh *dastar,* and a squat blond woman wearing a cat sweatshirt. I look up to find Tom staring at me. Grinning.

"So," I say, because there's nothing else to say.

"So!" he exclaims. "Which are we destined to be? Friends or lovers?" Still grinning.

"Friends." It's a knee-jerk response.

"Take your time. If you need to have a think—"

"No, I'm . . . good," I say with a smile, trying not to offend him.

He just shrugs, unfazed by my rejection. "Alas, the good ones are always taken, eh, Mags?" As if the only grounds for my rejection would be the existence of a boyfriend.

Maggie stares at the book-covered floor. She mutters, "Not always." Then she glances up at him, looking annoyed, frustrated, and something else that I can't—

Oh. I get it. Oh dear.

Oblivious, Tom continues to stare at me. Maggie stares at him.

"So," I push forward, "word on the street is you're selling a bike."

"Indeed I am! Who told you?"

Maggie huffs in affectionate exasperation. I playfully twirl a finger at her. Tom follows my finger.

"Oh, Mags! Right! Jolly good!"

There's a silence.

"So?" I prod, trying to get this ball—or bicycle—rolling.

"So?"

"Where is it?"

"Where's what now?"

Fortunately, Maggie takes charge. "The bike, Tom, can she

see the bike?"

"Why, s'right there!" He flails his hand at a space behind us. Next to the door, camouflaged by an array of papers, more books, and coats, is an adorable beach-cruiser bike, banana seat and all. I walk over to it. It's in good shape. Surprising for this guy.

"Duchess." Tom sighs. "A fitting name for the gal who got me through the thick and thin of my first six years."

My head snaps up. "You've been here six years?"

"Sorry," Maggie chimes in. "Tom came here to read philosophy, then started over in maths, then . . . well, I believe it was classics, wasn't it?" Her brow furrows. She looks to Tom.

"Linguistics, philology, and phonetics."

"Then classics?"

"Bang on, Mags."

Maggie beams. Definitely into him.

"Which college are you at?" I ask.

"He was at Magdalen with Charlie and me!"

I glance back to Tom. "And now?"

"Oh, no one will have me now." He leans in and nudges my shoulder with his knobby elbow. "Story of my life, eh?"

I think I'm understanding this. "So you don't go here anymore?"

"He's actually become quite the popular tutor!" Maggie enthuses. "Helping people apply to Oxford!"

Tom's open face turns wry. "I can teach 'em how to get in, just not how to get out."

He laughs, Maggie reciprocates, and I nod, murmuring, "Cool, cool." I look back to the bike. "So what are you thinking?"

"At present? In general?"

This is what happens when you're the book equivalent of the

crazy cat lady. "The price. What do you want for it?"

He chews his lip. "Forty quid." I pause, considering. I open my mouth to accept and Tom blurts, "All right, all right, you drive a hard bargain. Thirty."

I smile. "Done!" I dig into my pocket for cash.

He claps his hands and jumps up. "Spiffing!" I hand him the money and he clears a path so he can wheel the bike out into the vestibule, down the stairs, and onto the street. I look back at Maggie. I have to do something. "Tom?"

"Yes?" He's bent over the bike, examining some invisible flaw. He licks his finger and wipes at it.

"Maggie and I are meeting Charlie for tea. Would you like to join?"

His face lights up. "Spiffing!" He swings one long giraffe leg over Duchess, mounting her like a prize stallion. "Parsonage?"

Maggie and I look at each other. Maggie takes this one. "Tom. Ella would like to ride her bike now."

"Right!" He guffaws. "Just warming the seat." He dismounts and gallops up the stairs, calling, "I'll just grab Pippa!"

As he disappears inside, Maggie crosses to her bike and begins unlocking it. There's a silence. She clearly wants to say something. She doesn't.

"I can't thank you enough," I say. "It's perfect." She nods and smiles politely as we climb onto our bikes. She seems to be avoiding my gaze. I wonder if I've overstepped something. "Sorry if I . . . I probably shouldn't have just invited him to tea, considering—"

But Maggie shakes her head. "No, no. That's why I was coming here in the first place. To invite him. The battery on his mobile always dies, you see. He can go days without realizing no one's called him." Her tone is easy, but she still doesn't look at me.

I test the waters. "I've never met anyone like him. He's very . . . unique."

She finally looks at me, chewing her bottom lip, seemingly on the verge of a confession. "I don't know quite what it is. He's a bit doglike, really. As you saw, ready to be loved by anyone willing to give him a pat. It can be quite annoying, actually."

I smile, understanding where Maggie's coming from. "He did the same thing to you when you first met him?"

There's a moment of silence and something crosses Maggie's face. "No."

"No?"

"No. He didn't." She looks away. "Sorry. He just . . . gets to me."

Now I really understand where Maggie's coming from. "I can tell."

She sighs, reddens. "He does it with everyone! Literally everyone! Just not me. It's baffling. And maddening. And embarrassing! Sorry." She straightens her back, aligns her dress, smooths her cardigan, regathers her pride.

"There's nothing to be sorry about."

"Charlie says I should consider myself lucky. I mean, don't misunderstand, he loves Tom, but—"

I shake my head. "It's not about anyone else. If you want it, you should go for it."

"Oh God, no." Her eyes bug. She pauses, shakes her head, and groans, "He's just so damn sexy."

While that wouldn't be my takeaway from an encounter with Tom, to each her own. We look at each other again and both of us smile. I like this girl a lot. We already have each other's back. To protect, not stab. That's universal sisterhood, no matter which country you come from.

Tom returns while Maggie's describing the adjacent park to

me. I notice him staring at her. It's the first time I've seen him really look at her. She looks lovely right now, lit by the dappled late-afternoon sun filtering through the oak tree above her.

"Mags?" Tom says.

She turns from the park. "Yes, Tom?"

He considers her. "Your hair."

Her hand primps the right side of her pink beehive, and she flushes. I could make some popcorn and watch them all day.

"Yes?" she gently prods.

This is it. This is where he takes the plunge and asks her out, and I will tell this story in my toast at their wedding.

Tom leans in and peers at the left side of her head, almost quizzically. "You've a spot of bird shite in your hair."

CHAPTER 7

This love, wrong understood,
Oft' turned my joy to pain;
I tried to throw away the bud,
But the blossom would remain.
John Clare, "Love's Pains," 1844

G iven the lovely turn of your figure, it's quite gratifying you're not one of those dreadful American girls who subsist entirely on lawn clippings and glacier water," Charlie says.

My mouth is too full of scone to reply.

The four of us—Maggie, Tom, Charlie, and I—are settled on the charming patio of the Old Parsonage Hotel, having tea. This is Tea with a capital *T*. There's a three-tiered china platter filled with sandwiches on the bottom, scones, preserves, and cream in the middle, and bite-sized desserts on top. I haven't had afternoon tea since Ashley Carmichael's obsession with *Alice in Wonderland* forced me to spend her eighth birthday sipping pink tea out of tiny plastic cups, wearing a stupid hat, and being creeped out by a middle-aged guy in a dirty White Rabbit costume. This is better.

Tom, picking cranberries out of his scone, looks up, his attention drawn to something beyond our table. "Say, Charlie? Isn't that your rower?"

We follow Tom's gaze to one of the waiters (a strapping, square-jawed guy), refilling water glasses three tables over.

"In time." Charlie sighs.

Maggie's forehead crinkles. "But you fancied him last term," she says, as if it were another lifetime. "Surely you—"

"He's not ready."

"As if that's ever stopped you!" Tom guffaws.

Charlie shakes his head. "No, I need must tread carefully with this one. He still fears condemnation from his awful rower mates. He has months yet of realizations and dire haircuts. He's only just begun experimenting with colored trousers. So . . ." Charlie puts down his teacup and looks at me. "Considering you've been here all of twenty-four hours, and as I witnessed a sordid portion of them and can assume that they were not amongst your finest, how do you already know our delectable lecturer Mr. Davenport?"

I smirk at Charlie. "Is this why you asked me to tea?"

"No!" Maggie assures me just as Charlie says, "Obviously."

It starts drizzling, but no one seems bothered. Maggie slides the tiny bowl of clotted cream farther under the protection of the dessert plate. Priorities.

"Well, first, he almost hit me with his car."

Charlie nods. "You were looking the wrong way, of course."

I open my mouth to argue, but think better of it. "Then, later, he succeeded in nailing me—"

"There it is!" he cries.

I hold up my hand. "In the chip shop. With a plate of sauces."

Realization dawns in Charlie's eyes. "Davenport was responsible for that haute couture experiment of yours, was he?" I nod. "Excellent." He narrows his eyes. "But that can't be all. Because in class—"

I put my hand out again, hoping to abbreviate the inquisition. "He was an ass and I lost my temper. He just wanted to apologize. And he did. And it's fine."

Charlie glances at Maggie, assessing my story, seeming to weigh its narrative value. "But we must know exactly what he said. Words hold the clues."

Luckily, Maggie leans in and hisses, "Look!"

We all follow her gaze. On the other side of the low hedge, at a bus stop, stands Cecelia the English Rose.

"Cecelia Knowles," Tom murmurs reverently, as if he's caught a glimpse of a rare bird in the wild.

Behind his sunglasses, Charlie studies her. "I was surprised to see her in class. Starting over, perhaps?"

"Huh?"

"She did her undergrad here," Maggie explains to me. "Was a third year when Charlie and I were freshers. We'd notice her in lectures—"

"How could one not?" Tom and Charlie say in unison.

Maggie rolls her eyes. "But she was never here at the weekend, so I never got to know her well. Then she returned the following year to start her master's—we spent a short time together doing a bit of research—and about halfway through term . . . she simply disappeared. It was all a bit odd, really."

"She dropped out?"

Maggie shrugs.

"Obviously," Charlie begins, drawing the word out, "she found herself unexpectedly *enceinte*, stole away to the comforting bosom of an eerily-similar-spinster-aunt on the continent for her confinement, and entrusted the infant to the local farmer and his barren wife with the understanding that at the age of ten the child would be sent to England for her schooling under the care and protection of a mysterious patron. Obviously."

I love book nerds.

Cecelia glances at her watch as I take an obscene bite of scone, then she spots Maggie, who gives her a polite wave. Then she heads in our direction. Great. Tom drops the sandwich bread he's been scraping mustard off and attends to his frazzled hair, trying desperately to smooth it down.

Charlie can't help himself. "That's the way forward, Tom. Nothing like being well groomed."

Cecelia glides up to our table, smiling serenely. "Hello, Maggie."

"Hi!" Maggie bleats, a little too brightly.

"How are—" Cecelia begins, but Tom jumps up, as if just realizing he was sitting on a tack. Cecelia starts. He gestures to the chair next to him, imploring it to offer itself to her. Neither he nor the chair speaks.

Maggie saves the day. "Sorry. Care to join us?"

"Thank you, no," Cecelia says in her low, elegant voice. "I thought I'd nip in for a cuppa before I catch my bus. I was so very pleased to see you in class, I'd always rather hoped you'd continue—"

"Thomas Singh!" Tom finally says, thrusting out his hand. "Of the Yorkshire Singhs. Dirt farmers since the days of the Norman Conquest." He sees my confused look. "On my mother's side," he clarifies.

Cecelia inclines her head. "Cecelia Knowles. Of the Sussex Knowleses. Who resisted the Norman Conquest."

We all chuckle, trying to maintain the appearance of normalcy for Tom's sake. He still hasn't released Cecelia from his grasp. "So, which are we destined to be, friends or lovers?"

Cecelia smoothly withdraws her hand. "Friends will do quite nicely, thank you." The puppy, once again, has had its nose slapped.

"And, of course, you know Charlie Butler," Maggie says, trudging on. "And this is Ella."

Cecelia's eyes pop to me. "Oh dear," she says. "It *is* you. I wasn't sure."

She was sure.

I swallow the last piece of scone as I reach out a hand. "Ella Durran. Missed the Norman Conquest by a millennium." I smile. I don't have any animosity toward her. Honestly. But she seems to have taken an immediate disliking to me.

Cecelia smiles politely and briefly takes my hand. "Sorry, I must dash, I'll see you all next week in Jamie's class." Before I can say anything else, she disappears inside the lobby.

I take a casual sip of tea then ask, in a not-that-it-matters-in-the-slightest tone, "Do you think they're together? She and Davenport?"

Maggie shakes her head. "If they are, it won't last, I'm afraid." She says this the way a soap opera devotee talks about the love lives of the fictional characters.

My curiosity is piqued. "What do you mean?"

"Jamie Davenport's a legend," Maggie says, eyes wide. "The road between Oxford and Cambridge is positively littered with broken hearts."

Charlie considers this. "More like dropped knickers. The man invented the three-date rule."

"So just be careful there," Maggie says.

It takes me a moment to realize who she'd saying this to. "Wait, me?"

She nods. "Sorry, but there was an undeniable bit of chemistry going between—"

"No there wasn't!" I leap to my own defense. "I'm not remotely attracted to Jamie Davenport."

They all just look at me. Together. As if they'd rehearsed it.

I reach for another scone. "Besides, I'm only here until June. It's all about Oxford. And travel! The last thing I need is a relationship."

"Then maybe he's perfect, after all." Charlie smirks.

Maggie leans in. "I, we, just thought you should know. His reputation does in fact precede him."

I nod. "I appreciate that." And I do. But I had seen enough in the chip shop to convince me to stay away.

I TAKE A three-hour jet-lag nap back in my room and wake up groggy, disoriented, and weirdly thirsty. I pound two glasses of water and glance at the clock: 9:00 P.M. I'm wide-awake.

Might as well do some work.

I grab a huge anthology of poetry off my desk and climb back into bed. The book is a monolith, printed on those thin Bible pages. After tea, we all went to Blackwell's (coolest bookstore in the world) and picked up some of the texts that Jamie Davenport recommended for the term. Tom, who isn't even in our program, bought all the books, too. Unlike Maggie and Charlie, who just have a certain air about them, I can tell Tom doesn't come from money (besides the fact that Maggie paid for this tea). His accent is different from theirs, "oohs" instead of "uhs," "boos" instead of "bus." He had mentioned that his dad owns a shop—"knickknacks, odds and ends." A dad who pulled his patronage somewhere between maths and classics and begs Tom to come home so he can retire. Tom mentions at least three parttime jobs in addition to the tutoring—admin, shelving at the Bod, even coding for the university website. There's something timeless about him, as if, in the entire history of Oxford, there has always been a Tom, living in a closet of books, bicycling though the city in all weather, sneaking into lectures he doesn't belong in, changing courses a year shy of completing them.

Charlie, too, seems iconically Oxford to me. I have no idea where he might hail from or, as my mother would say, who "his people are." He likely just appeared as an infant in a basket of reeds at the Magdalen gates to be molded by Hugh and Eugenia, forged by the ghost of Oscar Wilde.

Maggie mentioned a father who clearly has something to do with banking and a mother who recently moved to France. She boarded somewhere Swiss-sounding for high school (or secondary school), mentioned doing theater in undergrad (though I can't imagine timid, baby-voiced Maggie treading the boards), and is obsessed with Thomas Hardy.

Now, tucked under my covers, I leaf through the poetry anthology, hoping something jumps out at me. Davenport asked us to describe how a poem makes us feel, so I do a quick scan for the words "feel" or "feeling" or "emotion," just as a starting point. My eye stops on Elizabeth Barrett Browning's "A Man's Requirements" and I begin to read.

> *Love me Sweet, with all thou art,*
> *Feeling, thinking, seeing;*
> *Love me in the lightest part,*
> *Love me in full being.*

It goes on to enumerate all the ways in which a man requires a woman to love him. Mentally, spiritually, eternally, completely, whatever. Then it takes a turn:

> *Thus, if thou wilt prove me, Dear,*
> *Woman's love no fable.*
> *I will love thee—half a year—*
> *As a man is able.*

Damn, EBB. Telling it like it is, like it's apparently always been, all the way back in 1846.

I have my poem. Even better that it basically describes the person who assigned the essay. *Do with that what you will, Davenport.*

Two hours later, I have five pages of double-spaced, twelve-point, Times New Roman, elucidating everything this poem represents. I dig my notebook out of my bag, find the page where I wrote down Jamie Davenport's e-mail address, and type it into a new message window. There are three more e-mails from my mother in my in-box. Later. I attach the poem and then pause over what to write in the body of the e-mail. I settle for:

> *Prof. Davenport,*
>
> *Attached, find the essay you requested.*
>
> > > *Best,*
> > > *Ella*

I consider adding "from Ohio," but I don't want him to think we have an inside joke. As the whoosh sound carries my essay across town to wherever Jamie Davenport is, I turn my attention to my mother's e-mails.

> *I saw Marni Hopkins in the store today and did you know that Bradley is doing graduate school at some place in Spain? Maybe you two*

I preemptively delete it.

Next e-mail:

Hi honey why haven't you called yet? Just check in when you have a moment. You know Marni was very impressed that you got into Oxford. She showed me a picture of Bradley. I think his ears

Delete.
Last e-mail:

Why does my computer do that color wheel spinning thing. What did you tell me to do the last time this happened?

I fire back immediately:

Restart it.

I sit back and stare at my computer. I could Skype her. It would be, what, five P.M. there? The e-mails came in an hour ago, I know she's around. But I really don't have anything to say.

Well, okay, I did get a bike, and found the Happy Cod, and I have a scout, and a Hugh the Porter, and I made friends, and I had a class, and there were scones. Not to mention a dream job.

But let's not forget that I called my unbeknownst-to-me professor an asshole (to his face), won't be studying with Styan, and have concluded that I'm not academically competitive here and will probably end up embarrassing not just myself, but also the Rhodes Foundation.

A lot has happened since my passport was stamped. I take a deep breath. It's okay. I have redeemed myself with this essay. Everything will get back on track. I just don't want to talk to my mother until it has.

I know her. Much better than she will ever know me.

My mother lives in a constant state of fearful anxiety. She thinks everything is falling apart, all the time, all at once, when there is nothing in her life that could possibly fall apart. She's had the same job for twenty years, she doesn't travel, she doesn't date, the house is paid for, she has two carbon monoxide detectors, she goes to the doctor, like, three times a year, and she avoids any public place where someone might ("you never know, Ella, the world has gone crazy") have a gun. Literally, unless a sinkhole opens up under her Volvo on her two-mile drive to work, nothing's going to happen to her.

She wasn't always like this. But it's been so long that it feels like always.

I'm just tired.

I just miss my dad.

The ding of incoming e-mail distracts me from this rabbit hole of familial failing. I lean forward to look, sure it's my mother saying she restarted the computer, but now the screen is looking at her funny—

My stomach flips when I see the sender: James Davenport.

Looking forward to reading. Have a good night.

Not "Surprised to see your work so soon"? Not "Very impressive, Ella from Ohio"?

He's being professional. As he should be. Because he's my professor now, not some mystery-eyed guy in a chip shop who looked at me as if I were the most delicious thing on the menu.

I'm not going to reply. What would I say? "*You too? I hope you enjoy it? What are you doing tonight?*"

I also won't Google him. And while I have to maintain a professional Twitter account, I'm not on any other forms of social media. Not only do I find it too much of a time suck, but it also provides too many opportunities to embarrass myself in front of potential clients; if they never see you do anything wrong, you never have to apologize.

I look back at the e-mail, my eyes inexplicably drawn to it, as if, instead of two innocuous sentences, there were a naked, beef-cake picture of the sender. He'd be Mr. September in the Hotties of Oxford calendar for sure. *Welcome back to school, ladies.* Jamie Davenport on a library ladder, rippling abs all greased up, inevitably holding a book in front of his junk.

At least I can still make myself laugh.

THE NEXT FEW days fly by faster than I can account for them. I finally feel like I'm in the right time zone and I can understand the accent now. Although I would have been happy to misunderstand the drunk guy who walked past me last night, then turned to his mate and loudly slurred, "Oi, that's a tasty bit." I've also managed to sleep through Eugenia's arrival three mornings in a row, and I've had my two other classes, but the professors didn't assign any work.

No, only Mr. Jamie Davenport does that, apparently. Then never reads it. Apparently.

I spend my days cutting through the course's suggested reading and fielding Gavin's requests. His e-mails come in at all hours. He calls at least once a day.

In the late afternoons, Maggie and I get on our bikes and she shows me the city. Maggie comes from London (she mentions an area and then apologizes in a tone that has me suspecting it's an embarrassingly posh neighborhood), but she did her undergrad at Magdalen, so she knows every corner of Oxford. She takes me through narrow, winding stone paths and special little places she's discovered over her years here. Now she lives in Exeter College's graduate housing complex, where she shares a kitchen and living area with four other students: two Chinese guys, a Rubenesque British girl who insists on only speaking Italian, and an older Middle Eastern woman who—as far as Maggie can tell—is never actually there. As a result, Maggie spends a lot of time with me.

At the end of our rides, we tend to join Charlie and Tom for dinner, so I've also been getting familiar with Oxford's hit-or-miss cuisine. I'm ashamed to admit that I already miss American food. I'd exchange sexual favors with anyone who could direct me to a decent cheeseburger.

Today Charlie and I are standing in the upper reading room of the Bodleian Library. Charlie gives me a tour, clutching a book on rowing to his side and whispering Oxford trivia. "The Bodleian has a copy of every book ever printed in the UK since 1611."

I silently repeat the way he pronounced it (Bod-lee-un), understanding why everyone just calls it "The Bod." The room is beautiful and cavernous, mostly filled with reading tables and chairs. I notice only a few stacks. "Where do they hide them all?" I whisper.

Charlie points down at the hardwood, seeming to indicate rooms and floors that live beneath us. He tosses a glance over his shoulder, then slips behind the unattended front desk. He reaches under the counter and pulls out a glossy magazine with the word "TATLER" in bold print. He hands it to me. "There's always a new issue stuffed under here."

I leaf through it and see picture after picture of people I don't recognize. It's like an alternate universe. It seems Britain has its own version of Kardashians. "You know what's interesting," I begin. "These people are totally interchangeable with—" but I'm interrupted by the sound of a book dropping down onto the counter next to me.

I look at the book that's appeared in front of me: *Dear and Honored Lady: The Correspondence Between Queen Victoria and Alfred Tennyson.* There's more to read, but it's blocked by the hand splayed across the cover. It's a nice, masculine hand. Long and tapered fingers, just the right amount of wrist hair, clean fingernails—

"Ella?"

Startled, I glance up and find the stabbing blue eyes of Jamie Davenport looking down at me. "My rooms, if you will. Today. Half three."

Not hearing what he says, I nod. He glances down at the *Tatler.* Raises an eyebrow. "Research?" he says, oozing sarcasm. Then he looks back at me, smiles tightly, and is gone.

"Masterful," Charlie breathes.

Wherever I just was, I come back to Charlie and the Bod. I'm completely lost. Maybe I overestimated my grasp of the British language. "What did he just say?"

Charlie's eyes are wide. "He wants you."

CHAPTER 8

Did he not come to me?
What thing could keep true Launcelot away
If I said, Come?
William Morris, "The Defence of Guenevere," 1858

I've made my way to Lincoln, a small medieval college with a converted church for a library in the middle of town on Turl Street. Maggie explained to me a few days ago that each professor is affiliated with a specific Oxford college, where they have an office and often teach undergraduates. Lincoln is where Jamie Davenport hangs his skinny jeans.

After making a right on Turl from the High, I step through a cutout door in a wooden gate and into a small portico. Beyond the portico's flagstones is a manicured quad surrounded on all sides by ivy-covered buildings. The college is smaller than Magdalen, but quaintly elegant and feels older (if that's possible). I go into the lodge, ask the porter for Professor Davenport's office and he directs me to staircase eight, off Chapel Quad, and up two flights of stairs.

Near the second-floor landing, I hear raised voices coming from behind a closed door. I stop climbing. Forgetting my nervousness for a moment, I find myself eavesdropping. Two men. One of them, I realize, is Jamie Davenport.

"I'm not interested in your opinion."

"James, this is absurd—"

"Add it to the list, then."

"We are your family!" the older voice yells.

"By birth! Nothing more, nothing less," Davenport shoots back, half as loud but doubly cutting. Then, more muffled, "Excuse me, I've got work to do."

"I came to you, in the middle of my workday—"

"Were you asked to come? Leave."

"You are, without a doubt, the most ungrateful—"

Now Davenport shouts. "Sodding hell, get out!"

I peek around the corner, and seconds later, the arched wooden door flies open and a barrel-chested older man storms through it. He stops and turns back toward the room. I press myself against the wall. "You're arrogant, my lad, and mark my words, it's going to be the end of you—"

"Christ, must I throw you out myself?"

"Speak to me as you will, I don't care, but if you dare hurt your mother any further, I swear—"

"No one can hurt her more than you already have!"

The door slams. From inside or out? I'm about to peek around the corner again when a silver-haired force of nature blows past me down the stairs without so much as a glance. His rage rolls over me like a tangible thing and I grab the banister to steady myself. I wait, holding my breath, trying to be silent. I give it a good ten seconds and then approach the door, knocking softly.

"Yes?" Davenport calls calmly.

I tentatively open the door and poke my head in. He's standing behind an antique desk, shuffling papers. He appears composed, as if nothing's amiss. "Hi. Is this a good time?"

I fully expect him to slam the door in my face. He glances up. "Yes, of course. Take a seat."

I walk into what looks like a parlor in an old English manor. Or at least what movies have led me to believe a parlor in an old English manor looks like. High ceilings partitioned with beams, insets painted in a Tudor pattern. A herringbone wood floor covered by a plush muted red carpet, rough stone walls, paned windows, and a massive stone fireplace. Two well-worn leather club chairs oppose each other in front of the fireplace, and a threadbare red love seat sits behind them. The desk sits in front of a bay window overlooking the quad.

I walk over to a club chair, trying to think of something clever to open with. "This is really nice. Homey," I say, missing the mark entirely.

He's still at his desk, rifling through the papers and books strewn there. "Well then, make yourself at home," he says.

I can't read his tone. *No need to panic*, I assure myself. Whatever just happened has nothing to do with me. I'm probably here because he wants to congratulate me on my first paper, or maybe further discuss one of the points I made that's piqued his curiosity. My being here will probably be good for him. Distract him from whatever that fight was about. Keeping the conversation alive, I say, "Do you live here?"

"No. Although it's set up for it." He finally turns, slips out from between the desk and chair, and crosses over to me. He's wearing a tucked-in charcoal-gray button-down with the sleeves pushed back to his elbows, and oxblood-colored pants that appear to be—can that be right?—velvet. The weirder thing? He looks incredible in them.

He's speaking. "Historically, teaching contracts here provided accommodations, as most of the lecturers were clergy. Or had to leave if they got married. Couldn't have a fellowship and a wife.

God forbid she proved too distracting."

Why is he telling me this? Why can't I stop looking at his pants?

He sits down in the chair opposite me, runs a hand through his hair. Then he gestures behind him at one of the closed doors. "There's a bed in the back."

Why is he telling me this? Why am I still looking at his pants?

He looks down at his knees. "Good for those all-nighters, I suppose," he mutters, making it even more awkward. "So. Of writing. 'A Man's Requirements.' What do you think of your paper, then?"

This catches me off guard. He's supposed to tell me what he thinks of my paper. "Um," I begin, and then clear my throat. "Well, since you've asked . . . I think I made some significant insights, observations, and analyses." He just looks at me. He has this ability to go still, as if he's stopped breathing. Like a vampire. Which makes me realize I'm not breathing. I look away and force myself to take a breath. "But enough about me, what did you think of my work," I joke.

"'Work' is a most appropriate word," he answers smoothly.

I stiffen. He's thrown my word back at me. I recognize the rhetorical technique and hold my ground. "That doesn't sound like a compliment," I reply, in what I hope is an equally smooth manner. "Did you find something wrong with it?"

"Wrong with it? No," he answers, shrugging, his casualness somehow stinging more than his criticism. I notice that he doesn't even have my essay in front of him. As if, after reading it through once, quickly, he's committed its mediocrity to memory. "In roughly twenty-five hundred words," he goes on, "you managed to explore the birth of feminism, the breakdown of arranged marriages, the celebration of the Peter Pan syndrome from an historical perspective, and the persecution of women's sexuality reaching its apex in the Salem witch trials." He pauses, but his eyes stay with me. Maybe he did commit it to memory. Maybe he wants to use it as an example for the class. Then he continues, "Extraordinary." I beam. "You managed to do everything other than the assignment."

I stare at him. The wrong kind of example for the class, then. He leans in. "Describe the poem as you would a friend. How does it make you feel?"

I blink at him, realizing the gravity of my error. "Oh," I say lamely. "I guess I . . . digressed."

"Digressed? Ella," he says, leaning fully forward, "you failed to do what was asked. You went wildly, tangentially astray. Impressively astray, but astray nonetheless."

I blink at him. This was my Hail Mary attempt to prove myself here, and I failed. His word. Failed. I've never failed. At anything.

I think Davenport must see the embarrassment on my face, because he shrugs and changes his approach, sitting back again. "Look, Ella. I wanted to chat with you about this before the full term gets under way." Horribly, I know what he's going to say. "You have the opportunity to—"

"Get out now and run back to the States?" My voice is as controlled as I can manage.

He quirks his head at me. "Why on earth would you suggest such a thing as that?"

"Well, clearly my work isn't up to par. The American is obviously out of her league." I can feel the defensiveness spewing out of my mouth. I mean, who does he think he is? I'm working for the presumptive nominee for the presidency of the—

"Why would you think you're out of your league?"

"Are you a shrink?" I snap. "Or is this just part of the Socratic method, answering-a-question-with-a-question teaching style here?"

"Sorry, was there a question in there?" He is completely calm, genuinely curious.

My eyes shift to the floor, but I can feel him peering at me. I take a breath, realizing I've stopped breathing again. I swallow, but something is stuck in my throat. My dream, probably. I think I'm choking on my Once-in-a-Lifetime Experience. My Oxford.

He's somehow managed to outmaneuver me.

Softly, he says, "Ella, this has nothing to do with . . ." He pauses, choosing his words. "The paper was terribly well written." I've noticed that Brits use negatively connoted words in a positive context and I'm not sure how I feel about it yet. "It was dreadfully insightful. But, here, it's not about displaying one's knowledge or academic prowess, or how convincing the argument may be. There are only ideas to discuss. The ideas are the wheat of the mind. Everything else is chaff, better left for the consumption of the sycophants who fancy themselves academics. For a thousand years, that's what this place has been about. Is it antiquated? Yes. Stodgy? Absolutely. Seemingly pointless? It would seem so in this new world order, and yet, Oxford is Oxford, and we persevere." He reaches over to the table sitting between us, picks up the poetry anthology. He ruffles its pages. "Tell me, Ella, why, out of all the poems in this book, did you pick this one?"

"Because it speaks the truth about men."

"Ah, right. So men are only capable of loving a woman for six months?"

"I think she rounded up."

This gets a small chuckle out of him. Then he sets the book on his lap, pauses, and looks up again. He does it methodically, deliberately, taking time for each movement. So unlike the freewheeling jerk I first encountered at the chip shop. "So, this what? Reminds you of an ex-boyfriend? You've most certainly had your heart broken. At least once?"

I snort. "I've never had my heart broken."

"Right. Sorry. How could you? Believing a man is only capable of loving a woman for six months."

"Oh, and you don't? Because from what I've heard, you're the poster child for—" I stop myself. That's too far.

His crazy-blue eyes flash with excitement, galvanized. "Poster child, really? How intriguingly scandalous. Please, do continue."

All I can do is shake my head.

He smiles. "So, we know each other, know all about each other." He sits back, grinning. "We sized each other right up in the chip shop, didn't we? Weighed and measured. Had someone of lesser intellect declared their knowledge of either one of us, he would be thought prejudicial or quick to judgment. Can't tell a book by its cover and all that. But we've sped-read each other, and, luckily, we're the clever ones. After all, we're Oxonians."

This wrings a tight smile out of me.

He looks up at the ceiling and appears to pluck his next words out of the air there, reciting from recent memory. "'Dismantling arts curriculum at such a crucial time both sociologically and solipsistically stunts the adolescent's complex comprehension skills, ultimately ushering in an electorate that only thinks in black and white at a time when, if we are to survive, we must think in technicolor.'" Now he looks at me. "I quite like that."

He Googled me. The bastard Googled me after I purposely didn't Google him. I don't know whether to feel flattered or betrayed. But now I look like a hypocrite, the Education Evangelist who can't even follow a simple assignment.

"Now I would have thought," he continues, "that the woman who wrote that article would have quite a bit to say, actually, about how a poem makes her feel."

I throw up my hands. "It was one article. I'm not even a writer. I'm not saying I know how to build an arts curriculum, just that it's a necessity, not a luxury!"

He leans forward, excited. "Exactly. It doesn't define you. But it is a first impression, isn't it? You're the hypercompetitive American, a Rhodes scholar no less, who sees Oxford as a series of hurdles to clear like levels in some video game, and I? I'm the hypocritical poetry scholar, espousing grand theories of love whilst shagging a different wench every night. Brilliant, glad we got that sorted. But who are we, really, eh? We've told each other what we think, but we've no idea what we feel. That requires a conversation. Having words, having language, to connect us to ourselves and each other."

He looks down at the book again and opens it. His rhythm has changed. He flips through it with excited purpose, some destination in mind. "To truly experience a poem," he mutters, almost to himself, "you need to feel it. A poem is alive, it has a voice. It is a person. Who are they? Why are they?" He sticks his finger in the book, and closes it, holding his place. Then he looks back to me. "Hearing her words, as she speaks to you, you think and feel certain things. Just as, hearing my words now, you think and feel certain things. Reading poetry is a conversation of feeling between two people. It shouldn't answer anything, it should only create more questions, like any good conversation. What did she make you feel? That's what I wanted you to examine."

I'd like to tell him that was a remarkable explanation of the assignment. Of life, for that matter, but all I can do is nod. I don't think I've been this quiet since I was in utero. Possibly not even then.

"Here," Davenport says, handing me the book with his finger

still trapped inside. He opens it and points to a piece of text. "Read this. Starting here. Aloud."

I take another breath, then read, trying to steady my voice.

> *"Ah, love, let us be true*
> *To one another!"*

I roll my eyes. "Give me something less obvious."

"Obvious? To whom? You've read it, brilliant. Now feel it."

This is too much. "Look, I get it, I get what you're doing, saying."

"Feel it."

"But, I get it."

He smiles impishly at me, those eyes twinkling. "Read it again, Ella. Please. You might be surprised."

"Please" does something to me. I look back down at the poem. The idea of being surprised in some way intrigues me.

> *"Ah, love, let us be true*
> *To one another! for the world, which seems*
> *To lie before us like a land of dreams*
> *So various, so beautiful, so new—"*

Davenport's quiet, measured voice fills the room:

> *"Hath really neither joy, nor love, nor light."*

I look at him. He recites from memory, gaze on the arm of my chair. He doesn't continue, so, after a moment, I do:

> *"Nor certitude, nor peace, nor help for pain."*

God, isn't that the truth? The words arrest me for a moment. I realize I'm not breathing. I forcibly inhale and continue:

"And we are here as on a darkling plain . . ."

My voice snags on the last syllable, like a bramble capturing my skirt. Davenport picks up the thread:

"Swept with confused alarms of struggle and flight . . ."

And I finish:

"Where ignorant armies clash by night."

Moving fast but steady, he scoots to the edge of his chair and reaches over, closing the book in my lap, his hand resting on its cover. That same hand that was splayed in front of me in the Bodleian. I stare at it. "Now tell me," he murmurs in a low voice, "what is Matthew Arnold saying?" I hesitate, thinking. "Don't think." I close my eyes. "If you don't open yourself up, how can you ever be surprised by life? And if you're not sur-prised, what's the bloody point?"

Breathe. "That in death . . . love is all there is."

"And how does that make you feel?" He presses into the book for emphasis and I feel the pressure in my lap.

I open my eyes, look up. His face is inches from mine, his eyes questing. The word falls out of my mouth. "Lonely." And I finally realize what it is about his eyes. They're the color of this swimming hole I used to spend summers at as a kid, at the end of a trail, at the base of a waterfall. The color was so magical I was convinced if I could hold my breath long enough, swim deep enough, pump my legs hard enough, I'd discover the bottom wasn't a bottom at all, but a portal to another world.

I feel my eyes fill, swelling to the brim. But nothing spills over.

Surface tension.

His eyes continue to bore into mine. I hear myself say, "How does it make you feel?"

For the briefest of seconds his eyes drop to my mouth before they blink back to my eyes. "Hopeful."

I can't stop swimming in those pools.

The realization comes at me sideways, like the buffeting of air from a semi on the highway:

I just lived years of my life in those eyes.

A voice: "Jamie, I've just had a ring from your—oh! So sorry, I didn't—"

He's standing, sweeping up the anthology with him. Only then do I hear my phone ringing. I stand as well, my legs unsteady, feeling as if I should be buttoning something up. I turn to the doorway and see Cecelia. She's looking at the floor, saying, "The door was open, I didn't—" I'm not sure if she is talking to me, or Jamie, or both of us.

"No, it's fine," I say breezily, taking my phone out of my pocket and walking to the door on shaking legs. "We're done. And I need to take this."

"Yes. Of course," he says, crossing in the opposite direction, back to his desk. "See you in class."

I slide past Cecelia, muttering, "You too." I answer my phone. "Yes, Gavin?"

CHAPTER 9

I'll walk, but not in old heroic traces,
And not in paths of high morality,
And not among the half-distinguished faces,
The clouded forms of long-past history.
Charlotte Brontë (possibly Emily), "Stanzas," 1850

The grilling began at the Bombay Curry House when, after being uncharacteristically quiet all evening and barely eating my chicken tikka Masala, I failed to dodge Charlie's loaded question: "How was the tute?"

Now, after thirty minutes of detailing and defending, I need a drink. Badly. "Guys! It wasn't a big deal. Really. Let it go."

Maggie looks at me. I can tell she senses that I was more affected by the tutorial than I'm letting on and, unlike Charlie and Tom, I think she also senses that the undertow of sexual chemistry is secondary to something larger. Something I don't even understand myself.

I stand up from the table and announce, "Well, I don't know about you locals, but this American's going to her first British pub."

Charlie and Maggie gasp. Tom drops his fork. They shout,

"You've never been to a pub?!"

ON THE WALK up St. Giles, Maggie informs me, "Pubs are like churches here."

"Right," Charlie replies. "Except we consider them sacred and attend them religiously." Then he pulls open the old, beaten-to-hell door of the Eagle and Child.

The Eagle and Freaking Child. This isn't just a pub, this is the legendary watering hole that hosted the Inklings, an informal assemblage of writers including J. R. R. Tolkein and Magdalen's own C. S. Lewis. I get a chill when I walk through the door. I turn to share the moment with my companions, but they're already halfway to the bar, immune to the ghosts of history.

The pub has beams that make the ceiling head-bumpingly low in places. Tom stands with his head at a constant tilt, unbothered. Rooms lead to other rooms, which grow progressively smaller, like caverns in a cave system. It smells like hops and rain.

Charlie turns to me, taking me by surprise. "Tipple, darling?"

I come back to reality. "Yes! Cider!"

He shakes his head. "Save your cider for Old Rosie at the Turf."

"Then a Grey Goose dirty martini, straight up, three olives."

Charlie attempts a kindly face. He fails. "This isn't a bar. It's a pub." He turns away from me, leans into the burly bartender, and says, "Gin and tonic for the missus."

We take our drinks over to Maggie and Tom, already halfway through their pints of thick black beer. Charlie waves at someone, his hand brushing the ceiling. I go up on my toes to see above the crowd.

Oh.

Cecelia.

I quickly scan the group she's with and ascertain that Davenport isn't among them. Surprising.

"Cecelia wants us to join her. Shall we?" Charlie asks, but is already walking over. Tom, seeing where we're headed, waves enthusiastically at Cecelia, as if welcoming a soldier home from war. She gives him a princessy three-fingered wave back.

As we approach the table, it occurs to me that Davenport could actually be here somewhere. At the bar, or in the bathroom. But Cecelia is making introductions and I force myself to pay attention. "This is Ahmed," she says, indicating a suave-looking guy with a pencil-thin mustache who gives us a cheeky salute. "His father's the Jordanian ambassador." Seems like unnecessary information, but no one else blinks. Ahmed puts his finger to his lips—*shhh*—and pretends to hide his beer. I smile at him. Cecelia then turns to a ridiculously hot guy sitting next to him, who I realize is Charlie's rower. "And this is my second cousin Ridley," Cecelia says, smiling. Of course they're related. Gorgeousness this obvious can't be coincidental.

Charlie elbows me and breathes into my ear, "When our children ask me, 'Funny Daddy, where did you meet Pretty Daddy?' I shall answer, 'Why, the back room of the Bird and Baby, of course.'"

"And this," Cecelia continues, gesturing to a guy slouched over at the end of the bench like a zombie, "is Ian."

Ian rouses himself enough to say, "Ian is arse over tits, at the moment." He gives us a smile that reminds me of one of Dalí's melting clocks. Then his half-lidded gaze finds me. "An' who's this?" He leers.

Cecelia brushes the hair back from her face as if she is being photographed. "This is Emma."

"Ella, actually."

"Of course," she says, not even glancing at me. "And this is

Charlie, Maggie, and Tom."

"Please, join us," Ahmed says gallantly, sweeping his arm at the table. They're collected around an L-shaped banquette with two chairs opposite the long side.

"I've been saving this spot for you all night!" Ian slurs, patting the space next to him on the bench, looking, unfortunately, right at me.

Charlie doesn't waste a second, hopping into the chair directly across from Ridley, as if joining him in a scull. Tom takes the chair next to Charlie, hoping that his newest "friend," Cecelia, places herself next to him on the short side of the banquet. No dice. She takes Maggie's arm and, in a very girlfriendy way, slides to the far side of the bench, pulling Maggie in after her, placing Maggie between Tom and herself.

And then there was one.

There's one spot left and its occupant has been preordained by Drunk Ian, who crawls out of the booth. "Ladies in the middle," he slurs. Reluctantly, I slide in next to Ridley, and Ian follows me in, already a bit too close for comfort.

"Thanks," I mutter.

Apparently that one word is enough to give me away. "A Yank!" Ian exclaims.

Ahmed leans around Ridley and addresses me. "Are you a Rhodes scholar, then?"

"That obvious?" I laugh.

He smiles tightly. "Always nice to have a Rhodie at the table."

He's saying the exact opposite of what he means. His father may be an ambassador, but Ahmed's diplomacy could use some work.

"I'm honestly curious." I shrug, wanting to play nice. "What exactly is the 'Rhodie' reputation here in Oxford?"

Before anyone can answer, Ian comes to life. "Bloody insufferable," he yells. "They think they're the cleverestest blokes in the room, but they can't wipe their own arse without a manual."

Silence.

"They're also loud!" Ian shouts.

Cecelia clears her throat. "I think what Ian is trying to say—quite poorly—is that Rhodes scholars are often selected for their academic achievement and professional drive. However, once here, they can have a difficult time adjusting to the freedom from structure that Oxford affords." She gazes calmly at me. "They don't know what to do with the rather significant amount of time between classes, the lack of syllabi, and such." She affords me a small smile. "Also, they often seem quite overwhelmed by the, shall we say, unorthodox relationships that can often occur between student and tutor."

I stare levelly back at her. Her face is a mask. I can't tell if she's judging me, if she's implying something about what she thinks she witnessed between Davenport and me a few hours ago, or if she's just being her.

"And they can't drink for shite," Ian sneers. "The gravest fault of all."

Charlie perks up. "Then we shall put our dear Ella to the test. Time for one of our infamous British drinking games." He looks at me, and gives a wink.

I nod, happy to move on from the subject of my Rhodie shortcomings.

"A shame Jamie couldn't come tonight." Cecelia sighs. "He so loves a good drinking game."

Pray tell, "Ce," what else does he love? Whatever. At least I know he's not going to suddenly pop out of the bathroom. I can relax.

A hand plops onto my thigh. I jerk, whipping murderous eyes to Ian, who withdraws his hand as if he's touched a stovetop.

"Sorry! Jus' trying to get your attention. I have a question for you, an immensely important one. Ready?" He gets serious, even though his eyes are floating in two different directions. "Do you go left or right?"

"What? I don't—"

"Your political leanings. What are they?"

Here we go.

CHRIST ALMIGHTY, THESE people can drink.

I'm a good drinker, I can hold my own. Still, I've had to sit out the last few rounds of Fuzzy Duck (deceptively innocent name) because I need to, you know, not die tonight. Ian, on the other hand, somehow gets drunker. He'll start talking to me, then forget why he started talking to me, go silent for a few minutes, and then start up again. It's excruciating. He also creeps closer to me every time he speaks.

Ian aside, I look around the table and find myself smiling. Maggie is red-cheeked and laughing, Tom's asleep with his head on the table and arms dangling down like a little kid. Cecelia is smiling. Charlie continues to work his magic on Ridley. He's a master. He's rigged the game so Rower Boy has to pour the shot into Charlie's mouth every time he "loses."

I'm at that place where I either need to drink more or I need to leave. It's the point-of-no-return portion of the evening.

"You completely *misunderstooded* me," Ian exhales onto the side of my face.

He's referring to the last fragment of conversation he doled out. I answer him in the hopes of shutting him up. "I *understooded* you perfectly. You're saying Americans are stupid. I get it."

"It's your disdain for intellectualism, your narrow-minded ignorance, your . . . your . . . your—"

Ridley leans across me. "You're pissed, Ian, go home."

Ian gets closer to my face, barreling on, "Your obliviousness to the imminent demise of your arrogant empire."

"Well," I say before I can stop myself, "if anyone's an expert on dead empires, it would be you guys."

While Ridley laughs, Ian takes the comment personally. "And you'll end up just like us, bloody irrelephant!" The table goes quiet. He seems to sense, through his drunken haze, that he's misstepped. He tries to regain some dignity by laughing at his malapropism. "Irrelephant! Now you've gone and done it, ol' boy. *Tusk, tusk.*" He bursts out laughing and everyone relaxes. But then he drops his hand on my shoulder. "Ah, let's not fight." His tone turns intimate and he moves closer. "Let's kiss and make up." He leans in, and I turn fully to face him, hoping to scare him with my eyes, bracing my back against Ridley's strong shoulder and arm.

In my deadliest tone, I say, simply, "Don't."

He throws his head back and laughs. "Ah, come now, let's be friends! We love our Yanks here. Don't we?" he spews to the table. Then, back to me, "Especially a tasty bit like you." I stare at him, recognition niggling. *Tasty bit.* Realization hits me: he was the drunk guy from the street the other night. *Oi, that's a tasty bit.* Instantly, my skin begins to crawl.

Before I can say something, Ian puts his hand on mine, leans in, and murmurs, "I, especially, love a good . . . Yank."

Of its own volition, my right hand sails through the air and clocks Ian right on his smug little chin. I was aiming for a push-back hit, but it ends up decking him.

Whoops.

The spectators gasp and Ian's head flops back. I think I knocked him out. Everything freezes. All eyes turn to me. Somebody do something. Somebody say something. Please. Help.

Charlie obliges. "I say, I haven't seen a right hook like that since Lennox 'The Lion' Lewis dropped Rahman in the rematch! Brava!" I have no idea what Charlie is talking about, but it breaks the ice. Everyone suddenly cheers.

"My dad, actually," I murmur, "taught me how to—I—I'm just gonna . . ." I start crawling over Ian.

Tom's eyes bug. "Wait. Your dad's Lennox Lewis?" But I'm up and moving toward the exit.

I hear Maggie sigh behind me. "Lennox Lewis is black, Tom!"

"Well, duh, Mags! I just didn't know Ella was!"

As Maggie and Charlie start in on him, I push through the front door and out into the night.

CHAPTER 10

That I could think there trembled through
His happy good-night air
Some blessed Hope, whereof he knew
And I was unaware.
Thomas Hardy, "The Darkling Thrush," 1900

It's drizzling on St. Giles, though I hardly notice it. I don't notice anything but the pounding of my heart and the sour turn of the beer in my stomach. I don't even notice that I'm walking in the wrong direction until I'm half a block away. I stop, but I don't turn around. I just stand there.

What the hell is wrong with me?

I've never done something like that before. Hit someone. Yes, he arguably deserved it, that's not what's bothering me. *I'm* bothering me. My reaction. I've never been that out of control.

I lean against the brick wall of a chained-up tuck shop, trying to breathe through this adrenaline dump. The cool dampness left by the constant drizzle seeps into my back, a makeshift cold shower. I close my eyes, tilt my head back, and take a very deep, very shaky breath.

I blame the damn tutorial. I feel as if a handful of marbles got knocked out of my grasp and went everywhere. And just as I'm gathering them back up, Asshat Ian comes along and knocks them out of my hand again, scattering them into corners and under furniture.

I feel like I've literally lost my marbles.

My anger surges up once again and I release a frustrated growl/grunt/yawp. "Men!"

A close voice answers, "Is that a call to arms?"

My eyes pop open.

Davenport. He's standing right in front of me, peering at me, looking amused.

"What are you doing here?" I demand, sounding like a scorned girlfriend.

His amusement fades. "Sorry?"

"You weren't supposed to be here."

Now he quirks his head at me, a look from him with which I'm already too familiar.

"They're all in there," I hasten to explain. "Your friends. My friends. Cecelia's friends. Cecelia. She'll be so happy you're here." My rambling has a tone.

He smiles again and it's nothing more than friendly, maybe even a tad pitying, all traces of our earlier meeting gone. It's like he's found one of my marbles under his chair and simply hands it back, as if he had nothing to do with knocking it out of my hand in the first place.

"Shall I escort you back in?" he asks.

"No. Thank you," I say, wanting to look away, at the ground, anywhere else, but I can't. Every time I see him I end up staring at him. "I've had enough for one day. Night. It was my first time in a pub, and there was a lot of drinking. But you should go, because they're waiting for you." Then, for reasons unknown to me, I bet the farm. "Especially Cecelia."

And there's the quirked head again. "Cecelia and I . . . we're not together. We're not a couple."

Does she know that? I want to ask. But I just shrug. He smiles at me and says, "One can't have it both ways, you know: a sordid reputation *and* a doting girlfriend." *Some men manage it*, I think, but he moves to the door. Then turns back to me once more, inclining his head at the pub, raising a brow.

I step away. "No, I should go. Really. Good night."

He won't stop smiling at me. Before I say something more embarrassing, I turn and walk away.

"Ella!" My name echoes down St. Giles.

I spin around. He's striding toward me. "Your first time in a pub, did you say?" I nod. He glances down the street, seeming to take stock of where he is. "Well, if you happen to be feeling a bit spontaneous, I'd quite like to introduce you to an authentic local." He looks back to me. "Local pub, that is. The Eagle and Child is a horrid tourist trap."

I'm feeling anything but spontaneous. "Oh no, that's okay." I back away from him. "Thanks, though."

"Are you quite sure?" He reaches up, pops the collar of his navy pea coat against the drizzle, and makes me feel like I'm in a movie. "Meet some real folk? Have a proper pint of real ale?" His eyes are bright, his voice a spark igniting kindling.

I back farther away. "I have a thing tomorrow." I have no thing tomorrow. "But, thanks. Again."

He isn't leaving.

I stop walking.

We look at each other.

WE'RE ABOUT TO walk into the pub and my phone goes off. I take a quick glance; it's Gavin. I turn to tell Davenport that I have to take it, but he's already signaling that he'll get us a table.

I answer my phone, standing under the dripping eave, my feet sinking into the waterlogged industrial mat.

"What was that thing in California you mentioned in the last call?" Gavin asks.

I know exactly what he's talking about. "Prop Thirteen."

"And it cut public school funding? Gutted the arts?"

"Among many other things, yes."

"Because . . . ?"

"It stipulated that the maximum amount of any *ad valorem* tax on real property could not exceed one percent of the full cash value—"

"English."

"Okay. Property taxes, which largely fund public education, can only increase at an annual inflation factor not to exceed two percent based on 1975 assessments—"

"Durran! Cut to the chase! Pretend I'm stupid."

I take a moment. "Who mostly goes to public schools in the U.S.?"

"The poor and minorities."

"Who pays property taxes?"

"People who own houses."

"Statistically, who owns all those houses?"

"Not poor minorities?"

"You win the washer/dryer. California, the state with the most expensive housing markets, has a public school system consistently ranked well below my home state of Ohio."

"Thanks, kid," Gavin says, and, per usual, hangs up without actually saying good-bye. I see a few *are you all right???* texts from Maggie and Charlie and answer them in the affirmative (without details like current location or company) and then enter the pub.

The interior of the place feels like any dive bar back in the

States. Granted, there are the ever-present low ceilings and beams, and ancient, uneven floors, but there's neon, and darts, and even a jukebox. The plaster walls are stained yellow with nicotine from centuries of cigarettes, cigars, and pipes. It looks as though the layers could be scraped off with a putty knife.

He's sitting at a booth next to the bar, and—surprise, surprise—a waitress has her arms around him, planting kisses all over his face. Undaunted, I walk over and slip in opposite him. The waitress—who I now see is middle-aged with spiky bottle-red and gray hair—turns to me and says, "Sorry, love, but he's spoke fer."

A potbellied, cow-necked guy pulling pints behind the bar calls out, "I heard that, Lizzie!"

"I weren't whisperin', Bernard!" she yells back. They share a laugh as she scuttles away.

I set my phone down on the sticky table, opposite his. Their presence makes this feel less like a date. Which is good. He points to my phone. "Everything all right?" he asks.

I take a breath and quickly fill him in. Talking about my job gives me confidence. About everything. His impressed, wide-eyed nod also helps. *See? Not a total disaster after all, prat.*

Just as I wrap up, Lizzie appears again, this time with a tray. "Here we are!" she sings, dropping everything off, then leaves.

I take in the haul on the table: two pints, a small bucket of bulk popcorn, and a basket of tortilla chips with a little plastic container of salsa. I stare at the array. The song changes to Nicki Minaj. "Give me a moment," I say. "I need to let the authenticity wash over me."

He grins and lifts his glass. "Welcome to England." I lift my (insanely heavy) glass and clink his.

Then there's a funny moment of silence. Which is unexpected. He takes a sip of his beer, and I take a sip of mine. He studies my face, gauging my reaction. "Well?"

It's not carbonated, it's room temperature, and it's really, really bitter. "Disgusting" is the first word that comes to mind. I venture in for another sip. It's weird, I don't like it, but I like it. I don't want any more, but I wouldn't mind another sip. *The beer*, I remind myself. *Not the man sitting across from you.* Finally, I answer him. "For pond scum, it's absolutely delicious."

He throws his head back and laughs. He's got a hearty laugh. I like that.

I grab a chip and open the salsa container, settling in, already glad I did this. "So," I begin. "How did you find yourself at Oxford?"

Just then, a lanky teenager sidles up to the table, smiling. "Had to dig it out the back," he says, dropping off a half-filled bottle of whiskey and two shot glasses. "Nobody's had a drop of the stuff since you left. See the pen line? Not a millimeter down."

Jamie slaps the kid's shoulder, gazing in wonder at the whiskey. "Cheers, Ricky. Grab yourself a glass, mate."

He's already pulling one out of his apron. "Couldn't possibly."

Jamie pours them a healthy shot. "Don't tell your mum, yeah?"

"Who?" They clink glasses and shoot them. Ricky turns to me. "And this lovely is . . . ?"

I jump ahead of Davenport. "Ella. It's a pleasure."

"Pleasure's all mine." Something silent passes between Jamie and Ricky. The kid looks away. "Well, I'll leave you to it. Welcome back, J.D. Cheers."

Jamie pours two shot glasses and nudges one over to me. I raise my eyebrow.

"An insurance policy against the ale," he admits. "Are you game?"

I pick up the glass. "I'm Irish."

He holds his up. "To being a credit to your race."

"Slainte," I say, and we clink glasses, splashes of whiskey coating our fingers. We belt it back. It's dangerously smooth. I wipe my mouth and watch him lick the knuckle of his pointer finger.

I should not be drinking with him.

"So," I say through the whiskey heat in my chest, "you did your undergrad here?"

"I did."

"Which college?"

"Christ Church."

I pop another chip in my mouth. "Fancy."

He shakes his head. "She's been here less than a week, but she knows Christ Church is fancy. I think it's evolved somewhat, but when I was there it was all sons of peers and grandsons of knights, that sort of thing."

I have to ask. "That's not you?"

He takes a sip of his beer, then says, "Lincoln is much more to my liking."

That was a bit slippery, but I let it go. "And you did your master's at Oxford, too?"

"At New College. Which isn't really 'new,' you know. I reckon it was the ninth college built at Oxford. It was just new at the time."

I can't help ribbing him. "Fascinating, Professor."

He shakes his head, takes the whiskey bottle, and fills our shot glasses again. "We should clear that up. I'm not a professor," he says.

"Fine, teaching assistant." We pick up our shots, clink, say "slainte" again, and belt them back.

"Nor that," he says. "I'm a junior research fellow, which means I've finished my DPhil—or PhD, as you would say—and

I'm in my first year of a three-year postdoc funded by Lincoln. I'm rewriting—" He's interrupted by the ring of his cell phone. I glance down and see "Dad" on the screen. He silences it.

"It's okay if you want to take that."

"It can go to voice mail. Anyway, I'm rewriting my dissertation. Making it less an academic defense and more suited for research consumption. Perhaps even readable by the general public. Though let's not get ahead of ourselves," he says, with a self-deprecating smile.

I return his smile. "And the teaching is part of it?"

"Yes," he says, reaching for a chip. "Originally just undergrads. This," he says, gesturing between us with his chip, indicating his teaching of graduate students, "has only happened due to circumstance. Styan is my mentor, which means she gives me an hour a month of her time and feedback on my dissertation. There was a bit of a palaver in the faculty a week ago, and Styan was asked to pop over to admin, so . . . here we are."

Here we are.

"Do you want to teach?" he asks. He reads the confusion on my face like a book. "Well, *The Atlantic* article. And when you said you were an education consultant—"

"Education policy," I clarify. "My background is strictly political. I started out working campaigns. Learned the ropes. But I always had the larger goal of wanting to change our education system."

"Is that all?" His tone is playfully sarcastic; he's probably too cynical for this American idealism. Nevertheless, he seems interested. "And how would you do that?"

"I'm glad you ask," I reply, with my own version of playful sarcasm. "To start, arts programs would be well funded. The research is incontrovertible. It all comes down to test scores, you know? Right or wrong, all anyone cares about is test scores. Well, fact: districts with robust arts programs also have the highest test scores."

"Really?"

"Really. And in districts with integrated arts programs—meaning incorporating music, art, dance, what have you, into the way we teach math and science—the achievement gap for economically disadvantaged students effectively closes."

"Well, it makes sense. After all, a wise man once said, 'Don't think . . . feel.' Who was that?"

I shrug. "Some posh prat." He chuckles. I take a sip of beer. "So, what's your, like, title?"

"Posh Prat." I laugh, and he smiles. "Technically, Doctor."

I raise one brow. "Dr. Davenport?"

"Sexy, innit?" he mocks, eyes twinkling.

I take another sip of my beer, which tastes pretty damn good now, and I notice, as if by magic, our shot glasses are filled again. How did he do that? We lift them up. "Slainte." We don't stop looking at each other as we shoot. He breaks eye contact only to hold his nearly empty pint glass and two fingers up to Bernard, who nods.

"So, where did you become Dr. Davenport?" I ask.

"The Other Place," he answers, grabbing a handful of popcorn.

"Where?"

"Sorry, that's what we call Cambridge. I'm just back, actually. Feel like a fresher again."

A scrawny, tattooed girl with platinum-blond hair and an unlit cigarette in her mouth appears at our table, crying "Well, loo' who's back from the bloomin' dead!" and bends over Jamie, kissing him on both cheeks, asking him where he's been. She keeps touching his arm, running her hand up and down his sleeve. Lizzie arrives with our beers and chases the girl off—

"Cain't ya see he's busy?"—but not before Jamie asks her to say hello to her sister for him.

He looks back to me, the picture of innocence.

"So this reputation of yours."

He practically leaps forward, elbows on the table. "Yes, this reputation of mine. What, exactly, have you heard? I'm fascinated."

I demur, shrugging. He counters by pushing a pint glass at me. I take a sip, drawing the moment out. "Well. For instance. I heard you have a three-date rule."

"A what?"

I give him an *as-if-you-don't-know* look. He gazes over the rim of his pint at me, truly clueless. "If a girl doesn't sleep with you after three dates, you never see her again."

He digs a chip into the salsa. "And if I have sex with her on the first date, must I have two more?"

I shake my head slowly, disapprovingly, teasingly. He grins. Then he relents, shrugging. "All right, yes, it's probably true that I stop seeing most women after three dates, but not because they won't have sex with me."

"Then why?"

He sucks a tooth, looking contemplative. "Because I'm no longer interested."

"And how do you know you're not interested?"

He levels a look at me, a wry, drowsy-lidded look. "I've a feeling you're one of those people who finishes every book she starts."

"You're not?"

"If you know how a book is going to end, why keep on with it?"

"If you don't open yourself up to life, how can you ever be surprised?" I say, quoting him back at him, doing an awful, tipsy imitation of his accent in the process. "And if you're not surprised, what's the bloody point?"

"I would love to be surprised. Alas, very few people manage to do so, in the end." He gazes at me, a challenge in his eyes. "I would reckon you feel the same way, actually."

He's not wrong.

There's a moment of silence and we both go for a chip, having reached that comfortable point of synchronization. Reflexively, I pull my hand away. He looks up at me, motioning to the chip basket, but for some reason I can't hold his eye right now. I look past him. Behind Davenport, attached to one end of the bar, is a freestanding, wood-paneled box of a room with frosted windows. Its closed door faces me. "Hey, what's that?" I ask, nodding my head in its direction.

He doesn't even look. "That's a snug." Off my blank look, he explains, "A snug was for people who didn't want to be seen drinking in a public house. Aristocracy passing through, the village vicar. Women. Young lovers. Grab your pint." I do, he stands, and I follow. Then a phone rings and I realize I left mine on the table. I go back to grab it and see that Jamie's is the one ringing. "Dad" again. "It's you," I say, picking it up and handing it over. He takes it, but doesn't even glance down, just silences it, and opens the door to the snug. He stands aside and gestures me in.

I step around him, entering the little room, no bigger than a large midwestern pantry. Just enough room for a rectangular table and plank seating. Jamie enters behind me and knocks on a panel of wood with a small knob attached. It slides open, offering direct access to the bar. Bernard's face looms through, framed like an old English portrait. "What can I get you?" he growls.

Jamie holds up his half-full pint. "Cheers, mate. Just showing

Ella the snug."

Bernard rolls his eyes and slides the panel closed with comical force.

"I love you!" Jamie calls.

"But you'll never have me," we hear distantly. We share a chuckle and I slide onto the bench on one side of the table. Jamie closes the door to the snug. The noise of the bar dims and we're left in relative silence.

Jamie settles in across from me. It's so quiet I can hear his breathing. The *shush-shush* of his velvet trousers as he crosses his legs. The snug's forced intimacy feels like a challenge somehow. Suddenly, in unison, we both say, "Can I ask you something?"

We share an awkward laugh. I sit back. "Go ahead."

He sits back, too. "I'm rather curious. You're going to run the world. Why are you here?"

I swallow. "I got a Rhodes."

"That's it?"

I shrug. "I mean, it's Oxford. Who says no to that?" Even to my ear, this sounds glib. Callous. Calculating. I can tell he's about to challenge me further, so I add, "Can't have a more recognizable name on your résumé. It's a network." Which also sounds horrible, and somehow like a betrayal of my childhood dream. I take a breath and say, before he can reply, "I also made a promise to myself—a plan—when I was thirteen. To come to Oxford."

He nods like this is the answer he was seeking, as if this one—the romantic childhood notion—is the reasonable and plausible explanation. I just hope he's not inclined to ask *why* I promised myself. Luckily, he isn't. But he does ask, "Why literature, though? Wouldn't PPE have been a better option?" PPE. Philosophy, politics, and economics. What every politico studies here.

"Probably," I answer truthfully, continuing to sip my beer. "But why do what I've already done? At Georgetown. In life." Then, before I can stop it, "Besides, I wanted a year of . . . of beauty, I guess. A year of humanity's better nature." I cringe. "Sorry, that sounds corny. I've never said it out loud before."

He shakes his head adamantly. "It's admirable. Not *corny*." His overpronunciation of the word betrays his unfamiliarity with it and in that moment I find him so disarmingly attractive that my mouth goes dry. He stares at me.

I look away. "My turn." But now I hesitate, unsure I want to ask him this after all. But then he says, "Please," in that voice of his and it just falls out of me. "Why don't you read the whole book? I mean, aren't you even the least bit curious? There's more to sex than sex, right?"

He studies me even more intently. I look down at the almost empty pint glass in front of me. I've lost count. I push it away, then blurt, "I'm not a prude, you know."

"I didn't think you were," he murmurs, as if he's thought about this. Thought about me. "Not having your heart broken and not being a prude aren't the same thing, are they?"

Exactly. I want to say this out loud, but I can't find my voice. See, this is what happens when you drink too much. You end up in a snug having an obtuse conversation with your tutor about sex you can only half follow.

He pauses, almost drains his beer. A lazy smile crosses his face. "We've a saying in the English faculty. Sex is literature, literature is sex."

"Metaphorically?"

"Elementally. If you're reading something, and you ask your-self, is this about sex, the answer's yes. It's always yes. Because everything is sex and sex is everything. It's love, and lust, and intimacy, yes, but it's also power, and violence, and domination.

Hell, it's creation. Genesis. The beginning of everything."

"The big bang."

He laughs, then continues. "It's the nexus of the human experience. Therefore it's at the root of everything man has ever written. I think we sometimes have to remind ourselves of that. We get so consumed with digging down, burrowing into the prose, that we forget what the story's actually about."

"Sex."

He tips his glass to me like it's a fedora in a 1940s movie and finishes his last swallow.

He sets it back down and faces me with a satisfied smile. About what I'm not sure. We sit in silence. The bar has grown quiet, the snug warm. Jamie's gone still, watching me. I open my mouth, but Jamie's phone rings once again. I glance down, expecting to see "Dad." It reads "Mum."

Jamie's jaw clenches. "Damn him."

"I can wait outside."

"No, absolutely not." This time, he shuts his phone off and puts it in his jacket pocket. "Trust me, it's nothing pressing. Just bothersome."

We look at each other. For too long.

I check my watch. "I need to go."

He stands abruptly. "Right. You have a thing tomorrow."

"Yes. Right." I stand, too. I pick up my phone, happy that Gavin has stayed away. "What do I owe you?"

He looks scandalized. "Oh God, nothing." I open my mouth to argue. "They never let me pay, it's family here."

I'm sure he's lying, but I'd rather not delay this exit any further. So I pick up my pint glass and ask, "Do we just leave it or—"

Jamie takes it from me, his fingers interlacing with mine. "I've got it." It takes me a second to release the glass.

We leave the snug and the cool air of the pub refreshes me. Jamie drops our glassware off at the counter and I wave to Lizzie and Bernard and Ricky. This place was perfect. I'll definitely be back. If I can ever find it again, that is. I move toward the exit and hear, "I'll walk out with you." He catches up to me.

I stop with my hand on the door handle. "Oh, you don't have to leave."

"I have a thing tomorrow as well." I risk a glance at him. He must see the doubt on my face. "Truly. I have an early lecture. My days of going to lectures still drunk are long over, I'm afraid." He gives me a wry grin and I push open the door.

It's still drizzling and the street is empty. Jamie approaches the curb and turns to face oncoming traffic, searching for headlights, for the boxy black body of an encroaching cab.

"What's it on?" I ask, testing him.

"Sorry?"

"Your lecture. Tomorrow?"

"Oh, you know." He sighs. "Tennyson. He's my subject." He pops his hand into the air as a cab continues past us.

"Why Tennyson?" I ask. "Why not, I don't know . . . Byron? Keats? Shelley?"

Jamie raises a shoulder. "I'm not a Romantic."

There's stillness between us. "Tell me about him. Tennyson. The man."

He seems relieved to speak of something other than himself. "Well, let's see. Fourth child in a family of twelve. Daddy issues. Went to Cambridge, wrote poetry, found acclaim, wore a sombrero and cape."

"Sounds colorful."

"But he was a complicated, difficult man. He suffered a trauma in his early twenties. His best friend, Arthur Hallam, died." Jamie rolls his eyes. "Best friend. That's an inadequate designation. They were more like . . ."

"Brothers?"

Jamie shakes his head. "He had brothers."

"Lovers?"

"Some say. I never found proof. I think it's a convenience for people who can't understand the depth of their connection. The loss of a platonic love doesn't bring one to one's knees for almost two decades. It doesn't keep one from living one's life, shutting people out, writing almost exclusively about death and grief for seventeen years. Damn cabbies!" Another one whizzes past his outstretched hand.

"Should we just walk? I can handle the rain."

"It's much too far. I'll get one for you soon enough." I want to say, *What if I don't want one?* But I don't. Happily, he continues.

"Tennyson didn't even marry until he was forty-one, and when he did, it was to the woman he'd been engaged to when Hallam died. The woman who Hallam had thought would be good for him. They had two sons. And, of course, named the eldest Hallam." Jamie's hand pops into the air yet again, but another cab, full to overflowing with rowdy students, sails past. He looks at me. "Do you mind if we share a taxi? It's enough of a challenge to get one, let alone two."

"Sure." I shrug. "So what's your work on, specifically?" No longer just making conversation, I'm enjoying the conversation.

"My dissertation was on *In Memoriam,* the grief poems. I was looking at one of Tennyson's rather specific physical details and how it might have affected his poetry."

"Which was?"

"He was dreadfully nearsighted. Couldn't see more than three feet in front of him without a monocle. So I was exploring the fact that his poetic descriptions tend to veer to either the micro-or macrocosm of existence. There's very little middle ground with him. It's either the veining on a particular flower petal or the, you know, universal suffering of death . . ." Jamie drifts off and steps boldly out into the street. "Oh, come on!" he shouts as a cab arcs around him. I can't help but smile at the contradiction of academics. He can discuss the minutiae of his research after how-many-shots and two pints but the act of hailing a cab proves too difficult.

Jamie sighs, coming back onto the sidewalk, and continues, barely skipping a beat. "Even his last words. You see this writ large. On his deathbed, right before he fell into unconsciousness, he said, 'Hallam. Hallam.' Now, which Hallam was he referring to? Was he calling out to the other side, the spiritual plane of existence? Or was he merely asking for his son? Was it the Hallam he was leaving or the Hallam he was joining?"

"Is it possible that he was calling to both?"

"Point taken. But I'd like to think the latter. When you feel more than you can say, when words fail you, when syntax and grammar and well-constructed expressions are choked from your mind and all that's left is raw feeling, a few broken words come forth. I'd like to believe those words, when everything's stripped away, might be the key to it all. The meaning of life. I'd like to think it's possible to remain so devoted to someone's memory that fifty-nine years later, when all the noise of life is muted, the last gasp passing over your lips is that person's name." Jamie looks at me. I just stare at him. "What?"

"And you're not a Romantic."

He smiles at me. I smile back. I imagine him kissing me. Not asking to, just doing it. Compelled.

The beep of a horn startles us both. We spin to find a black cab waiting patiently for us.

I sense a moment of regret in Jamie as he looks away from me and moves toward the cab. He says, to the cabbie, "Magdalen first, then up Norham Gardens way." Blame the alcohol, but this moment seems to lengthen, as if I'm consciously making a memory. I leisurely watch his back as he opens the door under the misty glow of the antique streetlamp, his damp hair curling against the wool collar of his coat, his broad shoulders and tapered waist, the clacking heel of a well-made brogue pivoting on the wet pavement as he turns back. I look up to find his eyes on me, his hand outstretched. "Shall we?"

CHAPTER 11

A man had given all other bliss,
And all his worldly worth for this
To waste his whole heart in one kiss
Upon her perfect lips.

Alfred, Lord Tennyson, "Sir Launcelot and Queen Guinevere," 1842

ornin' to ya, lass!"

I hear a woman's voice. Why do I hear a woman's voice? Am I dreaming? I must be dreaming.

"So tidy, y'are! It wouldn't knock a bother off ya to leave me something to do?"

My eyes pop open and I bolt upright, way too quick for my head's sake. "Eugenia," I say around the frog in my throat. The trusty scout moves through the room, muttering as I try to wake up. My blurry eyes begin to clear and I look down.

I'm naked.

I snatch the sheet to my chest.

Okay. Don't panic. Piece it together. Bar. Snug. Taxi. Then, nothing. Nothing happened. Right?

Eugenia opens my bathroom door. "Morning."

Not Eugenia's voice.

The honeyed tone kick-starts my memory. Something definitely happened. Images from last night roll over me. Nice images. Very nice images.

"Mornin', love," Eugenia sings. "Anythin' in the bin?"

"Not a whit," he answers easily.

Eugenia sighs. "S'as if the wee miss don't e'en live here." She bustles out of the bathroom, gives me a conspiratorial wink, and leaves.

I prepare myself for the impending awkwardness. Hey, at least he didn't leave before I woke up. I open my mouth to say something, anything, when I hear from the bathroom, "If you put your bin outside your door they won't come in."

"Like a sock on the doorknob?" I croak.

"What?"

"Never mind."

"Sorry, I would have given you a stir but you were sleeping so peacefully." He walks out of the bathroom and it all seems so oddly normal. Oh, nothing, just Jamie Davenport coming out of my bathroom wearing the clothes he was wearing yesterday, velvet trousers and all. God, was the tutorial only yesterday?

Rallying, I clear my throat. "How is Dr. Davenport this morning?"

He rolls down his sleeves and buttons the cuffs. "Good. Fine. Quite good, actually."

Relieved, I exhale. "Great. Me too."

Mutely, he slips on his jacket. Pulls a hand through his hair. He reaches for the doorknob, but turns back to me. "Sorry, I really must run. That lecture."

"Of course," I say breezily.

He turns back to the door, placing his hand on the knob. He turns back to me once again and says, looking at the floor, "Ella, I want to explain something to you—"

I cut him off at the pass. "Students are off-limits?"

He pauses. "Actually, technically no." He looks up and grins at me. "Unlike some, Britain is not a nation of Puritans when it comes to matters of carnality between two consenting adults."

I smile at him. "You're not looking for a relationship?"

He takes a step back into my room, sighing. "That would be it. Quite."

I clutch the sheet to my chest and leap irately out of bed. "How dare you!" I cry. "I thought you liked me! I thought we had something real! You're just like all the others!"

Jamie pales, puts his hands out like he's stopping traffic. "Oh dear God, please," he effuses. "In no way did—do—I wish to make you feel—"

I can't keep it up. I burst out laughing. "You should see your face!" Jamie blinks, finally realizing that I'm joking. He tries to chuckle, but it sounds more like he's being strangled. Maybe we don't know each other well enough for morning-after humor. "Don't worry," I assure him. "Really. I don't want to be in a relationship either." Then, for reasons unclear to me, I drop the sheet. Naked, I reach for the panties that have made their way to the back of my desk chair.

"Well," Jamie breathes. "Brilliant. Glad we're on the . . ." I bend over and pick up my bra."The same page."

"Totally," I say, knotting my hair on top of my head.

"I shouldn't like to have anything of a mess between us."

"Done."

He nods stiffly and turns back to the all-too-familiar door-knob. He pauses and says, to the door, "See you in class."

He leaves.

I refuse to feel disappointed.

RAGING HANGOVER ASIDE, I definitely have an extra spring in

my step all day. In fact, it's impossible for me to sit still long enough to get any work done, so eventually I give up and walk around town for a few hours, hungrily absorbing the sights, sounds, scents, and textures like a bear coming out of a long, soul-deep hibernation. On Cornmarket, I amble from one busking musician to the next, tossing a quid into their open instrument cases, enjoying the variety, the internationalism. The guy with the sitar. The blues guitarist. The flautist doing Mozart. The Afro-Caribbean drummer. They're all at home here.

It's starting to feel like home to me, too.

My phone buzzes with a text from Charlie.

> Hall for dinner at 7. Don't be late. Academic gown required.

I still haven't bought a gown (which is more like a sleeveless black vest with tails off the shoulders). Hugh had mentioned I could get one on Turl, so I walk over, and locate the shop right across the street from the Lincoln College gates. Jamie's gates. I find myself glancing out the lead-paned windows as the shopkeeper rings me up and I can't tell if I'm disappointed or relieved when I don't see him. I head back to Magdalen as the city's church bells start peeling.

A bored-looking woman propped on a stool by the door scans my college ID card and I enter Hall, which feels like a rite of passage. I force myself to keep walking and not stop in the doorway, gawking like a tourist. It's stunning. Soaring Gothic ceilings, flying buttresses, dark wood paneling, and three room-long tables with benches. At the front of the hall, on a dais, another table sits perpendicular to all the others, clearly reserved for invited guests. No one sits there yet, but the other three tables have begun to fill in with students. Despite my gobsmacked rubbernecking, I see Maggie waving from the front of one table. I wave back and hustle down the nearest aisle, taking in the white flatware, sparkling crystal, and three-pronged candlesticks.

Maggie, gown on over a vintage green sweater with cartoon owls on it, pats the seat next to her and I sit down, kissing her on the cheek. Charlie and Tom sit across from me smiling welcomingly.

"This is incredible," I say reverently, still looking around the room. "Why haven't we come here for dinner before?"

"Because the food's largely inedible," Charlie answers. "You must check the carte in advance. Only for lasagna do we make an effort."

Maggie touches my hand. "How are you?"

"Fine."

"Even after last night?"

I freeze. I don't allow my voice to have even the slightest tremor, my tone nothing more than inquisitive. "Last night?" I flick my eyes lightning quick to Tom and Charlie.

Charlie leans in. "Arse-Face Ian didn't ruin your night?"

"Oh!" I nearly chortle. I pour myself a generous glass of wine from the bottle they have open before them. "Completely forgotten."

Maggie sighs in relief. "Brilliant. We were ever so worried." Tom and Charlie nod in unison.

Charlie adds, "Ridley and Ahmed took him home after forcibly hydrating him for an hour."

"Ridley!" I cry. "How did things go with Row Boy? Does he paddle in the same current?" I waggle my eyebrows at Charlie and take a sip of wine.

"That remains to be seen. At present, he wants to see me cox." I choke on my wine slightly. Charlie squints witheringly at me and says laconically, "Coxswain, darling. The tiny loudmouthed wanker who sits in the front of the boat and yells at the rowers?" He downs the rest of his wine and pours more. "Anyway. Were you completely put off or did you venture forth in search of other diversions?"

Everyone in the room suddenly stops talking and stands up. Maggie, Charlie, and Tom leap to their feet and stand stock-still, like soldiers waiting to be inspected. Instead of asking what the hell is happening, I decide to follow suit and ask questions later. After a moment, a procession of people, in much fancier gowns than ours, walks down the center aisle. They are mostly older and distinguished-looking, except for one head of mussed brown hair that—

What is he doing here? This isn't his college. He doesn't see me, but I keep my eyes on him, wondering, in some irrational part of my brain, if he planned this. If he's trying to see me again.

The procession gathers at the front table, the "important" table. Then, from the back, a deep voice starts speaking quickly but purposefully in Latin, and everyone dips chins to chests and closes their eyes. The prayer is long. So long, in fact, that I can't help but open my eyes ever so slightly. His beautiful head is bowed in prayer, but his eyes are open, staring down at the table in front of him, the slightest smile on his lips.

The prayer over, everyone takes their seats again and the din of chatter resumes. I risk another glance and see Jamie talking with the woman on his right. She's laughing.

"So," Charlie says, and I snap my attention back to him. "Last night?"

"Oh, I just went home. Got some sleep. I really needed it."

I'm saved by the arrival of food. Servers descend upon us, dropping off plates. My eyes move to the front table again. Jamie pours the woman next to him some wine. Turning back, I find a plate of little fishes staring up at me accusingly. Anchovies. Whole anchovies. With the heads still on. "They still have eyes," I murmur.

Tom, already digging in, nods happily. "Best part!"

I slide my plate over to him. "I'll wait for the lasagna."

"You were saying something about needing it?" Charlie prods.

"Yeah! I was exhausted. Probably adrenaline or something." I don't know for sure if what happened last night is supposed to be a secret, I'm just assuming Jamie wouldn't want his students to know he slept with one of them. But Charlie's far too perceptive. He's a bloodhound. If there's the faintest scent of scandal in the room, Charlie will sniff it out.

He sips his wine. "Did you not hear that catlike screeching in the wee hours?"

The lasagna arrives and I dig in, buying myself some time. "Uh, no."

"No? It sounded as if it were being mauled right outside our windows. Maybe it was just in heat."

Unbidden, my eyes flit to Jamie yet again as I take a significant swallow of my wine. He's still in conversation with the woman on his right. He hasn't seen me yet. Which is good. It would probably be awkward. For him.

"Did it sound something like this, by chance?" Tom asks, and then proceeds to make the most ungodly screech, a cross between a cat, a siren, and peeling tires. It's ungodly loud, too, drawing attention to our table. I quickly pivot away from Jamie's sight line.

Maggie, suppressing a laugh, slaps Tom on the shoulder. "Tom! We're in Hall. Show some decorum, for God's sake."

Tom, oblivious, looks to Charlie and me for confirmation. "Mountain lion?"

"Perhaps it was the Magdalen Bridge troll," Charlie drawls. "Perhaps he found his larder bare of children and made a dash to Sainsbury's."

Tom shakes his head, licking his fork. "Trolls don't eat children. That's witches." I smile. I could listen to Tom being Tom for hours. I'm also relieved to have the focus off of me for the moment. The servers come back and grab our semi-empty plates. "Excuse me?" Tom asks one of them. "What's the pudding tonight?"

"Custard," she answers unexcitedly, already leaving.

"I'm well shot of it," Tom says, tossing his napkin on the table. "I could do with some chips, cheese, and beans, actually. I'm starved."

"I have chocolate," Maggie suggests. "My dad just returned from Brussels. Shall I go get it?"

"Do." Charlie jumps in. "Tom, get your coronary special from the kebab van and we'll all meet back at mine. Oh, and bring your Scotch, will you, Maggie? We shall have a proper night in." He smiles at me. "Ella? Will you join? After all, you've had plenty of rest. Got what you needed and all that."

"It's a plan!" I say, smiling back.

As we stand, Charlie pauses and drops his head to the side, gazing at the table as though it were a reflecting pool. "There was something else," he mutters. "Something I wanted to— Maggie, some help. Do you recall?" He looks at Maggie. "Oh, come, I said we mustn't forget to tell Ella."

Maggie squints. "Tom, do you recall? I'm sure I told you to remind me."

Tom puts his hands on his hips and looks up at the ceiling. "Bugger and blast, what was it? Wait! Might it have something to do with poetry?"

Charlie snaps his fingers. "Got it." He looks at me. "I saw

Davenport today."

"Yes, that was it!" Maggie cries.

"Bang on!" Tom exclaims.

I swallow. "Oh yeah? When?"

"This morning, actually. But where?" Charlie turns his gaze contemplatively to the ceiling now. "Ah, right." He drops his gaze levelly on me. "On our staircase landing."

I move to say something.

"Coming out of your room."

I freeze.

"Still wearing those velvet trousers."

My mouth drops open. Charlie, Maggie, and Tom are grinning like three cats that ate all the canaries. Charlie reaches over and taps his finger under my chin, closing my mouth. "Careful, darling. You wouldn't want to catch a foot in there, now, would you?"

They erupt in cackles. Maggie, at least, looks slightly repentant, her hands covering her laughing mouth as she says, "Sorry," but Tom fairly bounces down the aisle, hopping and spinning about on one foot, an uncoordinated Pied Piper. Charlie simply strolls out, his jacket draped casually over one shoulder, the very posture of self-satisfaction.

I can't tell which feeling is stronger: my mortification, or the relief that it's out in the open. I take a fortifying breath, glancing once more at the front table.

Jamie is looking directly at me while everyone stands up. He wipes his mouth, shakes someone's hand, and catches my eye again as he stands. He points covertly in the direction of the door. I nod.

I take a bracing gulp of my wine, then, before following everyone out, decide to finish it.

I STEP OUT of Hall and Jamie magically appears next to me. Barely touching my elbow, he guides me to a closed door marked BUTTERY. He opens it and sweeps me inside, closing the door quickly behind us. Cupboards and shelves are filled with glassware and other dining paraphernalia; napkin rings, candlesticks, saltshakers. It smells like a laundry room.

"Hi," he says quietly.

"Hi," I reply. "What are you doing here?"

He sighs, says in a rush, "Styan forgot she'd accepted an invitation to High Table, I stepped in, Ella listen . . ." He holds up a hand, looks me dead in the eye. "Last night was exhilarating. And surprising. Truly. All of it. I haven't had that much fun in the devil of a long time and I didn't adequately convey that this morning." This comes out in one breath and with unblinking eyes. Then he disconnects, glancing around the pantry as if mentally selecting glassware for a dinner party. Finally he says, "Forgive my bluntness, but—"

"You want to do it again?"

"No, I would never—" But his eyes whip to mine, surprised. "Actually, yes." He inhales. "But I can't. Is the point."

I look steadily into his eyes, making a decision. "Jamie," I say carefully, "I have a shelf life here. I hand in my dissertation and I'm on a plane to Washington. No matter what."

He shakes his head. "Those types of arrangements never seem to work out as planned."

I shake my head back at him. "They don't work because people don't know what they want. We do. Or, we know what we don't want. A relationship." We look at each other. "One condition." Instantly, he looks panicked, like a stray dog convinced that the food in my hand is just a ruse and I'm going to grab him by the scruff as soon as he comes near enough. "If we do this, we have to be honest with each other. If one of us is getting bored, or starting to have feelings they shouldn't, no lying. We need to be honest about it."

"You want honesty?" He looks me dead in the eye, eyes sparkling like they were last night. "When you dropped that sheet this morning it took every shred of my willpower to leave."

We stare at each other until everything around us blurs away and all I can see is him. Those swimming-hole eyes. I moisten my lips. I stick out my hand with a challenging smile. "Whaddaya say?"

He considers my hand, tempted. But shakes his head instead. "I still don't think it's a good idea."

"Don't think, Professor. Feel."

He tips his head, *touché,* a rueful acknowledgment, but takes a step back from me and I find myself wishing he'd kiss me. If this is going to be it, I want to have an accurate, sober memory of what his lips feel like. Our kisses last night were hurried, sloppy, means to an end. I'm better than that, and I'd like to think he is as well.

But he turns away, faces the door.

He stops. He pauses.

He turns around, strides back to me, takes my waiting hand, pulls me toward him, drops his head, and proves me right.

And then some.

CHAPTER 12

Your gypsy soul did beckon
To my fetid heart and made
A fearful conflagration of
The meanest kind to tame.
"Fragment," Unknown

Let's say you're not the most experienced of women. You can count the men you've been with on one hand. (Fine, both hands, but you know the exact number.) You've only had two one-night stands, but you've never had a "real" boyfriend either. By choice, mind you. You're smart, safe, and in control of the one thing you've seen derail everyone else: love.

Maybe you were damaged a little bit (not a lot, let's not overstate this). Maybe it has something to do with your family. Maybe someone left. Maybe someone died. Maybe the timing was arbitrary but critical and the fallout saw the normal adolescent goalposts suddenly moved in the night. Maybe boys became irrelevant. Maybe you don't know what you're talking about.

And then let's say, just for argument's sake, a decade later you meet this guy and he's unlike any guy you've ever met before, except for one thing: he doesn't want to be in a relationship. Which is just peaches 'cause neither do you. For you two, relationships are like decaf coffee: What, exactly, is the point?

So you ease into it.

Well. Relatively. He's like early-morning indian-summer sun on the back of your neck. Despite the chill, you know the day is shaping up to be a scorcher.

In the buttery, you're interrupted by the college butler, who stares after you witheringly as the two of you flee, looking pious. When you join your friends for Scotch and chocolate a half hour later, you realize you made no plans to meet up with him again. Which is fine.

Then Monday rolls around and you have your weekly class with him. He's professional; you're poker-faced. But he asks you to stay after class and then whispers warmly in your ear that he couldn't stop staring at your legs during his lecture. (You might have worn a skirt that day.) You suggest that the two of you have a tute about this matter. After all, you'd hate to be distracting in class. He tells you that's a rather good idea and an hour later you meet in his rooms, where you will continue to meet after class for the next six weeks. Other than this Monday-afternoon ritual, you never know when you're going to see him. You never make plans with him, because plans imply expectations, and for this thing to work between you, you can't be beholden to each other. You text him: *Hi. I have an hour before my lecture.* Sometimes your texts go unanswered. Which is fine.

Which is safe.

You always meet at his rooms in college, which you find preferable to your humble attic abode. After all, you have a twin bed and a shower you can barely fit in; he has a double bed, a clawfoot tub, and a corkscrew. What else do you need?

You never overstay your welcome. After your encounters, no

matter how passionate, how exhausting, you never stay. You always let yourself out. Not that he asks you to stay. Which is fine. Safe.

Then, at some point, your escapades are no longer confined to his office. He knows everyone. He can get in anywhere, anytime. Almost every college has a chapel and they're almost always empty and let's just say there's more to do on your knees in church than pray. Or maybe you find yourself on the center table in the Oxford Union library, all alone save for the murals of Camelot painted by young Pre-Raphaelites who, he explains while dropping between your legs as you gaze at the frescoes, were the sort of men who'd have heartily approved of what you two are doing here, right now, at this very moment. Or maybe it's one o'clock in the morning and he suddenly asks you, "Have you been up St. Mary's tower yet, the church of the virgin?" and an hour later you find yourself seventy-five feet in the air, clutching at the stone balustrade, crying out to the empty Radcliffe Square below?

Some people have friends with benefits. You have sex with benefits. You never pretend this is about anything other than what it is. Your benefits include everything you genuinely like about him: his voice, his humor, his mind. Afterward, you sometimes find yourself asking him about his research and you learn more about Tennyson and Queen Victoria than you ever thought you'd want to know. But you do want to know. You want to know everything.

You learn. You learn a lot about wine and you're surprisingly not bored by it. You learn not to prejudge a bottle with a screw top, and how to have just one glass instead of three. You learn that—your first night aside—he doesn't drink excessively, and you learn that you don't want to either. You want to remember everything. Like that thing he does with his finger that unfailingly pushes you over the edge. You learn what you taste like.

You never talk about the past, about family or exes or home-town humiliations, and neither does he. It's as if you both just materialized on each other's doorstep, fresh out of the box. That new-toy smell.

Sometimes you catch him looking at you and the floor of your stomach drops out like a carnival ride. It's not lust; lust you could understand. It's appreciation. It comes with a nearly imperceptible smile when he looks at you and he thinks you can't see him. It's the appreciation that separates him from all the other boys you've been with. It's the appreciation that makes him a man. And, in turn, you appreciate the hell out of him. For all of it.

It's not a secret what the two of you are doing. Your friends delight in teasing you about it. He's told you he has commit-ments on certain days, which you never know about ahead of time, which you don't ask about, and it mollifies your friends that you spend that time with them. Time spent telling you that you're an idiot, that you're falling for him, that you're go-ing to get nothing out of this but a broken heart. You smile because you know you're safe. You know this is different. You know you're leaving. You know you're going to be just fine and so will he.

You never thought you were a sexual being. You could always take it or leave it. You realize now that this isn't true. You don't want to blame the other men you've been with, but suffice to say, what you did with them shouldn't even be called sex. It's like hanging a Monet next to some doodle from kindergarten that didn't even earn a spot on the refrigerator. Is it all art? Maybe. But you'll take the Monet.

Then one day he asks you what you're doing the following night. You say nothing. He asks you to plan on spending it with him.

A plan.

He says he'll pick you up at your room, which he never does, and he tells you to dress warmly, which by its nature is the opposite of your usual operating principle when selecting what to wear around him: less is more. It doesn't sound like what you two do. It sounds like a date.

The next night you hear him coming up your stairs, the eager footsteps, the heavy breathing. You open your door and he comes to a stop at the final bend, looking adorably winded and peering up at you with that appreciation that makes your stomach feel like a centrifuge.

Then, in that voice, he asks, "Shall we?" and you know you'll never stop answering yes to that question.

CHAPTER 13

Let us hold the die uncast,
Free to come as free to go:
For I cannot know your past,
And of mine what can you know?
Christina Rossetti, "Promises Like Pie-Crust," 1861

Jamie," I whisper nervously, watching him scurrying around in the moonlight, "I'm pretty sure the terms of my visa preclude stealing a boat."

"Well, it's a good thing it's a punt and that we're merely borrowing it." He assesses a group of upside-down wooden boats that look like a cross between a raft, a canoe, and a gondola. He moves toward one, bending over and grunting slightly as he picks up an end and walks along the riverbank, peeling it away from the pile. The wood scrapes loudly. I cringe and hurry to his side.

He flips the punt over and slides it into the water, dropping his foot on the edge before it floats away, clearly a punting expert. He looks up at me, pushes the hair out of his eyes, and gestures, bowing slightly.

I give him my hand and he helps me step aboard, supporting

my arm as I find something resembling balance. He gestures to the two shallow benches set opposite each other in the center of the punt. Channeling my elementary school ballet training, I attempt a jeté, but go crashing into the bottom of the punt instead, about as graceful as a baby elephant falling into a mud pit. Abandoning all poise and dignity, I crawl to the far bench, right myself, and land unsteadily on the padded seat. I hear Jamie's slight chuckle.

"Catch." He tosses me his messenger bag then picks up a long pole lying on the side, thrusts it into the water, and pushes us out into the night.

We float under Magdalen Bridge, and he reaches up with the pole to touch the rough stone underside, pushing us along and out the other end. "Would you be a dear and open the bag?" he asks. "Take out the blanket and unroll it." I do, and find that a plaid woolen blanket is wrapped around a silver thermos. I hold it up to him, questioning. Jamie smiles. "Were this a summer afternoon, we'd have a pitcher of Pimms. We seem to eschew the concept of normality."

The night is actually quite mild; no rain, no breeze. Jamie slips the pole through the water and gently pushes us forward. He's watching me, gauging my reaction. I love this. I love everything about this.

Holding his gaze, I stretch my legs out in front of me, scootching down until I'm almost flat on my back on the bottom of the punt, my head settled on my seat. I tilt my head to the side coquettishly and pat the floor of the punt, my intention clear.

A telltale heat brightens Jamie's eyes. "Let me get us a bit further out," he murmurs, "Past the turns. I know a prime spot. Lie back." He affects a sonorous tone, like the voice in a guided meditation video. "Listen to the water lapping the boat. Lose yourself in the stars."

I flip over onto my stomach and look out in front of us. Our small river is heading toward a T, where a much larger river, the Isis, flows rapidly in front of Christ Church meadow. The moon shimmers off the wide expanse like a spotlight on a cymbal. I drift with the rhythm, the sloshing of the water, the faint creaking of the boards. Jamie's dreamy voice cuts through the silence. "In late spring you'll have to come back and punt properly. Before you go home."

I notice he doesn't include himself in this future outing. I don't turn to look at him.

Just before the Isis, he steers us left down a shallow offshoot, gliding onto the soft, silty bottom of the river. Oak trees stretch their bare, late-autumn limbs over our heads. I flip over as Jamie sets the pole down and crawls in next to me, his warmth seeping into my side as we both gaze up at the crosshatch of branches and stars. Our chests rise and fall in unison, breathing synchronized by some unknown force.

There's no need to talk, but I do. "Do you ever write poetry?"

"Oh God, no. I don't create, I appreciate."

I snort at his rhyme. Our hands find each other, our fingers entwining. My head lazily rolls in his direction. I gaze at his profile. That straight nose, those high cheekbones brushed by errant wisps of hair, that perfect jawline. "You certainly look the part."

"Yes, well, judging a book by its cover and all that. Striking covers often hide blank pages."

I playfully nudge his shoulder. "I bet you'd be a natural. Have you ever tried?"

He shakes his head. "The problem is I have standards. I have taste. That's what a bloody DPhil has got me. I'd feel like a fraud, writing something." He turns to me. "Do you know how hard it is? Writing good poetry? Condensing the wealth of human emotion into the sparsest of language? There's an alchemy that eludes me, a distillation. Boiling the content down, down, down until you're left with liquid gold. It's what Picasso did with a pen. One perfect, curved line and you have a woman in profile."

"Doesn't mean you can't try."

He sighs. "That's what being here does to people. Gods live among these spires. I spend my days with Tennyson, and he's a decent ol' chap and I learn quite a lot from him. We get on splendidly. But he still intimidates the hell out of me."

"He's dead."

He shakes his head. "We will leave Oxford, we will die. But they remain. They always remain. They are immortal."

"But, why not you?" He scoffs, turns away from me. "I'm serious. You don't know until you try. You could be the next Tenny—"

Jamie suddenly reaches over and grabs me, hauling me on top of him. The punt rocks, almost tipping us over. I open my mouth to cry out, but he captures it with his. We lose ourselves in the kiss for a moment, before we both stop and pull back, as if we have something to say. But Jamie doesn't speak. I stare at his bottom lip and touch it lightly, muttering, for lack of anything more important to say, "Well, I think you'd make a damn fine poet."

He looks at me, his eyes old yet also innocent somehow. Then kisses me softly. Small kisses landing on different parts of my face like individual raindrops. Then he unceremoniously flips me to the side.

"Hey!" I yelp as the punt rocks.

He grins, sitting upright slightly and fumbling around in the bottom of the punt. He comes up with the thermos. "And now we must try this. My specialty."

"What is it?" I ask, propping myself up on my elbows.

"Blast poetry, this may very well be what I'm remembered for. Liquid winter," he says, unscrewing the cap. "I drink this from Bonfire Night bang on through Hilary Term. Try it," he says, thrusting the thermos at me.

I take it and sniff. Instantly, Pavlovian, my throat tightens and my breathing halts. "What is this?"

"Guess."

"Chocolate, hot chocolate," I say quickly, breath still trapped, throat still closing.

"Yes, predominantly, but I've added—"

"I don't want it." I hold out the thermos.

He takes it quickly. "Oh no, are you allergic?"

"No."

"Then you simply must." He pushes it back toward me. "There's a special twist, you see, which no one . . . Ella? What's wrong?"

Even though I've turned away to look out over the water, I can sense Jamie peering at me. I force myself to breathe and turn back to him. "Nothing."

Jamie just looks at me. "What is it?"

"It's just my dad." I barely get the words out. The second I do I want to take them back. I look out at the water. In my peripheral, I can see Jamie's brow furrowing. "It's not a big deal," I assure him. "Really."

He's not buying it. "Tell me."

"It's not important."

"At least assure me that he's not on his way here to flatten me for taking advantage of his baby girl."

He succeeds in lightening the moment. We share a gentle laugh and I say, "No, you're safe, he's dead."

I can't believe I said it like that. We're both stunned into silence for a moment.

"Is that so?" Jamie asks quietly. All I can do is nod. He slides down onto his back, nestling in next to me. I join him, coming off my elbows and resting my head on the bench. Finally, Jamie speaks. "What was he like?"

I haven't heard this tone from him before. It's disconcerting; it's not sexual, or playful, or arch. It's comforting. It's the wool blanket he wrapped around the thermos. It's also different from anyone else who finds out my father died. The first question is always *"How did he die?"* Jamie wants to know how he lived. "He was the best," I say simply. "I know every little girl thinks that about her dad, but mine really was. He was funny and handsome and he had this energy and I was his partner in crime." The words come easily. Surprising. "He always said that waiting for me to learn how to talk was like waiting for his long-lost friend to arrive."

"That's wonderful. And as it should be. But . . ." Something resides in Jamie's voice. Personal reflection. I believe its source is the fragments of interaction I've witnessed between him and his father.

"But not as it often is?" I prod. Jamie is silent. I proceed with caution. "Were you ever close?"

He sighs. "Getting close to my father, one risks getting gored."

"I'm so sorry." I pause. "Why is he—"

"Futile. Utterly. Wasted breath. But, this isn't. What was your father's vocation?"

Obviously, this conversation is meant for another time. I inhale. "Ran a bar. Worked nights mostly. A real Irishman, you know? But he was a cause fighter, very politically active. If the schools weren't doing their job, he would show up at the school-board meeting. If there was a dangerous street corner, he got a traffic light installed. If the local PD had cops taking bribes—

which it did—he exposed it. He was a badass. And I helped him. Got signatures, approached people in front of grocery stores. People who were sure I was going to ask them to buy Girl Scout cookies."

Jamie turns onto his side and props his head on his hand. There's a silence, just the creaking of the planks and the lapping of the river. "When did he die?"

"Almost twelve years ago."

Jamie pauses. I can tell he's treading carefully. "Illness?"

"Mine, not his." Jamie's look of confusion pushes me onward. "It was my thirteenth birthday party. Except there was no party. We had to cancel it. I'd been sick for over a week and I was climbing the walls. No dragon slaying with Dad, just bed." I've never told this story before, but I don't stop talking long enough to convince myself that I shouldn't. "He felt bad that I wasn't having a party, so we spent the day watching our favorite comedy duos. We'd recite the routines and never end up getting through them because we were laughing too hard." Just saying this out loud has me grinning like an idiot. "Abbott and Costello, Laurel and Hardy, Martin and Lewis, Burns and—" I catch myself and shake my head. "These names don't mean anything to you, but for us—"

"Allen?"

I stop. "You know Burns and Allen?"

"I prefer Abbott and Costello."

That live-wire current between us charges again. That it's happening in the middle of telling Jamie about my dad's death is odd, to say the least.

"Sorry, please continue," Jamie urges.

"We're putting a pin in this discussion," I murmur.

"Noted."

I take a breath. "So, there was this place in town, this café that made my favorite thing in the entire world and my dad wanted me to have it for my birthday. After watching the videos, he only had about an hour before he had to be at the bar, but he was determined to get me my birthday treat. Eventually, I fell asleep on the couch. A knock on the door woke me up. Red and blue lights were flashing around our living room, coming in through the windows. My mom went to the door. And she started screaming. Just screaming her head off. I don't remember standing up or walking to the door. Just my mother on the floor with a policeman on his knees trying to hold her up." I pause for a moment, considering this, the genesis of the rift between my mother and me.

She just completely fell apart. Which I get, trust me, I get it, but she never got herself up off that floor. One of the policemen took her away, into the kitchen, and another one took me out into the freak, late-winter storm to my aunt's house and I didn't see my mother again for almost three weeks. I kept waiting for her to show up, to take me home. I went back to school, where I was suddenly the Girl Whose Father Died. I pulled away from everyone. I'd slip out through the gym at the end of the day so I wouldn't have to face anyone and I'd walk back to my aunt's house and I'd sit on the porch and wait for my mom to show up. I did this for two weeks. One day, to cheer me up I guess, my aunt bought me an issue of *Seventeen* magazine.

When my mother finally did show up, she got out of her car and I came to my feet, the chipped blue paint I'd been picking off the porch still under my fingernails. She walked up to me and I reached out my arms, but she stopped moving and started sobbing, bringing her hands up to her face. I went to her. I hugged her because I wanted—needed—to feel her arms around me. But her arms didn't move. I held her as she held her face and sobbed, and when she could finally talk all she said was, "Help me, Eleanor," over and over and over again, like a chant.

That was the last time I ever let myself need anything from anyone.

I realize I haven't spoken in a while. Jamie has been quietly waiting. I remember where I left off in the story; cops at the door, mother crying, father dead. I clear my throat. "First thing I remember thinking was, 'I'm never having my birthday hot chocolate.'" I had cried about that. I sobbed about it. I fixated on not having the hot chocolate so I wouldn't think about what else I'd never have again.

Jamie inhales slowly, bracingly. I chance a look at him. He looks thoughtfully at me. I speak. "They said he was killed on impact. So it could have been worse." Jamie just stares at me, looking for tears, I think. I stare back, trying to decipher what I see there. It's not pity, exactly. It's understanding. But it's laced with a tentative regret. Like looking at an aging family pet that's going to need to be put down soon.

"Anyway," I breathe, and roll over on top of him. I push myself up and straddle him in one smooth move, barely rocking us. I lean down and kiss him, a kiss that says I have some good months left in me, don't put me to sleep yet. I hastily undo his belt and lift my skirt up around my hips, reaching for the waistband of my wool tights.

"Ella . . ." he says, against my mouth.

"Yeah?" I pant.

He pushes me back slightly. Looks at me. "You don't have to do this now. We don't have to do this."

"This is what we do." I kiss him again, but he doesn't join in.

His hands find my hips, gently stilling me. "Ella, excuse me, but . . . well, one ought to use protection for sex. Not the other way round."

I flush with anger. Instantly. "What's that supposed to mean?" I climb off Jamie and cross my arms over my chest.

Jamie comes up on his elbows, shaking his head. "You told me you'd never had your heart broken, and clearly—"

"Oh God, this is why I don't talk about myself! 'Poor Ella, lost her dad and locked her heart away, never to love again.' Genius, Jamie. Really, very astute. You've got it all figured out. So tell me, why don't you want a relationship? What's your excuse, huh?"

Jamie's eyes drill into mine, hands fanned out in supplication, voice low. "I don't want to hurt you."

I don't know if he's answering my question or if he's just trying to stop the argument, but his gentle compassion takes some of the heat out of me. After a quiet moment, we both take a breath. Then we look at each other. He smiles tentatively and says, "Was that our first row?" I chuckle. He takes my hand and murmurs, "I have an idea. Let's do something a bit daft. I'm going to lie back down and you're going to lie down next to me. I'll set the punt adrift. Go where the current takes us."

"No talking?"

"No talking."

Jamie pushes us off the shore as I slide back down into the bottom of the punt. After a moment of stargazing, I find my head turning in toward him, resting on his chest. My body turns as well, my front finding his side. Immediately, his arm folds around me like a protective wing. I let my arm cross his body, my hand finding the curve of his shoulder and resting there. "May I say one more thing?" Jamie's chest rumbles with the richness of his voice. It vibrates through my head, almost making me dizzy.

"As long as I don't have to say anything."

"Just say yes, then."

I pause. "That depends on what—"

"Say it."

This makes me smile. I'll bite. "Yes."

"It's settled. My house. Tomorrow. Seven."

I lift my head to look at him. "Your house house?"

"You're talking."

"I'll bring dessert," I whisper.

His hand finds a perfect spot to rest on the curve of my ass as he murmurs, "You better." His other hand cups the side of my head, smoothing back my hair. With gentle pressure, he guides my head back down to his chest. I close my eyes.

The sounds of water, wind, trees, and night insects swell around us. Under that, the sound of Jamie's heartbeat in my ear, his breath lifting my head in an elemental cadence. There's a fragrance in the air that I didn't notice before, a constricting. Earth preparing for winter. I open my eyes slightly and can just glimpse the water over the side of the punt, the moonlight on the surface a study in light and dark. I gently rub the wool sweater at Jamie's shoulder, absently fingering the burls.

It's amazing how much you notice when you're not having sex.

CHAPTER 14

If I or she should chance to be
Involved in this affair,
He trusts to you to set them free,
Exactly as we were.

Charles Lutwidge Dodgson ("Lewis Carroll"), "Untitled," 1855

This is ridiculous."

"Yeah." Jamie scratches his eyebrow.

"No, I mean . . ." I walk into the center of the empty ballroom, throwing my arms out. "This is ridiculous, Jamie."

"I quite agree." He nods.

"You have a ballroom." A Victorian town-house-sized ballroom, but still. I stare at him. "How did this happen?"

Jamie worries his finger over a chip in the carved marble-faced fireplace. "My mother's aunt, Charlotte. She had no children. When I came up to Oxford for undergraduate I was kind to her. Went marketing, changed lightbulbs, did the washing up, that sort of thing. She died last year. I'd no idea she'd bequeath it to me. I started coming up from Cambridge at the weekends to work on it."

I take in the large room with its gleaming wood floor, huge

windows overlooking the quaint street, and very real crystal chandelier. "It's beautifully preserved. It's like a set from a Jane Austen movie."

"I'm rather proud, really. Charlotte absolutely gutted it after the war. She was a dear woman, but had no sense of history. I've endeavored to bring it back to its original state. It's almost done now. I've worked with a conservation specialist who refers me to accredited woodworkers, stonemasons, ironmongers, and the like. I also do a fair bit of the work myself." He looks up at the ceiling.

"And now you get to enjoy it. Live here. Raise a family here." He shrugs noncommittally. I blink. "You're not going to sell it, are you?"

"No." I relax slightly. "I'm going to donate it. It will make a fine museum once I'm finished. It's finished." He looks back to the ceiling for a quiet moment.

A moment I can't help but interrupt. "Seriously? But why would you—"

He cuts me off, looking at his watch. "Must check on dinner. Come with?" He holds out his hand and I take it, following him out the gilded double doors and down the grand staircase, back to the first floor.

"ARE ALL THESE old portraits decoration, or actual family?" I call out from the drawing room to Jamie, who is in the kitchen doing something miraculous with chicken.

"Actual," he calls back.

Amid all the staid paintings of women in ruffled frocks and gentlemen with their hands on sword hilts, there's a photograph above the fireplace. An elegant woman sits in a chair, three men fanned out behind her. The setting, a book-laden room. I recognize Jamie, tuxedo'd and in his late teens. The staging reflects the stoicism of the figures in the antique portraits, but there's one major difference: this family looks happy. Loving. Proud. Slightly mischievous. There's an ease in Jamie's face, something I only get glimpses of in adult Jamie. The mother and father are the definition of what the Victorians would call a "handsome couple."

I look more closely at the father, the man I saw barreling out of Jamie's office the day of our first tute. He's about twenty pounds lighter in the photo, his hair only silver at the temples. Seeing the comfort of the family, even with the manufactured aloofness of the setting and wardrobe, I have to wonder what happened.

"Your mother's gorgeous," I call out.

"She's taken, I'm afraid."

There's another boy in the picture, an athletic-looking younger one, also tuxedo'd. "Who's the handsome guy?"

"Me."

"No, the handsome one."

"Right, my brother."

I turn away from the fireplace, looking into the dining room. The table is large enough to seat fourteen. Jamie's set a place at each end, indicated by the full glasses of wine, silverware, and napkins, all expertly set. He's also lit a tall line of candles going down the center of the table, illuminating the swirling mahogany of the table's grain.

If I didn't know better, I'd think this was weirdly romantic. Wooing kind of stuff. Stuff that should have happened six weeks ago. Had we decided to actually date, that is. I tell myself that the setting is misleading. No wonder we haven't come here before. He probably didn't want me to misinterpret anything.

"Dinner is served," Jamie says, sweeping into the room carrying two plates, bringing the most delicious aroma with him.

Garlic and onions, wine and fire. "Please," he says, nodding at the chair as he sets a plate down. I eagerly take my seat. He glides to the opposite end and settles in comfortably. He belongs here. The environment in no way overpowers him. He fits.

"Jamie," I say reverently, staring at my plate. "This is amazing. Everything. Thank you."

"You say that now," he hedges. "You haven't tried it yet." He cuts gingerly into the tender chicken.

"What is it?" I ask.

"Coq au vin," he answers, inspecting a piece of meat on his fork.

I sip my wine. Delicious. I take a bite of chicken. I had no idea chicken could taste like this. "Oh my God," I moan. "Jamie!"

"Call my name like that once more and we shan't make it to dessert," he warns.

I look at him, raise a brow. "It's ready when you are." Even sitting fifteen feet away from each other, our eyes collide, threatening . . . what, exactly? I break first, turning back to my plate. "Where did you learn how to make this?"

"Smithy."

"And who's Smithy?" But Jamie's more involved with his chicken than the conversation. "Jamie?"

"Hmm?"

"Who's Smithy?"

"The cook," he says absently.

"What cook?"

"Our cook."

"You had a cook?"

"Have. Still works for my parents."

I narrow my eyes. "Do you have a butler?"

Jamie takes up his wine and says, smiling. "Who has a cook

and not a butler? Really, darling."

I smile back. "What about a valet? A scullery maid? A first and second footman?"

He sighs heavily. "Let us accept the fact that my family is, I believe the American vernacular would be, 'loaded,' and move on, shall we?" Jamie air-toasts me, that charming smile still on his face.

"Does your mom work?"

"Ah!" Jamie says, standing abruptly. "I know what I forgot." He disappears around the corner into the drawing room. Moments later, the opera *La Traviata* softly fills the house.

Goose bumps. All over.

Jamie returns and goes back to his food. I go back to mine. "So"—I try again—"does your mother have a profession?"

"She . . ." He searches for the word, scooping up broth on his plate. "Organizes."

"What does that mean?"

He waves his hand dismissively. "Charity things. Events. Life."

I'm not dense. He obviously doesn't want to continue this line of questioning. But I exposed myself rather spectacularly last night and his cageyness rankles. So I shift gears. "Speaking of mothers"—I go back to my plate—"I talked to mine today."

"Oh yeah?" Jamie holds his wineglass up to the candlelight, assessing the wine's "legs," as he taught me to do a few weeks ago. Honestly, I'd rather just drink it.

I nod enthusiastically. "She was happy that you were finally asking me over to your house."

Now his head snaps up. "You've talked with her about us?"

"Jamie. She's my mother."

He stops chewing. "What did she say?" He takes a careful sip of wine.

I smile broadly. "She's thrilled! She told her whole quilting circle. She's picking out onesies."

Jamie does the closest thing to a spit take I've seen in real life.

I laugh. "Like I'd talk to my mother about us? Are you insane?"

Jamie glares at me across the table, which just causes me laugh harder. He grins teasingly, silently promising retribution. "Not very nice," he lilts warningly.

I lift my wineglass, pretending to assess the legs as well. "I think we can agree that the last thing I am, Dr. Davenport, is nice." My tone is certainly anything but nice.

"I like that," he murmurs. Our eyes meet again. "I like you."

I look down at my plate. It's empty. I'm surprised there are even bones on it. I'm surprised that I stopped when I hit plate and didn't just eat my way through to the tablecloth. I can feel him staring at me.

Why not say it? I glance up. I shrug. "I like you back." He continues to stare at me. I look down at my wine, finish it. "Everything was delicious."

Jamie stands, picks up his glass, and walks over to me. He sits in the chair to my left, the table's corner between us. His silence is fraught.

"You did promise dessert," he murmurs.

"I did," I confirm, my breath already going shallow.

"And?"

I glance down at his hands, then back up into his eyes. "As I said, ready when you are."

THE NEXT MORNING, the bell over the door jingles as Jamie and I hustle in out of the rain.

"J.D.!" Simon bellows.

"Simon, my good man," Jamie says, moving to the side and

revealing me. I watch Simon's welcoming smile freeze, then bloom into something even bigger.

"Ella from Ohio!" Simon exclaims as we walk over to the counter.

I come here at least once a week, but never with Jamie. Simon and I haven't discussed Jamie, so the look on his face right now is priceless.

"Fish and chips for breakfast, is it? I knew it!" he says, pounding the counter. "That first day, sparks were flyin', they were!"

"We're just friends," I say. "He's my professor."

Simon cocks his head, eyeing us suspiciously. "And I'm Bonny Prince Charlie."

Jamie shrugs. "What can I say? She keeps turning me down. Can you imagine?"

Simon sighs and puts his hands on his hips, giving up on us. "The usual?"

"Cheers," Jamie says, sliding cash over the counter. I reach for my wallet, but Jamie shakes it off. I hesitate, wondering if I should fight this. I don't know the rules anymore. Especially after last night.

I stayed over. Actually slept. In his bed.

Two minutes later, Simon lumbers over to the booth with our meals. He plants a meaty palm on the table and leans in to me. "He's a decent bloke, you know. He's got quite the reputation and all that, but don't let him fool ya. There's more to him than that." Simon gives Jamie a firm clap on his shoulder. "Right, my lad?"

"I'll take that under advisement," I say, more seriously than intended. Simon nods once, like, *Nice doin' business with ya,* and returns to his post at the counter.

The bell above the door chimes, and before I have a chance to say anything or even take a bite, a man appears at our table.

"Jamie!"

Jamie looks up, startled. "Martin," he cries. A beat later, he pastes a smile on his face.

"Jamie, by God!" Martin beams, sticking out an eager hand. He's a big guy, solidly built, but somewhat goofy-looking. Jamie takes his hand and Martin pumps it vigorously. "Bloody good to see you, mate! How are you?"

"Well, well." Jamie nods compulsively.

Martin turns toward the door. "Soph! Babe! Come say hello!"

Unbeknownst to me, a pretty girl with impeccable makeup and clothes has been standing by the door as if she were guarding it. She removes herself from her post and scampers over to the table.

"Jamie, meet my fiancée, Sophie Elphick!"

"Pleasure," Jamie says, taking her hand. "And congratulations." He forces a smile and turns toward me. "This is—"

Martin interrupts. "How are you, dear boy? You all right?"

"Good, good!" Jamie chirps. "Martin, Sophie. This is Ella. Ella Durran."

They turn eager, smiling faces to me, tilting their heads identically, as only couples who have been together forever seem able to do. "Charmed," they say in unison. I wave slightly.

Martin is about speak, but Jamie says quickly, "Martin was a school chum of mine."

Martin's laugh sounds like a machine gun. "School chum! As if we were jumping rope and plaiting each other's hair." Jamie chuckles uncomfortably and looks down at the table. "We were hellions! Do you know, just the other day I was remembering those German girls we met in Paris and took to Les Chandelles! We were, what, nineteen?" His rat-ta-tat-tat laugh continues.

Sophie gives Martin a playful slap, exposing (and possibly showing off) a rather large diamond ring. "Martin, you're incorrigible."

Rat-ta-tat-tat. "Far too long, old chap!" He drops his hand on Jamie's shoulder. "You look grand. Didn't want to be a bother and all that. You've been rather incommunicado."

Jamie nods and smiles as if his life depended on it. "Indeed, indeed I have been. Sorry, it's just been mad. I meant to—"

Martin immediately holds up his hands. "No, no!" he declares. "It's completely understandable,"

"Oh!" Sophie claps. "We're having our stag and hen this coming Wednesday. A joint one."

Martin holds up a finger. "The first one. Informal, just for the Oxford people. We're having a proper do in London next month." He grins at Sophie. "Separately, thankyouverymuch."

She ignores him. "Why not come, both of you!"

"Yes, well, I'll be sure to give you a ring," Jamie says quickly. "Ella, we really should be off." And with that, he quickly stands.

I look down at my untouched fish and chips.

"Ah, Happy Cod for breakfast," Martin says with a wistful sigh. "That was always a milestone, wasn't it?" He winks at me.

"You must come!" Sophie reiterates, taking my hand in her diamond-encrusted one.

I smile at her. I look down at our hands. "What a beautiful ring."

"Isn't it just grand?" she hisses, pouncing on the compliment like a tigress lying in wait for its prey.

"Where's the party going to be—"

"Actually," Jamie interrupts. "Would you mind texting me the details? We really must be off." Jamie picks up our two bouquets of breakfast. "We'll take this along with us, Ella. Sorry for the rush. Lost track of time."

My stomach clenches. Is he embarrassed by me? Or worse, ashamed?

"I did try texting a while back—" Martin holds up his phone.

"Really? Must not have received it. Vodaphone were complete shit for a while there, finally switched, couldn't take it anymore. Ella?" He's looking beseechingly at me. I quickly stand and slip out of the booth. "Apologies, must get Ella to her lecture."

Sophie turns to me, beaming. "Oh, what do you teach, then?"

"I—I don't actually, I'm a student," I stammer.

They both look at Jamie.

"Graduate student," I clarify, trying to make it better somehow. Why is everything awkward?

"Anyway, lovely to meet you," Jamie says, reaching for Sophie's hand and then Martin's. Their eyes meet and it feels like the first time Jamie has actually looked at him since he came into the chip shop. "You look happy," he murmurs.

Martin takes a serious tone. "I am. We are. Thank you."

Jamie smiles tightly once more and we head for the door. "Mate?" Martin calls out. "Any improvement?"

Without stopping, Jamie glances over his shoulder and non-answers, "Brilliant. Cheers."

CHAPTER 15

You have been mine before,—
How long ago I may not know:
But just when at that swallow's soar
Your neck turned so,
Some veil did fall,—I knew it all of yore.
Dante Gabriel Rossetti, "Sudden Light," 1863

We're in Jamie's classic convertible—which I've figured out is an Aston Martin—and almost to the English faculty, when I finally decide he isn't going to offer an explanation for the elephant in the chip shop. So I ask, "What was Martin referring to?"

"Sorry?"

"Martin asked if there was 'any improvement,'" I huff, "and I have no idea what he's talking about and you obviously do."

He doesn't answer. We stop at a red light and Jamie goes vampire still, staring straight ahead. He finally mutters, "It's my brother. Oliver. He's undergoing treatment for multiple myeloma."

My tone immediately shifts. "I'm sorry." Then, when he doesn't continue, "What is that exactly? If you don't mind my asking."

"It's a blood cancer. Specifically of the plasma cells."

"Oh God," I exhale. "I'm so sorry."

Jamie stoically shakes this off as the light turns green and he accelerates through the intersection. "Best not linger on it."

"But he's so young."

"There's nothing logical about disease." Jamie pulls over in front of the St. Cross building.

I ask the follow-up question, even though I'm afraid to. "So? Has there been any improvement?"

"No," Jamie answers bluntly. "There is no cure, actually." I stifle a groan, feeling Oliver's condemnation at my core. Jamie looks at the steering wheel. "I'm sorry, Ella, I should've been more forthcoming. I'm simply not one to go on about such things. But now you can better understand the demands on my time. I take him to treatment in London and stay on with him afterward."

I reach over and take his hand, which still rests on the Aston's shifter. "You don't have to hide things from me, Jamie. I'm a big girl. I can handle it." Jamie nods quickly, but doesn't look at me. "Jamie," I try again, leaning into him. "If you need anything, I'm here for you. I could come be with you in London. Run errands, make meals, I don't know, watch a bunch of Abbott and Costello?"

"It's quite all right," he says, braving a glance at me and smiling slightly. "I appreciate that, honestly I do, but we've a routine. And Oliver is rather private about the whole thing." He looks down at our hands on the shifter. He turns his hand around in mine and grasps it. "Actually," he says slowly, "now that we're on the up-and-up about all this, I'm terribly behind in my work and Oliver has a break in treatment coming up. I hesitate to even ask, but would you be terribly offended if we gave"—he gestures between us—"this, us, a brief hiatus?"

"Of course not. Like I said, whatever you need." My answer is so automated it sounds like a customer-service call-center recording. Press one for disingenuous pandering, press two for passive-aggressive bullshit—

"You're just too damn distracting, you see," he says, leaning in charmingly.

Now I look out the window. "Actually, I could use some time, too. I need to start thinking about my dissertation subject and I've barely cracked *Middlemarch*."

"Ah, my favorite." Jamie sighs.

"But it's not poetry," I tease.

"I beg to differ. You'll see. For whose class?"

"Hughes."

Jamie rolls his eyes. "Here's a fun game with Hughes. Count the number of times he feels the need, apropos of nothing, to remind everyone how spectacularly unattractive George Eliot was."

I chuckle and gather my bag off the floor, still holding on to his hand. "So, how long do you think you need?"

Jamie looks outside, considering. "A month?"

"A month!" My surprised yelp is out of my mouth before I can stop it. Jamie doesn't respond, just keeps staring out the window. I can't help the ugly pang of hurt collecting in my stomach. I'm not proud of it. I know I'm being unforgivably selfish. But I need to know. "Jamie. Are you done? Because we said we'd be honest when it was over. Which is fine. And understandable. I mean, you obviously have—"

Without warning, Jamie grabs the back of my neck, closes the distance between us, and pulls me in for a kiss. I go molten inside, forgetting anything I might have been saying. Eventually, he pulls away, looks me right in the eye, and says, "I'm not done." The husky promise settles deep inside me.

"Okay," I whisper. He releases my neck and I open the door, reluctantly getting out. I sling my bag over my shoulder, lean down, and look at him. "So. I'm gonna go listen to Saunders lecture about the importance of margin notation in early modern manuscripts and you're gonna get your Tennyson on and we'll . . . be in touch."

"It's a plan," he says, quoting my standard line, a teasing smile playing at his lips.

I SPEND THE weekend getting a little too drunk with Charlie, Maggie, and Tom. I don't text or call Jamie and he doesn't text or call me. I've turned our lack of communication into a drinking game: if you look at your phone and he still hasn't contacted you, drink. It's very effective.

Gavin throws a lot of work at me. Things I probably shouldn't be doing. Things outside my auspices as the education consultant. Over the past six weeks, I've answered every one of his calls and returned every e-mail within an hour. I think he's come to rely on me, especially when it pertains to staffing suggestions for young and hungry (i.e., cheap) field-office coordinators. He even asked me the other day for my opinion on a campaign ad. It's odd imagining where I'll be this time next year, if I'll still be working for the senator, or if she'll be the president-elect? Or if I'll have some other client by then. The new people I'll meet. Will I still be in touch with the ones I've met here?

I Skype with my mother and hear all about how it's already snowed once, not much, only an inch or so and it didn't stick, but she panicked and put the snow tires on and now she's driving around with snow tires and she doesn't know if she should take the snow tires off or just wait for it to really start snowing and why haven't they invented temporary chains yet? They can put a man on the moon but they can't invent temporary chains? I tell her they can and they have. I tell her my set from D.C. is sitting in her garage right now with the rest of the stuff I packed up before I left the country. This discussion takes a good thirty minutes and I'm able to disconnect the call without actually having told her anything relevant. But not before my door bursts open and Charlie walks in, wearing a new shirt and no pants (which my mother can't see). He wants to know if the collar should go up or down. My mother tells him down. Satisfied, he leaves. My mother says he's cute and asks if I'm seeing him. I tell her not yet, but my fingers are crossed.

After class on Monday (where I receive nothing more intimate from Jamie than a furtive wink) and logging a few library hours, I gravitate to the pub with Maggie, Charlie, and Tom. We're at the Turf drinking cider in front of the temporary fire pit outside when I see a familiar head ducking through the door and coming out onto the patio.

For a moment I can't place him. He's handsome. Could it be as simple at that? I just haven't had my head turned in six weeks and I'm mistaking that with familiarity? But his eyes find mine and, after a moment, he smiles in recognition. He lifts his beer at me in a toast.

It's the beer that does it. He's the cute D.C. guy from the Rhodes House. His hair is longer than it was seven weeks ago, blurring his corporate edges. I find myself standing up, telling my friends I'll be right back. Just as I step up to him, his name flashes into my head and comes right out my mouth. "Connor Harrison-Smith."

He turns away from the group he's with. "Ella Durran, long time." He smiles and it lights up his whole, gorgeous face and I suddenly remember that I have his number in my phone. I never used it. A flash of regret wells in me. Jamie hijacked my life. Connor studies me, smiling. "You never come to any of the Rhodes events."

"Yeah, I . . . I think I've enjoyed not being around other Americans."

He lifts a brow, nods. "Fair enough. How's English literature and language 1830 to 1914 treating you?"

Remembering my name is one thing; remembering exactly what I'm studying is another. I'm impressed. "Good," I answer, nodding. "How's Global Health?"

"Disastrous. Something about AIDS and unclean drinking water?" he answers cheekily. "I don't know. I'm just here for the beer."

I hold up a finger. "Let us not forget the overpriced food."

Connor chuckles, takes a sip of his beer. He really is cute. He absently rubs his chin, and when he removes his hand I notice a thin, white scar running horizontally across the tip of it. My type of guy—the guy with character, the guy with a face that tells a story. He takes a breath and says, "Hey, speaking of food, I don't have any classes on Thursday. I was thinking of going to London for Thanksgiving. There's a hotel in Mayfair that's doing a full turkey dinner. 'With all the "fixins,"' it said online. Want to join me?"

I'm caught off guard. "Is this a Rhodes group outing?" I ask carefully.

"No. Just me." He grins. "Who wants to be around a bunch of Americans, right?"

Despite myself, I like him. He's nice, he's funny, he's cute. This could be good for me. "I still haven't been to London," I admit, biting the inside of my lip.

Connor's eyes bug. "What?"

I shake my head. "Haven't had the time."

"Hmm. No American friends. No time. Hasn't been to London yet." He turns his head, side-eyeing me. "Is there a guy I should know about?"

The word "no" crawls up my throat, morphs into "not really," but I still can't push it out of my mouth. Connor must see my deliberation, because he says, "Look, no pressure. It's Thanksgiving. It's turkey. It's 'fixins.'" There's that smile again.

I smile back. "Okay, I'll let you know."

Connor grimaces, considers. "I tried leaving the ball in your court once and it never got returned. How about this time you serve, and I'll follow up on Wednesday?" He's already taking out his phone. "Okay?"

This makes me laugh. "Fine. It's a plan," I say, and give him my number.

THAT NIGHT, CHARLIE, Maggie, and I get takeaway pizzas, a big jug of wine, and sit on the floor in Charlie's room eating our feelings. The theme of the night is "Walls." Charlie's hit a wall with Ridley the Rower, Maggie's banging her head against a wall with Tom, and I'm ignoring the wall that's suddenly appeared between Jamie and me.

I love Charlie's room. It looks like something out of *Brideshead Revisited*. Oriental rugs cover the hardwood, a four-panel screen hiding the bed, a red velvet couch, and antique floor lamps. He has a collection of drippy candles in wine bottles (surely against code) and he's put a portable washer/dryer combo in the corner. He even has a tea chest with an assortment of loose-leaf teas that I'm slowly working my way through with Charlie's guidance. He lived here all three years of his undergraduate and was able to keep it this year as well. The college usually requires students to vacate their rooms not only over the summer, but even between terms, so they can be rented to tourists or conference attendees. Charlie must have done something for someone (or to someone) for the privilege, and I don't want to know what it is.

"How can he be so daft?" Maggie whines after a hefty swig on the bottle.

"Have you met Tom?" Charlie retorts.

"I simply don't know what else I can do. It's embarrassing how forward I've been with him!"

"How so?" I ask.

"Well, for instance, we talked of finding that special person, and I said to him, maybe she's right in front of you if only you'd open your eyes!" She looks between us. "I was right in front of him at the time, you see."

"Were you naked?"

"Ella!" Maggie cries.

"Look, baring your soul isn't working. I say bare your ass."

"That's the way forward," Charlie chimes in. "He needs to see you as he's never seen you before. You know. Attractive." I kick him. "What I mean to say is we've never any cracker of an excuse to look our finest. I mean," he says, plucking at the lapel of his tweed jacket, "one tries, but it can only be taken so far amongst the troglodytes in tracksuits and trainers. No, we must find a way to the nines, as it were."

I nod. "Yes, we need an event. An opportunity for transformation. Like Cinderella at the ball."

"Yes!" Charlie gasps, inspiration striking. "The Blenheim Ball!"

"There's an actual ball? I meant metaphorically."

"Is there a ball, she asks. Read your *Tatler*. It's the highlight of the winter social calendar, a proper black-tie, all the unspeakably rich people up from London."

"For what?"

"Some unfortunate charity."

I shrug. "So, let's do that."

Maggie's brow furrows farther as Charlie scoffs and says, "It doesn't work like that. You have to be invited."

"Well, how do you get invited?"

"No one knows. It's like MI6 . . . they find you."

Maggie, distraught, drops her head into her hands. "Oh, Charlie, don't tease me with what I can't have."

"Yes, Tom's done quite enough of that," Charlie drawls. "Look on the bright side. At least yours knows which team he plays for. Straight as an arrow."

"So is yours," I remind him.

"Bottle, please," Charlie groans. I pass him the bottle and he takes a swig.

"You could make your life so much easier if you'd just fish in more familiar waters."

Charlie comes back at me dryly, "Where's the sport in fishing from a stocked pond? I much prefer the open sea." He peers at me. "So where might our dear professor be baiting his hook this evening?"

There's a moment of silence. Charlie hands me the bottle knowingly.

"We were spending too much time together," I say, taking a sip. "We're taking a break. It's a good thing. We thought it was for the best." Charlie opens his mouth to speak again, and I cut him off. "Maggie, you need a plan."

IT'S LATE WEDNESDAY afternoon and after a full day of sitting on my ass writing about the portrayal of female beauty in *Bleak House* and *Middlemarch,* I feel anything but beautiful. So I take a long walk over to the hippie salad stand in the Covered Market for an early dinner of quinoa and falafel. Nice and healthy. And then I detour to the unconscious reason I came to the covered market: Moo-Moo's. I collect my Cadbury's caramel milkshake and walk aimlessly by the stalls as vendors close up for the night, sucking on the pink straw until the only sound in the building is the sweeping of brooms, the clanking of security gates, and my unadulterated last-dregs slurping.

When I emerge into the crepuscular light of Market Street and turn right onto Turl, I find myself at the Lincoln College gates. Coincidence? Yes. No. Maybe.

The door in the gate opens before me. Not pausing to consider what I'm doing (or why), I hustle over and catch it just in time, slipping into the lodge. The porter, who knows me well at this point, nods hello and I casually continue past him. I scoot over to Chapel Quad and up staircase eight, finding myself in front of Jamie's door. I take a breath. I knock.

No answer.

I'm simultaneously disappointed and relieved.

I head back down the stairs and pause in the shadows of the quad. What am I doing? I should've called him first.

I take out my phone and search through my call history for his number. I have to scroll back six days. I hesitate. I take a breath and press the button.

If he seems weird, I'll tell him I had a question about the reading. Why are we reading William Barnes? (No, but seriously, Jamie, why?). I won't leave a message if he doesn't pick up—

"Well, hello, stranger. What a pleasant surprise," he whispers.

His voice torches that ever-ready kindling in my stomach. "Why are you whispering?" I ask instead of a million other things.

"I'm in the library at present."

"The Bod?" I ask.

"No, Lincoln's," he breathes, and I'm moving. I don't even know where I'm going (Jamie's never formally taken me around the college), but I know the library is the big church on the corner of the High and Turl Street.

I walk through a narrow arch in the medieval wall and into Front Quad. "Working on the thesis?"

"Eternally." Jamie sighs.

"And how's it coming?" I ask, exiting the lodge and turning left on Turl.

"Brilliant."

"Really? That's great. Good to hear."

"No, not really," Jamie whispers. "I think it's only appropriate at this point to give back my doctorate and self-exile in ignominy to the Isle of Elba."

I come to an iron gate that looks like it leads to the church. I push on it. It won't budge. That's when I notice the card reader attached to the latch, blinking its red eye at me. *Dammit.* "I'm sure it's not that bad," I say, hoping someone will exit the gate so I can slip through.

"How are you and George Eliot faring?" Jamie asks, just as a girl approaches the gate and opens it. I smile confidently at her, as if I belong here, and slip inside.

"I'm in love," I answer truthfully, but distractedly. "She's the voice of God in my head." I walk up to the sliding glass doors of the library and find yet another card reader. I grind my teeth.

"I told you," Jamie purrs.

"Forgot your card?" I hear behind me. I whip around and find a lanky acne-riddled boy grinning sheepishly at me.

I tightly cover the mouthpiece on my phone and flash my winningest smile. "Yes! I'm such an idiot. You're my hero."

He flushes red and, ducking his head, swipes his card. The doors slide open. "Thanks," I mouth.

"Anytime," he whispers.

"What's that? Where are you?" Jamie asks.

"Just getting some food," I lie as I close in on my unsuspecting prey.

"Doesn't Moo-Moo's close at five?"

You think you know me so well, Dr. Davenport. "Tell me exactly where you are in the library, the precise spot," I whisper, entering the main room of the converted church.

Wow. I was not expecting this. It is gorgeous. Soaring white marble ceiling with painted blue insets, high arched windows, an open floor with wooden stacks jutting inward like ribs, and a long table in the center. Religion for bibliophiles. There's even a late-medieval tomb topped with the horizontal carving of a knight, sword clutched atop his chest, a mirror image of the bones the sarcophagus contains. Eerie, but I love that it's still here. Someone clearly doubted the spiritual wisdom of removing it. A few books sit atop it, waiting to be reshelved.

"Shall I tell you what I'm wearing as well?" Jamie chuckles.

"It does kind of turn me on. Imagining you sitting there, working away. I can see myself—"

"Right." Jamie coughs. "Well then, allow me to assist." He drops his voice, murmurs, low and sweet, "In between the stacks are study carrels. Last row in the back. I like the one on the right, closest to the window overlooking the High. Sometimes there's an unfortunate fresher in my spot and I challenge him to a duel."

"Ooh, blood sport. Hot," I coo, padding lightly down the center aisle.

"I take my chair, prepare my tablets and books . . . er, unbutton my jacket, and then I, well, I suppose I sit down—" He stops abruptly, voice suddenly less phone sex and more awkward telemarketer. "This can't be remotely exciting."

"You have no idea."

"I want to see you," he groans. "I hope soon."

"Sooner than you think," I say smugly, closing in on the final stack.

"Bollocks. The librarian's onto me. I have to go. Chat soon, yes?"

"Uh-huh," I answer, grinning. I hang up just as I turn the corner, his carrel, no more than fifteen feet away, coming into view.

It's empty.

CHAPTER 16

But though with seeming mirth she takes her part
In all the dances and the laughter there,
And though to many a youth, on brief demand,
She gives a kind assent and courteous hand,
She loves but him, for him is all her care.
Charles (Tennyson) Turner, "A Country Dance," 1880

What did I say to him? What did I say when this whole thing started? I said don't lie to me. Simple. I said honesty is the only way this is going to work. Honesty about when we've reached the end of the road, honesty about what we're feeling for each other. I ignore the obnoxious little voice inside my head that points out I haven't been entirely honest about that last bit and focus instead on Jamie's duplicity.

I even gave him the benefit of the doubt. I walked every aisle, looked in every carrel. He lied to me.

As I wend my way through the throng on the High, I group-text Charlie, Maggie, and Tom:

> Meet me in 20. We're going out.

"HUGH!" I EXCLAIM, banging into the lodge. "Put the champagne on ice! Ella Durran's hitting the town tonight!"

He pauses in his nightly ritual of powering everything down, gazing at me over the tops of his glasses. "Indeed, Miss Durran?"

I keep walking. "Indeedy-do, Hugh! I'm blowing this Popsicle stand!" I abruptly halt. There's a long-stemmed rose sticking out of one of the pidges.

My pidge.

"Hugh," I breathe. "When did—"

"This morning, Miss Durran. I was growing rather concerned it might wilt. Just about to place it in a bit of water for you, actually—"

I yank the rose out of my pidge, throw it to the floor, and stomp on it. Repeatedly. He dares sully my pidge with his lies? The nerve!

The smell of crushed roses brings me back to myself. Breathing heavily, I look at Hugh. His expression hasn't changed in the slightest during my tantrum. He still watches me as if I've entered the lodge with the sole purpose of boring him. "No water, then?"

I look down at the rose in disbelief. "Sorry," I mutter, bending over to scoop up its masticated petals.

"I'll attend to it," Hugh says quietly.

"I'm so sorry, I don't know what—"

"Miss Durran."

I look up and see Hugh standing over me with that same dulled expression, but a changed tone. "Allow me." He squats down next to me with a slight grunt, knees creaking. His kindness overwhelms me and my throat tightens. "I'm so sorry—" I offer again, but Hugh just shakes his head.

"'Tis nothing. Best be off, Miss Durran. You've Popsicle stands to blow."

This kind man reaches into the ashes and pulls a smile out of me. "Thank you, Hugh. You're a keeper, you know that?"

"My ex-wife would disagree with you there, Miss Durran."

I muster one more smile and flee the lodge.

I hoof up my staircase. Charlie's door is open and, upon hearing my footsteps, he emerges, dressed in his Gatsby suit and smelling like a French hooker, bless him. He holds a bottle of whiskey by the neck like a dead duck. Maggie, brow perpetually furrowed in worry, appears behind him, Tom—still wearing his bike helmet—beside her.

I smile brightly. Too brightly. "Great, you're all here! Let's go! Let's go dance!" I start back down the stairs, but when I don't hear them behind me, I turn around. "What?"

Maggie smiles placatingly, as if she's about to talk a jumper off the ledge. "Sorry, but it's half five, love."

"So?"

"No clubs are open at half five, Love."

I huff out a breath, devastated. "Well . . ." My voice breaks as I toss my hands out helplessly. "What should we do?"

They all look at each other, then back at me. Charlie holds up the whiskey bottle. "Pray about it?"

BY THE TIME the club opens, we're drunk. Drunk enough to think riding our bikes there is a good idea. Only Charlie doesn't have a bike, so he perches on the handlebars of Tom's bike, Pippa. The entire ride there, Charlie mutters about the decline of the monarchy and the ascent of the "feckless bourgeois heathens" (I can only assume he means the Middletons).

We drop our bikes in the alleyway leading to the club and stagger to the front door, where a handsome, smiling face awaits me. "Ella," he says warmly, "beautiful night for a bike ride."

I forgot to mention it's pissing rain.

I also forgot to mention that about an hour ago Connor texted me asking if I'd thought any more about going to London tomorrow for Thanksgiving. I didn't answer his question, but I did tell him he should meet us at the club.

Apparently, he did.

Smiling back at him, I wipe the rain off my face and introduce my friends. Maggie blushes shyly and Tom gets all bloke-y, slapping Connor on the shoulder and editorializing about women and dancing, something like, "What are you gonna do, eh? They like it when we shake it." I'm not really paying attention, because I'm watching Charlie elevator-assess Connor. Thoroughly. When he finally sticks out his hand, he side-eyes me, conveying a silent but nonetheless very loud, *He's no Jamie Davenport.* I glare back with an equally loud look that says, *Shut up.*

Charlie brushes past me, murmuring, "Just so long as you recognize it," and continues forward into the dark entryway of the club. We all follow.

I'm not a club expert, but as soon as we're inside I can tell this one is a dive. First, it's a dance club in a town with argu-ably the highest nerd-per-capita ratio in the entire world. So I wouldn't call what's happening in the middle of the floor danc-ing so much as controlled convulsing. Second, instead of being sweltering as most clubs are, this one manages to retain that bone-deep chill that's uniquely British. Third, it's a Wednesday. So nobody is here because they should be. There's either a very good or a very bad reason.

Given the state I'm in, it's perfect.

"Drink?" Connor whisper/yells into my ear.

"I'm good for now," I call back.

"You sure?"

"Yeah, we pre-gamed."

"Just let me know if you want something." He turns to the bar.

Connor is so nice. So unaffected. I miss American men.

I should dance. Dancing would be good right now.

I leave everyone at the bar and slip into the throng, letting the body heat (minimal though it may be) lure me into the center of the dance floor. Within a minute I'm fully assimilated, just another rain-slicked body in the crowd.

I love to dance. Ever since I was a kid. It was therapeutic. Why did I stop? I used to dance every day after school. Put on the radio and just go to town. When did I become the serious adult who runs five miles a day instead of dancing by herself in her own damn apartment?

I don't know how much time passes, but enough to work up a sweat and no longer feel quite so tipsy. At a song break, I slowly resurface, opening my eyes and finding myself back in this awful club. I see my friends at the bar. With Connor.

I catch his eye. He smiles at me, sets his drink down on the bar, seems to tell the group he'll be back, and walks directly toward me. A warm rush travels through me as he arrives. Right now, the fact that he's no Jamie Davenport is a good thing. A very good thing. He boldly brushes a still-damp lock of hair back from my face and says warmly, "Dancing becomes you. You look happy."

A smile takes over my face. "Do you dance?" I ask him.

"Does any man, really?"

I start moving again and he joins in. He's not bad. Who would have guessed? We smile at each other. He leans in to be heard, his breath stirring the hair at my ear. "You've got some moves." He pauses. "And there's no way to say that without sounding like a total creeper. Sorry." I laugh. I pull away and flutter my hand at my face like an antebellum fan. He gives me a big, luscious smile. Now he shouts, "Really like your friends. Who needs Americans?"

I laugh and lean into him. He seamlessly drops his hands to the back of my waist. They settle on that no-man's-land between lower back and ass. It's neutral territory in the way demilitarized zones are technically neutral territory: a hair-trigger away from not. I'm weirdly proud of Connor in this moment. He clearly has more game than he lets on. My guess? He's had a few serious girlfriends, a couple of years each. He's experienced, but not in a promiscuous way, unlike Jamie and his legion of dropped knickers. There's just something solid about Connor. Predictable.

There's a tap on my shoulder. I stop dancing and spin around.

A cute girl in a strapless white dress and a neon-pink veil beams at me. It takes me a moment to realize it's Sophie from the Happy Cod. "Hi!" I yelp, my mind racing. Oh God. It's Wednesday. It's Martin and Sophie's joint bachelor/bachelorette party. I rein in my panic. So what if Jamie's here? I have nothing to be guilty about.

Sophie's cheeks are apple red, her eyes slightly unfocused. Not too unfocused to dip down and catch Connor's hands slowly dropping from my body. She looks momentarily confused, but keeps smiling. Nothing can derail her festive glee. "You came!" she cries.

"I came!" I cry back, gluing a smile on my face.

"Where's Jamie? Martin'll be thrilled!" she yells happily, looking around.

"Jamie didn't come with me." I'll just leave it at that.

Apparently something *can* derail her glee and that something is the absence of Jamie Davenport. Sophie's face suddenly slackens and she looks as if she's going to cry. Silently, she grabs my hand (or attempts to; she finds my elbow and haltingly makes her way down to my hand) and trots me off the dance floor in unsteady four-inch heels, like a newborn colt. I glance back at Connor, giving him an apologetic smile. He points toward the bar and slinks off in that direction.

Sophie throws open the restroom door (momentarily losing her balance) and spins around on the filthy tile floor. For a moment she merely stares at me, looking overwhelmed and incapable of speech. Just as I'm about to break the uncomfortable silence, she blurts, "Martin told me everything, Emma."

Because she looks on the verge of tears I choose not to correct her on my name. And not having any idea what she's talking about, I say, "Oh?"

She nods emphatically. "It's dreadful. Simply dreadful."

I am so not in the mood for this, whatever it is. Does that mean I'm a terrible person? I just want to get back to my friends, to Connor. To a cocktail. "I'm sorry," I say, a good thing to say when you don't know what to say.

She's coming toward me, arms out. She drapes herself over me and pats the back of my head. The vodka is wafting out of her pores like an evergreen car freshener.

"The things we endure," she murmurs into my hair. Ah, I think I got it. Martin cheated on her. That must be it. I lift my arms, resting my hands on her back, giving her supportive little friend-pats. She continues, "I saw it with my own mother and father." I inwardly groan. *Poor girl.* "My mother kept asking, 'Why me?' Why her, indeed. Why any of us? And what does one do in such circumstances?"

I pull out of our embrace and look her dead in the eye. "You leave. You leave is what you do."

Sophie appears horrified at the notion. "It's not as if it's his fault." *Poor, brainwashed girl.*

I take hold of her upper arms, restraining myself from trying to shake the doormat out of her. "Well, it's certainly not your fault!"

She grabs my arms in turn, equally strong. "It's not anyone's fault when it comes down to it. Besides, Martin told me how he is. That he retreats, pushes those he loves most the farthest away."

I shake my head. "That's not an excuse!"

Now she steps back, getting emotional again, whirring her hand ineffectually. "No, of course not, it's just . . . here you are with a new man—who's terribly fit, by the way, but that's not the point—and it just . . . it makes me . . . so . . ." She stops whirring and just stands there, in the middle of the bathroom, arms hanging limply at her sides like a little girl who's lost her doll. Her voice goes up an octave and her face crumples in on itself. "Sad!"

I go to her, once again, this time taking her hands. I'm not this person, usually, but she's so distraught. And it's her hen do. And Martin's an asshole. "Leave him, Sophie. You don't deserve this. None of us do." My words of wisdom seem to be working. She stops crying. She sniffles. She looks at me.

She sounds as if she has a clothespin on her nose when she says, "What?"

Her tone is a mix of surprise and confusion, as if I'd just brought a complete non sequitur into the conversation. As if we had been talking about the state of the world and I had suddenly belted out, "Shoes, shoes, shoes, I love shoes!" We stare at each other for a second and what I see in her eyes causes my stomach to flip over like a terrier. "You're talking about Martin, right?"

"No! Oh God, no, I don't know what I'd do if it were Martin. No, Jamie."

Jamie? I quickly replay the conversation in my head. "What, exactly, did Martin tell you?"

"Everything. All of it, I'm afraid. Jamie phoned Martin later that day, the day we saw you in the chippy, and told him every-thing."

"Which is?"

Sophie sighs sadly. "How god-awful it all was. And still is, for that matter. And that poor girl, what was her name?"

I knew it. IknewitIknewitIknewitIknewit. I do my best to remain calm. "What's what's-her-name's name?"

Sophie sighs so hard her lips motorboat. "I can't remember."

I implore her, through gritted teeth, "Try."

Her hand starts whirring again. "Sarah?" There's a Sarah? "No, that's not it. See?"

"Oh, trust me, I see. Clear as day—"

"No, no, See. Something with a *C*."

Lightbulb. "Ce? Cecelia?"

Sophie snaps her fingers. Or tries to. She essentially just rubs them together. "That's it! Martin said she was inconsolable after the funeral and that Jamie took her on, rather. It's been years now, apparently."

My stomach coils. I knew it. Of course. Cecelia. Years! Why did I ever believe him? He's such a—"Funeral?" I say. "What funeral?"

"Well, Oliver's, of course." Sophie shakes her head, looking bewildered.

My mouth falls open, but other than that, I'm paralyzed from the neck down. I can't move. I can't breathe.

Oliver's dead?

Jamie's brother, whom he's been religiously taking for treat-ments in London all this time, is dead?

I want to scream, but to do that I'd have to be able to breathe, to draw oxygen into my lungs. Words tumble out instead. "Oli-ver's dead."

"Dreadful, isn't it?" she replies, as if I were merely stating a fact, not asking a question.

Reeling, I barely notice Sophie stagger to the sink, turn on the dingy faucet, and splash cold water on her face.

I excuse myself from the ladies' room, all calm serenity. The calm of shock. The calm of betrayal. The calm before the storm.

One thought breaks through this calm, the first darkening cloud on the horizon, the telltale electricity that lifts the hair on your arms.

Jamie's soft, pleading, moonlit voice in our set-adrift punt:
I don't want to hurt you.

CHAPTER 17

No other man
Can know a man
Such as this.
For a woman knows a man
In ways a man
Knows not exist.
Ay, she knows her man,
Such as he is.
Unknown, "Fragment"

The first campaign I ever worked on was for a city council seat in Nowhere, Virginia. I did it for the experience. I'd drive down there in the early evenings of my freshman year, knock on doors during the dinner hour, sleep in my car, then canvass the gas stations and bank parking lots in the prework hours, before driving back to D.C. for my lunchtime classes. I was an animal. I created inventive campaign literature, I engaged constituents who'd never been engaged before, I ate endless amounts of barbecue, and I paid for it out of my own pocket. I did everything. Everything but vet the candidate.

Turns out, he was a pedophile. And a meth addict.

I felt horrible. Horrible about what I'd nearly done. But what really stuck in my craw as I took that final drive back to campus, what I could not for the life of me understand, was this:

Why would he put himself in this position to begin with?

If you have a secret (or secrets, in this case), why run for public office? Why open yourself up to the scrutiny of others? Why set yourself up to disappoint those closest to you?

Did he want to get caught?

Fifteen minutes after leaving Sophie in the filthy bathroom, I'm standing at Jamie's door, sopping wet and no longer calm. That vanished when I turned off Banbury Road onto Norham Gardens, my wet clothes chafing with every step, the wind wrapping my hair around my face and throat like clingy fingers. In its place, single-minded, near-homicidal rage.

We were better than this, Jamie and I. We weren't much, maybe, but we weren't this. This cliché. This statistic. This sadly predictable inevitability. As Jamie had said in our first tute, "We're the clever ones. We're Oxonians."

This is not the way the clever ones end.

I don't knock on his door. I don't ring the bell. I feel entitled to shatter his sense of safety the way he's shattered mine. So I reach for the doorknob. Surprisingly, it turns in my hand, as if this is all preordained.

I push the door open and stride in, making a left out of the foyer and into the drawing room, following the low hum of voices. Male and female. Cecelia? I stop under the archway and stare at the tableau before me.

Jamie sits in a chair. Shirtless. He gazes up at a girl. In a nurse's outfit, of all clichés. Holding Jamie's hand.

Both Jamie and Nursie jump and turn to me.

"Ella," Jamie breathes, a compendium of emotions crossing his face in the space of a second.

The girl drops Jamie's hand, holding some kind of tubing in her own, and takes a step toward me. "Miss, I'm sorry, Mr. Davenport isn't to be disturbed at present."

"Stephanie," Jamie says lowly. "It's all right." The strain in his voice, its airy thinness, prompts me to take a closer look at him. I haven't seen him in almost a week. He seems altered somehow. I take a curious step toward him as Nursie steps off to the side. Her move reveals something else in the room, something previously blocked from my view.

An IV stand.

I look more closely at the nurse and realize the outfit she's wearing isn't remotely sexy. I caught the stethoscope around her neck and her little white dress with black piping, but I didn't notice the demure length, the industrial-strength material, the sensible square-toed sneakers.

I focus back on Jamie. "What is going on?"

"You shouldn't have—"

"What the hell is going on?!" I start to shake, rain flicking off me with each tremor. My heart goes from zero to sixty in a single beat, so loud I'm sure he can hear it across the room.

For the first time since we met, I know we both wish we were looking at someone else.

"Dammit!" Jamie barks, loud enough that the nurse moves back toward him, placating hand outstretched, trying to calm him. "This isn't what I wanted—"

I cut him off again. "I thought we both wanted honesty! Remember?"

Jamie swallows, looking like all the blood has left his body. "God, Ella, this is not the time. Please just leave."

"Leave?! You don't think you owe me—"

"Ella—"

"You know what?" I shout. "It doesn't matter. I don't care

anymore—"

A roar starts in the back of Jamie's throat and barrels out of him like a freight train from a tunnel: "Get out!"

This silences me. I've never heard him yell before. It scares me. I've never been scared of Jamie. Silently, reeling, I turn and walk out of the drawing room.

I can hear Jamie's groan from all the way in the foyer. "Come back! Ella, I'm sorry, wait!"

Too late.

I slam the door on my way out, rattling the entire house behind me.

CHAPTER 18

Sweet, never weep for what cannot be,
For this God has not given.
If the merest dream of love were true
Then, sweet, we should be in heaven,
And this is only earth, my dear,
Where true love is not given.

Elizabeth Rossetti (née Siddal), "Dead Love," 1899

I rush down the front steps, but stop at the bottom, feeling completely lost, as if I slipped into another universe and found myself on this rainy sidewalk. Do I go left or right? Or up or down?

The door opens behind me.

"Ella, please, I'm sorry, stop."

I hear his panting, strained voice, but it has no effect. I'm still trying to find my way out of this black hole.

"Ella, please, you must allow me to explain."

My anger spikes again and brings me present. I spin around to face him. "Oh, must I?!"

"All I ask is that—" He stops talking. He lists into the door-jamb. He's pale, shaky. He attempts to play it off, righting himself, pointing into the house. "I'll put the kettle on, yeah?"

"I don't want tea, Jamie!"

"Might I offer you something a bit stronger?"

I fold my arms. "An explanation. Offer me that."

His eyes are gentle and weary, his face long and drained. I can't stop looking at him. He's morphed in a week, but I don't know how exactly. Is it just because I'm seeing the person he actually is, not the person I thought he was? Or is there something else?

"All right." He takes a shallow breath, moves away from the door, and takes a deliberate step down the stairs. "I'm in the midst of a rather serious medical circumstance. It's—"

"You know who isn't in the midst of a rather serious medical circumstance? Your brother. Your dead brother." I bite back a cringe. That came out more callous than I intended.

His brows snap together. "How do you know that?"

I shake my head. "I'm asking the questions." I begin to pace, organizing my thoughts. Or trying to. "What is it? What do you have?"

"Multiple myeloma."

I stop pacing. "Isn't that . . . what Oliver had?"

Jamie nods.

"Isn't that what killed him?"

Jamie nods again.

"So, you're dying?" How is my voice so calm? I might as well be asking him why he wore those particular pants today. I know I'm not handling this well, but I can't find any rationality, any objectivity, any of the skills I usually have at my disposal. I've never felt this untethered. Well. Not in twelve years, anyway.

Jamie just stares at me, the answer unavoidable in his eyes. I can't look at them. He takes another tentative step down the stairs. Unstable, he grabs at the iron handrail. It shifts against his weight, old and rusting and dangerously loose. He clutches at it with both hands, seeking balance. I want to leap up the steps and help him, but I don't. I can't right now. I glance down at his hands. A Band-Aid sits on top of one of them, a crimson dot in the center. "Was that chemo in there?"

"Saline."

"Saline?"

"The chemo—this particular chemo—is a quick injection. And pills. But it requires a saline flush after—"

"How long have you been in treatment?"

"Six weeks. This is my third round. Might we go inside?" He's still shirtless. Though the rain has abated, the wind has picked up.

"Go if you want."

"No, merely a suggestion." With that, he takes yet another tentative step. The railing could go at any moment. Jamie, aware of that fact, mutters, "I really must repair this."

A tsunami of questions swells in me. I grow relentless, my tone like a trial lawyer. "Why do you have your hair?"

"I don't—I don't know. Some people get lucky."

"Lucky?" A sarcastic laugh falls from my mouth. "Why aren't you more ill?"

"I'm quite ill, Ella."

"Well, why didn't I notice? Why haven't you been throwing up? Staying in bed? And who has chemo at home? With their own personal nurse—"

The gentleness in Jamie's eyes disappears, replaced with a weary exasperation. "Ella, do you want real answers to these questions? Because I will gladly sit with you and explain myself, but I'm asking you to attempt a modicum of gentleness. Please. I've got an unrelenting headache at present."

I barely hear him because something he said swoops back

around and lands. "You've been in treatment for six weeks," I say. "So, like, the entire time we've been together?" The words "been together" hover over us like a fog. The phrase is a misnomer, a placeholder term devoid of actual meaning. It could mean everything or nothing.

The tiniest smile curls his lip. Rueful. Verging on remorseful. "My first treatment was actually the evening after we . . . the Buttery. You'll excuse me, but I must sit." He uses the unstable railing to lower himself, taking a welcomed seat on the third step up from the sidewalk, which puts us, oddly, at eye level.

I remember his protestations in the Buttery. *I can't. Is the point. Don't think it's a good idea.* "Why would you ever start something—"

"You were supposed to be my last hurrah." He dares a look at me. Then, horribly, he chuckles. "My send-off. My bon voyage party." He continues to laugh, and drops his face into his hands. "Bugger, how foolish."

I'm not laughing. "Why didn't you tell me?"

"Why would I have?"

The top of my head blows off. "Because it affects me, too!"

He looks up at me, liquid-eyed, no longer laughing. His voice is hoarse. "How? You don't want a relationship. You're leaving. You have a plan. So did I."

In the ensuing silence, Jamie picks at the Band-Aid and I notice the spot has gotten larger. I feel myself splintering, cracking open into a gaping crevasse, and I realize in that moment that I've never hated anyone as much as I hate him.

When my dad died, my mother made it quite clear that I had to be the strong one. That I couldn't fall apart, because she needed me. It was the ultimate bait and switch. For twelve years, she'd been the mom and I'd been the child; those were the rules of our world. And she just decided those weren't the rules anymore and I was trapped. I stare at Jamie. Another rule change. Another bait and switch.

"You thought you were going to trap me," I level.

His eyes flash. "Trap you?"

"That I'd fall for you. That I'd stay. That I'd take care of you."

His mouth falls open and I know instantaneously, viscerally, that I'm wrong. "You think that little of me?"

The hurt in his eyes only fuels my anger. Now I'm the bad guy? "You clearly thought that little of me!" I snap.

Suddenly he levers himself off the step and I'm sure the railing is going to rip out of the cement. I stiffen. He tries to speak. "You . . ." But he can't continue. His face pales, he bends, clutches that useless railing. Drops his head, tries to breathe. The dot of blood on his Band-Aid spreads. *Stop!* I scream inside.

Giving up, Jamie sits back down, breathing through flared nostrils like a bull struck with too many banderillas. Finally, he looks up at me. He reaches out his bandaged hand. Beckoning. "Please."

Instead of going up the three seemingly insignificant steps between us, I back away, the matador after the kill. Jamie watches my retreat, quirking his head at me the way he always does. Except this time there's no endearment in the gesture. There's only bewilderment. And hurt.

I can't deal with his hurt right now; I'm still trying to understand mine. Why does this hurt so much?

"Wow," I hear myself say. "It's a good thing I don't love you."

"Magdalen," is all I say to the cabbie.

I feel like a wax figure of myself, as if all my body's faculties are busy processing and can't be diverted to the mundane task of speech. Questions pile up, crowding in, pushing me up against the backseat of this cab, suffocating. I can't finish one thought before another shoves in.

Then this thought, a glaring light scattering the others like roaches: I just walked out on a dying man.

Correction: I just told a dying man it's a good thing I don't love him, and then I walked out on him.

My phone rings. All robot arms, I fish it out of my coat pocket even though I'm not going to answer. I'm not talking to him ever again.

But it's not Jamie. It's Gavin.

"Gavin," I croak.

"Just thought I'd call before the holiday, in case there's anything we need to go over. I'm going to my sister's and she won't let me so much as turn my phone on tomorrow."

What's tomorrow? Then I remember. Thanksgiving.

Thanksgiving! Shit! Connor! "No, yeah, I—I think we're good," I stammer. "I'm working on a—a plan right now, the vouchers thing. I'll send it in a few. A few days, that is."

There's a beat. "You okay?"

"Yeah! Just . . ." *What?* All thought has fled. "Sorry, Gavin, can you hold on one second?"

"Sure."

I lean forward, toward the driver. This I can at least handle. "Excuse me? Sorry, but can you turn around? I need to go to . . ." I can't remember the name of the club. I can't remember anything right now. "What's that club? Over by the castle?"

"The Castle."

"Yeah, by the Oxford castle."

"The Castle."

I huff out a breath. "You know, with the murdery back alley—"

"That's the Castle, love."

Oh. All right, then. My extensive Abbott and Costello training failed me there. "Right, yes, thank you, that's the one." I sit back and try to focus on one thought, just one. It's not working. I've never felt this discombobulated. I've never done drugs, but I imagine this is what a terrible trip feels like. One of those questing nightmares where stairs lead nowhere and doors take you back to places you haven't actually left. I'm trapped in an Escher drawing.

Then, compounding the surreality, I hear my name. Soft. Distant. As if underwater. "Ella? Hello?"

I look down at my phone. "Hi, sorry!" I shout, fumbling it up to my ear. "I—I'm here."

"Listen," Gavin says. "I want you to start thinking about some hires, okay? Especially deputy political director. We need someone young—because we're old and tired—but experienced. Any idea where we could find this unicorn?"

"Let me think about it," I say, thinking, *Why don't you just hire me?* And then I wonder why I think that. Would I really want that job? I thought I was done with the campaign side of politics.

"Who knows," he says. "Maybe I'll just hire you." He laughs. "All right, have a nice holiday. Good luck finding turkey in that country."

He hangs up. I stare at my phone. Was he serious? My phone rings again, startling me so completely that I drop it on the floor of the cab. I shakily retrieve it, noting the caller ID. "I'm so, so, so, so sorry," I answer preemptively.

"She's alive!" Connor does a bad Dr. Frankenstein impression, but there's no mistaking the genuine note of concern in his voice.

"I'm fine, I went to the bathroom and . . ." There's no way I'm dragging him into this story. I wish I could drag myself out of it. "I wasn't feeling well. So I left." Worst lie ever. I should take lessons from Dr. Davenport.

"Why didn't you come find me? I would have walked you home," Connor says. What a good guy. What a handsome, good guy. Connor Whatever-His-Last-Name-Is knows just what to say. "So," he continues, "I'm standing here with Charlie and we're looking at very sad, very abandoned Duchess. Would you like me to bring her by?"

"So you're—you're still at the club?" I start snapping my fingers at the cabbie like a complete asshole. He just looks confused.

"Yeah, we're all still here. Charlie's been texting you."

Dammit! I stop snapping, mute my phone, and tell the cabbie, "Stop! I mean, go! Magdalen! No Castle!" Cavemen got nothing on me.

"But we're almost there, miss."

I can see the alley where they're all waiting just up ahead. "No, I know, I don't want to—just no Castle! Magdalen!"

The cabbie slams on his brakes, begins a three-point turn, and mutters, "All right, all right, don't get your knickers in a twist."

I unmute my phone. Connor is saying, "Ella? Ella, are you there?"

"Sorry, listen, could you ask Charlie to bring my bike back to college?"

I hear murmuring before Connor returns. "Yup, no worries. Are you sure you're—"

"I'm fine. Thanks, Connor. Again, I'm sorry. Have a good—"

"Ella, wait." He chuckles. "You never gave me an answer."

"To what?" I have no clue what he's talking about.

"London? Thanksgiving? You, me, 'fixins'?"

This is not the time, I think. *I can't. I just can't. Maybe another time, when I'm—*

"Ella? It's not a big—"

"Yes, I'd love to."

The moment I say it, the second the words leave my mouth, I want to die. I shut off my phone. I throw it to the side. I look out into the blurry darkness, the rain sheeting down the window of the cab.

Then the tears start.

Soon I can't contain the sobs. The sound ricochets around the cab.

The cabbie peers at me in the rearview. "Cheer up, love," he tries. "Whatever it is, life's too short, yeah?"

LONDON FEELS LIKE a different country. I've become so comfortable in Oxford that only in a new city do I realize how much it's become home to me. London reminds me of Washington, a thriving, pulsing, global metropolis. And yet there are smatterings of quaintness, an unexpected charm that sneaks up on you. *Oh, look, a palace! Oh, look, a double-decker bus! Oh, look, an obsolete-yet-still-iconic call box!* Connor's been to London before, so he's an excellent tour guide. He's also an excellent conversationalist. There have only been a handful of awkward silences between us, which under normal circumstances would be a good sign. But these aren't normal circumstances. There are far too many instances of "Ella, did you hear me?" and me saying "Sorry, what?"

I didn't sleep much last night.

After walking around for hours and building up a solid appetite, we gladly sit down to our dinner at a swanky hotel in Mayfair overlooking Grosvenor Square. It's mostly empty, except for a couple of American tourists and, directly next to us, a family of four. An American mother trying to explain the holiday to her very, very British children.

"But, Mummy, why are we eating turkey? Turkey is for

Christmas," they say. The woman looks to her English husband for assistance. Together they try to answer their adorable children. I imagine myself in her position: British husband, British kids, stranger in a strange land. I'm surprised to find that there's something appealing about the notion. When the husband leans over and kisses her forehead, however, I turn away.

"Ella?" Connor's voice brings me present. Again. The waiter is standing beside me with a tray, holding two glasses of champagne. "The hotel is offering us some complimentary bubbly. Want one?"

"Who are we to refuse?" I say, attempting enthusiasm. We clink glasses. We look into each other's eyes and take a sip. I can tell Connor's having a good time. And I am, too. Really. He's an interesting guy. On our walk, we talked schooling, past jobs, D.C. neighborhoods, restaurants, bars. I think these things, the details that technically define you, are what you give to people in exchange for not talking about the real things.

Connor comes from a good family. His father's a judge and his mother's a surgeon. He's had two ex-girlfriends worth mentioning (I was right), he's impeccably educated, politically moderate, well traveled, well read, fluent in Spanish, likes Ethiopian food, and spends two weeks every summer at the family "cottage" on the Vineyard. His post-Oxford plans are uncertain. As we sip champagne and listen to harp music wafting in from the lobby, Connor describes his dilemma: go back to Washington and make a ton of money or go to India on his own dime and volunteer, becoming "just another white dude mansplaining how to use a water filter and wear a condom." His dismissive tone belies the excited spark I see in his eyes.

"Have you read *Middlemarch*?" I blurt.

"No," he answers, seeming relieved that I decided to speak, taking a breath and a sip of his champagne.

"First of all, you should. Secondly, there's this one part," I begin, but the server interrupts us, dropping down a plate of Thanksgiving. It's a decent effort, but as Bentsen told Quayle in the 1988 vice-presidential debate, "I knew Jack Kennedy and, Senator, you're no Jack Kennedy." Yes, there's turkey, but the potatoes are roasted reds. There's a puddle of pink sauce with the consistency of mint jelly (the cranberry, I'm assuming?) slowly making friends with everything else on the plate, including some unidentifiable wet bread (stuffing?) and, of course, courgettes. Always with the courgettes in this country. It's all topped off with a culturally incongruous bubble of Yorkshire pudding.

"Happy Thanksgiving," Connor says, lifting his glass.

I lift mine and try to maintain eye contact. "Happy Thanksgiving." We smile at each other. I put my glass down without drinking. It's turning my stomach and I seem to have acquired a headache just by looking at it.

He cuts into his turkey. "So, *Middlemarch*?"

"Right! So, the book is, like, eight hundred pages and the main character has been in love—" next to my plate, my phone rings. "Sorry. Thought I'd turned it off." As I pick it up, I glance at the name on the screen. *Mom*.

Connor can see it, too. "Take it," he says.

"It's okay."

"Ella, it's your mother. It's a national holiday. You're not going to at least say hi? Really, I don't mind."

He thinks I'm not answering because I'm trying to be polite. He has no idea. Connor probably talks to his parents all the time. He probably sent them a Thanksgiving cornucopia. Great. Now I have to answer it.

"Hi, Mom."

"Hi, honey!" she bleats, obviously surprised I picked up. There's a suspended moment of silence. "Well, Happy Thanksgiving!"

I tear off a piece of Yorkshire pudding and pop it in my mouth. "Happy Thanksgiving to you. Are you going to Aunt Mal's today?"

"Yes, soon. And how are you? Are you celebrating Thanksgiving over there? You sound like you're eating something."

"I am. I'm eating turkey at a hotel in Mayfair. Which is a sentence I never thought I'd say."

"You're not all alone, are you?"

Her suddenly worried tone instantly grates. I look at Connor's handsome head bent over his plate. "No, actually," I answer, because what the hell, "I'm on a date." Connor's head lifts and he smiles at me.

"Ooh!" she exclaims instantly, just-add-water excited. I can sense across an ocean all the questions lining up in her head. I never talk about my love life. If that's what you'd even call it. "What's his name, is he English, what—"

"His name is Connor, he's American, he's a doctor." Connor raises a brow at the inaccuracy. I wave my hand; whatever, close enough.

"He sounds perfect," Mom breathes. "I didn't know you were seeing someone, El. You never tell me—"

"We're not 'seeing each other,' Mom. Unless you mean naked." Connor almost chokes on his champagne.

"Oh, for cripes sake." Mom sighs, well acquainted with my irreverence. Of all the traits my mother possesses, prudery is actually, surprisingly, not one of them. She works in a medical office, after all.

"You know me. No strings, just sex." Connor leans back in his chair with his champagne and a huge smile.

"Eleanor! That mouth of yours."

"What a coincidence, he said the same thing last night!"

She tsks at me. "I know you're just joshing, but you be nice to him. You know how you can be."

Yes. I do. I hurt men. I leave men. I lead them on and then walk away. *It's a good thing I don't love you* crashes through my head like a buffalo stampede. I ignore it. As much as one can ignore a buffalo stampede. "He's fine," I grit, my mood souring. "He can handle himself." A misplaced flash of anger directs itself at my mother, and I try to dial it back. It's not fair to blame her. I'm twenty-four years old. I need to be over this.

The bubbly suddenly seems like a good idea, after all. I take a large sip and, lightening my tone, say, "Look, we're both leaving at the end of the year, going our separate ways. It's stupid to start a relationship." I almost forget who I'm talking about, but Connor gives me a cheeky thumbs-up, like he heartily approves, and I try to smile.

"Well, don't be afraid to make the most of it," she lilts. I repress a sigh. Here comes the lesson. "It's like that fella says. You know, 'Tis better to have lost your love—no, wait. What is it? 'Tis better to—"

She's attempting poetry? Really? "''Tis better to have loved and lost than never to have loved at all,' Mom."

"Yes it is, yes it is. And he was right, too. Believe you me. I should know." She goes quiet, then sighs. "The holidays always make it worse." Her sudden sadness guts me. It also irritates me, which is unfair. I take another sip of champagne as she asks, "Who wrote that again?"

Who did write that? Before I can finish the thought, the answer comes to me, as does a tightness in my throat. I swallow the bubbly. "Tennyson. Alfred, Lord Tennyson, Mom."

"Right, right. Listen, honey, I need to leave for Mal's. They say it might snow and I don't want to be on the road if it does. Say hi to Connor for me. I love you."

"Love you, too," I reply. I wish it weren't so automatic a response, but I can honestly say it's not a lie. I do love her. In my way. Whatever that is. However I love.

I hang up and look at the phone. "My mom says hi."

We take a moment to regroup. We both take a few bites and eat in silence. Finally, Connor says, "So, an eight-hundred-page book that I have to read . . ."

"Right." I take a breath. I could just drop it at this point, but something compels me to continue. "So, the main character's been in love with this guy for basically all eight hundred pages, even though she was married to this other guy. Then that guy dies, but she still can't be with the guy she's always loved because her late husband put it in his will that if she marries him—he's a starving-artist type—she'll be destitute, because all the money her late husband left her would have to be forfeited."

"What a dick," Connor observes, forking a potato.

"You have no idea. But, finally, as the love of her life is about to walk away for the last time, Dorothea—that's the girl—finally breaks down and decides, screw it, and leaves everything behind to be with him."

"Why?"

I look at him. Why? "Because love." Connor takes another bite. I can feel the rambling coming on. I'm powerless to stop it. "It's raining and storming and he's about to leave and she just starts sobbing. She realizes in that moment love has a cost. And she knows that she's going to have to figure out what that cost is. And that's exactly what Dorothea says. 'I will learn what everything costs.' End of chapter."

Connor nods, brings the champagne to his lips. "Because she'll have to be poor to be with him."

I pause. "Well, yes, but it's also a metaphor." I take a big bite of turkey and continue talking anyway. "See, Dorothea never really lets herself feel anything. She's pious and thoughtful and she's always doing things for the betterment of humanity, but that just means that she never gets too close to anything really important. Like, personally important. The distance protects her. I mean, you can't hurt that much if you haven't lost that much, right?"

Connor chews on this. "Right, okay."

"But it's a cosmic joke! Because we're going to lose it all anyway. There's no protection! There's only death! That's the cost!"

Connor stares at the tablecloth for a moment while I breathe, trying to muzzle the crazy. He smiles sheepishly up at me. "Sorry. The last book I really understood was *The Hungry, Hungry Caterpillar*. I'm terrible at analyzing literature."

I move the turkey around in my mouth. "I'm beginning to think I am, too." I sigh. I pause for a second, then smile. "This is about India. You and India. You'll learn what everything costs. That's the point." He nods pleasantly. I turn back to my plate, thinking about Dorothea, about *Middlemarch,* about the awful explanation I just gave. I wish I could talk to Jamie about this. He'd get it. What am I saying? There's a reason it's his favorite book. He already gets it. Deeply. Somatically.

"You know," Connor says, "your conversation with your mom . . . I've never had a no-strings, friends-with-benefits kind of relationship. Maybe I should try it." He's teasing, yes, but he's also testing the waters. Here I am thinking about love and death and cost, and Connor's thinking about getting laid. I don't blame him. Hell, I wish I could be thinking about it, too.

I push back from the table and ball up my napkin, wondering belatedly what, exactly, I'm doing. I dig in my purse for money as I find myself saying, "Connor, if I were going to have another no-strings, friends-with-benefits thing with anyone, it would definitely be with you. I mean, look at you. But I'm not." Then I add, sounding weirdly surprised, "I'm going to leave."

He looks mortified. "Ella, I didn't mean—wait, stop, I'm so sorry—"

I throw a fifty-pound note on the table, my hand shaking slightly. "No, no, it's not you. Trust me, it's so not you. There's something I need to . . . attend to."

He relaxes slightly. We look at each other. "You mean someone?" he asks. Reluctantly, I nod. He grins. "What'll we tell your mother?"

We both chuckle, happy to relieve the tension. I pause. "This was lovely. You're lovely. I'm sorry, Connor."

"Don't be," he says, a little too easily. His jaw tenses as he adds charitably, "He's a lucky guy."

I squeeze Connor's shoulder on the way past and head out into the new night, thinking, *Jamie is the furthest thing from lucky I've ever known.*

CHAPTER 19

How many loved your moments of glad grace,
And loved your beauty with love false or true,
But one man loved the pilgrim soul in you,
And loved the sorrows of your changing face . . .
William Butler Yeats, "When You Are Old," 1891

Jamie doesn't seem surprised to see me on his stoop. He opens the door (I knocked this time) and steps back, gesturing me in. He's wearing flannel pajama bottoms and a ratty Christ Church College T-shirt. I've never seen him in clothes like this. In my experience, he's either dressed like he's just stepped out of a photo shoot or he's naked. As I walk past him, I notice that his coloring is off. He somehow looks thinner than he did yesterday, hollowed out.

He silently leads me into the kitchen, crossing to the sink. I hover at the island. He pops the tab on the electric kettle, the British assumption of tea. Then he turns back around and we look at each other.

"How are you feeling?" I ask.

He shrugs, crossing his arm over his stomach, rubbing his other forearm. "I believe Happy Thanksgiving is in order.

Happy? Is that how you say it?"

"Yes. It is. Thank you."

We're stiff together. Formal. For the first time, I feel more English than American. I watch my hand run along the island's marble top, studying the white and gray and black veins. "So, I'm sorry."

"As am I."

I look up at him. He's looking at the floor. "For how I re-acted," I say.

He looks up at me. "I'm sorry for everything." We assess each other, these people we thought we knew. His eyes tell me that the simple apology is enough for now, and I agree. The problem is, now I want to go to him, hug him, hold him. But I stay where I am. I don't know who we are to each other anymore.

The kettle begins to hum, heating up.

"Will you tell me the story?" I ask.

Four years ago, Oliver was diagnosed with multiple myeloma at the age of twenty-one. Two years after that, he died. Although there can be a genetic component to the disease, Jamie says it's rare, and he had been tested when Oliver needed possible stem-cell donors and his results were clean, so he didn't think he needed to worry. Within a year of Oliver's death, Jamie—then in Cambridge and helping a friend with her doctoral research in biology—got a blood test. This is how he found out. Jamie's case is just as aggressive as Oliver's was, but was caught earlier. He explains that he immediately began treatment, doing what Oliver had done: stem-cell replacement therapy. This entailed a few rounds of chemo, the harvesting of his own cells, and an implantation procedure that required him to stay in a hospital, completely isolated, for fear of his contracting an infection, for a month. It bought him a year of remission.

The day I arrived in Oxford happened to be the day Jamie

found out the myeloma had come back. He went to the Varsity Club for a drink on the rooftop, met a blond distraction, took her for fish and chips at "the best restaurant in Oxford," and found himself running into a jet-lagged Ella from Ohio.

The kettle bubbles, the hissing escalates. I have to lean over the island to hear Jamie's low voice.

He explains his decision to pull away from me a week ago. He's doing an eight-week round of "maintenance" chemo before deciding, in December, whether he's going to try stem-cell replacement again. He was two rounds into this treatment and losing the ability to hide the effects. He was tired all the time and he wasn't reliably keeping his food down and his hair was beginning to thin. He worried he might become impotent. He asked me for a month break, because that's how long he had left in treatment.

Jamie knows everything about this disease and its cycles. He lived through it with Oliver and now he's being forced to live through it himself. He's a pro. He's orchestrated his treatment the way he wants to have it: in-home, on his schedule. Of course, having money helps. He can pay a nurse to come at night so that as soon as the IV comes out, he can go right to sleep. He can have her come on a Sunday, for instance, so that he can get through his class the following day before feeling the effects.

Jamie, whom I always saw as spontaneous and haphazard, is actually a planner of the highest order. He puts my abilities to shame.

The kettle's automatic shutoff pops, loud as a gunshot. Tightly wound, both of us jump. But instead of lifting the kettle off its base and making tea, Jamie just stands there, back against the refrigerator, looking at the floor. "I suppose you want to know why I didn't tell you," he says.

I don't, actually. I already know why he didn't tell me. I figured it out during my sleepless night, while walking around London with Connor, on the interminable bus ride back to Oxford tonight. "You thought we'd be over before you ever had to explain anything. Which would have worked out perfectly if not for . . . how it worked out." It's the closest I can come to revealing how I feel about him. That this has become more for me, surprisingly more, than what we shook on back in the Buttery.

Jamie shakes his head. "I wish I could say that were true. I'm afraid it's more selfish than that." He looks up at me. I hold my breath. "With you, I was able to pretend I wasn't sick. The disease didn't exist. It's pathetic, really." His crisp voice cracks like overdone toast. "I convinced myself I deserved you. Not just because of the last eighteen months, but because of the last four years. And because of the future, too, I suppose. You were my prize. My gift. My last chance to feel . . ." He pauses, and I begin filling in the blank. Lust? Excitement? Heat? He settles on, "This . . . again. One last time." He quickly turns to the counter, where a box of Kleenex sits, plucks a few tissues out, and turns back to me. I didn't notice he was crying. "Christ, Ella, I'm so sorry." He holds the tissues out to me and that's when I realize my face is wet. I'm the one who's crying.

"But you're not actually dying," I say.

He quirks his head at me, as he always does. "What do you mean?"

"I mean, if you're in treatment and you were in remission once, you're not actually dying. You're fighting." It just doesn't make sense to me. How someone so full of life can have it leaking away.

"There are stages," he says, "But this particular disease is a life sentence. There's no cure." He rattles off platitudes to make me feel better. Glass half full, it's not over till it's over, don't throw in the towel, et cetera. "The trick," Jamie says, "is to bounce from treatment to treatment, like playing the net in a tennis match. Keep the ball in play, racket against racket. Just don't let it get past you or it's game over. Stay in the volley long enough and hope for a breakthrough. A winning shot. That's the strategy."

He sees the question in my eyes: If that's the strategy, how is it that Oliver is dead?

"He was more advanced than I. Also, the years since Oliver was diagnosed have seen an exponential advancement in treatment." He pauses, swallows. "If Oliver had been diagnosed when I was, if the order had been reversed, he might still be alive." The color suddenly drains from his face. His eyes go glassy, and just as I'm about to hand him a tissue, I realize that what's happening to Jamie isn't emotional. "Will you excuse me?" He slips out of the kitchen, down the hall, and I hear the bathroom door close. Then the sound of retching.

My own stomach clenches. My face heats. We've done everything—everything—together, but this somehow feels too intimate. I try to breathe. Tears start escaping again. My hand comes to my eyes, then my mouth, then my chest, in an attempt, I think, to keep all of my feelings in, unsure which way they might escape.

I focus on what Jamie just said. If Oliver had been diagnosed last, he might still be alive. Which means the reverse is also true: if Jamie had been diagnosed first, he would be dead. I would have never met him. I would have come to Oxford, lived at Oxford, studied at Oxford, drunk at Oxford, had sex at Oxford, but not had Jamie's Oxford. The idea that I could have missed him in this life by a matter of years, two small insignificant years, an infinitesimal moment in the history of the earth, a geological blink, paralyzes me.

A toilet flushes, a door opens, socked feet pad down the hallway, and Jamie returns, his previously pale face now blotchily flushed. "Sorry," he says.

I rapidly shake my head. "Please. Do you want to sit?"

"Yes, quite. Thank you." We move into the drawing room and he says, "I'm better in the mornings." We settle on opposite ends of the couch. I curl my legs up under me. Jamie leans forward, props his elbows on his knees. I stare at his profile, small in this vast house. He looks so isolated, so alone. "What about your parents?" I ask.

"What about them?"

I don't actually know. It just feels like I should ask about them. He never talks about them, won't talk about them. How did things deteriorate to this point? "This must be killing them," I say. He doesn't confirm or deny. A horrible thought occurs to me. "They know you're sick, right?"

"Yes."

"Well, are they involved——"

"Ella," Jamie says, "the room is starting to spin. Might we continue this tomorrow?"

"Of course."

"I'll call you when I'm awake."

"No, you won't."

He nods tightly, like he was expecting this. "I promise. I won't disappear again. We have more to——"

"You won't call me because I'm staying right here." I can't immediately decipher what I see in his eyes. Relief? Regret? Hope? Fear? Maybe a bit of everything. "Do you want to go upstairs?" I ask softly.

He slowly shakes his head. "I like sleeping here. I save my bedroom for when I feel well." His eyes lock on mine and I have a sudden flash of the last time we were together, in that very bedroom upstairs. Was that only a week ago? "It limits negative associations. The drawing room being the hospital room keeps the bedroom a bedroom."

I stare at him. "You really have it all figured out, don't you?" He leans back, pivots half toward me. His eyes start to close. I settle into the couch, and reach over, taking his legs. He opens sleepy eyes. "Here," I say softly, "stretch out." He sighs in relief and pleasure at my touch.

"You can sleep upstairs. Take any shirt you want. The remote for the telly's in the nightstand drawer." He drifts off.

He looks peaceful, like the carved sculpture atop the knight's tomb in the Lincoln library, the sarcophagus. His long, tapered fingers entwined over his stomach; his head centered on a throw pillow. I determinedly push the tomb image away.

I stare blankly at his feet. Long. Thin. The perfect punctuation mark to his allover elegance. I've never looked at his feet before. How is that possible? I find myself thinking of things he's said. Seemingly insignificant things, like how he's going to donate his house, or suggesting I go punting in the spring and not including himself. I realize now, with a sickening lurch of my stomach, that he isn't betting on being here.

Questions start descending upon me. How does this change things? Can I still be with him knowing all this? How could I not? And what happens next? I'm obviously still leaving in June, but how does this work for the next six months? For instance, I'm traveling in December. Am I really just going to leave, knowing he's sick back in Oxford? Do I even want to leave now?

As Jamie's breathing evens, and the grandfather clock in the foyer ticks distantly, I try to take stock of everything that has led me here, to this city, to this man. To this. My Once-in-a-Lifetime Experience.

CHAPTER 20

James Thomson, "Mr. MacCall at Cleveland Hall," 1866

"Ella?"

I'm in a dream and I hear my name in chocolate-covered-caramel tones.

"Sorry, but my leg's quite gone to sleep."

I crack open my eyes and see a blurred Jamie on the other side of the couch. We've tangled into each other in the night. "Sorry," I mutter. I shift so he can extricate his leg.

As I wake more fully, I notice that he looks almost completely normal. As if one night of sleep has magically cured him. I realize that this is the reason I never noticed he was sick; if he avoided me on certain days, I really couldn't have known. I open my mouth to say good morning, but Jamie's smile fades and he murmurs, "I wasn't trying to trap you."

I take a second. "I know." I have to clear the morning out of my throat before continuing. "I knew it when I said it."

Jamie tentatively reaches out and rests his hand on my ankle. "Please understand, you are no part of this. You and I are separate from this."

I digest this. In one sense, he's absolutely right. What if he had continued to hide his illness? We might have fizzled out. I might have left on June 11 none the wiser. This is his illness, not ours.

"Nothing has to change," he says. "Except that I don't have to lie anymore." He grins wryly. "We can continue on. If you want. Nothing has to change," he reiterates.

I think of something he said the other night, that this—me—was his last hurrah. I realize that I feel the same way. Before I go back to my life, before I continue on my preordained path, my plan . . . I want this. Whatever this is. My first instinct was to run away from it, but now it's the opposite. Being with him seems imperative now. Like being given the opportunity to hold time in your hand.

At my silence, Jamie swallows. "I understand, obviously, if you don't want any part of this. If you don't want to continue the intimacy with which . . ." He pauses. "Perhaps we might be friends?" He looks down at his hand on my ankle like he's memorizing it. Like it might disappear before his eyes.

"I don't want to be your friend."

He removes his hand, nodding reflexively.

"I want to be your girlfriend."

He looks up at me. "Truly?"

"Whaddaya say?" I stick out my hand. It's how we do things.

He takes my hand, beaming, and gently pulls me toward him. "It's a plan."

AFTER SOME BREAKFAST (which, for Jamie, was just coffee and two slices of thick-slab bacon on toast) we're lingering at the kitchen table, Jamie looking like he could fall asleep again. I'm back to thinking. Specifically, about the trip I have planned in December. I still really want to go, but am I being selfish? It would be amazing if he could come with me, but it's over the holidays and surely he has plans. And would he even be well enough to travel?

Jamie breaks the silence. "Tuppence for your thoughts?"

I shake my head. "I was just thinking . . . about a trip I'm supposed to take over break."

He perks up. "Where are you off to, then? Back to America for the vac?"

"No, actually. Europe."

"All of it? Really?" I throw a bit of bacon at his head and we both smile. "Where exactly are you going?"

"Everywhere."

"You've obviously put rather a significant amount of thought into this."

"Considering I've never been anywhere, everywhere is a per-fectly reasonable answer."

"Hang on," Jamie says, straightening. "What do you mean you've never been anywhere?"

"Ella from Ohio's never been outside of the good ol' U.S. of A. Until she arrived at Heathrow on September twenty-eighth, that is."

Jamie now sits ramrod straight. "Are you taking the piss?"

"Nope."

"But you seem so . . ."

"Worldly?" I suggest, putting on an air. "Sophisticated?"

"Opinionated."

It feels so good to laugh with each other again. "Do you want to hear the plan?" I ask.

"Absolutely."

I'm excited again. I tuck my leg underneath me and resituate myself. "All right, on December twentieth, I'm taking the Eurostar to Paris, where I'll spend Christmas, and then I'm training to Brussels for three days—"

"Brussels? Why Brussels?"

I shrug. "It's Brussels."

Jamie's mouth forms a confused moue. It's the same look I'd give him if he said he was coming to America and wanted to see Ohio. I persist. "Then I'm heading to Amsterdam for New Year's, spending four nights—"

Jamie interrupts again. "What happened to the rest of France?"

"I don't want to rent a car. Too expensive."

Jamie makes the same face again. I persist again. "Then from Amsterdam, I'm doing the overnight train to Venice—"

"Hold on, you're going to be that close to Bruges and you're not going?" I huff, growing exasperated. "Tell me you're going to Ghent, at the very least?" I glare at him. He shrugs and says, "Sorry, but it just seems a waste. Hilary Term doesn't begin until January eighteenth, you have almost a month, and you're going to simply take trains back and forth between major cities, which all have the same McDonald's and the same cheap T-shirt shops and fake gelato and Irish pubs called the Blarney Stone and everyone you meet speaks English?"

A silence hangs in the air, that anticipatory moment right before the curtain goes up at the theater. And then I say it. "Well, if you have such strong opinions about it, you should come with me."

Without missing a beat, Jamie reaches across the table and grabs his phone, tapping the screen and studying it. "My final treatment is on December the sixteenth. I'll most likely need three days to recover." He looks from his calendar right at me.

"Ah. What a coincidence. That's the twentieth. Shall we leave then?"

My heart quickens. "For where?"

"Everywhere. Or was it anywhere?"

That pang of guilt comes round the bend again. "Jamie, hold on. We're acting like you're fine, like everything's normal. I think, just to be safe—"

He leans in to me across the table. "Nothing. Changes. That was the deal."

I rub my forehead, wanting so badly to believe him. But something else occurs to me. "Also, there's no way I can afford the Jamie Davenport version of this trip." We've never discussed money, and Jamie doesn't flaunt it, but it's clear he has it, that it comes from somewhere other than his meager JRF stipend. The classic car (which he's said he's had since he was eighteen), the ability to renovate the town house however he wants, the wine habit. The velvet trousers.

He waves me off. "I'll take care of it."

I bristle. "No. Absolutely not. Are you insane?"

"What?"

"I'm not taking your money."

"Who said anything about taking it? I'm sharing it. 'Can't take it with you,' and all that."

"Stop it," I snap. "That's not funny."

Now Jamie really looks at me. I'm not ready for jokes about his illness. I swallow, soften a bit. "Look, no one's ever paid for me, for anything. If you're going to come with me, we're going to do it on my budget. I won't be, like, some . . . kept woman."

Jamie looks at me. I'm gratified to see that he gets it. He's not rolling his eyes or belittling what's clearly a matter of pride for me. He's just nodding slightly, thinking. Before he even opens his mouth, I know a negotiation is coming. "If any of the plans you've already made can't be refunded, I'll pay for that."

So far, so fair. "All right."

"We'll take the Aston. A car's the only way to access some of the more remote hill towns. You can pay for petrol?"

I nod. "Done."

"And I get five trump cards."

"What does that mean?"

"Five instances where, if you're whingeing about how much something costs—hotels, experiences—I get to trump it and we must do it. Because there are some things you'll regret not doing when you had the chance, and I can't have that."

I narrow my eyes. "Three trump cards."

"Am I a genie?"

"The number three has a nice fairy-tale symmetry to it, don't you think?"

He snorts. "Deal. And one more thing. If I want to do something for you along the way, buy you something small, take you to a nice dinner, you'll let me because I'm your boyfriend now and that's the sort of special preferment boyfriends are afforded."

I'm unable to contain my smile, excitement bursting through me like a supernova. But almost immediately it's doused. I peer at him. "Don't you need to be with your family for the holidays?" A whisper-like sound comes from the foyer, followed by the gentle slapping of something landing on the floor. Before I can question what it is, Jamie stands, unconcerned, and walks out of the room. I call out after him, "Because we could leave after—"

"I really have no need to be with my family at present."

I chew on this as he reenters the kitchen carrying a pile of mail. I persist. "But you're . . . you know."

"Dying?"

I give him a reproachful look and he drops back into his chair and starts sorting the mail into three neat piles. "All I'm saying is if my mom lived in the same country and I didn't show up for Christmas, I'd hear about it for the rest of my life."

"Yes, but if you knew the rest of your life was to be significantly abbreviated, I should think you could bear it."

He actually has a point. Sarcastic, macabre, but a point nonetheless. Eventually I want to discuss his family, especially his father, but not right now. Right now I'm too excited. The possibility of traveling with him is a dream come true that I didn't even know I had dreamed.

Jamie drops the last piece of mail on what's clearly the discard stack and stands, going to the counter for more coffee. It's a very ornate card to be so casually thrown onto the discard pile. It's square, gilded around the edges, and made out of a thick cream-colored card stock. There's calligraphy on the front. I pick it up as Jamie says, "Would you like a spot more?"

"Huh?" I turn the card over in my hands.

"Coffee." Then, in a bad truck-stop diner accent, "'Warm up on the joe, darlin'?'"

I smile but don't look up. The card I'm holding is a final invitation. A reminder invitation. To the very ball Charlie mentioned when we were trying to help Maggie: the Blenheim Ball. The don't-tease-me-with-something-I-can't-have Blenheim Ball that's happening in two weeks. "Jamie?"

My voice has him side-eyeing me suspiciously. "Am I correct in assuming my name is going to be followed by a request of sorts?"

I hold up the card. "This invitation, it's to the Blenheim Ball. I've actually heard of it, and, well . . . I've never been to a ball. And actually—"

"You can't imagine how much I detest these things," he interrupts.

I soldier on. "But it's a palace. And I've never been to a palace."

Jamie waves his cup dismissively. A drop splashes over onto the floor. He uses a socked toe to wipe it, and says, "We shall see many palaces. Wait until you see Versailles. In fact, let's go there first. We'll start in Paris, take the train out, I know a lovely little inn in the village there."

"I want to go."

"And we shall. The weather might be crap, but—"

"Jamie!" He finally looks up at me. I hold the postcard up with fervor, like it's a map to some buried treasure. "I want. To go. To the ball."

He looks appalled. "Why?"

"Because I've always wanted to!" This is probably true. I guess. I mean, who doesn't want to go to a ball? "I'm from Ohio!"

Jamie shakes his head, sitting back down. "Ella, these things are dreadful. Awful rich people affirming to each other how awful and rich they are."

"Right! Great!"

"And my parents will be there." He says it like a warning.

"So?" Jamie sighs, looks at the floor. I go coy. "Unless . . . you don't want them to meet me."

"Oh, you are a sly one. You know it's not that."

I switch effortlessly into wheedling political-operative mode. "Are things so bad with them that you can't fulfill the simple dream of your American girlfriend"—I stutter slightly over the word—"because your parents might be on the other side of the room?" Jamie levels a look at me. I push it further. "Either tell me why it's impossible to be in the same room as them or take me to the ball. Your choice."

Jamie's jaw flexes. After a moment, he sighs. "Fine. We'll go."

"Really?!" I'm surprised by his response and even more surprised to find that I'm genuinely excited.

"Just let me—" But I'm jumping into his lap, coffee splashing everywhere. Jamie lets out a laugh as I kiss his face all over.

"Thank you, Jamie. Thank you so much."

Jamie adopts a princely affectation. "'Twill be my sincerest pleasure to escort you, madam." Then he drops it, looks at me seriously. "But do understand, I may find it necessary to leave early." I tilt my head at him. "If I'm not feeling well I won't stay there making a spectacle of myself, providing grist for the gossip mills." I can understand that. These are the things I need to start considering. Jamie tips his head back slightly, eyes thoughtful. "You know, it might be wise for you to bring along a companion, just in case."

"Excellent idea!" I say, a bit too quickly and loudly.

Jamie looks at me, suspicious or confused, I'm not sure which. "Yes, a buffer of sorts."

I bite my lip. It's time. "Can there be more than one buffer?"

Jamie looks imperiously down his nose at me. "How many buffers?"

"I know three buffers that would make some seriously questionable, Faustian-level bargains to go."

"I knew it!" he says with a smile, oddly triumphant. "I knew you had some ulterior motive."

"No, I really do want to go, it's just that—"

His smile broadens. "I'll put the tickets on my parents' tab."

"Are you sure?"

"Absolutely. The shock of my attendance will cause them to buy everything at the silent auction just to gloat. A case of Rothschild, a chef's-table dinner at the Dorchester, yet another round of golf at St. Andrews my father will never use. We're single-handedly contributing to the prosperity of the foundation."

I throw my arms around him.

He mutters into my hair, almost to himself, "I ought to see if Cecelia will be coming."

"Cecelia?" Even now, after everything, her name still doesn't sit as well with me as I would like. Which I'm not proud of.

"Yes. I'm sure my father took care of it, but I'll ask."

I pull back and look at him. "Why would your father take care of Cecelia?"

"He does whatever he can to be kind to her."

"But why?"

Jamie quirks his head at me. "Because Cecelia was Oliver's fiancée."

CHAPTER 21

What is he buzzing in my ears?
"Now that I come to die,
"Do I view the world as a vale of tears?"
Ah, reverend sir, not I!
Robert Browning, "Confessions," 1864

Blenheim Palace is mind-bogglingly big. Trying to understand how the massive horseshoe-shaped structure used to be—and a portion of it still is—a home, makes my brain hurt. Yes, America has its great mansions, but they're provincial by comparison. Cute colonial attempts. Summer cottages. Cabins in the woods. And we're only twelve miles from Oxford. It was a fifteen-minute drive. A drive in a sleek, black Mercedes limo.

With Jamie's family crest on the door.

Which he tried to block from view by standing in front of it and insisting, "No, please, by all means, after you."

Today is a "good day." He woke up feeling normal, much to his chagrin. I know he would have loved to have an excuse to cancel.

But damn, does he look good in his tux.

Everyone looks good. The gowns aren't sparkly and flashy, they're understated, the material thick and sumptuous, the cut impeccable. The suits are throwbacks to double-breasted days of yore. As we follow the crowd toward the front door, two giant braziers on each side dart firelight across the guests. Maggie slips her hand into mine and squeezes.

We were in Hall when I told Maggie, Charlie, and Tom that Jamie and I were officially together, and they were happy for me. When I told them I got us tickets to the ball, they had a collective psychotic break. Tom fell to the floor in a giraffe-like sprawl, Charlie stood and slowly ascended to the tabletop, arms outstretched, singing "Jerusalem," and Maggie just started quietly weeping.

I look over at Charlie in his tails and the Salvador Dalí mustache he grew (or attempted to grow) for the occasion. Tom, in a top hat that adds an unnecessary eight inches to his height, bounces on the balls of his feet, and just misses bumping the little blue-haired biddy in front of him. His attentions are elsewhere. At present he's eye-darting Maggie, glancing at her and then quickly looking away before being caught. She looks like Veronica Lake, decked out in a floor-length, cowl-neck, ruby satin dress. Her hair's dyed platinum blond for the night and styled in long 1940s waves cascading over one shoulder. When Tom first saw her, his eyes goggled and he yelled, "Oi, Mags, you're gorgeous! You look nothing like yourself!" Charlie and I both swatted him and he turned immediately silent. He kept an openmouthed stare going all the way to the limo before seeming to decide—after giving her a hand to help her into it—never to look at her again. Until now. His eye darting looks slightly repentant. And confused. I catch Charlie's eye and we share a hopeful grin. So far, so good.

I'm in a vintage yellow gown that Charlie picked out for me

and Maggie did my hair in some intricate pin-curl updo. She also did a smoky-eye thing that I would have never attempted on my own and can't stop looking at in any mirror I pass. *I* definitely look nothing like myself.

We enter the palace and I have to remind myself to breathe.

It's decorated for Christmas. The marble floors are like glass, reflecting light from two twenty-foot Christmas trees standing sentry in the entry hall and the garlands strung across the gallery railing. The soft orange glow emanating from the vaulted and frescoed ceiling forty feet above bounces off the stone columns and refracts in the paned windows with hushed luminescent whispers.

Everywhere I turn there's another statue, another piece of art, another tapestry, bookcase, alcove, mural. Jamie guides us through the rooms and hallways (the ones we're allowed in) as if he grew up here, pointing out historical architectural details, recounting the palace's ancient scandals, hinting that one or two of his ancestors may have been key players in them. It's unnerving how unaffected he is by all of this, how easily he moves in this setting. Servants open the door for him, take his jacket, hand him champagne, and Jamie moves through them by rote. Conversely, I've turned into a parrot, compulsively squawking, "Thank you! Thank you! You don't have to do that, thank you!" He wears his tux like a second skin; his posture straightens, his head tips back slightly. He's like an actor slipping into character.

Jamie's words come back to me: it's just awful rich people affirming how awful and rich they are. As someone who wasn't raised with money, or even remotely near it, I'm simultaneously awed by this kind of wealth and also deeply uncomfortable with it. As much as I may choose to ignore it, Jamie is a product of this system. I'm only now realizing just how much. And yet he's chosen to toil away in academia, researching, writing, teaching.

I wonder if this is the source of some of his familial tension. Maybe they want him to have done something more . . . fitting with his life? Something more profitable? Prestigious? Where I come from, ending up with a Ph.D, teaching poetry at Oxford, living in an inherited Victorian town house would be inconceivable; but maybe that life is just as inconceivable where Jamie comes from, only for the opposite reason: it's a failing.

Jamie must see some of this transpiring on my face, because he peers at me and asks, "You all right?" We're alone now. Maggie, Charlie, and Tom have wandered off to find a bar and we're scouting for a place to situate ourselves.

I turn to answer him, but my eyes are drawn to a middle-aged woman about ten feet behind him. She's wearing one of the more colorful gowns, a paisley floral pattern. She also holds a fan. Like, an actual fan. Like it's *Gone with the Wind* and she's about to tap someone flirtatiously on the shoulder with it. She drips money like a leaky faucet.

"Don't look now," I murmur lowly, "but the very definition of 'awful and rich' is standing right behind—oh shit, she's looking at us. Let's go."

"Steady on, chin up," Jamie murmurs, a smile playing at his lips. "I'm sure whoever she is, she's simply thinking how stunning you look tonight." I lean in to kiss him, but the woman heads decisively toward us. She winks at me (odd), then breaks into a run, and attacks Jamie, grabbing him around the waist. Jamie's face registers shock, but he looks down at the bejeweled fingers entwined on his stomach and smiles. He quickly spins, enveloping the woman in a hug. They pull apart and she clasps his cheeks between her hands. She gazes into his eyes, her face lit from within by that combination of love, pride, and joy that only exists in one person: a mother looking at her child.

"Gorgeous boy," she breathes.

"Beautiful mum," he says back, clearly echoing some child-hood game.

Looking at her love for him is like looking directly into the sun.

She steps back like a general, assessing her son fully. "You're looking quite well, my love, quite well." She pokes his stomach. "I can't tell you how delighted I am that you came."

Whatever I was expecting Jamie's mother to be like—their relationship to be like—it wasn't this. At all. I'm so confused I've been standing here with my mouth wide open since she grabbed him.

She eyes me. "Shall you introduce me, or must I do everything myself?"

"Yes, of course." Jamie touches my shoulder. "Eleanor Durran, may I present my mother, Antonia Davenport."

She takes my hand with gusto. "Eleanor! How lovely. You don't often hear that name anymore."

I smile. "That's why I go by Ella."

She chuckles. "Family name?"

"Eleanor Roosevelt," I answer. "My father had delusions of grandeur."

Jamie chimes in. "You'll appreciate this, Mother, Ella actually saw you standing—"

I grab the sentence out of his mouth. "Standing over there and wanted to tell you that I absolutely love your dress!" I smile hugely and quick-flash my eyes to Jamie, silently threatening death if he contradicts my story.

"Likewise," she says, still smiling. It's as if she's physically incapable of not smiling. It's natural, real, written on her face with caring penmanship. There's a mischievous quality to her, a whimsy that I've seen in her son when he's at his happiest. It's infectious. "That yellow is extraordinary. In truth, it was the first thing I noticed, and I thought to myself, 'Who is that stunning light of a woman standing there?' And then I realized you were standing with my son." She pokes Jamie's stomach again. "Well done, you!"

Jamie grabs her wrist and peers at the fan hanging off it. "And what is this?"

"Oh, Jamie, I've discovered the most exquisite escape hatch." Her wide eyes and open enthusiasm strip thirty years from her face. "If I find I'm unable to extricate myself from a particularly dire conversation, I simply wave this and insist that I must get some air. Menopause is truly the most miraculous excuse."

Jamie lifts an eyebrow. "Is it? I must try it sometime, then."

Her eyes flit behind me and she calls, "William! Come say hello!"

I look over my shoulder and find the man who stormed out of Jamie's office, looking as though he has been forcibly stuffed into a tuxedo. A rugged, feral man tortured into elegance. I smile at him as he approaches. He barely returns it, the side of his mouth spasmodically jerking to the left. I don't wait for an introduction, extending my hand gamely. "Ella Durran. Nice to meet you, sir."

He takes it, brief but firm. Unisex. He's not changing his greeting because I'm a woman or, more, his son's girlfriend. I can respect that. "William Davenport," he intones, low and rumbly, like a cartoon lion. "I had heard my son was dating a beautiful American girl," he continues, trying to be endearing, but like his tux, this, too, seems unnatural. He doesn't look at me.

"I had heard those rumors, too, sir, but I didn't let them stop me." Antonia laughs, Jamie smiles, but William gives me nothing more than a tight smirk. He glances at his son. "Jamie." I can't tell if it's a greeting or a reprimand.

"Father," Jamie replies, suddenly austere, as if he's mimicking

William.

Antonia steps in. "Eleanor, have you ever been to Scotland?"

"No, ma'am."

She turns to Jamie. "Invite her at Christmas! We'd adore having her."

"Most kind of you, Mother, but actually"—Jamie softens his voice—"Ella and I are going on holiday." A flicker of disappointment crosses Antonia's face and she turns back to me.

I stall, trapped. Jamie hasn't talked with them about this? "Thank you so much—really—but you see, I've never been to Europe," I say. "It might be the only chance I'll get while I'm over here."

Her smile returns. "Oh, then you must go!" she cries. "Another time." What a gracious, lovely woman. Antonia's gaze catches something behind me and she rolls her eyes slightly. "You'll excuse me, but duty calls. I really must say hello. Be back straightaway," and she moves off, leaving Jamie, William, and me in a loose triangle.

Wasting no time, William immediately leans in to Jamie. "Dr. Solomon said you weren't willing to do another round of stem-cell replacement."

Even though he has one round of chemo left, and he won't have conclusive test results until January, Jamie has decided not to try the stem-cell replacement therapy again. He says it only gave him a year of remission last time, and it was painful, and depleting, and required him to live in a hospital for a month in total isolation. The only other option is a different kind of chemo, which Jamie seems to prefer. I'm doing my best to stay out of it.

At Jamie's silence, William presses, "Care to explain?"

Any ease Jamie had been feeling has disappeared with his mother's departure. He's gone cold. Dead-fish cold. He gazes dully past William's shoulder into the party. "No."

"Even though it's your best chance of remission?" William doesn't even glance at me. Apparently, I don't belong in this conversation.

But Jamie murmurs, "There's Cecelia," and waves to her across the room. "Come, Ella. Let's say hello."

"Jamie," William says lowly, tightly. "This is not a time to gamble, to be reckless. What about trying the—"

Jamie turns to me as if his father has evaporated. "Shall we?"

I glance guiltily at William and say to Jamie, "Join you in a sec."

"Be quick about it." Jamie leaves before I can even metabolize my annoyance at his command.

I take a breath and turn to William, smiling, ready to mollify, to assure him that I'm there for his son. "I guess it's fair to say that Jamie's a bit stubborn about his medical decisions. But we're handling it. In fact, he didn't get a chance to tell you, but his numbers are really promising right now—"

"Are you quite finished?" William's gaze snaps to mine like a laser, like he's scanning me. I freeze. Before I can unfreeze, Antonia returns, all easy smiles, touching her husband's arm.

"So sorry to interrupt, but we really must go find the table now. The Beauchamps are waiting and you know Matthew won't have his Scotch until you do and you know how insufferable Caroline finds him until he has had it. Please be sure to find us later, Eleanor," she says, smiling. "And do take my invitation seriously. We would simply love it if you came to visit us. Wouldn't that be splendid, William?"

William breaks his stare and then, as if nothing but warmth had passed between us, says, "Splendid."

Antonia leads him away and I, still mulling over that encounter, cross to Jamie and Cecelia, who stand about thirty feet away, heads huddled together. My unease with William is replaced by a sudden nervousness at approaching Cecelia.

I have no idea what to say to her.

Jamie told me that Cecelia met Oliver, who was studying at King's College London at the time, during her second year at Oxford. They were on the same train, which broke down somewhere between London and Reading, and, with nothing better to do, they began to talk. According to Jamie, his brother phoned him when the train started moving again and simply said, "I found her. The One. Call off the search." They'd been dating for six months when Oliver was diagnosed. They immediately got engaged. "The romantic impulse of youth," Jamie had said, rolling his eyes. But I found the story remarkable. That a young woman, twenty-one, obviously smart as a whip, her whole life ahead of her, would choose to commit to a future where there, quite simply, wasn't one.

What do you say to that?

I smile as I join them, and Jamie slips his hand into mine. "Sorry to abandon ship," he mutters, kissing my bare shoulder. "But I simply can't listen to him."

I don't argue, I don't absolve. We'll talk about it later. I turn to Cecelia. "Awesome gown. Great color!" Truthfully, I haven't even glanced at her gown. Or the color. She could be wearing a bathing suit for all I know.

"Yours as well," she says with that smile that could freeze lava in its flow.

"Why don't I fetch some drinks," Jamie says, touching both of our elbows. "God knows I need one. What'll it be?"

"Grey Goose martini, extra dirty, three olives," I answer. Jamie smiles and turns to Cecelia.

"Whichever white they're pouring."

"Sauv Blanc?" Jamie asks, beginning to move away. "Chard if

it's not too oaky? Gewürztraminer?"

She looks levelly at him. "White."

Chuckling, he leaves. Cecelia turns back to me with a slightly more genuine smile. "Jamie and his wine."

I respond with far too hearty a laugh. "It's been an education." I've never taken the time to actually see her, to go beyond how pretty she is, into who she is. I try to do so now. It's slightly easier than before. The door's no longer locked and bolted, just closed.

"I'm sure it has, rather," she says knowingly. There's a sincerity there that feels like an offering.

I seize it. "Look. I can't imagine what you've gone through, I wouldn't even pretend to know . . . but I have . . . experienced loss before. And if—"

She places her hand on my arm. "Understood. Consider me available. If you have questions, or simply want to chat. I only wish I'd had someone."

There's softness in her voice, in her. I like her, I realize. Her coldness, her aloofness, what I mistook for jealousy, I now see was just her protectiveness of Jamie. "Can I just say?" I blurt out. God, where's Jamie with the drinks? This would be so much easier with vodka. I swallow. "I am so, so, so sorry."

"Thank you," she replies immediately, and I recognize it for what it is: the involuntary response of someone who hears "I'm sorry for your loss" every single hour of every single day and for whom it has ceased to have any meaning. But the look in her eyes tells me she knows this one is sincere.

But then she changes tack completely. "Which C course will you be taking next term?"

"W-what?"

"I was thinking I might take Senses of Humour: from Wordsworth to Eliot." She regards me and, finally, smiles slightly. "I'd quite like to learn how to laugh again."

I DON'T THINK I've ever laughed more in my life. My earlier discomfort has eased. I've acclimated to the ostentation and not just because I've had a few drinks. We've staked our claim in a corner near the dance floor and Jamie has been telling us who everyone is. Charlie then spouts a completely ridiculous falsehood about them. Jamie will point to a portly, balding man, say something like, "That's Geoffrey Mondale, seventh Earl of Sheffield," and Charlie will instantly add, "Geoffy Sheffy to his friends, been known to run naked through his woods in Maori-inspired face paint stalking squirrels, which inevitably manage to elude him." Even Cecelia's laughing, shaking her head and murmuring, "Oh Lord, enough." Of course the one time Charlie holds back after Jamie's introduction, it's Cecelia who swats him on the arm and says, "Come now, Charlie. Don't be a bore."

When Jamie runs out of people to talk about, Maggie asks Charlie to dance with her. They're turning to leave when Tom— yes, Tom!—steps forward, saying grimly, "I'll do it," as if it's a chore. As if he's a soldier in the trenches and someone has to run behind enemy lines to rescue a fallen comrade. We all look at him. "What? I'm . . ." He fizzles out. "Taller." Charlie steps back, hands up, relinquishing. Maggie instantly blushes and puts her hand out for Tom to take, only Tom's already turned heel, making a beeline for the dance floor. She looks at me, hopeful. I give her an encouraging smile and she turns, plodding in her heels to catch up with Tom. Charlie and I raise an eyebrow at each other. We watch them begin to dance, arms fully outstretched, middle school style, leaving four feet between them. Maggie starts to say something just as Tom starts to say something. She—predictably—apologizes, and Tom looks down at his feet. From which he doesn't look up again. Maggie's eyes find us, forehead more deeply furrowed than I've ever seen it.

"I give up." Charlie sighs, turning to me. "Right. To the bar. Statistically, there's not enough alcohol in the world to make watching that"—he gestures dismissively toward our friends—"comfortable, but I shall happily endeavor to prove the exception." He leaves.

Jamie turns to me and extends an arm. "Shall we?"

About to answer, I catch a glimpse of Cecelia. She's watching the dancing couples, wearing a slightly melancholy, nostalgic look. I nudge Jamie and tip my head at her. He quirks his head at me. I try again. He quirks further. I incline my entire head in Cecelia's direction. He gets it this time. "Ce?" She turns that serene face to him. "Would you care to dance?"

I half expect her to demur, but her face lights up, a smile emanating from it. She nods quickly, almost embarrassed. "So much."

Jamie offers his arm and she gratefully takes it. As I watch them step out onto the dance floor I can't believe how happy I suddenly am. Against all reason, given the circumstances, how blisteringly happy I am in this moment, watching these people I've come to care about congregate on a dance floor. There's something magical about it.

On a sigh, I turn to go find Charlie, and run straight into William.

"Whoa!" I cry, keeping control of my glass as I step back from his battering ram of a chest. "Sorry."

"Didn't mean to startle you," he says.

"No, it's fine!" I remind myself to smile. "I was just on my way to—"

"Dance with me." He offers his arm, looks out at the dance floor.

"I'd love to." And I mean it. Mostly. I want to start over with him, get to know him. I set my drink on a table.

Just as I extend my hand to him, my purse vibrates. *Shit.* "Sorry," I say to William, and his head turns toward me. "I just need to . . ." I dig my phone out and look at the display. Gavin. Of course. "I'll be quick."

"I'll wait," William says, looking back out, something ominous in that declaration. I wince apologetically, but he doesn't see it.

Yes, it's a Saturday night, and yes, I'm at a ball at a palace in England, but this is who I am. I'm the person who takes the call. Besides, I know what it's about and it'll be quick. "Gavin."

"Did you see the numbers I sent?"

"I did." In the limo on the way over here. "They're great."

"Just great?" He sounds so excited I have a feeling he might be a few Manhattans into his evening.

"A net positive favorable—even a net twenty—doesn't matter when it's hypothetical," I say. I glance at William. He's assessing the crowd, but I can practically see his ear tuned to me like a dog's. "We're basically asking people if they'd vote for Santa Claus over the Tooth Fairy. It's fiction." I catch the beginning of a reluctant grin on William's face. Boldly, I raise my voice a little. Am I preening? Sure. "Come on, Gavin, you're supposed to be the battle-worn vet who doesn't count chickens, I'm supposed to be the doe-eyed idealist."

Gavin laughs. "Oh, what do you know, you're just the doe-eyed education consultant."

"Then why'd you send me the numbers?" I fire back. "Why are you calling me?"

"Because you're the only one I know will answer." There's a moment of quiet and I swear I hear ice clinking in a glass. It's five P.M. on a Saturday and Janet's probably in Florida with her boyfriend and youngest son. Thrice-divorced Gavin is calling me. "You're doing good, kid," he says. "Really. You're doing good—no, you're doing great—work for us."

"Thank you," I say, stealing another glance at William.

"We're gonna need you in the administration."

Weirdly, my ears heat. Just my ears, just a rush of anticipatory blood to a random part of me. I laugh it off. "Don't start measuring the drapes for the Oval just yet."

He chuckles. "I'll call you tomorrow. I got a list of possible hires I wanna run by you." Per usual, he doesn't say good-bye. He's just gone.

I slip my phone back into my purse. I turn to William and tap his arm, and he looks as if he's surprised to see me there, as if he hasn't been listening to my entire conversation. An actor, he is not. "Sorry about that."

"Quite all right," he says, and offers his arm to me. I tuck my hand into his elbow and we move to the periphery of the dancing crowd. William turns to me, taking my right hand lightly in his. My left immediately goes to his shoulder and his other hand finds my waist. I send a silent thanks to my mother for making me take ballroom dance as an elective sophomore year.

I scan the crowd for Jamie and Cecelia, but they must have drifted to the other side of the floor. I see that Maggie and Tom have inched closer, but they gaze in opposite directions, glancing at each other occasionally and then looking away quickly if they happen to meet the other's eye. Needless to say, they don't speak. I peer at William, hoping he'll look back at me and smile. He does neither. So I study him. He's quite striking for his age. He has Jamie's jaw and shoulders. But his eyes are dark. Opaque. He begins rolling his neck, back and forth, like a boxer warming up for a fight. Before I can ask if he's all right, he unclasps my hand and reaches for his bow tie. We pause in our dance as he struggles to loosen the knot without completely undoing it. "Damn constricting," he mutters.

I smile at him and blurt, "You think that's bad, try a bra."

He narrows his eyes at me—it wasn't funny, I know it wasn't funny—and retakes my hand. We start moving again. In silence. Just as I'm about to say something to dispel the awkwardness, he beats me to the punch.

"Enjoying your time in Britain?"

"Yes, very much. I love it." We dance. "This is a beautiful event. Thanks for letting my friends join in tonight. They're having the best—"

"I fell in love with Antonia before I knew she was a Lady Duncan. She was just a uni girl in a disco who made me tea at three in the morning. We dated for six months before I found out her title went back fifteen generations and she had hundreds of thousands of acres and five estates spread over this godforsaken island. I thought I'd struck gold." He's not looking at me. He stares over my shoulder into space. I wait for him to continue. Clearly he has a reason for launching into this story. Not that I know what it is. "I was twenty-five then. I had nothing, all the money I was making went right back into the business. The first ball she took me to? I had to borrow her father's suit." A wry smile finds its way to his lips, but quickly disappears again. "We eloped. I gave her a ring I'd fashioned out of a crisp bag."

I like this William, the young romantic.

"But the following year her father died and I discovered just how much hundreds of thousands of acres and five estates costs a person and just how much he didn't have. We lived in the Argyll kitchens—that's the house in Scotland—for two years because it was reliably warm. Which couldn't be said for the rest of that pile. Toni gave birth to Jamie in those kitchens. Nothing but a bucket of boiling water, me, and Smithy banging on about putting a knife under our mattress to cut the pain. This is

1989, mind you, not 1389. Then my company went public. That fifty quid I'd stolen out my father's till when I was sixteen had multiplied itself by a million. Oliver was born in a private suite at St. Mary's in Paddington."

Why is he telling me this? I'm not saying I'm not charmed, but why?

He looks at me for the first time since we started dancing. It's riveting. "Do you know why Jamie won't do the stem-cell replacement therapy again?" Jarred, I open my mouth to engage, but he continues. "Not because it's painful and tedious and, according to him, futile. It's you. He doesn't want to isolate himself, unglue himself from you for a month. That must make you feel quite valued?"

I obviously disagree with his assessment, but I know he's trying to get a rise out of me and I won't take the bait. "It's Jamie's choice."

The corner of William's mouth lifts. I can't tell if it's a smile or a sneer. "I see. You've never loved anyone before." I bristle. This is like when I criticize my cousin's horrible kids and my mother pulls the you-don't-know-what-it's-like-to-be-a-parent card. Nothing irritates me more. Except for this. Once again, I open my mouth, but William says, "It's all right. You're young. Love is still firmly about hormones." Everything this man says is rooted in criticism. "You're a Rhodes scholar, yes?"

"Yes," I reply cautiously.

"Good. I like dealing with clever people. You have a ticket back to the states on June eleventh, if I'm correct? You will be back in America, working twenty hours per day, in a different city every night, possibly, getting Janet Wilkes elected president." I want to ask him how the hell he knows any of this, but I'm too stunned to speak. He charges forward. "Do you see yourself and my son gallivanting through Europe until then?

Cruising the Seine? Skiing the Alps? Let me burst this bubble. He will either be too ill to travel or he will be dead. After you're done with him, you will still have a life. He, very well, might not."

My steps falter. William tightens his grip on my waist, keeping me moving. I try to breathe through my astonished anger. You don't often get blindsided in slow motion.

"I understand the appeal of lineage," he murmurs. "Privilege. Access. Believe me. We're more alike than you realize. My father, too, was a barman."

My heart nearly explodes out of my chest. How does he know this?

"We both know the embarrassment of a meager upbringing."

Instantly, my hackles go up. "I am not embarrassed by my father."

"Had he lived longer you very well might have been."

I stop dancing and move to wrench my hand out of William's grasp. His grip turns to iron and he bites out, "Keep dancing, Eleanor. We shouldn't want to draw unnecessary attention."

He's right. I can feel the eyes on us, the curious stares. I seethe as we continue to dance. Face-to-face. Eye to eye. I silently dare him to say more. He finally continues. "What I mean to say is that we can understand each other. We have both suffered a significant loss in our lives—"

"We're not going to talk about my father." My voice is steel. "William," I call him by his first name because if he can talk to me like this then I can dispense with the formality bullshit. "Just because you somehow have some facts about my life doesn't mean you know me. Or what I feel for your son. I have no interest in your money. Or you, for that matter."

"You feel for my son, do you?" The word "feel" oozes disdain. "You have inserted yourself into the very thick of our lives. But you are transient, a squatter in our house. We, Antonia and I, are here for the duration. We are responsible for our son's life. For his life. Do you hear? Listen carefully. You don't take a son, an ill son, my-unfortunately-only son away from his mother for Christmas. You don't tell a father who's been down this blasted road before that you're 'handling it.' You are fleeting. You, dear girl, are a distraction. A potentially fatal one. Can you live with that? Is it worth it? Riding in crested limousines and going to balls in yellow frocks and having your poor man's grand tour? Is it worth my son's life?"

I take a steadying breath. He's being brutally unfair and insulting, but I understand where he's coming from. If I were in his position I'd be worried about the sudden appearance of a girl in my wealthy, dying son's life as well. In retrospect, I can't believe I didn't expect this response from him. The unexpected response is actually Antonia's effusive welcoming.

I center myself, mentally editing what I really want to say. The ugly thing I want to say.

But then I look into his eyes, and I see the deadness there, the smugness, the righteousness, everything Jamie constantly battles when he shouldn't have to—when he should just be assured of his father's love—and it makes me angry. And I say the ugly thing anyway. "You know, it's funny. I didn't understand how Jamie could have such little regard for his own father. Until now."

William's face instantly reddens. Those dead eyes spark to life. "Who do you think you are?" he seethes. "I have already lost one son. I do not intend to lose another."

As if a glamour had magically dropped away, I suddenly see how ravaged he looks. His eyes moisten with angry, frustrated tears, which I know must embarrass him. It softens me a bit. Just a bit. "You don't get it. If Jamie wants to do chemo, I'll sit with him. If he wants to do stem cells, I'll wait for him. If he wants to swim with dolphins, I'll get my towel. This isn't about me. It's Jamie's choice, not mine. You have to let—"

"I have to let those choices be guided by an artful little girl who hasn't the faintest bloody idea what she's talking about? No, sweetie, I don't believe I must."

And I no longer care about appearances. I'm done dancing. I start to pull away, but he tightens his hold on my waist. "Wait—"

"No, sweetie, I don't believe I must," I hiss, pulling away from him and leaving the dance floor. William immediately follows. He won't be left standing alone. The illusion only works if we both leave at the same time.

I'm almost to the safety of the ladies' room when I feel William right behind me. His voice, though quiet, cuts sharply through the din, right at my ear. "Are you listening to me?"

I bang into the restroom and say, over my shoulder, "No. And neither is Jamie."

CHAPTER 22

Madam Life's a piece in bloom
Death goes dogging everywhere:
She's the tenant of the room,
He's the ruffian on the stair.
William Ernest Henley, "IX–To W.R.," 1877

We're about thirty miles outside of Oxford when Jamie says to me, for the hundredth time, "You have your passport?"

I take a moment, as if I'm thinking about it. Then I sit forward suddenly, straining against the seat belt, frantically patting the pockets of my jeans and jacket. "Oh no!"

Jamie tries to stay calm. His eyes snap to me. I raise a wry eyebrow. He exhales wearily and faces front again. "Not the first time I've asked?"

"Not even close."

"Sorry," he mutters.

We call this "chemo brain," his uncharacteristic forgetfulness. Sometimes it's as simple as not remembering he's already asked a question; sometimes it's hours of not being able to locate his keys only to open the refrigerator and find them sitting next to the cream that's still in a grocery bag.

I reach over and playfully tousle his hair. When I pull my hand back, I notice a few strands on my fingers. Jamie's final round of treatment was three days ago and I know he feels more ill than he's letting on. Still, there's an air of victory in the car, and we couldn't be doing anything better for him, for us, than driving through the countryside to Dover to catch a ferry to France.

We're still going away for the holidays.

While locked inside a bathroom stall at Blenheim, I thought long and hard about telling Jamie everything that had transpired between William and me. I decided absolutely not. Not only do I refuse to throw more logs on whatever fire smolders between William and Jamie, but I also refuse to play any part in manipulating Jamie's choices. It would have been playing directly into William's hand, and that's not how this is going to work. Not on my watch.

So I downed a glass of champagne and danced with Jamie until he said he was "rather tired" and we left. Jamie located Antonia—who was luckily a good distance from William—and gave her a kiss good-bye. She then turned that warm, smiling, welcoming face to me and insisted that I take her card, call her, and she'd take me to tea. I put her number in my phone, but haven't called her yet. Because one thing William said stuck with me: that I am, to a certain extent, a transient. I don't know the history between William and Jamie, I don't know why things have deteriorated as they have, and I won't be here to deal with the fallout. I'll be pulling up stakes eventually.

So if Jamie's fine not being with his parents for the holidays, then so am I. In fact, I'm excited. So excited.

We're starting in Normandy for two days, then heading to Paris for four. Then we'll head south, into Jamie's beloved wine country, and end up along the Riviera for New Year's. Every time I say this (out loud or to myself, doesn't matter), I giggle. Legitimately giggle. After New Year's, we'll decide where we go for the next two weeks. No plans, just wandering. Perhaps Switzerland, or down into Italy, where it'll be warmer. I'm game for anything.

I look out my window at the passing scenery. Beautiful. Rolling green hills dotted with oak trees and fluffy sheep. There's a fine winter mist caressing everything. The sky is broken up into pockets of light gray and stormy blue, like a quilt. "I love this," I murmur. "This country is a novel come to life. It's timeless. It's rugged and slightly wild, but elegant, too. Hmm, sounds like someone I know," I tease. Jamie doesn't respond. "Hey, you wanna stay in your lane, buddy?" We're starting to inch over the solid white line of the motorway's shoulder. A slight curve in the road puts us solidly over it. "Jamie, seriously." I glance over and find that his face has gone ghost white, his eyes hooded, a sheen of sweat covering his brow. "Jamie?"

His head drops to his chest.

"Jamie!" I shout, lunging for the wheel. He startles awake, but just as quickly drops out again. "Jamie, brake! Brake!" He jerks his head up and pounds his foot onto the floor, missing the brake. Instinctively, I grab the wheel with one hand while lifting his foot onto the brake pedal with the other, the car kicking up gravel on the shoulder. I press down on his leg as hard as I can and we start slowing, but not quickly enough. I yank up the emergency brake. We skid to a stop in a cloud of dust.

Jamie flops forward like a rag doll.

I unbuckle my seat belt and grab him, taking his head in my hands and forcing him to look at me. "Jamie!" He mumbles something that sounds like "sorry." I keep a hand on his chest to brace him upright and dig into my back pocket for my phone. "Jamie. Jamie! Stay awake! Please!" He attempts to speak, but his head falls to his chest again.

I gently lean him against the driver's-side window. "It's okay, it'll be okay!" Hands shaking, I start to dial 911, but stop myself. *Shit!* Is 911 the emergency number in this country? How do I not know this?! How can I have a boyfriend with cancer and not know how to call for help?! *Idiot!*

I start slapping the side of Jamie's face, staccato little strikes, trying to wake him. "Jamie, Jamie!" His eyes open. Barely, but open. "How do I call an ambulance?" He mumbles something. "An ambulance, Jamie! How do I call?!" I slap him again. Harder this time.

"Nine-nine-nine . . . and stop. Slapping." And out he goes again, this time with the faintest of smiles.

"Funny," I croak. "Jerk." But it gives me a momentary reprieve from my panic as I dial. When I have the phone to my ear, I grab one of his hands and bring it to my mouth, kissing it. "Everything's gonna be okay, just try to breathe. All right?" My heart has left my chest. It's flopping around on the floorboards. "Don't worry. Help is coming. Stay with me, Ja—Yes, hello!"

Just as I connect to the dispatcher, Jamie faintly squeezes my hand. I look up into his eyes, searching. "Don't call my parents," he breathes with his last bit of strength.

Then he passes out for good.

CHAPTER 23

Say not the struggle nought availeth,
The labor and the wounds are vain,
The enemy faints not, nor faileth,
And as things have been, things remain.
Arthur Hugh Clough, "Say Not the Strug-
gle Nought Availeth," 1862

You can do this. It's just a car.

A car that probably costs more than my entire education, but, still, a car.

A car with everything reversed. Like a goddamn fun house.

I check the mirrors yet again, automatically and absently reaching to the right for the shifter. Instead, my hand hits the door.

Jesus. Focus.

When the paramedics had asked me if I wanted to follow, I had nodded. Why did I nod? Because I'd needed to feel useful. They said the hospital was only three miles away. I can do anything for three miles.

But now the ambulance's lights are flashing and the siren comes on and it's go time. I depress the clutch and, with my left hand, shift into drive. I follow the ambulance back onto the motorway and we slowly pick up speed. The transmission grinds and I cringe.

As if driving a stick for the first time since I learned to drive on my aunt's old Volkswagen Beetle wasn't bad enough, driving on the opposite side of the road, sitting on the opposite side of the car, takes every single ounce of attention. The problem is, I don't have an ounce left. Every part of my mind is consumed with Jamie. What signs did I miss? Is this normal? Is he all right? Is this just a glimpse of things to come?

We have to switch lanes and my eyes instinctively glance up and to the right, seeing nothing but the patchy clouds. Forcibly, I look left, to the rearview mirror.

I'm not cut out for this. I've never been around illness before. I'm useless. And for whatever reason, I'm the only one Jamie wants near him.

And I'm leaving.

Someone will have to take care of Jamie when I'm gone. Whether he wants to admit it or not, as he gets progressively worse, he's going to need more help. It's a fact. Decisions are going to have to be made.

Jamie's going to need his family.

Oh God. A roundabout. White-knuckled, I follow the ambulance through it.

This is how crisis works, I think. In one instant, priorities can change.

Beliefs can reverse.

Somehow, some way, his relationship with his parents has to be fixed. I can't leave him, come June 11, like this, like some animal slinking off into the woods to die alone.

Miraculously, we've made it to the hospital. The ambulance driver sticks her hand out the window and points at the adjacent, nearly empty parking lot. We're somewhere in the wilds of Kent and it appears that we're pretty much alone in the world.

Even without having to navigate around other cars, I swing too wide into the parking spot, and end up straddling the line. Screw it. Let them ask me to move. I've parked right in front of a sign that cautions no overnight parking and I think, Oh God, I might have to drive at night. With Jamie in the car.

Distracted, I turn off the Aston and open my door, stepping out into the crisp winter air. The distant sound of a train whistle reminds me, for the first time, of the ferry we're not catching. Should I call the company? I don't have the number. I'll look it up on my—

The ground moves beneath my feet. An optical illusion. In reality, the car is rolling forward. "Shit!" I leap back into the car and yank the brake. But not before the Aston rolls into the "No Overnight Parking" sign, tipping it backward thirty degrees with a mournful creak.

I drop my head onto the center console. I don't even want to look at the bumper. I take a deep breath.

Knowing what I have to do, I pull out my phone.

"I AM SO bloody sorry," Jamie mutters yet again as I arrange and fluff a pillow behind his back, doing my best to make him comfortable on the couch in the drawing room.

"If you didn't want to go you should have just said so," I joke. "You didn't have to pull a stunt like this."

He sighs heavily with the faintest sound of a laugh.

Anemia. Severe Anemia. Turns out he'd been feeling faint and lethargic for the past week, he just didn't tell anyone (i.e., me). Before we left this morning, he'd been dragging, which I'd noticed but thought was just a side effect from the chemo. Or maybe I just didn't want to notice. He didn't tell me he'd nearly passed out in the shower. I feel horrible, as if this were my fault. Was I being selfish, or stupid, or . . . ?

The doctors had wanted to give him a blood transfusion, which would have involved staying in the hospital and had potential repercussions that made his oncologist nervous. Plan B was a series of shots that encourage the body to create more of its own red blood cells. Which is great. Except it'll take two weeks before they can tell if there's any improvement. So Jamie's relegated to the couch. Indefinitely. We've been home for about an hour and so far Jamie's really pissed and I'm really disappointed and both of us feel guilty about the way we're feeling.

That's as far as we've gotten.

"There's no point in you being here. You should go," he says.

I stop my fussing. "Go where?"

"On holiday, you dolt!"

"Don't call me that!" I snap, nerves beyond frayed. The teasing grin on Jamie's pale face instantly drops, and I take a breath. "I'm sorry. About everything, okay? I should have realized you weren't—"

"No, please. Stop right there. You feel bad, I feel bad, but we will not plague each other with guilt. It's an absurd emotion, reserved for those who we fear might feel less than they ought." He looks in my eyes. "You and I, we carry on. If we stop, it is to only catch our breath. Well, breath caught."

"Jamie, I'm not leaving you."

He groans slightly. "You have our itinerary, everything's confirmed. Please." I straighten and sigh. He takes my dangling hand. "I couldn't live with myself if you didn't get to travel because of this."

"So much for *no guilt*, huh?" I tease. He rolls his eyes. "We still have the Easter vac in March. It's not a big deal."

"No, Ella." He sweeps a hand over himself. "*This* is not a big deal. I simply overexerted, that's all. By the time you get back in a month, I'll be right as rain."

He looks so much like a little boy right now—optimistic, vulnerable, and so completely untethered from reality—that tears spring to my eyes. Tears that I turn away from him to hide. "We'll see."

He tugs my hand, urges me look at him. "Carry on. Yeah?"

Before I can reply, there's a knock at the door. "That's the food, be right—Sit!" I bark incredulously when he moves to get up. Worst patient ever.

We'd ordered Indian food as soon as we got home. I can't vouch for Jamie's appetite, but I'm starving. All I want is a huge bowl of rice and tikka masala and approximately fourteen pieces of naan. I reach into my pocket for some money and open the door, muttering "Sorry, I don't have anything smaller than a fifty—" I screech to a halt.

Antonia.

And William.

Antonia exudes calm, but her face is etched with worry. "My dear girl, how are you? Is he all right?"

"Yes, yes, he's fine." Then, reflexively, we throw our arms around each other. I don't know who initiated it, but it causes me to tear up again. I had long since forgotten the relief and comfort a mother can bring to a situation. I'm shocked to discover how much I needed it. "I'm fine," I breathe into her hair. "I just wasn't expecting—"

"You'll pardon me." William pushes past us, his impatience as obvious as his anger. "James?"

Antonia quickly escapes our embrace, squeezing my arm as she mutters, "Sorry." She chases after her husband. "William, don't make me ask you to wait outside."

I close the door and quickly follow. As I round the corner to the drawing room, Jamie exclaims, "Bloody hell!"

William stands over Jamie's prone figure on the couch. "Enjoying your holiday?"

"What are you—"

"Are you happy now?" William seethes. "Do you see what your recklessness has done?"

Jamie pushes himself up into a proper sitting position, less exposed. "What are you doing here?" He looks angrily to me. "I said they were not to be called."

Antonia steps in, saving me. "Yes, and I could throttle you for asking it of her." She drops on the couch next to him, taking his face in her hands, forcing him to look at her. "Are you all right?"

Jamie grabs her hands and lowers them gently, his agitated gaze darting at William. "I'm fine. Really. It was just a dizzy spell. No need for the cavalry."

My eyes bulge. A dizzy spell? He can't even be honest with them.

This is why I had told Antonia to be patient, to let me talk to Jamie, warm him up to the idea of their coming down here. For one very obvious reason, which happens to be standing behind her right now, scowling. I never thought they'd just show up. Scotland is a six-hour drive. They must have gotten in the car as soon as we hung up. Or maybe there's a private plane I don't know about.

William won't be put off. "Against all advice, doctor or otherwise, you insist on frolicking off to the continent," he booms. "When were you planning to have your follow-up? Hmm?"

"When I returned. Obviously," Jamie bites out.

"In January? After a month? Splendid! A month of eating whatever you want, running yourself ragged, drinking to excess, and shagging like a teenager who's just discovered his cock?"

I wince. Not at William's crudity, but at his accuracy. Said this way, leaving for a month does sound reckless. Jamie jumps off the couch and starts pacing, fueled by adrenaline.

"Jamie, which treatment will you be starting in January? William, don't be crass," Antonia says, the voice of reason.

"Chemo," Jamie replies tightly.

"Chemo?" William barks. "What about the stem cell?"

Jamie takes a breath. "I already told you—"

"Dr. Solomon said he'd convinced you to reconsider—"

"I did reconsider and I came to the same conclusion." I look at Jamie. I didn't know this. He glances briefly at me, looking slightly embarrassed when he says, "I'll revisit the idea when Ella's gone back to America—"

"If you're not dead."

"William," Antonia snaps. "I forbid you to say that." There's flint in her voice. "Do you hear me? I won't have it."

William rolls his eyes and spins away, facing the far wall.

Was he right, what he said at the ball? Is Jamie not doing the stem-cell therapy because he doesn't want to be away from me? A sick feeling begins to settle in my stomach.

Antonia sighs. "What is your plan, my love?"

Jamie waves his hand dismissively at his mother. "I'll keep on with the chemo, as maintenance. In six months, I'll assess my options."

"You stubborn sod!" William bellows, spinning back around. He advances, smacking his fist into the palm of his hand at each beat for emphasis, as if angrily tracking the iamb. "You don't keep the dog at bay, you wring its bloody neck!"

Jamie, losing his strength, sinks back into the couch.

"At the very least, do the trial," William implores.

"What trial?" I hear myself ask.

A look of smug superiority fills William's face. "It seems Jamie doesn't share everything with you, after all." It takes all my control not to remind him that he's only standing here because of me. He looks back to Jamie. "Shall I tell her? Or would you prefer to?"

Jamie clenches his jaw. He speaks quietly. "It's a new drug, for people who are terminal. My father would have you believe it's a game changer—"

"They've seen very promising—"

"Good God!" Jamie exhaustedly snaps. "It's not a cure. There *is* no cure. We're talking about something that may, *may*, buy me more time."

"Why didn't I know about this?" I ask, temper flaring. "Why haven't you mentioned it?"

Jamie stares at the coffee table. "Because of the cost."

"The cost!" I shout, louder than I intended. "Are you serious—"

Jamie clenches his eyes shut. "Not financial cost, personal cost. Side effects."

"Which are?"

"They have no bloody idea! It's a trial. That's the point." He sits forward suddenly, elbows on his knees. He stares at William as he draws a steadying breath. "Oliver did a trial and it killed him. Slowly, painfully. He bled out internally, drowning, suffocating on his own blood—"

"The drug didn't kill Oliver." William interrupts yet again.

Suddenly Jamie's finger pops out like a gun, pointing accusingly at William. Hand shaking in repressed rage, he glares at his father. I'm taken aback. I've never seen him this angry.

William alters his tone. "I'm only saying Oliver was too advanced. You're the perfect candidate for this."

Jamie's voice shakes when he says quietly, "I won't submit Ella to unknown side effects. I won't abide her turning nursemaid—"

"This isn't about me!" I cry, appalled at his reasoning, just as

William yells, "This isn't about her!" We glance at each other warily, uncomfortable in our agreement.

Antonia shakes her head. "You'd think we'd all have learned something from the last time round." The moment she speaks Jamie and William demagnetize, separate like two boxers going to opposite corners once the referee steps in. There's silence. It feels like this roller coaster is slowing, pulling into the station. Though I'm not unfastening my seat belt just yet.

She looks between them. "This illness is not easy on any of us. Decisions are not easy for any of us. Yes, Jamie, you will decide your future, but we will all live with it. There is no right answer. Wouldn't it be relieving if there were?"

Her diplomacy is inspiring. I could take a lesson from her.

"So, my love. Listen. Consider. Don't discount something simply because your father is suggesting it. Then make your choice. And we shall support it."

William has retreated to a corner of the room, looking at the floor. Jamie absently rubs his forehead. He looks exhausted, yet contemplative. I'm still in awe of Antonia.

Jamie goes completely still for a moment. Then:

"I'll do the trial. On one condition." He looks up at his father. "You are to stay out of it. You are not to talk to my doctors. You are to neither call nor visit. I am to be left alone for the next three months."

William looks as if he's going to detonate.

"Jamie, is that really necessary?" I ask.

Jamie's eyes never leave William's. "Yes."

"Why?"

He doesn't answer. William finally speaks. "I'll be outside." He leaves. Not another word. No "I'm sorry." No "Jamie, please." No "I love you." He doesn't look at anyone. He just exits.

Antonia turns to Jamie on the couch. She kisses his cheek. She lingers there. Then they embrace. Just hold each other. Standing behind Jamie, I watch tears leak out of Antonia's tightly shut eyes. This is what was inside her the whole time. I hear a choked, fractured voice say, "I love you," and in this moment I can't tell if it came from Jamie or Antonia. It doesn't matter.

I've only felt love like this once in my life, and I can't bear to think of it right now.

Antonia pats Jamie on the back, and pulls away. "Gorgeous boy."

"Beautiful mum."

She gets up and reaches for my hand. We don't dare hug. I think we both know we'd lose it. She inclines her head in the direction that William exited. "Apologies, Eleanor."

What the hell is she apologizing for? I shake my head, try to lighten the mood. "He's a bit of a bull in a china shop, isn't he?"

"That's generous, my dear." She smiles slightly, seems to think about this for a second. "Though sometimes one must ask one-self why the bull is in the china shop in the first place." She leaves.

As her footsteps recede I debate going after her. I want to know why he's in the china shop. I want to know what is going on between father and son. I glance at Jamie and see that he's tipped his head back, closed his eyes.

"Jamie—" I begin.

"I need a moment."

He's angry. I get it. I'm angry, too. I step out into the hall-way just as the front door closes behind Antonia. Too late. She's gone.

I won't go out there. That would be asking for trouble and we've had enough of it for one day. But I find myself gravitating to the window beside the door, curtained with a simple muslin panel. Standing to the side of it and looking through the space between the window and the drapery, I can see directly onto the front stoop without having to push back the material. I know I'm snooping, but I can't help it. This feels necessary.

Antonia has paused on the top stair and gazes down upon William, who, at the bottom of the stairs, has taken hold of the handrail and is violently pulling at it until it breaks free from its rusty bolts. He throws it down into the bushes next to the stair. He stands motionless for a moment, panting with flared nostrils. He kicks the railing for good measure, then just looks at it. Eventually, he reaches into his jacket pocket, takes out a cigarette, lights up, and begins pacing. Kicking up dirt. Forcing air and smoke in and out of his body, clearly wanting to do more damage, but not sure to what.

Antonia slowly but deliberately descends the stairs. William points his cigarette at her, his face contorted, a bomb ready to go off.

I reach for the door handle; I think better of it. Because Antonia calmly takes one more step down to William, bringing herself eye level with him.

I've never seen two people speak so clearly, yet wordlessly, to each other.

William finally moves. He goes to toss his cigarette, but Antonia snatches it from him. She takes a long drag, tips her head back, and exhales. She looks back at William and tosses it onto the pavement. William hangs his head, but looks up at his wife, a conqueror who has been conquered. She is right there for him.

She takes his shoulders as he falls forward, the top of his head finding a place to rest between her breasts. His hands find her hips, settling there with long-held familiarity. She runs her palms down the length of his back, up and down, up and down, the way you rub a dog when it's come and put its head in your lap. William turns to the left, toward me, and I see his eyes are closed, his lips a tight, straight line, a mask of tension. Antonia drops her head back and looks up at the sky, mouth open, sucking in air.

I don't know whether it's the sight of their unguarded pain or intimacy that causes me to finally turn away, but I do.

I walk back into the parlor to find Jamie still on the couch. His eyes open as I approach. "Listen," he begins.

"No, stop. Just stop, Jamie. Enough. I'm sorry they ambushed you. Just to be clear, I didn't ask them to come. But I'm not sorry I called them. They have a right to know what's happening to their son."

"You don't want to get involved in this, Ella. It doesn't concern you."

"It does. You know why? Because I'm the one who's here now." I'm channeling Antonia. So when Jamie opens his mouth to protest, I continue. "You told me nothing's changed. And I believed you in that moment because I wanted to, but, Jamie. Everything's changed." I watch this land in his eyes, the sad recognition of a truth denied. "It doesn't have to stop us, this." I gesture between us. "But we can't ignore it either."

I sit down on the edge of the coffee table, right in front of him, knees to knees. "You know me well enough by now to know that I like having opinions." He snorts at this. "But luckily for you, I'm good at it. People pay me for my opinions, but I'm giving them to you for free. So keeping things from me isn't going to keep me from having opinions. It's just going to keep me from having informed opinions. Which is pointless." I take his hand. I take a risk. "Do you want me here?"

He looks into my eyes and I get a flash of the Jamie from our first tutorial. "Of course."

"Then treat me like I'm here. Don't shut me out. Don't act like it's already June eleventh. Because it'll come soon enough."

After a moment, Jamie sighs. "So we carry on, then, together?"

I nod. "Together. We'll go in March. The weather will be better anyway." *Everything will be better*, I tell myself.

After a moment, he picks up my hand, bends it back at the wrist, and kisses the palm. He lets his lips linger there. His eyes close. He inhales. He murmurs, "'We are here as on a darkling plane. Where ignorant armies clash by night.'" He opens his eyes, looks over my hand at me. His eyes, though tired, call to me like midnight pools. The hardest part of this is the fragility. The shroud of look-don't-touch over these moments of connection. The are-you-all right-how-do-you-feel filter.

He drops his head. I reach out and run my hand through his hair. He turns his head into my palm, like a cat. He leans forward, and places the top of his head on my chest, between my breasts.

"I swear," he mutters. "If that man is day, I'm night."

His hands find my hips.

He turns his head to the left.

As I begin rubbing my hands down his back all I can think is, *Day and night are just two sides of the same planet.*

CHAPTER 24

Be near me when the sensuous frame
Is rack'd with pangs that conquer trust;
And Time, a maniac scattering dust,
And Life, a Fury slinging flame.
Alfred, Lord Tennyson, *In Memoriam, L,* 1850

Ever thought about what it would be like to set up shop on a bathroom floor? I hadn't either. Now I'm an expert. I could teach workshops.

The secret is cushions. Pillows don't cut it. They're for amateurs. You want a big, sectional, one-piece cushion off an Oxfam couch placed perpendicular to the toilet. You'll want a blanket that's breathable (no microfiber, even though it would be easier to clean) that he can throw off depending on his internal temperature. You'll also want a space heater for the cold days, an oscillating fan for the adrenal fatigue days, and—this is crucial—find a cleaning product with a scent that doesn't make him more ill than he already is. Last but not least, find a video online that teaches you (step-by-step, it's harder than you'd think) how to convert a regular light switch into a dimmer. Why? So that, when he's dashing into the bathroom at three A.M., he can avoid that refrigerator-light-right-in-the-face experience. You'll learn that light can be painful.

I like to sit, as I am doing now, on the marble countertop, my back against the mirror, a book on the 1832 Reform Bill in my lap. Jamie moves slightly, restlessly. My senses attuned, I know what's coming. He throws off the blanket and pivots toward the toilet. I sit forward, but he holds out a hand. Wait. He hovers over the bowl for a moment, testing the waters, so to speak. I give him space, but I watch him like a hawk. Sometimes Jamie gets faint when he vomits, and about a month after he started the trial he lost consciousness and cut his forehead open on the edge of the toilet-paper holder. That face I once thought was too perfect to be handsome now has a white scar right through its left eyebrow. I got my man-with-a-story face, after all. After that, I insisted (and he finally acquiesced) on joining him in here.

Turns out, we have some of our best talks in this bathroom. We talk history (the world's and our own), George Eliot (I'm writing my thesis on the concept of education in Middlemarch), culture, science, philosophy, and, of course, literature. Occasionally we watch Abbott and Costello. I pratfall. Badly. Anything for a laugh.

Jamie sits back, propping himself against the wall. It was a false alarm. His legs sprawl in a wide V as if he's just run a marathon. He pretty much has.

According to Jamie, the trial's side effects have been "rather manageable." He averages five good days for every two bad ones and he's only been hospitalized twice (anemia again and a sepsis scare). He's managed to not break any bones (a pretty common feature of myeloma's bone-weakening havoc) and though he sleeps a lot, his energy levels when he's awake are almost normal. He's not teaching this term, but he's been getting revisions done, and he's even lectured a few times. I think what irritates him most is that he's never able to count on his body's cooperation. He'll be feeling fine one day, but there's crippling acid reflux the next, then a good day, then constipation. The unknown is relentless.

Somehow he still has his hair, which brands him a pariah in the group sessions. He tries to show people where it's thinning in the back. He's like the narrow-hipped, all-belly mom-to-be in a Lamaze class who assures the other women that she gained a little weight in her upper arms this week. *Bitch.* I don't have the heart to tell him his ingratiating explanations only make it worse.

"You know the Oxfordshire History Centre?" Jamie asks, voice witching-hour quiet.

This is the way of things; long strings of silence punctuated by non sequiturs. We both do it. In the last three months we've acquired backstage, VIP access to each other's brain.

"Never been," I answer.

"We ought to go."

I jump off the counter. "I'll get my purse."

He chuckles. That's good. Then he's puking. Not so good. I wait. He steadies himself. He continues talking. "I haven't been in ages, but there's this . . . thing, this . . . historical footnote I rather enjoyed. I keep thinking about it." He leans back against the wall.

I slide down onto the floor across from him. I hand him the water bottle, he rinses his mouth, turns, spits into the toilet. Rituals. I tentatively take his feet into my lap and try rubbing them. I watch his face, looking for any sign of discomfort. One of the weirder side effects is a transient nerve pain that comes and goes. When it's happening, Jamie can't be touched. He can't even touch surfaces—a chair, the couch, the bed—everything hurts. He wanders, zombie-like, from room to room, betting on his stamina to outlast the neuropathy. Now he moans in pleasure, indicating that I can keep rubbing his feet. "God, I miss you," he exhales.

Impotency. The big, scary, demon-conjuring word whispered in the group sessions. The wives slinking up to me. "And how long have you two been together?" My prevarication: officially together or sleeping together? At either answer, their eyes goggle, these women who have long since measured their relationships in years, in decades even, not months. "What, that's all? Poor lamb." Their advice: Don't talk about it. Don't bruise his ego. Take a romance novel into the bath, they said. So I did. Only I varied it slightly: when I took a romance novel into the bath, I had Jamie read it to me.

By hook or by crook. Or, in this case, by book, we've found ways to make it work. But honestly? It's still not enough. I feel fundamentally empty. I can only imagine how he feels.

Trust me, I understand the irony, considering how this relationship started.

But, Jamie had his final treatment yesterday. There's a light at the end of the tunnel. A big, red, Amsterdam-style light. Open for business.

Jamie is silent and I realize he might have nodded off. He does that. Some days he sleeps around the clock (literally, from ten one night to ten the next). We've long since moved the sickbed from the drawing room to his actual bed. So much for negative associations. While he sleeps, I'll sit in his bed and do work, either on my thesis or the campaign. Or I put my earbuds in and watch *The West Wing* for the thousandth time. On the bad days, I don't like leaving him while he's sleeping.

But on the good days, I'm out and about, at the Bod or the English faculty library, meeting with my adviser, going to classes and lectures, grabbing a pint with Maggie, Charlie, and Tom. I stay at Magdalen about half the time, and when I'm there I catch up with Hugh while I sort through my pidge, and chat with Eugenia in the early mornings. My Three Musketeers love that Jamie and I are together, but, at Jamie's behest, they still know nothing of his illness. He's immensely private and he should be. Because of Oliver, telling people Jamie has myeloma doesn't elicit looks of sympathy; it elicits looks of ghoulish horror, as if they're standing in the presence of a ghost.

Charlie's Blenheim Ball plan backfired. Now Tom just seems confused around Maggie. He barely speaks to her, is aloof and distant, which leads Maggie to believe that he's infatuated with someone else. Best-laid plans and all that. Having dinner with my friends, hearing college gossip, talking about their theses, watching Charlie try to make Ridley jealous by parading other guys in front of him . . . it gives me a chance to feel uncomplicated again. I'm just a girl studying abroad, unwittingly adopting an insufferable mid-Atlantic accent (especially after a few drinks), living in a rented attic room with the bare essentials. I have no roots in these moments. But I leave it all behind in a heartbeat to get back to Jamie and the old Victorian in North Oxford.

Some days he seems fine. Nearly normal. We laugh. We touch. We share a glass of wine. We get out of the house. We walk around the park, up to Port Meadow. We go see Lizzie, Bernard, and Ricky, have a finger of Jamie's whiskey and popcorn. We go to the Happy Cod, share an order of chips. When it's raining (so much of the time), we go to the Ashmolean or the Natural History Museum and stare at Anglo-Saxon treasure, illuminated manuscripts, dinosaur bones.

Watching Jamie go through this has been a lesson in fortitude. He doesn't ask the big questions. Why me? Why my brother? What's the point of it all? What's next? I've never heard him ponder, doubt, rail. I can only assume he got all of that out of his system the first time around, with Oliver. That first great loss, like a first love, I suppose, that prompts the questioning. Maybe, once you come to realize that there are no answers, you learn to live with the questions.

I get lunch with Cecelia at least once a week. I honestly don't know what I'd do without her knowledge and advice. (It doesn't hurt that she also happens to know everything about women's property rights in nineteenth-century Britain, because of her work on Elizabeth Gaskell, so she's helped me break through the more esoteric aspects of my research.)

Frankly, I'm kind of in love with her.

Frankly, I'm kind of in love with this life.

This unexpected life.

You would think I'd be running in the opposite direction, that I'd be checking my watch, waiting for that bus to take me back to Heathrow on June 11. But it's the opposite. I don't know why; I can't explain it.

Especially when I still love my job. I get a call from Gavin and the excitement kicks in, energizing me like a drug. Against all odds, Janet's survived the early primaries (even winning, to the pundits' shock, the Iowa caucuses) and all the candidates other than Vice President Hillerson have dropped out. But we haven't seen the numbers move one way or the other in about seven weeks; the two candidates just keep trading primary victories back and forth. The final debate is tonight, and a week from Tuesday there are primaries in five states, which should be the deciding factor.

Everything, it seems, is coming to a head. The final debate, Jamie's final treatment, my final term here . . . and I have no idea how any of it is going to end.

Life.

Jamie's eyes open and he continues talking as if he never paused. "At the Oxfordshire History Centre there's an old map of what Oxford used to look like at the very beginning of the university. A population of about five thousand, which isn't insignificant considering London was hovering around twenty thousand at the time. The river gave it strategic importance and the Normans built a castle here, on a mound that had already been used by the Danes when they routed the city in the—" Jamie stops himself, as he often does when he realizes he's lecturing. He thinks I mind. I don't. I think it's cute. "Point being, there had to be something here already, something unique to the place. The Saxons used Oxford as a center of trade and transport. Specifically, as a place to cross the Thames with livestock, such as oxen. Oxen fording the Thames. Which, obviously, is how Oxford was derived."

I nod, my attention still on rubbing his feet. "Oxenford."

"Right," he mutters as if coming out of a dream. "It's just that. That concept of a ford in the river. The place, the exact place where it's easiest to cross. How desirable it was. Is." He places a gentle hand on my thigh. It feels so good I practically purr. But he doesn't continue speaking and I glance up.

He's looking at me with what I can only describe as weary resignation. It's everything I never wanted to see in his eyes. It terrifies me. My heart beats once, loudly, like an animal surprised in the bush.

"Oliver was forced away from that place," Jamie murmurs, and I clench my fist to keep from reaching out and covering his mouth. "Dragged kicking and screaming. Forced to continue a fight he'd already lost. He didn't have the strength to override my father's insistence. Dominance. Lies. 'You're strong yet, Ollie, you're young, lad, you owe it to us, to those who love you. C'mon, one more fight, my boy.' He gave in. And he suffered. My rugger brother became a skeleton. He shat blood. He hallucinated hellfire. He tried to kill himself and they revived him. He was dragged further and further upstream. Past his Oxenford." Jamie's eyes refuse to leave mine, his jaw working, his teeth grinding. Angry, yes, but also righteous. "That will not happen again."

I can't reply. He's been so even-keeled these past few months, more stoic than I could ever imagine being in his situation. I know he's tired of being sick; I know he's been beaten down by this. Intellectually, I know all of this. But I haven't felt it, really understood it, until now.

"It's said we live longer now. Fallacy. We're simply kept alive longer. Death with dignity. Every culture had it. The Greeks drank hemlock. The Romans fell on their swords. Samurais and seppuku. Medieval knights, so armored there was no conceivable way to suicide on the battlefields, gave that honor to one another, a misericord slipped between the plates and straight into the heart. But us? No misericord for us. We cure people to death." He pauses. "This is where the ones who truly love you ought to step in, champion you. They ought to." Jamie swallows. "In those awful final days, the one who might have been able to give Ollie some comfort, the one he loved most, Ce, he kept away. He couldn't bear having her see what he'd been reduced to. By my father."

In the ensuing silence I can hear Jamie's breathing begin to thicken, grow more audible, more rasped, choking down the long-repressed emotion and losing. Finally, he says thinly, "He would have had him plugged into those bloody machines forever. So Oliver made me his Lasting. His Power of Attorney." Jamie swallows. "Truth? I had hoped that Oliver would die before it became my decision. Cowardly? Yes. But we might have come through the whole palaver without William ever knowing we'd switched the paperwork. We could have preserved the illusion that he was still in charge. When he found out . . . things were said." He stops. That's it. That's all I'm going to get.

Jamie can be obtuse, especially where feelings are concerned. He speaks in fragments, pieces that he leaves for me to put together.

To his credit, William has held up his end of their bargain. For the last three months it's been as if he doesn't exist. While Antonia visits often, and though I know William's been in London a lot for business, he's exiled himself from his son's life just to ensure Jamie does what, he believes, Jamie needs to do to keep his life. My translation? William loves Jamie. And William loved Oliver. That's evident now.

Tears seep from the corners of Jamie's eyes. I want to say something to help, to make it all better, but what would that be? Nothing helps the loss of a brother, the betrayal of a father. So I rub his feet while his hand kneads my thigh.

Jamie looks up, watery blue eyes finding mine. "Don't worry. I'm not giving up. That's not what I'm implying by any of this . . . natter." He chuckles once, softly, self-deprecating. "You're not rid of me yet. I'm only saying, when the time comes, let it be my Oxenford." He looks back down at his feet. "'*Sunset and evening star, and one clear call for me! And may there be no moaning of the bar, when I put out to sea.*'" Jamie closes his eyes.

Tennyson. Always Tennyson.

Everyone has his metaphor. For Tennyson it was a sandbar, for Jamie it's a ford in the river. For me?

I don't know yet.

I can't think about it.

I'm not ready to think about leaving this world. Right now I'm just struggling with the thought of leaving Jamie in June, and there is no metaphor for that.

Jamie's invited me to move in with him, but I haven't brought more than a toothbrush and pajamas over here.

Because when I pack up in June, I don't want to do it in this house. It has to be at Magdalen. The place I originally came here for and the place I will leave behind. I'm shallowly planted there; here, the roots have taken and will be harder to remove when the time comes.

"Relinquish," Jamie says, more calmly, more composed. "Knowing when to let go. Release oneself. There's nothing worse than being caught, trapped in indecisiveness." These random thoughts that come and go as he slips in and out, are little cherry bombs that he sets off in me.

When my father was dying, did he relinquish? It happened so fast. He probably spent his last moments cursing himself for taking an icy corner too quickly. But he knew his daughter and wife loved him, I'm certain of that. In that moment, was that enough?

I can't imagine the terror William must live in, that he could get a call in the middle of the night and it's me—me, whom he loathes—telling him Jamie's gone. Antonia's words come back to me. *Sometimes one must ask oneself why the bull is in the china shop in the first place.*

There's no right or wrong. No judgment to be passed. Life just gets complicated when people love each other. To take sides is an exercise in futility. How do we get rid of the sides?

How do I, in good conscience, leave Jamie at the mercy of his father if nothing's been resolved?

I will fix this. I will figure out a plan. It's my gift, after all, and it will be my parting gift to Jamie and his family. And, in truth, to myself as well. The gift of a plan duly executed. The gift of a clear conscience.

In the deathly quiet, my phone rings. My head drops to my chest. "I'm so sorry," I murmur.

Jamie squeezes my thigh, letting me know he doesn't mind. "The final debate. Just the two of them, Wilkes and Hillerson. It's tonight?"

"Yeah," I say, standing. "It's crunch time." I pull the phone out of my pocket, step out of the bathroom into the bedroom, and answer softly. "Gavin."

"So. Janet's pregnant."

What. "What?"

"She's pregnant." I've never heard his voice sound like this, detached, just reporting the facts. It's so unlike him. Which is why it takes me this long to realize he's not joking.

"It's not mine," he states.

Jesus, maybe he *is* joking. "Gavin, please, if this is your idea of a—"

"It's the boyfriend's. Peter's."

I don't even know where to start. "H-how far along is she?"

"Four months."

"Four months!" I yelp, turning farther away from the bathroom.

"Apparently, she's not very—how am I having this conversation?—'regular,' some premenopausal thing, so it took her a few months to figure it out. The goddamn doctor's office leaked it, just in time for the debate tonight. Not that she could've hid it forever." He sighs. A measure of Gavin comes back into his voice when he says, "It's done, kid. We've overcome a lot, but . . ." He sighs again. "This is just a bridge too far." I'm silent. "I gotta make calls."

"O-okay," I finally answer, but he's already hung up. I bring the phone down from my ear and just look at the blank screen.

It's over.

I should be surprised, and I am.

I should be shocked, and I am.

I should be angry. I am.

I should be afraid of what comes next; that too.

But with all that churning inside me, my only thought as I stare at the blank screen is: now I can stay in Oxford.

It trumps everything.

And that scares the hell out of me.

I turn back toward the bathroom and see Jamie. He's nodded off, back against the wall, chin to chest. The way a toddler can fall asleep. I stare at him for a moment. A long moment.

Then I step back out into the bedroom and call Gavin back.

"Yeah?" he answers.

"Why?" I ask.

"Why, what?"

"Why is it over? Why is she dropping out?" It's so quiet I think we've been disconnected. "Hello?"

"Oh, I don't know, Ella, just spit-balling here, but maybe because we can't have an unmarried, single mother for president?"

He's shouting by the end. I don't shout back. "Why, Gavin? Why can't we have an unmarried, single mother for president?"

He sighs, not listening. "Hillerson will eviscerate her tonight if she doesn't drop out, I won't put her in that position—"

"You'll excuse me but that's not for you to decide. Or Hillerson. Or the party. Or anyone else other than the American people. Give them the chance to decide. We'll never know what they want if we don't give them the choice."

There's a beat. "Ella, forgive me, but you're out of your—"

"Is she there?" I swallow. "Gavin, please, I know this is outside my wheelhouse, I know you didn't ask for my opinion, but I have one."

After an eternity, he exhales. "Hold on."

There's shuffling in the background and then I hear, on speakerphone, Janet's resigned voice. "Ella?"

"Don't drop out."

"Honey," she breathes, "I want this baby, with Peter. I thought it wasn't possible at my age. This is a once-in-a-lifetime—"

"Have your baby. And don't drop out." Though unsure how to read her silence, I forge on. "Do the debate."

"I appreciate your enthusiasm, but I don't see us overcoming this."

Anger bolts through me. "No, see, there's nothing to overcome! There's only something to become!" I pace. "Become the woman who stands up to this bullshit. Become the woman who challenges the patriarchal playbook."

"Ella—"

"We have to stop pretending that there are rules, that anyone knows anything. No one knows shit!"

There's a faint chuckle when she says, "I agree, trust me, but—"

"If nothing else," I huff, "if this ends next Tuesday, if we find out this is just too much for people to accept, then at least we elevated the discourse when we had the chance. That you were the candidate who didn't just have the answers, but dared to ask the questions. Do the debate. And. Ask. Why. Make Hillerson say it, make him say 'you're unfit,' not only to *your* face, but to the face of every woman in the country. All his arguments are specious: 'We can't have a pregnant candidate, we can't have a baby-mama POTUS.' Why? Because we've never had one before? And then ask him if he'd have a problem with a new father taking office? And then, once his own misogyny has painted him into a corner, ask him if he's suggesting that you'd only be fit to be president if you'd had an abortion? Socratic method his ass."

After a long moment, I hear the smile in her voice when she says, "Socratic method. Oxford's rubbing off on you." She sighs. "I'll think about it."

This stops me in my tracks. Really?

Oh God, what did I just do? I'm pretty sure I just asked a wonderful woman to go up onstage and lash herself to the feminist mast on national television.

I swallow. "It's a plan."

We hang up.

I stand there, my legs suddenly shaky. When I step back into the bathroom, I'm surprised to find Jamie looking at me through hooded lids, smiling slightly. "Are we watching the debate tonight?" he asks.

"If there is one," I hedge.

He nods at my phone. "I'm dying to know what that was about."

I drop back down at his feet, resuming our previous position. "I'd tell you, but then I'd have to kill you."

He cocks an eyebrow at me. "Why do you think I asked?"

I snort. It's sad, it's funny, and I'm suddenly exhausted. I drop my head. Then I feel Jamie's fingers in my hair, his palm cupping my cheek. I lean into it, let it strengthen me for a moment. "So," Jamie purrs. "Your birthday."

I look up at the abrupt change of topic. His eyes twinkle like they used to. He's feeling a bit better.

I smile, trying to rally. "Now we're talking."

"It's next week."

"Yes, it is."

"I want to take you somewhere. Shall we go somewhere?"

Is he kidding?

Despite the promise we both made to postpone our December trip to the Easter vac, it became clear about two weeks ago that Jamie could not travel. His oncologist flat-out prohibited it. Jamie is still having a hard time accepting it. Obviously.

After my birthday next week, I have a couple of weeks off before Trinity Term starts and Charlie, Maggie, and Tom have invited me to join them when they go to Morocco at the end of the break. I could, I guess, but I feel like I'm on countdown. I want to spend every last minute with Jamie. I want to watch him get better. We've earned it.

I shake my head at Jamie's suggestion. "We're having a stay-cation, remember? Recovery, get your strength back, have sex, write, have sex, follow-up blood work, have more sex."

He grins. "We'll be sensible, I promise. Just a few days. I'll get checked out before we go. We'll keep close. We could go to the Lakes or Cornwall. Or Bath! How about Bath? Or I could show you around Cambridge? Choose something, anything." I'm silent. "Anywhere you want. Anywhere you want that doesn't involve a boat or a plane. It's your birthday."

An idea forms. "Anywhere?"

He nods once, decisively, happily. Sure he's won.

I hold out my hand to shake. This is how we do deals in this relationship and I want him bound by this. "Anywhere?" I confirm.

Jamie shakes my hand and smiles. "You can't frighten me," he boasts. "Anywhere."

Before I can tell him, my phone dings. I look down at it. A two-word text from Gavin:

It's on.

CHAPTER 25

Be the green grass above me
With showers and dewdrops wet;
And if thou wilt, remember,
And if thou wilt, forget.
Christina Rossetti, "Song," 1848

taly, Greece, Croatia, New Zealand . . . these are the places you hear are beautiful. Why didn't anyone ever tell me that Scotland is gorgeous? I mean, mouth-droppingly, eye-buggingly, slap-yo-mama stunning.

We've been ascending the mountain for thirty minutes when Jamie finally deigns to speak. A welcome change from the grunts and sighs he's afforded me this whole week. "My mother's going to give you a tour of the house. Everything she tells you will be wrong."

An overeager laugh rips out of me, like ripping open a bag of Doritos so zealously that every last chip goes flying. Jamie, unaffected, continues. "She also invents clan names. The Mac-Grubberlochs had the finest herd of cattle in all the land, that sort of thing."

I risk taking his hand. He doesn't recoil. A major victory.

"She's so excited," I wheedle.

"As well she should be. This is the first time I've brought a girl home. She's likely arranged a parade."

Look, I get it. I tricked him. I sucker-punched him. I done did him dirty. But sometimes you have to hide the medicine in the peanut butter to get it down the dog's throat. (And if that doesn't work, well, grab its muzzle, pry its jaw open, and shove the pill all the way to the back of its stubborn gullet). But to his credit, he kept his word. Not once did he try to back out of his promise to take me anywhere I wanted to go.

That night, after I had told him I wanted to go to Scotland, we watched the debate on my laptop in the bathroom. The vice president saved the issue of Janet's pregnancy for the end, because—at his core—he's a showman and a media whore. Which means that when he dug himself into the hole I'd predicted, there was no crawling out of it before the end of the debate. It ended with Janet looking unfazed and Hillerson refusing to shake her hand as he walked off. When someone got him on camera and asked him how he thought it went, Hillerson, flustered, exclaimed, "She just kept asking, 'Why!'" Which became a viral meme within the hour. "She just kept asking why" is now Janet's unofficial campaign slogan. When I got the text from Gavin that said, *That was all you, Kid, tip of the hat,* I finally let myself have a moment of profound personal pride. Though still miffed with me about Scotland, Jamie opened one of his fancy bottles of wine (that he couldn't drink) and toasted me with a water glass.

I bring his hand to my mouth now and kiss it, noticing the stains around his cuticles. He's been feeling much better, almost completely back to normal, so he insisted on stripping and staining the floors on the second story of the house over the past few days. A psychologist would probably have a field day with the symbolism, but he just wanted to use the time away to let the floors cure and the odor dissipate.

I look up at him through my lashes, adopt a coquettish kitten voice that never fails to get an eye roll. "Do you hate me?"

On cue, Jamie rolls his eyes. "I've survived worse than a weekend with my family."

I glance out the window. "You seriously grew up here?"

"Partly. Summers, holidays."

"Shut up!" I screech when Jamie turns a corner and reveals a vista of craggy gray cliffs leading down to spring-green pastureland divided by low stone walls and dotted with shaggy highland cattle. I notice an old, abandoned gatehouse on our left, gates open. Before I can comment on its beauty, Jamie turns the Aston and we drive through it.

Oh my God.

The road stretches straight before us, bordered by towering oak trees, boughs arcing over us, tipping their leafy hats in a grand gesture of welcome. Jamie picks up speed, blowing down the lane.

Openmouthed, I stare at the house that's just revealed itself through the copse of trees. I'm sorry, did I say house? I mean, estate. Castle. Compound. Ecosystem.

Jamie accelerates and we screech up to the house as if making a pit stop in the Indy 500. Gravel sprays as we skid to a stop. He throws the car in park, looks at me, and takes a deep, bearing-up breath. He opens the door and steps out. I can't. Not yet. I can only gaze, in awe, at the sheer stone front of the house. This part of it looks like Blenheim (probably from the same time period), but the wing to the right looks older and castle-y, turrets and battlements.

As I get out of the car, the double front doors of the house fly open and Antonia steps out, clapping her hands. Another woman, as wide as she is tall with a crop of bushy white hair, waddles purposefully down the steps behind her. Wearing an apron and a towel thrown over her shoulder, she makes a beeline for Jamie, coming at him like a brick wall and engulfing him in a bosom-centric hug. She pulls back, looking stern.

"Let me look atcha!" she demands. Jamie stands up straight and holds out his arms like he's at an army induction center. "Just as I s'pected. Too thin," she declares, shaking her head. She jabs a pudgy thumb behind her. "Me broth's in the house. Made it especial."

Jamie glances at me with a warm, genuine smile I haven't seen in a week. "Ella, this is Smithy, the love of my life. Smithy's broth has curative properties."

Smithy grunts in the affirmative. She takes a closer look at me, sticking out her hand. I take it. "You must be the birthday girl everyone's makin' such a fuss about."

Antonia slips in to hug me, announcing, "So you've finally rid yourself of that dreadful stuffed-shirt professor, have you? What was his name? Doesn't matter, you've done quite well for yourself. You've brought a gorgeous boy with you."

"I could easily get back into this car and be off," Jamie says, not entirely joking.

Antonia huffs. "Well, if you're going to be a priss about it." She goes to her son and takes him full around. Jamie kisses the top of her head. No matter what happens, I'm already so happy. Just seeing them together, here, meeting Smithy, makes the last week worth it.

Jamie puts one arm around Antonia and the other around Smithy and turns toward the house. "Now, Mother, I've promised Ella the grand tour and she's quite keen. You know how she loves history, and you're the perfect person to . . ." He trails off and stops walking. I follow his gaze to the open doorway.

William looms over us. He jerks his head. "Hello." He looks to me. "Welcome, Eleanor."

"Thank you," I reply. "I'm very happy to be here."

He turns back to Jamie, takes him in, assessing. "Jamie."

"Father."

"You're looking rather well. As it were."

"You as well. As it were."

In the silence, they stare at each other. Two bulls on opposite sides of a pasture.

"Boys, please," Antonia stage-whispers, jerking her head toward Smithy. "Must you be so effusive in front of the staff?" Smithy cackles, her laugh sounding exactly like I imagined it would. I have to bite my lip to keep from joining her.

William reddens. "Yes, well. I'll have Colin take care of the bags and such." With that, he turns back into the house. Jamie takes a breath and we all follow him.

ANTONIA, PEEKING INTO an under-the-stairs bathroom, says with a sly grin, "The wood on these walls was nicked from Warwick Castle during the Reformation." Then Jamie whispers to me, "Kennilworth." Antonia continues, "Right before my great-great-great-great-grandfather was given the house and land by James the Sixth." (Jamie whispers, "The Fifth.") In a fifty-foot-long gallery overlooking the pond, Antonia points to a portrait and declares, "That is Jamie's ancestor, a MacTartanish, who hid from the English during the Troubles by dressing as a woman and living in the kitchens with the servants." (Jamie whispers, "MacTavish; stables.") Antonia points into a rock-walled, dungeon-looking room in a turret and announces, "Elizabeth imprisoned Mary Queen of Scots in these rooms in 1437."

Jamie: "Absurd."

Antonia: "She escaped by rappelling down a bedsheet tied to

the radiator."

Jamie: "A medieval radiator, you see."

Upstairs, we come to a long, wide hallway with rows of tall white doors on each side. Two across from each other are open. "This will be your room," Antonia says, sweeping into the one on the right. I follow her and notice that my bag has appeared on a settee at the foot of a massive canopied bed, curtained with heavy antique brocade. Four huge windows overlook the vast property, all the way to the cliffs beyond. Every piece of furniture belongs in a museum.

"This is stunning."

I'm about to gush further, but Jamie, who's ventured farther in to the room, searching for something, speaks first. "Mother, where's my valise?"

"In the Rose Room, dear."

Jamie's hands find his hips. He levels a look at Antonia. "Is that so?"

She slinks for the door, coming back to me. "Your father and I thought it best. There are traditions of the house, long-standing traditions."

"All the way back to the Eskimo invasion of 45 BC," Jamie mutters.

Antonia leans in to me. "I've put slippers by your bed. The hallway floor gets rather chilly at night. Wouldn't want you getting cold feet." She exits to the hallway, leaving Jamie and me alone.

"What did she say?" he asks. He sounds stroppy, impatient. Jesus. Get him anywhere near William and it's as if he filches only the most unpleasant aspects of his father's personality.

I squeeze his arm. "We'll be fine."

Jamie exhales. I know why he's upset at being separated. We haven't had a chance to be together yet—what with his recovery, and the floors, and my, you know, sucker punching.

Jamie seems to relax. "Right. Well, then." He looks around the room. The fleur-de-lis wallpaper, the gilded vanity and mirror, the abundance of decorative pillows. He seems reflective. It's obviously been a while since he's walked these rooms. When I go back to the house I grew up in, I'm always shocked at how small it is. This is clearly not that experience, but I can relate to seeing something so familiar with new eyes. "It's rather . . . fussy," Jamie mutters. "And cold."

"I love it. All of it. Every corner." I look up at him. "I love her."

He looks down at me, finally meeting my eye. A heat sparks there, a heat I haven't seen in months. A heat that isn't banked or contained. A heat like "Dover Beach." Like the Buttery. Like his dining room. A heat with potentiality. "I love her, too," he murmurs.

I don't know why we can both say that so freely about his mother, but haven't yet said it to each other, about each other. Maybe he doesn't feel it. Maybe he's just English. Maybe he's protecting himself.

I know which reason is mine.

I go up on tiptoe. I kiss him softly. He kisses me back. Not so softly.

"Are you two coming?" Antonia calls from the hall.

Jamie groans in the back of his throat, like a discontented bear.

Antonia leads us back downstairs, describing the frescoes and the battle they depict (which even I can see is, in fact, a hunt). We stop in front of two solid oak doors.

"Last stop." Antonia smiles. "The library. Where Jamie once locked his brother in a suit of armor."

"He asked me to!"

"Overnight?"

I laugh. Antonia nods toward the doors. "You do the honors."

I happily grab hold of the round knobs and push the double doors open with purpose, as if I were presenting mother and son to the room—

Why are there balloons?

Why are there streamers?

Why is William smiling?

What are they doing here?!

"Surprise!" everyone cries.

Charlie, Maggie, and Tom (wearing some kind of hunting outfit and waders) charge over and sweep me into a group hug. Tears spring to my eyes. Over Charlie's shoulder I see Jamie's smile become a laugh as he and Antonia embrace. I hear him say to his mother, "Completely surprised."

"Couldn't have come off better," she confirms.

I disentangle one arm and reach out for them both. Jamie laces his fingers through mine. He leans forward and finds the space to kiss my cheek, warming me to my core, a roaring fire on a winter night. He planned this. Even though he was pissed at me, even though he didn't want to come, he did this for me.

I love this man. I love everything about him.

I promise myself that I'm going to tell him that.

AFTER A BIRTHDAY tea in the library, I open presents. I get a collection of (used) philosophy books from Tom, a leather-bound journal from Maggie, and a bottle of fine Scotch from Charlie, which manages to get William's nod of approval. Although he keeps leaving the room to take a call, he always comes back. While we haven't said anything to each other, we've exchanged a number of tight smiles and nods. Progress?

Jamie hands me one final card. "From Ce." I look at the envelope, my name written in cursive on the front. As I slip my finger under the flap, Jamie continues, "She desperately wanted to be here, but she had an obligation from which she couldn't extricate herself."

Maggie, sitting across from me on a love seat next to Tom, nudges him in the ribs. "How sad for you."

Tom seems distracted, preoccupied. He's still unable to meet Maggie's eye. "Cecelia Knowles? Ancient history."

Her mouth forms a confused moue, although she continues to tease him. "Oh, is that so?"

Tom nods tightly. "I've moved on. To more fertile ground."

Charlie, who's been inspecting the first editions around the room, doesn't even have the wherewithal to turn to Tom when he groans, "Oh, good God, who now? Vegetable, mineral, or beast?"

"I'm not at liberty. To say. At present."

Maggie faces forward again, placing her hands primly on her knees, out of things to say. Even as I extract from the envelope a gift certificate for a spa in Oxford (and silently thank Cecelia for knowing just what I need), my eyes are drawn to Maggie and Tom, who now sit next to each other like two owls sharing a stumpy tree branch, staring straight ahead. Maggie meets my eyes, brow furrowed.

But then Jamie leans over and whispers in my ear, "My gift will come later."

I turn to him, raising an eyebrow, whispering back, "It better."

"It's not that." His eyes drop to my mouth. "Well, it very well could be that." He looks back up. "I have a present, of sorts. Rather silly and sentimental. Not for public consumption."

Before I can reply, my phone rings. I dig it out of my pocket as the room goes quiet. "Don't mind me!" I urge, and everyone resumes their conversations. Everyone except William, who continues to watch me. It's like the Blenheim ball all over again. I stand and walk to a corner of the library as I answer. "Gavin."

I'm greeted by a tinny, speakerphone rendition of "Happy Birthday." Janet's horribly off-key and Gavin's deep bass drowns her out, but it's still sweet of them. When they're done, they applaud. For themselves. Why do people do that?

I laugh. "Very nice! Thank you. Both of you!"

"How old are you now?" Janet asks, a chuckle in her voice.

"Twenty-five."

Gavin groans. "I have socks older than you."

"Now, Gavin," she reprimands. "This is actually good news. Her being twenty-five and all."

"Why, Janet, you're right. Very good news."

My ear pricks, like hearing a different frequency. They sound rehearsed. Teasing and wink-wink-nudge-nudge. "How so?" I ask.

"Well . . ." Gavin sighs theatrically. "You know the trouble we've been having filling the deputy political director position." God, do I. It's practically all we've talked about for months now. Janet doesn't like any of the people Gavin and I and everyone else have thrown at her and we're running out of suggestions. "We've realized that there's one detail, one quality, that none of them have."

My mouth dries. "Oh yeah?"

"None of them have been twenty-five."

"Not a one!" Janet chirps.

"And we've agreed that's a deal breaker. We just can't have someone who isn't twenty-five."

I feel as if the smile taking over my face is going to run right off it. "I completely agree," I manage to say.

"Good," Gavin says. "We thought you would." Now they

both laugh. "So, you're in?"

It's a funny thing, clocking the moment your life changes forever while it's happening. Usually a moment's significance only matters in retrospect. Seeing the exit you meant to take in the rearview mirror, that sort of thing. Not this time. I suppose it's like seeing your boyfriend go down on one knee, or watching a plus sign appear on a pregnancy test. Or, on the other side of life, opening your front door to find a sad-eyed cop with his hat in his hand.

Which just makes me think of another birthday, twelve years ago. I push it down.

"I'm in! Thank you! Both of you!"

"Just remember," Gavin says, his stern-father voice on. "Enjoy the rest of your time there. But, on June eleventh, the carriage turns into a pumpkin and the footmen into mice. You come home and help us change the world. We're counting on you."

"It's a plan," I answer.

We hang up and I float back to my friends in a daze. I sit down once again next to Jamie; he takes my hand.

"Everything all right, Eleanor?" Antonia asks.

"Yes!" I chirp. "Sorry about that."

"No need, love. But, if we may . . . we have something for you. William and I," she clarifies.

William moves to stand behind her chair. They look as if they're posing. In fact, I'm reminded of the photograph in Jamie's dining room and realize that it was taken in this library. William sets his hand on her shoulder while she reaches into her pocket and takes out a small blue velvet box. Its edges are threadbare, showing its age. As Antonia extends her arm, presenting the box palm up, my heart drops into my stomach.

"It appears they're proposing," Jamie drawls.

At my hesitation, Antonia thrusts the box closer to me. "Go

on, then."

I take it. I try to keep my hand from shaking. I try to breathe. I open the lid. It's exactly what I didn't want to see. It's a ring. A diamond ring. I move to hand it back. "Antonia, please, this is—"

"The diamond is flawed," Antonia blurts. "It has no monetary value, really. No need to refuse. Jamie told us that you're not a jewelry person," she says, smiling. "It's for your love of history, a keepsake that you might find of value."

I gaze up at her.

She takes a breath. "Before the war—the first one—a wealthy American woman married into this family. Quite unwillingly. She was more than content with a young clerk she had decided upon, but her father refused their engagement and shipped her off to the wilds of Scotland. This was the ring her clerk had given her."

I look back down at it. Emeralds encircle the diamond, which is small but well set. The band looks brand-new. Never worn.

"She kept that ring in the back of her nightstand drawer. Now, you might pity her, but don't. She had a surprisingly happy marriage here. Had four children. My father was her eldest, actually. My grandmother and I were quite close."

William interjects awkwardly, "She was my grandmother-in-law, you see."

The entire room pauses. Antonia looks up at him and smiles, giving his hand a loving pat. "Yes, dear, very true." She turns back to me and continues: "She never heard from her clerk again. She did what was asked of her—well, if it comes down to it, what she was told—yet she had a fine life regardless. Now, we don't always get to choose what happens in life, don't we all know. However, we can choose what we do with what we're given." Antonia pauses. "And so this ring is for you. A thank-you from two parents who are quite impressed with the choices you've made in this situation you've found yourself in." She glances quickly at Jamie and smiles back at me.

I'm caught in her eyes. Eyes that hold the weight of her two sons. One here, one not. And still, she chooses to smile at me. To thank me. To give me a family heirloom like a daughter.

I know my mouth is hanging open. I turn to Jamie. He shrugs, says, "That story's correct."

I see Maggie, Charlie, and Tom exchanging confused, curious glances, but they're too polite to speak up, to ask for clarification.

Then, as if none of this ever happened, Antonia glances at her watch and stands. "I must talk to Smithy about the roast. Happy birthday, love." She bends down and kisses my stunned cheek, straightens, and walks to the door.

Jamie calls after her, "Aren't you going to tell her your grandmother's name?"

"Oh, bother, of course." She sighs, turning back to me, briefly. "Carolina Vanderbilt."

I AM SO full of so many things right now and none of them have anywhere to go. "Jamie, where's the bathroom?"

"I'll take you."

"No, just point the way." It comes out sharper than I intended.

Jamie shows me where to go and I take off across the grand foyer and down a long hallway. I want to bolt out the front door, a horse out of the corral. Instead, I'm going to go lock myself in one of the twenty-seven bathrooms for a minute. Just a minute.

I finally find it, and close the door, leaning against it, breathing. In and out. In and out.

I see myself in the exquisite mirror over the sink. It's as if I can see the thoughts running in and out of my head like Metro

Center at rush hour.

I want to look at the ring again, focus on that for a moment. I take the box out of my pocket and pop it open. The ring really is beautiful, trinket or not. I gently take it out and—*dammit!*—it slips from my hand, falling into the copper sink. I dive after it, trying to grab it before it goes down the drain. It escapes one hand and I pounce with the other, trapping it with my palm. I slowly lift my hand, pinching at it with my thumb and forefinger, but end up shooting it closer to the drain. *Jesus!* I lurch forward with both hands, a final, desperate grab before it disappears into drain hell. Got it!

I steady my hands before I oh-so-gently pluck the ring out of the sink and carefully put it back in the box.

I'm never taking it out again. It's as if the ring knows I'm unworthy of having it.

I look in the mirror. A newly appointed deputy political director stares back at me.

THERE'S NOTHING LIKE the smell of good food being prepared by people who know what they're doing. Smithy is one of those people. "Before we leave, will you show me how to make coq au vin?" I ask her.

Her face lights up. "You like it, do ya?"

"It's the best thing I've ever had." I'm not blowing smoke either. I've become addicted to Smithy's coq au vin.

Charlie, Maggie, and Tom are exploring the grounds and Jamie is taking a nap, tired from the drive. I watch Antonia and Smithy put the finishing touches on dinner. They've given me a menial task, folding napkins. Which they had to teach me how to do first. I had no idea there were so many wrong ways to do it.

Suddenly William walks into the kitchen, his determined gate interrupted by my presence. He has a moment of hesitation, as if he's stumbled into the women's bathroom at a restaurant. "Hello," he mutters. "I've finished for the day. I came to see if there's anything I can do."

I glance down. "Wanna help me fold?"

"Surely one person is more than enough." He looks to Antonia. Then, seeming to hear his answer on a delay, he glances back at me. "But thank you."

Antonia bustles over to him, wiping her wet hands on her apron. She takes him by the elbow and steers him toward a beautiful old door with handcrafted ironwork, which I've been peering at, trying to figure out where it leads. "Go down to the cellar and pick out some wine. Champagne to start."

"Colin can choose, you know I'm not the best at—"

"I have complete faith in you," she drawls. "Now shoo!"

William sighs, looking like a reprimanded child, and leaves through the iron door, disappearing down a spiral staircase. It's endearing, the way this overbearing, hotheaded man defers to his wife.

Antonia goes back to the island where she's been chopping an onion. After a moment, she says, "William is actually quite happy to see you. He knows you had everything to do with getting Jamie here. He's thrilled. He's talked about it for days."

"Have they said anything to each other yet?"

Smithy glances between us as she kneads dough, lips pursed, tracking everything. "When the two o' thems don't speak a word is when they say the most, if ya ask me."

I lean forward. "They need to be locked in a room somewhere until one of them crawls out bloodied and victorious, eating the other's heart."

Antonia snorts. "They might do, it wouldn't surprise—" She looks up and her face lights up with that special smile she reserves for Jamie. "My lad! You're up. Feeling better?"

He's loitering in the doorway, looking adorable. Hair still rumpled from his nap, misbuttoned shirt. His voice is throaty when he says, "Yes, cheers. Slept quite soundly, actually." He crosses over to me and kisses the side of my head. I lean into him, loving the smell of sleepy Jamie. "What can I do?" he asks.

"Fold?" *He* won't refuse me.

He nods and scoots out the chair next to me. The easy silence that fills the kitchen gives me a sense of calm that I haven't felt since I don't know when; members of a family, working together, preparing a meal. It's all so . . . right. Except for William. He belongs here and yet his presence would be disruptive. If only these two men could see what I see in them, a boyishness, a tenderness. They've lost sight of—

"Jamie, can we have champagne? Now?" I ask. "I'm feeling celebratory."

"Of course." He stands, kisses me. "I'll just run upstairs for a jumper. Bit dank in the cellar."

He leaves and the kitchen goes silent.

Antonia and Smithy look at each other and, as one, turn to me. Antonia, wide-eyed, whispers, "You clever, clever girl."

Panic sets in. This wasn't the plan. The plan was to have a mediated sit-down, a Camp David–worthy summit. "You think? It was totally spontaneous, I didn't really think it through—"

"It was brilliant."

"Shall we ready the whiskey and bandages?" Smithy quips, slapping her dough onto the table.

Antonia takes a stuttered breath, her casual bravado gone. "What now?"

"We wait, I guess."

"All right, we wait." We all go back to our tasks. Smithy continues to work her dough. Antonia begins chopping anything in front of her.

"What if they need a referee? I mean, you're so good at that." My voice has accelerated.

Antonia stops chopping and peers at me. "They should have their time. Some privacy, don't you think?"

"Yes. Absolutely. Of course."

"We'll give it twenty minutes. If they don't reappear, we'll take the back stairs down."

"There are back stairs?" I sound desperate.

Antonia nods once.

I fold. Antonia chops. Fold. Chop. Dough slap. Fold. Chop. Dough slap.

"Twenty minutes is a long time," comes out of me.

"Ten minutes, then. We'll give them ten minutes."

Fold. Chop. Dough slap.

Smithy looks between us, her eyes moving like a metronome.

Fold. Chop. Dough slap.

Antonia and I stop. We look at each other.

Without another word, we both leave the kitchen.

CHAPTER 26

And we were in that seldom mood
When soul with soul agrees,
Mingling, like flood with equal flood,
In agitated ease.

Coventry Patmore, "The Rosy Bosom'd Hours," 1876

The "back stairs" are encased in one of the turrets. Timeworn stone spirals downward into what might once have been a dungeon. I'm definitely coming back later to explore. If we're still here, that is. Or if I'm not being questioned by police.

Antonia precedes me, and at the last stair, just before we step through an archway, she stops. I hear footsteps coming toward us, echoing in a tunnel. We tuck back into the staircase, hidden from view by the curve of its rough wall. There's a small cough, which I immediately recognize as Jamie's. The footsteps turn before they reach us, and stop. "Oh! Sorry."

"Not at all," I hear William say, and realize that the cellar must be on the other side of the wall we're leaning against. "Can I help you?" William's voice sounds even more ominous in the cellar's echoes.

"Ella asked me to fetch champagne." Jamie pauses. "Though

I'm beginning to think . . ."

Antonia and I grimace guiltily at each other.

"Right," William mutters. "Well, since you've come, you might as well—"

"I'm sure you have it well in hand." Jamie's shoes click, as if he's turning to leave.

"Jamie." William's voice is tight. "Might we have a word?"

I hold my breath. Antonia and I stare at each other, on tenterhooks. Jamie sighs. "Must we?"

Antonia's eyes close, looking as disappointed as I feel. *Dammit, Jamie.*

"Of course not," William huffs. "I thought you might have an opinion on the wine, but I'm perfectly capable—"

"I believe it was champagne she . . ." But even talking about wine seems too overwhelming. "Never mind." Jamie's footsteps fill the ancient stone tunnel and then diminish.

Antonia and I look at each other. Should we leave? Should we stay? On the other side of the wall, we hear William root through wine bottles. The sound of glass knocking against wood, of bottles yanked from a rack and pushed back in. Then, an unnatural stillness.

Then, an explosion of shattering glass.

Antonia and I both jump. It's not the sound of something being dropped; it's the sound of something being dashed. William's breathing grows so loud we can hear it from around the corner, guttural and choked. The bull has entered the china shop.

Then he's sobbing. Feral, bestial sobs. A pained little groan slips from Antonia's lips and she turns to go to him. I grab her hand. She looks at me, bewildered. I point toward the hallway and then to my ears.

Jamie's returning footsteps.

William must hear them, too, because he swallows his sobs. Jamie's heels turn the corner into the cellar and, once again, stop dead. "Not one of the Château Lafites, I hope." Then, "I thought I heard something as I topped the stairs." William doesn't reply. Jamie doesn't move. "Everything all right?" Jamie ventures.

"Smashing," William chokes out.

"Rather."

"It slipped. Nothing to fuss about."

"I'll get the broom." Jamie's voice deadens as he moves deeper into the cellar.

"Leave it, I'll have Colin or one of the—"

But I hear the creak of an old hinge and Jamie says, "I've got it."

"Don't. Let it be. The last thing I need is you cutting yourself." The sound of glass scraping against the floor. "Damn it all, I said leave it!" William explodes. "Might I be allowed to run my own ruddy house?"

"For Christ's sake, I'm only—" A heavier set of footsteps strides toward the tunnel hallway. "Right, of course! Walk away. God, I hate . . ." Jamie falters. I imagine him clenching his jaw, his fists, every part of him in one tight coil ready to spring.

"Go on," William dares. "You hate . . . ? You obviously have something to say, so say it, you ungrateful—"

"Stop!" Silence. Then, "Oliver's last word, remember?"

"What are you dredging up now?"

Antonia's hand finds mine.

After a moment, Jamie continues. "We were standing on opposite sides of his bed, arguing over him, and he said, 'Stop.' You pretended not to hear it. 'Stop,' and then he passed out. Never regained consciousness. Four hours later he needed the ventilator and I had to make the decision. And you hated me for it. 'Stop.' His word, not mine."

Antonia squeezes my hand and I watch her eyes fill and overflow, tears trickling down like a roadside waterfall.

"I wasn't aware," William blusters. "I couldn't hear—"

"'Stop.'"

After a moment, the sound of tinkling glass resumes. "Hand me the bin." Jamie sighs. A metal pail scrapes across the floor, followed by the tinny ring of glass dropping into it.

"You routed me," William says more strongly.

"And you gutted me," Jamie fires back.

"How so?" William shouts. "Maybe, had you consulted me, instead of behaving like some petulant child—"

The bin crashes to the floor. *Oh God, are they going to come to blows?*

"You said," Jamie yells, "his body still warm before us, you said, 'Why Oliver? Why did it have to be Oliver?'"

My eyes pop open. As do Antonia's. She doesn't know this either?

Even William sounds appalled. "I never said such a thing!"

"You did."

"I would never!"

"First you blamed me for killing him and then you salted the wound by wishing it were me in his place."

"No! Untrue! A father doesn't favor—"

"Oh, come off it, you would have gladly exchanged—"

"I was talking about myself!" William roars. "I wanted it to be me lying there! Me! Not you! God forbid, not you." Rasping breath and then, "I said what I said, Jamie. I did. I blamed you, yes." William's voice is as tight as an overwound clock. "But wish you dead? I love you! It was just . . . the pain had nowhere to go, you see, nowhere to—"

A sob rips through the cellar, echoing off the stone. I look to Antonia, but her eyes are closed. Jamie struggles for breath, for control. "Apologies," he chokes out. "What you said. Was just . . . unexpected."

When he speaks again, William sounds mystified. "What have I done, honestly, Jamie, what have I done to make you think I would ever wish—"

"Not that." Jamie clears his throat. "I mean, yes, that. But no, it was the word 'love' what surprised me."

"Oh, please," William scoffs. "Don't act as if you don't know that."

Eventually, the tinkling sound of glass being swept up breaks the silence. Again. Jamie, voice more controlled now, speaks. "I've heard every other bloody thing. Your disappointment. Your anger. But love? No. That stays bottled up inside you like all these wines, just sitting here, waiting to be shared, enjoyed, but too valuable to open. You're so afraid that once they're drunk, there will be no more, it will all be gone. Well, one day, it'll be gone anyway whether you drink it or not."

"You're quite the poet, I'll give you that," William drawls. Jamie sighs, defeated, muttering something that prompts William to counter, "Oh, come now, I'm joking. I . . . I do understand. What you're saying, I do. But my father—"

"Dammit!" Jamie hisses. "Bugger it all to hell." Antonia and I both look up, panicked.

"Christ, d'you cut yourself?"

"It's fine."

"Let me see."

"I'm fine."

"I have a handkerchief. I'll wrap it."

"It'll stain."

"I don't give a mouse fart, give me your hand."

Silence.

A long silence.

William speaks first. "I believe I may have made a bit of a mess of things."

"It was a crap vintage anyway."

William snorts.

Jamie sighs, all the heat seeming to have left him. As if, having volleyed those barbed words back and forth with William, having purged them, they've been dulled, rendered inert. "Dying is awful business."

"Don't say that."

"It's not true?"

"You're not dying."

Jamie scoffs. "We're all dying."

Silence.

"I can't lose both of you, Jamie. I won't allow it." William's voice breaks.

"You won't allow it."

"Sons do not die before fathers. It's not the order of things. I've done what I've done, I do what I do, because I refuse to accept that this is my lot. Simply can't fathom that I can't fix it. I can't buy the cancer out of you. I can't pay it to go away, I can't bully it away. What have I done in this life that I'm forced to watch both my sons die before me?"

When Jamie finally replies, his voice is strangled. "I'm sorry. I truly am. But there is no order to things. I can't let you do to me what you did to Oliver, just so you feel like you've done everything you can. I won't have 'stop' be my last word."

"Live and let live, is that it?"

"Live and let die, more like."

Antonia leans her head against the wall, turns into it.

William swallows, his tongue clicking against the roof of his mouth, betraying its dryness. Betraying his fear. "It all seems rather pointless. We fix and repair, fix and repair, only to have it break again. I don't know what to do, Jamie. Tell me what to do."

"Open the bottle. Open every damn bottle you can, while you can. Then let me go. In love. That's what you can do."

Unbidden, I think of "*Dover Beach*" and Jamie asking me what Matthew Arnold is saying, and me replying, *In death, love is all there is.* He asked me how that made me feel and I, stupidly, naively said, *Lonely.* But not Jamie. No, Jamie answered, *Hopeful.*

Because Jamie knew all of this already.

After a time, I hear them pulling away from each other and I realize that they were embracing. The sound of a hand pounding on a back as William says hoarsely, "Damn stiff upper lip. Everything comes out eventually, I suppose."

"Try being with an American," Jamie quips. They chuckle.

William clears his throat. "How's your hand?"

"I'll live." They both snort at that. "I feel rather better, I must say."

"If only feeling better made it easier."

"Well," Jamie argues, "at least it doesn't make it harder."

William groans slightly. "Ever the optimist."

"Quoth the pessimist."

They share a chuckle. William sighs. "We better get back up there. Your mother's probably called the coroner. Here, we'll take this one up for supper."

"We're not drinking this."

"What's wrong with it?"

"It's more expedient to ask what's right with it."

"You know," William growls, "where I come from, we drink ale. All this fuss about wine, with the year and the vintage—"

"They're the same thing, old man."

Antonia and I look at each other, unable to contain our smiles as they begin bickering. I point up the stairs with a nod, indicating that we should leave them to it. But Antonia tugs my hand. I look at her. She tugs harder and pulls me into her, our hands unclasping and her arms enveloping me. She kisses the hair above my ear and croaks, "Thank you."

I swallow. To be hugged by a mother and have nothing but gratitude and joy there; it's heady stuff. I squeeze her and then, for some reason I don't understand, nudge her back. We look at each other and she smiles again. She whispers, "Shall we join them?"

I'm about to go with her, but something inside me—for a reason I now understand—whispers back, "You go."

She looks disappointed, but wipes her eyes, takes a breath, and turns away, stepping through the archway and to her left, into the wine cellar. "Ah, splendid!" she cries, sounding chipper. "You haven't killed each other."

They laugh. They speak easily. They tease, they prod, they poke.

I find I can't take a step. I find I have to lean against the wall for a moment. Just a moment and then I'll leave. I promise. I just want to appreciate this.

The three of them, on the other side of the wall, are a single unit now. Unseeable, unknowable, by me. I got what I wanted. I'm free to leave now.

So why don't I want to?

I take a breath. I force my foot onto the next stair, and then the next, and the next. Leaving them behind.

"So, Professor Davenport," Charlie says, holding his champagne flute up by his face and leaning across the table toward Jamie. "I should like to know your intentions."

"Charlie, please," Jamie replies. "My parents don't know

about us yet."

Everyone chuckles, including Charlie, who huffs, "They'd have to be blind not to see the way you look at me." We're sitting in the grand dining room, the seven of us spread out around a table meant for twenty, Antonia and William at each head, Jamie and me on one side, Charlie, Maggie, and Tom on the other. We've gone through two bottles of bubbly and three bottles of wine. And that's just since the start of dinner. Smithy's delicious quintessential English roast dinner, of which she took only one considering bite from Jamie's plate before declaring it edible, wished me happy birthday, slipped into her coat, and excused herself for the night.

Charlie has recently begun resting his elbows on the table, something he would never do sober. The avidity in his eyes makes me nervous. That, and the fact that he's pouring himself more champagne.

"Seriously now," Charlie continues. "Tell us your plans."

Jamie is less comfortable with this question. "Don't have any, really." He holds his empty glass up to William, who wordlessly refills it.

"Sorry, but you'll be teaching?" Maggie prods.

"Well, that remains to be seen—"

"Cease this prevaricating!" Charlie bangs his fist on the table for effect. "What's to become of Ella from Ohio, our dear Yankee orphan?"

I slide my glass to the right. "William?"

He turns with the bottle. "Pleasure."

Charlie wobbles a hand at Jamie. "Will you move to Washington? Surely they need skinny-bejeaned, schoolgirl-fantasy liabilities in America as well."

"Actually"—I jump in—"I'll probably be traveling with the campaign, so there's no point in Jamie moving—"

"You're not breaking up!" Charlie shouts, this possibility just occurring to him. Jamie just drinks his wine. My eyes flash to his parents, whom I don't really want to discuss this in front of and who are pretending they've gone deaf. "Take him with you! He can revise his sodding thesis from anywhere!"

Maggie taps his forearm. "Charlie—"

He's unmoved. "What's a year or two in America?" He turns glassy eyes on Jamie. "Go explore the colonies, then come home and take your rightful place as lord and heir of . . ." Unable to remember the name of the house he's sitting in, he swirls his hand, "This, and then marry Fanny Brice over there"—he means Fanny Price—"and promulgate"—he means "propagate"—"the line as befits a man of your exalted birth!"

"Charlie's a bit of a monarchist," Maggie murmurs.

"I'm only saying—"

That's it. I'm done. "This isn't just a job, Charlie. It's my life. If she gets elected, I hopefully get a position in the administration, where I can have some impact. Best case, she gets two terms. Then we get our next guy in and the cycle starts over. I can't put in for a transfer. There's no London office in American politics." Why am I so defensive? Why am I justifying this? Why do I sound bitter when I say, "Decade after decade after decade, keeping my country going in the right direction, that's my life."

Charlie, impervious to fact, just looks bewildered. "Surely, someone else can do that!" I open my mouth, but he keeps going. "What, you think you're alone on this mythical hill with your magical education sword raised against the advancing illiterate hordes? That the issue of education in America can only be fixed by you and your merry band of arts teachers—"

"I care, Charlie, I care about what happens to my country—"

He rolls his eyes. "For someone who loves her country so

much, you seem rather keen to change it. Now listen, you silly tart. I love you, I do, but you are a class-A idiot if you think that's life. This . . ." He gestures between Jamie and me. "What you two have, that's life."

The table goes silent. I open my mouth to try, once again, to explain this (or at the very least end it), but he stands. He winks at Jamie and looks back at me. "You have a think." Then adds, inspired, "While I have a tink!" He staggers out, laughing to himself.

I open my mouth, but Tom—good, ol' reliable Tom—steps right into the fray. "Might you devise a suitable travel schedule? Whereby an equal amount of time is spent at key intervals traveling to see one another? I could help you devise the algorithm—"

"I'm not disposed to travel, I'm afraid," Jamie pipes up, finally setting his glass down. He gazes steadily at Tom. "I'm ill."

Tom looks down at his plate, scrutinizing his food. "I feel fine."

I lean in to Jamie. "You don't have to do this."

He just keeps looking at Tom. "I've terminal blood cancer."

Maggie's fork drops to her plate with a clatter, her hand finding her mouth. Tom cocks his head like a puppy. "Is it serious?"

"He said 'terminal,'" Maggie whispers, looking to me for confirmation. I try to nod, but can't meet her eye.

"I've been in treatment for quite some time—" Jamie begins to explain, but Maggie's sob interrupts him. Her loud, gasping wreck of a sob.

We all stare at her.

She cries harder, gasping for breath. Tom, little boy lost, drops his head to his chest. Jamie glances at me and sardonically lifts his glass. We clink.

Charlie, of course, reenters the room at this moment, staggers back to his seat, takes one look at Maggie and Tom, and mutters, "Jesus, who died?"

William abruptly stands, barking, "A toast!" He turns to me and raises his glass. Everyone follows suit, even Maggie, who covers her mouth with one hand while holding her trembling glass aloft with the other. William grimaces at her. "No need to cry about it, my dear, I'll be brief." This elicits a relieved chuckle from everyone. Except for Maggie, who sniffles. And Charlie, who peers at her, flummoxed.

"What the hell is going—"

"Eleanor . . ." William's tone stops even Charlie from continuing. He regards me and his eyes soften. "Ella," he revises. "I wish to thank you. For being . . ." He pauses, seems to change tack. "Happy birthday. May we all celebrate many more around this table."

My eyes fill.

Maggie releases a fresh sob.

William raises his glass again. "To Ella from Iowa."

"Ohio," Jamie whispers.

"Oh, bugger, to Ella from Ohio, then!"

Laughing, everyone choruses, "To Ella from Ohio!" and clinks glasses.

I nod at William. He nods back.

It's a start.

Before he regains his seat, Maggie jumps up like a jack-in-the-box, blurting, "Sorry, can I just say—" She draws a shaky breath. She turns and looks down at Tom. "You're an idiot."

Tom's still looking at me.

"Tom!"

He jumps, "Here!" Now he looks up at her.

Her face falls, suddenly sad, deflated. "I don't have it in me. I simply cannot endure it, waiting for you to go through yet another one of your infatuations. I'm done."

"But—but it's you!" Tom stammers.

"I know, yes, it's me," she hisses, "never-good-enough, never-pretty-enough, never-one-of-your-propositions—" Tom opens his mouth to interrupt, but she keeps going. "No, I'm going to finish, because I'm done, I'm done always being patient, always there! Don't you see, we could die tomorrow and we'd never—" Poor Maggie, realizing what she has just said, spins to Jamie and me. "Sorry! I just meant—"

"Keep going!" I cry.

She spins back to Tom, but before she can speak, Tom says, "Yes."

"Yes, what?"

"What?"

"Why are you saying 'what'?"

"Because I said yes and then you said 'what.'"

"Why?!"

I catch Jamie's eye and mutter, "Third base!" He gets the Abbott and Costello reference and we bite back a much-needed laugh.

Tom is sputtering. "Why? Because, okay, okay, here it is: Maggie?"

"What!"

Tom's hand shoots out. "That wasn't Maggie question mark. Well, it was, but it was meant to be Maggie full stop."

"All right, yes?"

Tom squeezes his eyes closed like he's doing calculus in his head. "Shh! Don't speak! I really must concentrate."

"Tom, this is—"

He completely melts down. "No! Stop!" He's beginning to hyperventilate. "Just let me—gather all of my—it's just, you see . . . All right, going back, just a bit, you know, to what you just said, the thing about never-pretty-enough, and never-whatever-enough and never—what was it? Propositioned!—don't you see, Mags? From the beginning it was . . . it was you, wasn't it? It was always you, but I couldn't have, I wouldn't have, I mean, I would have, if you'd wanted, of course I would have, but if you hadn't wanted to, with me, I would have—well, I couldn't have taken it, I couldn't, I wouldn't . . . oh, bugger and blast!" Tom stands. He takes her face in his hands, leans down, and kisses her. Just lays one on her. Arms hanging at her sides, Maggie melts, Tom holding her up by her head for a moment. Then she springs to life, grabbing his shoulders and leaping up, wrapping her legs around his waist.

We stare at them.

Antonia stands, smooths her dress, folds her napkin. "Cake in the library?"

AFTER ANOTHER HOUR of festivities, of cake and coffee and Charlie opening my present of Scotch for another toast, we stumble (some of us more than others) upstairs for the night. I kiss both Antonia's and William's cheeks and thank them, without reservation, for the best birthday I've ever had. As we walk down the hallway, we peel off into our traditional, separate rooms. I take the opportunity to shower quickly and brush my teeth. There's a robe in the bathroom and I slip it on. I toe into the slippers Antonia provided.

I can't do anything about the smile that seems etched on my face.

I crack the door open. The coast is clear. I slip out into the hallway, closing the door behind me as quietly as I can. When I turn around, I see the door next to Jamie's room open. Maggie shuffles out of her room. I smile. She turns, sees me, startles, and smiles guiltily back.

We meet in the middle of the hall, our shared look like two knowing sorority girls. Then her brow furrows, her smile turns sad, and she pulls me into a hug. "I'm so sorry," she whispers.

I manage to whisper back, "Not tonight. We have nothing to be sorry about tonight. Okay?" I take her hands in mine, pull back, and look into her swimming eyes. "I couldn't be happier. For both of us."

I can tell she's excited but nervous. Possibly even worried. As she probably should be. Time for some sisterly advice. "Remember," I whisper. "It's Tom. Be literal and explicit. And patient. Also, don't make any sudden moves." She chuckles and takes a breath, dropping my hands. When she walks past me, I slap her ass. Stifling a laugh, she slips into the room.

My turn. I quietly open Jamie's door and close it behind me. It's dark. The light from the hallway creeps through the bottom of the door, only illuminating about three feet in front of me. I have no idea where the bed is.

"Jamie?" I whisper, taking tiny steps forward.

"Who goes there?" he growls playfully, his voice coming from the left.

I continue forward, keeping my hands in front of me as I reply, "'Tis none but I, sir."

"Ella." He hates it when I do my Dickensian orphan accent. Which only makes me do it more.

"Wot, sir? Does I displease you? Evuh so sorry, guv'nuh."

He groans as my eyes begin to adjust to the moonlight slipping in through the curtains. I can see him lying in bed, turned toward me, propped up on an elbow. Waiting. The sexiest silhouette in the history of light and dark.

I stop walking when I get to the side of his bed. I look down at myself, illuminated by the ambient silver light. I untie the terrycloth belt around my waist and drop the robe.

It's an echo of our first morning-after, when I dropped the sheet just to be shocking. I'm not even sure he remembers this until he says throatily, "The last time you did that you were telling me how much you didn't want a relationship."

"Oops."

He leans forward and snakes his hand around my wrist, tugging me onto his high, plush, inviting bed. I giggle. "Oi, guv! I likes me a bit of a rough tumble ev'ry now an' den, but—" Jamie puts his finger to my lips and I go quiet. I feel his encroaching heat as his other hand slips up and over my shoulder, grasping the side of my neck. His thumb trawls up my throat, stroking the underside of my jaw.

I liquefy.

"Haud yer weesht, lass," Jamie murmurs in the flat-out sexiest Scottish accent I've ever heard. His breath warms my throat and his lips find the hollow at the base. "Yer in Scotland now, ye ken?" His tongue flicks out, sending a spike of need shooting through me. "None of that sassenach glaiber here."

I can't take it anymore. I haul his face up and kiss him, pushing myself into the heat of his bare chest. He's so warm, I want to burrow in there and hibernate.

But, later. Right now I have other plans.

Jamie's breathing has quickened and shallowed, there's a slight rasp. Even though his hands are kneading my hips eagerly, I tip away and ask, "Feeling up for this?" Wordlessly, he brings our mouths back together, throws a long leg over my hip, and slides me toward him, pulling our lower halves flush and answering my question.

Wasting no time, Jamie rolls me onto my back and nudges my legs apart with his knee. He rises up on an elbow, the fingers of one hand tangling into my hair, his other hand finding my stomach. I reach out and card my fingers through his hair.

His hand trembles slightly on my abdomen, his breathing still hoarse.

I'm transported. Blame the house, blame the events of the day, blame the ring Antonia gave me, but I suddenly feel as if I've slipped into another era. The two of us, in this timeless room, finding our way back to each other. There's a feeling of reverence in the tilt of Jamie's head, in his attention to my body. It feels sacred, blessed, even matrimonial. The awareness of centuries of wedding nights that may have passed in this room swoops in on me, and I shiver. Which prompts Jamie to look at my face. His eyes glitter in the dimness. "Thank you," he murmurs.

I don't have to ask for what. It doesn't matter. It ripples through me like a stone dropped in a lake, compelling me to say, right back at him, "Thank *you*." For all the same reasons, whatever they are.

"I love you."

"I love *you*."

My seamless reply seems to catch him off guard. He's not the sort of man to clarify, to ask, "Really?" But I can see it in his eyes. How could he doubt it? In response, I tighten my fingers in his hair. *Yes, really.*

He drops his head and kisses my stomach. Then sweeps his lips upward. He pivots over me, settling fully between my legs. He lifts onto his palms, rising above me. I bend my knees, wrapping my legs around his hips, so very ready. But he pauses. I notice that his arms are shaking. He's weak still. He drops his head, hanging it between us. I stretch my neck and kiss his forehead. It's so warm. He's overexerting himself.

Before he does something ridiculous like apologize, I grab his shoulders and push him off me, flipping him onto his back. His surprise alone is worth it. He laughs. Without skipping a beat, I straddle him, sliding myself down on him in one go. He sucks in a breath and throws his head back.

I can't help but grin. We may be timeless, but something tells me this room hasn't seen many women on top.

MY EYES OPEN slowly, leisurely. Early-morning light finds its way through the gap in the heavy velvet curtains. Jamie's turned away from me. Caught up in the memories of last night, I slide over and rest my face between his shoulder blades.

I lurch backward. He's covered in sweat. He's trembling. "Jamie, you okay?" I whisper. He doesn't respond. I grab his shoulders and turn him onto his back. His breathing sounds like there's a baby rattle stuck in his chest. "Jamie!" I hiss. No response. I shake his shoulders. "Jamie, wake up!" I reach for his face.

His skin is on fire.

I bolt upright. "Jamie!" He doesn't open his eyes. I crawl over him, straddling him in a tragic reprisal of last night, and open his eyelids.

His eyes are rolled back in his head.

I scream.

CHAPTER 27

A sickle for my friend, the weary,
A sickle quick and true,
A sickle, by God's grace in heav'n,
A sickle waits for you.
Unknown, "Fragment"

t's the waiting that gets to me. Waiting for William and Antonia to come bursting through the door. Waiting for someone to call 999. Waiting for the medevac helicopter to come. Waiting for Jamie to get strapped to the gurney. Waiting for William to tell me what I already know, that I should go with Jamie and they'll meet me at the hospital. Waiting while the EMTs force oxygen into my boyfriend and the helicopter finally arrives in Glasgow. Waiting in an uncomfortable chair after seeing him whisked away behind doors that shut with a frightening finality.

A lot of thinking happens while I'm waiting, but it's not productive thinking. It's fragmented. It's heightened, panicked, often without context. *How did this happen so fast? Thank God I threw on my robe before his parents came in. I forgot to tell the EMTs about the anemia.* In and out and between these thoughts, another one keeps looping in my head, unattached to any other thread, bobbing and weaving and coming in for the occasional jab:

If he comes through this . . .

The phrase just appears and disappears and reappears again. *If he comes through this.* Like a pledge, a deal in the making. With whom or with what and to what end, I don't know. If he comes through this . . .

What?

Am I bargaining? Already experiencing one of the five stages of grief?

Finally, Antonia and William arrive. They want to know everything, and I know nothing. All I can say is that he was unconscious but breathing when we arrived. They collapse in relief and I think, *This is the gold standard now? Unconscious but breathing?* We huddle together, a triad of hope.

Now the waiting really begins.

If he comes through this . . .

An eternity later, a doctor appears, mask hanging down at her tanned-leather throat, paper hat atop her platinum spiked hair. Her voice is Scots steel. "I'm Dr. Corrigan, I've been attending to James. Mr. and Mrs. Davenport?" She looks to Antonia and William. They nod. She turns to me. "And you're . . ." She checks the chart she's holding. "Eleanor? I'm sorry to say I haven't much information at the moment. I'm waiting to receive his records from Oxford. The medic said that he's just finished a drug trial?" I nod. She looks again at the chart, her crow's-feet crinkling. "And you say he was fine last night?"

I answer. "Yes. I mean, he was warm and his breathing was a little strained, but—"

"Was he exerting himself? Doing anything strenuous?"

I pause. I don't know if I want to go there right now.

"Doctor," William interjects. "Any idea what this is?"

She glances up from the chart. "Pneumonia."

All of us sigh in relief. "Thank God," Antonia breathes.

The doctor holds up a hand, urging restraint. "It's acute."

"It's not the cancer," William says. "Pneumonia is curable."

"Under normal circumstances, yes."

William steals the words from my mouth. "What does that mean?"

Dr. Corrigan takes a breath. "Firstly, I've never seen it come on this quickly, this aggressively. Secondly, your son's immune system is severely compromised. He's very few resources to fight this. We've put him in a medically induced coma."

"What?" For the first time since I've known her, Antonia looks terrified. Which in turn terrifies me.

"It keeps him from struggling," the doctor assures her. "It gives him, and us, the best chance of fighting this." Her tone shifts, turning more sympathetic. She must see our fear. "Please understand, it isn't uncommon to contract pneumonia after a round of chemotherapy. It's the severity that's unsettling." She looks at me and continues. "Does he drink?"

I look at Antonia and William. "Not much. But he had more alcohol last night than he's had in months."

The doctor considers this, then asks, "Has he had any recent exposure to chemicals? A cleaning agent? Paint thinner, glue—"

"Oh God. The floors." Everyone looks at me. "He stripped and stained an entire floor of his house a few days ago."

Now the doctor nods. "Did he wear a mask?"

"N-no, but we had every window open, we ventilated . . ." My voice rasps, running out of steam. I feel terrible. But why is this the sort of information you get after the fact?

"That's quite helpful," the doctor says, as if she's found the missing piece to a puzzle. "The next twenty-four hours should tell us more. I'll run some blood tests, do an MRI, a liver scan, and wait for his files. Feel free to go home and we'll ring when we know more."

William and I both say, "We're not going anywhere."

Corrigan nods once. "Then sit tight and I'll come back as soon as I know anything."

"Anything, Doctor. Please," Antonia is compelled to say. I hate seeing her this helpless.

The doctor leaves.

We sit and we wait.

The waiting turns into doing. Nothing important or relevant, just doing. Go to the bathroom. Go get some gum. Go stretch your legs. We're a constantly shifting constellation. William rises and leaves for an hour, comes back with ruddy cheeks, cigarette breath, and a newspaper. Antonia curls into a corner on the floor and pretends to sleep. I pace. Occasionally, when we cluster, we exchange words, though honestly I don't know what they are.

Sometime in the late evening, after an hour or so of silence, Antonia says softly, "Ella? Just curious, what do your parents do?" My eyes flick to William. He gazes impassively back at me. Clearly he hasn't told her everything he discovered about me. Probably because he'd have to admit he "discovered" it in the first place.

"My mother's a receptionist." I have to clear my tired, unused voice to continue. "At a medical office. My father's dead."

Antonia's eyes go soft. "So sorry. I had no idea."

"Thank you." Her sincerity prompts me to continue. "It was quick. Car accident."

"How awful for you."

I'm about to say, *No, not at all. It's better that way.* That's my standard response whenever someone finds out about my father's death. But this time it's different. Her tone makes it feel different. Why? Before I can formulate a response, Antonia continues.

"I can't imagine enduring the pain of death without having been able to love someone whilst they were dying."

I'm not prepared to have this discussion. "Well, there was nothing to do about it. It's not like you get a choice." Antonia simply nods. "Anyway, when he was alive, he ran a bar."

She smiles. "A bar. How fun. William's father ran a bar."

I act as if this is new information to me, but William says, "He was also quite community-minded, your father, yes? A politician of sorts. A bit of a cause fighter?"

Antonia looks to her husband, surprised. As do I. "Yes. That's true."

Antonia turns back to me, grinning. "So that's where you get that fire from. Apple and the tree and whatnot. Do you love your job?"

I inhale to answer, but hesitate. My concept of love has so altered these past few months, I'm not sure the answer is the same as it once was. It's complicated. Loving anything is complicated. I choose my next words carefully, as if I'm being interviewed. "I love believing in something and fighting for it."

Antonia nods. "And are you happy?"

"Yes," I reply, and only after it's said do I realize it's a rote response.

Antonia just nods again. "Very good. I'm sure your father would be proud. Every parent merely wants their child to be happy. And healthy," she adds. "Besides, you're keeping your father alive. In you. That's lovely."

Antonia goes back to fiddling with the remote for the suspended television in the corner, oblivious to the impact of what she's said. Is that why I do what I do? Am I keeping my father alive in the only way I can?

What if he had survived that car crash, even for a day or two?

What if we had talked to each other, held each other, loved each other, and *then* he died? Would that have made any difference? Would I be someone other than who I chose to—

My eyes catch William's. He's watching me as if my skull has been cracked open like an egg, my thoughts on full display.

"Excuse me?" We all turn to the voice behind us, coming from the archway at the nurses' station. A young, petite woman in scrubs looks at me. "A Sebastian Melmouth is asking for you, miss?"

MAGGIE, CHARLIE, AND Tom have stopped by the hospital on their way back to Oxford. We stand in the warm vestibule between the double sliding doors of the entryway. They give me my suitcase, as well as Jamie's, and I thank them. Maggie, who hasn't stopped holding Tom's hand (even when she keeps reaching out to hug me), says, with a tone that suggests this question has been weighing on her, "You're not going home, are you?"

"No, I'll stay here." Her face lights up. She pulls me into a hug yet again and I pat her back. "I don't need to be at Oxford until term starts."

She pulls away and looks at me, that perpetually wrinkled brow further creased in confusion. Charlie interjects. "She didn't mean Oxford, darling. She meant your actual home. America."

"Oh. Oh!" I clarify, "Well, yeah, of course. In June. I have to." They exchange a look that I'm too anxious and tired to parse. "I want to. Jamie wants me to." I pull them all into a hug, promise I'll update them, and watch them walk back toward Maggie's car. "Charlie!" I call. He pivots back to me. "Please let Cecelia know what's going on?"

He takes his phone out of his pocket and crosses back to the vestibule. He takes off his sunglasses, looking at his screen as he says, "Yes, I have her number." He looks up at me. He doesn't turn back to the car. His head tilts and the look in his eyes is too much.

"Don't," I warn, tears burning.

"About last night. What I said."

"I know, you were drunk. Apology accepted."

"Oh, I'm not apologizing. In the words of the immortal Piaf, *'Je ne regrette rien.'* No." Charlie considers his words. "It doesn't make you weak."

"What doesn't?"

"Love."

I can't help but roll my eyes a little. "From you of all people?"

He shrugs. "You have what everyone wants. What even I want." He helicopters his sunglasses. "I mean, not right now, but, you know, eventually. When I'm thick around the middle and thinning on top and living in"—he shudders—"the real world."

I smirk. "And in the meantime: Ridley?"

"Who?"

I level a look at him. He smiles, slips his sunglasses back on, and looks into the middle distance. "Yes. Sure. Why not?"

IT SEEMS THAT only a few hours later Cecelia appears, bursting into the predawn flatness of the waiting room, pink-cheeked and red-eyed, her scarf trailing behind her. I look up from the book of Matthew Arnold's poetry I found in my bag, which I've been reading like a Bible. I stand as she beelines for me, throwing her arms around my neck, her cheek against mine still cold from outside. I cling to her. "I got the first train as soon as Charlie phoned," she breathes.

"I thought you had to be in Oxford?"

"This is more important." She pulls back. "Is he all right? How is he?"

"We don't know."

She sees Antonia and William napping in the seats across from me, Antonia's head resting on William's broad shoulder, his arm around her. He's been doing that a lot, putting his arm around her, kissing her cheek, holding her hand. I always thought Antonia was William's keeper. Helping him through emotional moments, reminding him to breathe, taking him to task when he'd gored those around him. But I was only seeing one side of the coin. How foolish. No coin has only one side. Cecelia's voice cuts through my musings. "How are they?" she asks.

How are they? They're facing an all-too-familiar firing squad. My eyes fill with tears. Seeing this, Cecelia wordlessly takes my hand and leads me out of the waiting room.

Ten minutes later we're ensconced in the cafeteria, Styrofoam cups of weak tea clutched in our hands, acting as if it's warming us when we both know it's not. We chat. We even chuckle. I let Cecelia's calmness anchor me. I let her tell me everything will be okay. Even if it's not, even if everything goes wrong, she—by her very presence—assures me that, in the end, it will be okay. She's still here, isn't she?

Antonia wanders into the cafeteria. She lights up at the sight of Cecelia, but her usual enthusiasm is dimmed, a soldier who, though still committed to the cause, is battle-weary. She gives a little wave as she approaches and leans down to kiss Cecelia, saying, "You're such a dear to have come."

"There's no place else I'd be."

Antonia drops into a chair. "Never thought we'd be here again so soon." She sighs.

Cecelia presses her lips together. In her low, composed lilt, her pioneer core is on full display. "No. But we loved Oliver. And we love Jamie. And, as you're wont to say, we carry on with it all."

Carry on. I look to Antonia. So it's a more personal, familial motto for Jamie than I'd assumed.

The shared silence feels almost prayerful. Finally, Antonia's soft, warm voice says, "I can't help but think of your words at Ollie's funeral just now. 'Love well those who are dying, so that they may die in love.' In all my sadness and grief, that gave me comfort. How fortunate I was to have had that time with Oliver." Antonia turns her eyes to me. I know she's thinking about my father.

I never saw my dad's body. I never even saw what was left of the car. To this day I have no actual proof that he died. Who knows? It could all be an elaborate hoax. Which is exactly what it felt like for a long time. My last memory of him is shrugging into his coat at the front door, the rattle of his keys, his voice (that fades in my memory a little more each year no matter what I do) promising to be back soon. So, I made all the rookie mistakes. I'd read something and think, *Dad will love this.* I'd call his cell before remembering. Then there were the dreams. He was just gone. In an instant.

Compelled, I speak. "I've never had that . . . time. Before. I—I don't know . . . how—" I'm not sure if the catch in my throat is stopping me from crying or throwing up. I'm about to excuse myself before either happens, when Cecelia takes my hand. Just as Antonia takes my other one.

Sitting around the table holding hands feels tribal, ritualistic. A ceremonial ring of unity. Antonia leans in and repeats Cecelia's words. "We carry on with it all."

"We carry on with it all," I repeat. Only, when I say it, I start to cry. The two women unclasp their hands from mine and place them on my shoulders.

I can't stop crying. And I don't want to stop.

For the first time, crying feels good.

BACK IN THE waiting room, we find William pacing. Cecelia goes to him. He hugs her (something I haven't earned yet) and she kisses his cheek. He turns to me.

He says, "Ella, might we have a word?" and my stomach drops onto the floor.

CHAPTER 28

I am weary of days and hours,
Blown buds of barren flowers,
Desires and dreams and powers
And everything but sleep.
Algernon Charles Swinburne, "The Garden of Proserpine," 1866

We find an empty room and sit opposite each other on two twin hospital beds. William grips the edge of his mattress, head hanging, looking at the floor. I breathe in the stale, antiseptic air, bracing myself. "I've decided," he begins, and my cell phone rings.

I dig it out of my pocket.

Gavin.

I side-button it.

I put it back in my pocket.

"Sorry," I say. "Go ahead."

William stares at me, clocking the fact that I didn't answer my phone. I see it in his eyes. He takes a breath. He looks at me. He begins his sentence differently. "If they tell us that this is the end of the line, that he can't come back from this . . . knowing him as we do, as you do . . . do we let him go?"

No! Of course not! He can fight this! How could you? We have to do everything we can!

I haven't said good-bye yet.

"Yes."

For twenty-five years I was a child. Now I'm an adult.

"Right, then." William stands, clearing his throat. He moves for the door.

"William," I croak.

His body turns a half click back to me, but he won't meet my eye.

"Thank you. For asking me."

He says, to the floor, "Thank you."

"For what?"

Now he looks at me. "He wouldn't have done the trial if not for you. If not for you, Ella." He looks back down. "Thank you . . . for giving him a reason to fight."

I stand and tread my way to him. I wrap my arms around his neck and rest my chin on his shoulder. Eventually, one of his hands finds the center of my spine. The other finds the back of my head, a paternal cupping.

We weep as one.

LATER, MUCH LATER, I drag my suitcase into a bathroom and change in the accessible stall, trying to feel, in some small way, fresh and clean again. I brought Jamie's suitcase in here as well, wanting to find something of his to wear, something with his smell on it. I find a navy V-neck sweater that will do nicely and throw it on over my long-sleeved T-shirt. When I go to zip his suitcase, I notice a brown paper bag between the layers of clothing. Curiosity gets the best of me. I slip it out.

The bag is actually wrapping paper, covering a rectangular package about half an inch thick. The front, in Jamie's scholarly scrawl, reads: *To Ella from Ohio on the Occasion of Her Twenty-Fifth Birthday.*

It's the present he wanted to give me. The one he wouldn't give me in front of people. The one he told me he'd give me later, in private.

I hesitate only a moment before slipping my finger under the tape at one end and sliding the item out of its wrapping.

It's a journal.

I open the front cover. An inscription greets me:

> You said I could do this. I had a go.
> (See below)
> In posh pratitude,
> Yours,
> eternally,
> JD

I turn the page.

The journal is filled with poems. In Jamie's handwriting.

The first poem is centered to the page, short and sweet, titled simply "E.D."

> *Your gypsy soul did beckon*
> *To my fetid heart and made*
> *A fearful conflagration of*
> *The meanest kind to tame.*

The next page: "Thanksgiving."

> *No other man*
> *Can know a man*

Such as this.
For a woman knows a man
In ways a man
Knows not exist.

Ay, she knows her man,
Such as he is.

The hairs on the back of my neck rise. My hand begins to shake. The title of the next one wrings a sob out of me and I do my best to catch my tears before they fall on the page.

Oxenford

A sickle for my friend, the weary,
A sickle quick and true,
A sickle, by God's grace in heav'n,
A sickle waits for you.

I turn through at least a dozen more, "Slainte," "Buttery," "Don't Think, Feel," "Coq au Vin." One makes me laugh out loud. It's broken into numbered sections like an epic Victorian poem, except there are only three and the title is intentionally cumbersome:

On Philosophy, or the Eternal Debate, or Amongst Friends upon the Boards of the American Theater (1938), or Wisdom.

I
Who's on first?
II
What's on second?

III
I don't know's on third.

Laughing, I wipe my eyes and turn to the final page, reading through the blur:

Hot Chocolate

*Will you let your bindings
Bind?
Blindly for eternity?
Or will you snip the
Rotted lines,
'Fore they be snipped for you?*

I'm trembling by the time I turn the last, crisp page. As I do, I close my eyes for a moment, taking in his words, his life. Our life. This book is us. Jamie has immortalized us; a too brief encounter made eternal. I open my eyes and see what looks like an inscription, at the end of the book, carved into the hardness of the back cover. Two simple words:

Carry On

I close the cover and place the book, our book, back in his suitcase. As if this hasn't been enough to process, I notice another item, an envelope tucked into the side of his bag. There's no way I'm leaving it there. I'm ready to take his whole damn suitcase apart. I open it and find a thirty-day rail pass with my name on it, but no destination. And of course there's a note. It's not signed, or poetic, it just says:

Starting Tomorrow: Anywhere, Everywhere. Happy Birthday.

This was his gift. I imagine Jamie before me, handing over his book of poems, a shy grin, saying something self-deprecating. Then, after I've thanked him profusely, kissed him, he urges me to open the envelope. *Oh. What have we here?*

It's the sweetest, most thoughtful thing anyone's ever done for me. But it's also infuriating. Why would he do this? Why would he send me away during the vacation, during his recovery, during our time to reconnect, our time to savor what we have left?

Because I'm leaving in June. Because he knows this is my last chance to travel like I've always wanted to. Because he knows that he can't go and he won't be responsible for holding me back. Because he loves me more than he wants to spend what remains of our time with me.

What do you do with that kind of love?

CHAPTER 29

Think of me as withdrawn into the dimness,
Yours still, you mine; remember all the best
Of our past moments, and forget the rest;
And so, to where I wait, come gently on.
William Allingham, "Untitled," 1890

Eventually, I clean myself up. I go back out to the waiting room. Cecelia is curled up in a chair like a cat tipped vertically. Antonia sleeps on William's shoulder as he stares at the floor.

Before I can go to them, Dr. Corrigan appears around the corner. William rouses Antonia, and Cecelia wakes up, senses the stirring. We all go to the doctor. She looks grim, causing my heart to beat erratically, a child on the kitchen floor banging pots and pans.

"No sign of improvement as of yet," she states, and my heart stops beating. "We're still keeping him under and intubated. He's not responding to the antibiotics yet. But . . ." She looks confused. "I received his blood work. And while his white-blood-cell count is still quite low, it seems that the trial may have had an effect."

"What do you mean?" I ask.

"Compared to the files that were sent to me, I'm seeing relatively little incidence of the myeloma. He's remarkably clean."

A small gasp comes from the back of Antonia's throat. I can't move. "He's in remission," William utters.

The doctor shakes her head. "I'm not his oncologist. I have the barest of tests in front of me. But I can say that I see a definite shift. The next twelve hours are critical. If he pulls through the pneumonia—"

"I want to see him." My voice is calm but edgy, as if I could tip over into hysteria at the slightest provocation.

"He's in isolation—"

That does it. "Now! I'll see him now!"

"He's deeply sedated, he won't know you're—"

"I don't care!" I shout.

Antonia tries to grab my shoulder, but I shake her off. Cecelia's hand slips into mine, offering strength, support. I hear her voice, low and calm. Capable. "Give her a mask, Doctor. Whatever you need to do. Surely, she can be let in."

Dr. Corrigan considers us. She nods, once. She purses her lips, but says, "Follow me."

AFTER DONNING A pair of scrubs, having a nurse help me wash and dry my hands, and being given a surgical mask, I'm taken to Jamie's room. Dr. Corrigan points at the window in the door. "Just prepare yourself." I peek into the room.

Jamie looks like death. Plain and simple. He's as pale as the bedsheet, his face covered by a ventilator, an IV in his hand. He's surrounded by machines. Dr. Corrigan moves to the door and opens it softly. "I'll be back in ten minutes to fetch you out again. You mustn't touch him. The risk of further infection is too great."

I hover at the threshold. "Can I ask you . . . how long he has?"

She's taken aback. "What do you—"

"I mean . . ." I pause, glancing at Jamie. "Let's say he comes through the pneumonia and we're just dealing with the amount of cancer that you saw. How long?"

The doctor shakes her head. "It doesn't work that way."

"Please. How long?"

"I don't know."

"Approximately."

The doctor snorts, as if I'm amusing her. "Eleanor." Her voice takes on a more real tenor, dropping the doctor filter. "What you're asking is unknowable. His oncologist probably gave him timetables, ay? He has this long if he gets treatment, this long if he doesn't? Well, the oncologist wasn't expecting pneumonia, now, was he? Asking me how long Jamie has to live is like asking me how long you have. Do you know how long you have?"

All I can do is shake my head.

"Exactly. Neither do I. What I can tell you is that, now, you have ten minutes." She turns and disappears down the hallway.

Reeling, I enter the room.

There's not even a chair in here. I look down at him and edge closer to the bed. My hand snakes out before I remember that I can't touch him. I grab it with my other hand, clasping it in front of me.

Everything I wanted to say to him evaporates. What am I doing here? What's the plan? Bludgeon him into recovery with invectives and recriminations? Cry and plead until he wakes up just to shut me up? Beat my chest? Tear out my hair?

Looking at him, eyes closed, head tipped back, tube down his throat, breathing artificially, I can't believe it's only been six months since I first met him. Since he doused me with condiments in a chip shop. Since I hated him at first sight. Since

that first class, our tutorial, whiskey and ale, drunken first fum-
blings, Buttery kisses and chapel trysts. Dry English wit one
minute, gallows humor the next. His eyes. Those pools of every
shade and depth.

Eyes, it suddenly occurs to me, I might never see again.

Carefully, I perch at the foot of his bed. I look at him for a
moment.

"Jamie?" Just saying his name brings a flood of tears. "Jamie,
I hope you can hear me. Please. This isn't your Oxenford. Okay?
This isn't where you cross."

I don't know when it is, or where it is, but it's not here. It can't
be here.

Please don't let it be here.

*Stay, Jamie. If you can, if you want to, please choose another
time. Choose to stay. Choose to stay with me.*

Stay with me and I'll stay with you.

This catches me up short.

It came so effortlessly, but is it true? Because I can't say that—I
can't even think that—if it's not true. It's not fair, to either of us.

After all, that was our one rule: be honest.

Maybe that means, first and foremost, being honest with myself.

And honestly? When I think of leaving on June 11, it feels
as if I'm preparing to amputate an essential part of me. It feels
sacrificial. Like death. Sudden death. The car-accident kind. The
twig snap that drives so quick and true into your heart you don't
dare remove it for fear of how much it will hurt. You just leave
it there. You walk around with it. And when people stare at it in
pity, you look down at your chest and you shrug. *No, really, it's
better this way.*

This is what Antonia was saying.

Losing someone is hard enough. But death without the process of dying is an abomination. It takes nine months to create life; it feels unnatural, a sin against nature, that the reverse shouldn't also have its time. Time to let go of the known as we take hold of the unknown.

Maybe in this, an Oxenford can be shared. Maybe it's not just for the person crossing the river, but also for those left on the bank. Looking into a loved one's eyes, seeing the knowing there, the inevitability, and telling them, I love you. My love is with you to your end; yours will be with me until mine.

Because the love doesn't die, does it?

What Cecelia said at Oliver's funeral: *Love well those who are dying, so that they may die in love.*

In love.

God, Jamie, please wake up.

I look down at him, his bony shoulders, his ravaged face, his chest rising and falling artificially, and I realize that there are two possible narratives: he can be a boy I knew during my Oxford year, the first boy I ever loved, who I heard went on to die sometime later.

Or he can be the boy I journeyed to the end with.

When I first found out Jamie was sick, I believed that his disease mirrored my obligations back in America. We were both otherwise engaged. We both had commitments we couldn't get out of.

The difference is Jamie doesn't have a choice. My father didn't have a choice.

I do.

And when you get a choice, you're a fool not to take it.

But, I'm going home. Come June, I hug Antonia, hug William (now that I can), kiss Cecelia, say farewell to my three companions, and leave. Click my heels three times and go home.

But what if I want to stay in Oz?

What if Oz is home now?

Here with this man before me, and everything that comes with him. Parents. A sister. Friends. Oxford.

It's just not the plan.

My father taught me how to care passionately about things, how to fight for them. *I love believing in something and fighting for it.* That's what I told Antonia and that's true. It's what I counseled Janet to do, on a national stage, no less. Believe in something and fight for it.

Well. I found my next fight.

Love.

That's my choice.

"Eleanor?" The doctor's soft, imploring voice cuts through my thoughts.

"Be right there," I say. I swallow. I whisper, "Jamie. Please hear me. This isn't your Oxenford, our Oxenford. But I promise, we'll find it. Together. Because I love you and I'm not leaving you. You're going to have to leave me first. Choose to stay with me, and I'll choose to stay with you."

I'm surprised how sacred these words are to me, like wedding vows.

And if you're not surprised by life, then what's the bloody point?

I look down at his hand lying beside him on the sheet. The same hand splayed across a book in the Bodleian, that offered me "Dover Beach" to read aloud, that helped me into a punt, that lay on my stomach last night when he told me he loved me for the first time.

I reach out, but stop just short of touching it.

I glance back up at his face. Sunken cheeks, shadowed eyes, a day's worth of stubble.

Still alive.

I lean down, inches from his ear. "I will learn what every-thing costs."

CHAPTER 30

The story of the Oxford scholar poor,
Of pregnant parts and quick inventive brain,
Who, tired of knocking at preferment's door,
One summer morn forsook
His friends, and went to learn the gypsy-lore,
And roam'd the world with that wild brotherhood,
And came, as most men deemed, to little good,
But came to Oxford and his friends no more.
Matthew Arnold, "The Scholar-Gypsy," 1853

ours later, while I'm distracting myself in the gift shop by perusing awful—truly, awful—"Get Better Soon" greeting cards, my phone buzzes. It's a text.

From Connor.

As I read it, confusion quickly eclipses my surprise.

> Congrats! Holy shit!

What is he talking about? For a crazy moment, I think that he must know about Jamie and me, about my decision to stay. Obviously, I'm a sleep-deprived idiot. I text back: *Hi! But . . . ?*

He replies with a link to a CNN web page. I click on it.

I only read the headline before striding out the double sliding doors and into the parking lot, pressing call.

Gavin picks up on the first ring. "There you are!" he says. As if I'm a kid who wandered away from him at a department store instead of someone who didn't answer her phone once—once—because she was deciding whether or not to kill her boyfriend.

"Hillerson's out!"

"Yeah, I saw," I say.

He's barely listening to me. "It was the debate, his numbers tanked! We just won all five primaries!" I'd totally forgotten about the primaries. Is today Tuesday? I look up at the cloudy sky for a clue as to what time it is. "God, I wish I could see his smug bullshit face right now. Anyway, we're officially in full-on general-election mode. Things are moving quickly, kid, and we're gonna need you to come home. I know it's early, but you had a good run. And I remember that I spent my Trinity Term just drinking." He laughs. I don't. "Look, I know it's not exactly sticking to the plan, but plans are subject to change without notice." I can tell my silence is unfamiliar to him and for the first time I sense discomfort in his voice. "Okay?"

I wasn't going to do this now. I wanted to wait until I'd had some sleep, until I could be articulate and diplomatic, because, frankly, I'm a verbally incontinent mess at the moment.

But now, like Hillerson, my hand has been forced.

Here we go.

"No."

Gavin's silent. He's never heard that word come out of my mouth before. "I don't understand."

"I'm not coming home."

"Let's not make this a thing, Ella. You don't want me to find an interim deputy political director, because, I gotta be honest,

I don't think that's gonna be good for you—"

"No, I mean I'm not coming home. Period. Now or in June."

More silence. Then he says, "What's this about, Ella? It can't be another job. There's no better opportunity—"

"No, I wouldn't do that to you. Or Janet. I'm so grateful to you both . . ." I can't finish. I choke up. It turns out, the act of making a choice, of choosing a path, doesn't mean the other path disappears. It just means that it will forever run parallel to the one you're on. It means you have to live with knowing what you gave up. Which isn't a bad thing; if anything, it only serves to strengthen my resolve.

But I would have killed this job. I would have been a superstar. I know it.

Gavin knows it, too, because, after a lengthy pause, he tries to save me from myself. "Ella, here's what I'm gonna do. I'm gonna give you a day to think it over before I start looking for someone else."

"I don't need a day."

"Yesterday, we promoted you. Today, you quit. Did you get spooked? Doesn't this opportunity mean anything to you?"

Resenting the hell out of his guilt-tripping takes a backseat to my encroaching realization that actually, no, it doesn't. It occurs to me that I never told anyone I'd been promoted. When Gavin and Janet gave me the news, I went back to the company of my friends, my boyfriend, and his parents, who gave me a ring, and I never had the urge, not once, at any point in the evening, to tell anyone. It was irrelevant before I decided it was irrelevant. "You would think," I answer.

"You're too smart for this!" Gavin says, impassioned. "You're not one of those girls."

I bristle. "What girls would those be?"

He pauses. His tone rhetorical, he asks, "Is this about a boy?"

My anger comes hot and quick. What an awful, reductive thing to say. I take a breath. "No. This is about a girl. This is about a girl choosing her life."

"Oh, really? Choosing her life over making history? Over helping get a fellow woman elected president? Those are your priorities?"

He might as well have punched me in the stomach. "Gavin—"

Suddenly another voice takes over the line. "Ella?" Then she whispers, away from the receiver, "Take a walk."

Still reeling from Gavin's assault, hearing her voice makes my eyes swim. "I'm so sorry—" I begin.

"Don't apologize," she says fiercely. "You hear me?"

I don't think I can stand any longer. I drop to my knees on the asphalt, frigid air sawing in and out of my lungs, clouding in front of my face. "It's just . . . things changed. I changed," I gasp.

"Ella, Ella, stop. It's your choices at the end of the day that make you who you are. Be that. I admire that." She's silent for a moment, letting her words sink in. I struggle to breathe. "I have to go."

"Thank you."

"My door is always open. Okay? That's a promise."

"That's a plan," I say, and she's gone.

I let the cold seep into my knees for a minute. I clock my breathing, wait for it to settle. I look at the bare branches above me, the gray mist of a sky, the cars, the Dacias and Minis and Vauxhalls, which I realize seem more familiar to me now than their American counterparts.

I lift the phone up, stare at the screen for a moment.

And then turn it off.

It occurs to me now, in this blisteringly cold hospital car park on the outskirts of Glasgow, Scotland, that being called upon to do something because you're good at it is not the same thing as having a calling. My calling is education, not politics. Politics was my father's calling.

I feel like I'm waking up from one of those dreams, the revelatory kind, where you carry with you into waking the sense that all secrets were revealed and all mysteries were solved, and everything *feels* different . . . but what the hell was it about? You struggle to remember the context, you chase the clues left behind, you hold on to the threads of the revelation hoping they'll lead you back to the source, and when you finally give up and let it go . . . it finds you.

Maybe my dream of Oxford, the planning, the career building, the Rhodes, everything that went into getting me there was really about: just getting there. Maybe the City of Dreaming Spires—the foundational lifeblood of education in the Western world—wasn't itself the dream, but the entry point to something I could have never imagined, never seen until now.

Love. Family. Connection.

A life.

And the freedom to decide, on my own terms, what I want to do, what I'm going to do with my calling.

For the first time in my life, I don't have an immediate plan.

Well. Except for one.

I go back into the hospital, stopping by the commissary to buy a round of coffee for my fellows in purgatory. Reentering the waiting room, I see Cecelia and Antonia sitting side by side, talking. William's next to his wife, nominally reading, but mostly just teeming with ineffectual worry.

I hand out coffee and then plop down across from all of them. "William," I say. He looks up from his magazine. "We have some business to discuss." He nods once, as Cecelia and Antonia look at me warily. "When Jamie comes out of this, when he feels better, I don't care if it's in the middle of term, I'm taking him traveling. We're going to travel until we feel like stopping. You're not going to make him feel bad about this. In return, I promise that I won't let him be reckless."

Antonia perks up, her face radiant with hope. "Dear girl! Are you staying?"

"Sorry, yeah. I'm staying." Should have led with that.

Antonia gasps, leaps out of her chair, and throws her arms around me. Over her shoulder I continue to stare at William, waiting for a response. Finally, after an eternity, he says, "Your terms are acceptable," and goes back to his magazine.

"Really?" I can't keep the surprise out of my voice as I pull away from Antonia. "Because I mean it. We're going to go and keep going. Jamie's shown that he cares about his health and we'll do whatever needs to be done, but—"

"First rule of business," William murmurs, flipping a page. "When they say yes, stop talking."

The barest hint of a smile crosses his face, but before I can return it, Dr. Corrigan walks into the room and we all flock to her like imprinted ducklings.

I can't read her expression.

I have a horrible, sinking, high-seas feeling in my stomach. What if he's gone? What if I made all these life plans for us and there's no more us?

Honestly? I wouldn't change a thing. I look around and realize that there is so much more us than I ever realized.

A peace settles over me, causing me to meet the doctor's gaze with strength.

Luckily, she smiles. "It's time to wake Jamie up."

IT TAKES A few hours to bring him out of the anesthesia. So while Jamie is being un-anesthetized, we four do our best to get completely anesthetized with my half-consumed bottle of birthday Scotch from Charlie, which we happily drink out of Dixie Cups in the hospital lobby.

When we're finally allowed to enter Jamie's room, I take the lead, coming around the corner and finding myself halted by the beautiful sight before me. Jamie's sitting up, the head of the bed elevated. He looks absolutely wrecked. "*Rode hard and put away wet*," as my father would have said. But when he sees me, I'm rewarded with a big, loving, living smile. He reaches his hand out. It's only a few inches off the bed, but it's enough. More than enough.

I cautiously walk down the aisle, approaching his bedside.

Seeing his eyes open, alert, blue, twinkling, and wanting weakens me. My chest blows open and a gust of love rushes through it.

I thought the hardest thing I'd have to do was leave him in June.

But the hardest thing is staying. The hardest thing is living with dying. Loving with dying. The hardest thing is love, with no expiration date, no qualifiers, no safety net. Love that demands acceptance of all the things I cannot change. Love that doesn't follow a plan.

I take his hand gently and kiss it. He tries to speak, but his voice is raw from intubation and sleep. Nothing comes out but a small, endearing squeak. I resist the urge to jump on him. Probably not medically sound. So I whisper, "I love you."

I watch him smile. Then, by sheer force of will, he slowly pulls me close to him, bringing my ear to his mouth. He takes a shaky breath, mustering all his strength, and I close my eyes, ready to hear those words repeated back to me.

Instead, he whispers, "It's a good thing I don't love you, Ella from Ohio."

EPILOGUE

And, while she hid all England with a kiss,
Bright over Europe fell her golden hair.
Charles (Tennyson) Turner, "Letty's Globe," 1860

'll always remember Jamie this way:

Standing in a raging waterfall. We'd hiked up a canyon not far from the Amalfi coast. After a bracing dip in jewel-toned pools, I went to warm myself on the sun-drenched rocks. Jamie refused to get out. He dove in and out of the water like a dolphin, at one point even making the sound to accompany it. He was a boy again. Exploring, playing, having the time of his life. He was healthier, not nearly as thin as he was right after the pneumonia (hard to be when you're living on pasta, wine, and gelato). I watched him for what felt like an hour as he called out to me, "Watch this, Ella!" and then did some physical feat that would have been impossible months earlier.

The waterfall was a distance away, but that didn't stop him. He climbed up on the rocky base and stood directly under the pounding water. He cried out in primal tones, so alive. He would not let the waterfall defeat him. If it pushed him down he would fight his way back up. At times he'd stand tall, as if he'd found a place of balance between himself and the rushing water. I couldn't take my eyes off him. His face would go in and out of focus, now in front of the waterfall, now behind, slipping between the curtain, back and forth, back and forth between the vale, and every time my heart would stutter.

That day, that image, the waterfall as a curtain between life and the after, became my metaphor.

When Jamie woke up in that Glasgow hospital, life as he knew it had changed. He happily accepted the news that the trial might have bought him some time. But when I told him I had decided to stay?

He balked.

We fought.

He banished me from his room for a whole day. I overheard him telling Antonia that he felt guilty that I was giving up my dream for him, what if I regretted it, what if I grew to resent him for it, what if—until finally Antonia had drawled, "She's clever, she'll always be clever, she can do anything she wants with her life, so, impossible though it seems, have the grace to consider, gorgeous boy, that her decision might not have been entirely about you."

That is why I love her.

Six weeks later, after journeying back to Oxford and physical therapy and countless tests and gallons of Smithy's frozen broth, we seized our moment, our window of health, and slipped, like thieves in the night, out into the world. Into its cities and villages, its mountains and valleys, its waterfalls.

Today, as I sip my coffee, a kiss lands whisper-soft on my shoulder.

Oh, good.

Jamie's awake.

His kisses continue up my neck and I offer my cup to him,

never taking my eyes off the morning light on the rolling vine-yards. He takes the coffee and sits next to me on the veran-dah. Absently twirling the ring around my finger, I calculate distances in my head. We have a full day of driving ahead of us. We're aiming to be in Switzerland by nightfall. Of course, we'll stop and do some tastings on the way. There's also a house in Annecy where Tennyson once stayed, which Jamie wants to check out. Maybe we'll grab lunch there. I've grown addicted to saucissons aux pommes and have to make sure I get at least one more helping before we leave the Rhône Valley.

Jamie tips his face up to the morning sun.

I came to Oxford looking for a Once-in-a-Lifetime Experience. I chose to experience a lifetime.

I know that one day he will lose to the waterfall, slip behind its turbulent curtain forever, lost to me like something out of a fairy tale. But in our story, there's no villain, no witch, no fairy godmother, no moral imperative or cautionary conclusion. No happily-ever-after.

It just is. It's life.

The water keeps flowing as we come and go.

We were never forever, Jamie and I. Nothing is in this life. But if you love someone, and are loved by someone, you might find forever after.

Whatever and wherever that is.

AFTERWORD

To know and love one other human being is the root of all wisdom.

—Evelyn Waugh, *Brideshead Revisited*

ACKNOWLEDGMENTS

I'ld first like to thank Allison Burnett, upon whose original screenplay this book is based.

Also, thank you to Clint Culpepper for hiring me to further the screenplay in part for my background and love of Oxford.

Thank you so much to the crew at Temple Hill. Tracey Nyberg, for that call that changed everything: "What do you think of Oxford The Novel?" To Annalie Gernert and Alli Dyer, for book-ending the life of this project with your notes and insight. To Jaclyn Huntling for all your work bringing the film to life. Petersen Harris: we both jumped on a moving train and I couldn't have had a better co-conductor. To Marty Bowen and Wyck Godfrey, two wonderful guys who have always had the vision for this project, and the faith in me to execute it. Marty, I love how much you love romance.

I would be remiss if I did not acknowledge the role that the Oxford University Society of Los Angeles, and especially the inimitable Bea Hopkinson, played in this process. It is Bea who originally fielded Clint Culpepper's request for screenwriters who'd gone to Oxford and it was through OUSLA that I first met writer/director Medeni Griffiths, friend, Welshwoman, lover of all things with fringe, and fellow Oxonian, who partnered with me on the screenplay.

Thank you to everyone at and from Lincoln College, Oxford, for always making me feel like I'm home. To Dr. Daniel Starza Smith for taking the time to give me a tute on the esoteric rungs of the Oxford academic ladder. And especially to Dr. Jem Bloomfield for his copious notes and attention to detail that I've come to expect in our decade of friendship, but which never fail to surprise and delight me.

To Dr. Breda Carroll for all the help you lent along the way when it came to medical research and advice. And to my friend, the fine young actor Jimmy Brighton, who unfortunately became rather an expert on cancer and its myriad treatments while I was writing this book. I am sincerely grateful for your honesty, courage, and heart. But still: F.C.

Thank you to the business people, without whom we creatives would never have anyone we need to put pants on for. Attorney Paul Miloknay, and everyone at Writers House, especially Simon Lipskar.

To the HarperCollins/William Morrow team. Liate Stehlik, for believing in this project from the beginning and Kate Nintzel for championing it. Julie Paulauski, Katherine Turro, Molly Waxman and everyone else who shepherded me through this process. And, of course, to Elle Keck, an editor I feel so lucky to have partnered with.

Thank you to the authors I've meet and befriended during my years as an audiobook narrator. Your generosity is truly humbling. I learn from you every day.

To my friends, family, and audiobook colleagues who put up with me during this very hectic writing process. Little things, like a healthy work-life balance, fell to the wayside. Especially to Mom and Ken, who watched me go round the dark side of the moon on this one. I love you and I'm back.

And finally, to Geof, my partner in all things. You are the

surprise of my life. For many reasons, this book would not exist without you and it is as much yours as mine. Some wise writery person once said, "don't write what you know; write what you want to know." Well, I learned about choice right alongside Ella, and G: I choose you.

TK